SIERRA WEDDINGS

THREE-IN-ONE COLLECTION

JERI ODELL

BARBOUR
PUBLISHING

Always Yesterday © 2008 by Jeri Odell
Only Today © 2008 by Jeri Odell
Until Tomorrow © 2009 by Jeri Odell

ISBN 978-1-60260-637-1

Scripture quotations are taken from the King James Version of the Bible.

This book is a work of fiction. Names, characters, places, and incidents are either products of the author's imagination or used fictitiously. Any similarity to actual people, organizations, and/or events is purely coincidental.

Cover Design: Kirk DouPonce, DogEared Design

Published by Barbour Publishing, Inc., P.O. Box 719, Uhrichsville, Ohio 44683, www.barbourbooks.com

Our mission is to publish and distribute inspirational products offering exceptional value and biblical encouragement to the masses.

 Member of the
Evangelical Christian
Publishers Association

Printed in the United States of America.

Dear Readers,

What an honor it is to have you reading my compilation of Nevada stories. Both Delanie and Lexi have been dancing thru my imagination for quite a few years. Lexi was actually my first heroine in the first fiction book I ever wrote. After much evolving, she finally lives on the printed page. I'm glad you're joining her there.

I'm always awed by the Lord's grace that he allows me to write. I count it a great privilege to get to teach His truth in the form of fiction. And I count it a great privilege to work with Becky, JoAnne, and the whole Barbour crew. But you, dear reader, are the best, because without you, I'd have no one to write for. Thanks for allowing me that honor.

I want to dedicate this book to my mom. She has been a faithful Heartsong reader for years. And she helped proof this book. Thanks, Mom. I love you.

Jeri Odell

ALWAYS YESTERDAY

Dedication

This book is dedicated to Camden, my first grandson. I have waited a very long time for you, and love you more than you can even imagine. I cannot wait to hold you close, pray over you, and share sweet stories about Jesus. This grandma couldn't be more thrilled. Many thanks to Marti, my cousin, for her medical expertise, to Adam, my son, for his legal expertise, and to Kelsy, my daughter, and Crit group 11 for their editorial guidance. And last, but not least, the Reno police department for their valuable information about the inner workings of the department. If there is any glory to be had, may it go to my Lord and Savior, Jesus Christ.

Chapter 1

*A*searing pain tore through Eli Logan's left shoulder. Warm blood trailed down his chest. Woozy, he grabbed for something—anything—to hold on to. Stumbling toward the warehouse wall, he leaned against it for support. He searched for any sign of his assailant but only caught sight of his partner's pale face and terror-filled eyes. Bernadette had frozen when he needed her most.

The throbbing in his shoulder increased with each erratic breath. Eli holstered his gun and placed his right hand over the bullet wound, feeling a soggy shirt beneath his fingers. "Call for an ambulance!" he yelled at his middle-aged partner, who still hadn't moved. The growing red stain soaking his shirt meant he was losing blood at a quick pace. His knees gave way, and a black fog fought to overpower him. He slid down the wall and hit the ground with a thud. "Dear God, help me."

Eli jerked to a sitting position, sweat drenching him. He touched his left shoulder, expecting blood but finding only a three-month-old scar. Would this nightmare never stop? Untangling himself from the sheets, he headed for the kitchen and a cold drink of water. When would he ever get a full night's sleep again?

His hand trembled when he took the glass from the cupboard. Outside the window a full moon shone overhead, illuminating a cloudless Nevada sky. He filled his glass and let the cool liquid slide down his parched throat. Inhaling deeply, he attempted to slow his pounding heart and calm his breathing.

The clock mocked him. Five minutes after three. Maybe he could still catch a few more hours of shut-eye. Of course, he doubted he'd accomplish that feat. Once the nightmare awoke him, the adrenaline surging through his body guaranteed his day started now.

Lying back down, he stared at the ceiling. Was he ready for tomorrow—his first day back at work since the shooting? He'd undergone surgery, physical therapy, and counseling. All of the professionals said he was good to go, but he remained unconvinced, though he'd never verbalized his doubts. *No, I can do this. I will do this!*

"At least I won't have a woman partner anymore." He mumbled the fact aloud to reassure himself. "Some guy named Delaney." That news brought relief. Women were pleasant to look at, maybe even fun to date once in a while, but they didn't belong on the force. Nor did they belong in his life. He just wished he wasn't so attracted to the pretty ones.

There were three women in his life he'd counted on, and none of them came through when he needed them most. When he was twelve, his mother taught him his first hard lesson about the fairer sex. She packed up and left the day after his sixteen-year-old brother's funeral. Ronny died of a drug overdose. She said she wasn't hanging around to watch Eli do the same. He'd lost both his mother and his brother in a week, and God had done nothing to intervene. So for almost two decades it had been just him and his old man, and his dad had spent most of those eighteen years in a drunken stupor. But he was all the family Eli had, and he loved his dad, tried to watch out for him—at least as much as his dad allowed.

Eli turned his pillow over and punched it, longing to forget, longing to sleep, but the memories kept coming. Amy—his one and only love, or so he thought—taught him lesson number two. She didn't want him; she wanted his best friend. When he caught them together, he walked away from the pair and never looked back, but he never recovered either. By seventeen he'd learned three hard truths: You can't count on God, you can't count on family, and you can't count on friends.

And let's not forget Bernadette. Good ol' Bernie. She'd grown tired of the traffic scene and wanted more excitement. Well, she'd gotten her wish—only she couldn't handle the thrill. Now that she was restricted to a desk job at the precinct, cruising around writing tickets probably didn't seem so boring to her anymore.

"Sarge, I'm here." Eli rounded the corner into the sergeant's office a few hours later, but his chair sat empty. A movement by the window caught Eli's attention, and there stood one fine-looking woman. His breath caught in his throat, and had he not been trained to school his emotions, he'd have stood there gawking. *Sarge, how do you do it? She must be half your age and a real looker—something you're definitely not.*

"Hi." The velvet-voiced, honey-haired woman crossed the room, her hand extended. "As you probably guessed, Joe stepped out for a moment. He should be back any second." Turquoise eyes welcomed him, and her sincere smile relayed openness. Her fresh looks appealed to him, and when his big hand swallowed her small one, he felt something akin to voltage pass between them. "I'm—"

"Good. You two have met. That'll save me time on introductions." Sergeant Joe Wood stepped through the office door. His large frame dwarfed the petite beauty standing next to Eli. Though a great guy, Sarge had some rough edges. What must have intrigued the sergeant was obvious—perfect, petite features in a natural presentation and eyes that reminded Eli of the tranquil waters of the Caribbean.

"We haven't actually met," she corrected. "I was just about to introduce myself when you walked in."

As Sarge settled into his squeaky chair, Eli again found himself drinking in all he could of her face. If he ever decided to look for a woman, one like her couldn't be more perfect—small, feminine, and au naturel. But of course he had no plan of ever looking for a woman.

"I'm Delanie Cooper."

He dropped her hand as if it had suddenly transfigured into a poisonous snake. *Delanie? This can't be!* He turned to face Sarge with an accusing stare. "This isn't..."

Sarge nodded, confirming Eli's suspicions. "Eli Logan, meet Delanie Cooper, your new partner."

"No way!" Eli moved toward the gray metal desk. He bent over until he and Sarge were eye level. "Absolutely no way!" He glared into Sarge's small, round eyes.

"I told you on the phone you'd been reassigned."

"When you said my new partner was Delanie, I thought you meant like Tony Delaney or Sam Delaney—not Delanie as in a female!" His voice rose, as did his frustration level. "I won't work with another woman." Eli crossed his arms over his chest to underscore the determination of his words.

"You don't have a choice, pal. I call the shots."

"Then I'll go over your head." Eli headed for the door, turning just before his exit. "I'll go all the way to the chief of police if I have to." Reality struck him with a force that stopped him dead in his tracks. "You're Frank Cooper's daughter, aren't you?" He'd heard the chief had one on the force.

Delanie nodded.

So much for plan B. How could he tell his superior he refused to work with his daughter? He glared at Sarge and shook his head. "Why? Why are you doing this? You know how I feel about women cops."

"Delanie is one of the best we have. She's intelligent, quick—"

"She's barely five feet and a hundred pounds. What if I'm wounded and need her to carry me out of the middle of gang crossfire?"

"I know what happened with your last partner." Delanie's velvet voice no longer sounded like a caress; now it just irritated Eli. "But I've never frozen, and I don't think I ever will. I'm strong as an ox and promise I'll work hard not to let you down."

"Have you ever been face-to-face with a forty-five and a guy on the other end who wanted you dead? Let me assure you, talk is cheap." He doubted she'd ever faced more than a routine traffic stop.

"Not only have I looked down a barrel at close range, I took the guy's legs out from under him with a sweep." The two of them stood in a face-off, both refusing to back down. Her eyes lost their serenity and now reminded him of a stormy sea at sunset, but he refused to be impressed by her looks or her claims.

"Eli." Sarge's voice came from right beside Eli, but he didn't break eye contact with Ms. Cooper; she didn't blink an eye either. "Delanie is a black belt in Kajukenbo. She can take care of herself. You, my friend, have a new partner and an assignment that starts tomorrow. You go home now and think long and hard about this decision. Either you show up tomorrow and join Delanie undercover, or you empty your locker, pal." Sarge pushed his way between them and forced their gazes to break.

Anger coursed through Eli like rapids in a river. How could he walk away when this job had been his life for the past ten years? How could he walk away when his sole purpose had become avenging his brother's death by ridding Reno of drug lords?

"I'll be here," he promised, walking to the door. Pausing, he directed his parting words at Delanie. "And you'd better hope you're a good cop, because if you're not, it won't matter whose daughter you are."

His long strides carried him down the narrow hall to the exit. Once outside, he sucked in a huge breath of fresh air. Delanie Cooper had better watch her step, because he'd covered more than one error for Bernadette, and where had that gotten him? He touched his shoulder, remembering.

Slipping on his sunglasses, Eli trekked across the parking lot toward his hog. He'd balked at having a female partner since the day he'd left the academy. He'd watched them, and they weren't as strong or as capable out on the field. Sure, most could shoot well enough; many were better marksmen than he, but they were too emotional for a job that required a cool head and decisive action. Bernadette proved his theory when she forgot her training, gave in to fear, and nearly got him killed.

Eli slipped on his helmet and straddled his bike. Pulling out onto Second, he headed for Virginia Street, making himself a promise: Delanie Cooper wouldn't be the fourth woman on his list to fail him. The next fiasco might cost him his life, and he wasn't willing to pay that high a price. A few mess-ups and he'd be rid of her. Eli Logan never broke promises to anyone, and he wouldn't break this one to himself either.

∞

Delanie glanced from Joe to the door and back again. "Well, your warning that Eli might resent my assignment as his partner now seems a bit understated."

"I told you he had issues." Joe settled back into his chair.

"Issues? The man's a woman-hater." Delanie claimed the green vinyl chair facing Joe.

"He's really a great guy. Has a lot of strength as a cop. Probably one of the best on the force."

"You couldn't prove it by me." Delanie shrugged. "But I don't think I'm the answer to your dilemma. How am I going to help him?" She leaned forward, waiting to hear.

"You're not the answer, Delanie. God is. The police psychologist believes the only way Eli will get past his fear and find true healing is to pair him with a strong, dependable female partner. I chose you because you not only fit the description, but you also have a strong faith in God. You see, I only agree with the psychologist to a point. True healing comes from one source and one source only—God. You can barely get through a sentence without your faith spilling into the conversation. Eli needs a strong dose of what you have to offer."

"That's a big order, Joe. What if I fail him? What if I let him down, too? I'm only human and have lots of room for error."

"I prayed long and hard about finding the right partner for Eli. I'm convinced you're the one for the assignment, so I'll trust that whatever happens is part of God's plan to draw Eli to Himself." Joe tapped his pencil against his desk several times as if to underscore his words.

"I sure hope you're right." Delanie let out a long, slow breath. This assignment looked as if it would be the toughest one she'd had to date. Not the police work, but the friendship evangelism assignment that came with it. How could a woman befriend a woman-hater and lead him to Christ?

God, this one is up to You. I'm willing, but You'll have to handle all the details. And, Lord, I'm sorry I let Eli goad me into a contest of wills. So far on this assignment I've crashed and burned. I failed as a shining light pointing to You.

"I'm going to take off. I'll see you in the morning." Delanie rose and strode to the door. "Do you think he'll be here?"

"Eli—he'll be here, all right. He's a cop through and through. It's all he knows, and frankly, it's his whole life."

The news made Delanie a little sad. Being a police officer was a great job, even a wonderful ministry, but someone's entire life? She needed to know more about Eli. An idea formed.

"Where does he live?"

"Eli?" Joe's wrinkled brow verified his confusion at the abrupt subject change.

"Yeah, Eli." She grinned at Joe's perplexed look.

"What difference does that make?" His brows drew even closer together.

11

"I want to get a feel for him. Drive through his neighborhood and try to understand this new partner of mine."

"He won't appreciate you snooping around."

"Too bad. He's not willing to sit down with me, get to know me, work out our differences."

"He lives in an apartment—off Ralston just north of I-80."

The news surprised her. "Why? I know the pay's low, but not that low. He could live in a better area than that."

"Two reasons. To keep a pulse on the drug activity in the area and to befriend young boys in his neighborhood, hoping to help keep them off drugs and out of gangs." The admiration in Joe's voice was apparent.

"So Mr. Logan has a caring side." Delanie considered this new information. At least it made him almost human.

"Not for you."

"No, not for me, but at least for someone." She turned to leave; now she had a plan. "See ya," she called over her shoulder on her way out Joe's door.

Delanie took the stairs to the second floor, pondering her new partner. She let out a long breath, feeling overwhelmed by the man. He was so negative, so antiwoman, and yet she couldn't deny the interest she felt, the chemistry when their hands touched. It would take a lot of prayer to maintain a good frame of mind around him.

She popped in to say hi to her dad and obtain more information regarding Mr. Logan. With her other partners, she'd spent time with them over coffee so she could get to know them. That wouldn't be the case here. Whatever she wanted to know, she'd have to ferret out on her own. Her dad said little, except that Eli was a good man and a good cop. He did, however, provide her with Eli's address.

Leaving the precinct, Delanie drove straight to Eli's stomping grounds. After a little searching, she found parking curbside a half block or so from his apartment building—the place Eli called home. It was old and somewhat decrepit, certainly in need of work. Parking down a bit, she smiled as she thought how conspicuous she was in a sports car, even a white one. Hers was not a nondescript surveillance car at all. She watched people come and go. Many were Hispanic and young kids.

Eli exited, wearing sweats and a sleeveless shirt and bouncing a basketball. A group of ten or so boys who looked to be junior high age surrounded him. His hair, almost black and slightly too long, glistened in the sun. Laughter filled the air as he and the boys wrestled over the ball. The scruffy beard that looked like several days' growth still covered his jawline and chin, but somehow it added to his rugged attractiveness. For Delanie, seeing his playful side and watching his interaction with the boys made him all the more appealing.

He glanced in her direction once but apparently didn't see her. Delanie waited until he was a half block away, then followed on foot. At Eleventh Street Eli and his entourage made a left. Delanie jogged to catch up. Unfamiliar with the neighborhood, she had no idea where they were headed.

Just before she rounded the corner where Eli had turned, someone grabbed her from behind. Muscular arms wrapped around her neck and waist, holding her in a choke hold. *Don't panic! Stay calm!* Immediately all of her senses were alert, alive. She sucked hard to take in a breath; the arm across her throat made it difficult. Why hadn't she been paying attention to her surroundings? As a cop, she knew better, especially in this neighborhood. She'd wait. Sooner or later this guy would make a mistake, and she'd make her move. Heart pounding, she prayed for help.

Chapter 2

Sarge didn't tell me your nickname was Coop the Snoop."

Eli knew the moment Delanie recognized his voice—some of the tension left her body, and she relaxed a little, but not completely. He loosened his hold the slightest bit, and she inhaled a gulp of air. He didn't want to notice the smell of her—clean with a hint of lavender—or the touch of her—small and soft in his arms—but neither eluded him.

What is it about this woman? He released her, needing to put space between them. She swung around and, using her legs, swept his out from under him. He hit the ground—hard. Dazed, he replayed the last few seconds. One instant he was contemplating her femininity, and the next he was sprawled out on the pavement with a throbbing head and an aching back, listening to a group of boys chuckling somewhere nearby. He'd never hear the end of this from them.

"Man, she's quick," he heard Miguel say.

"Did you see the way she knocked his feet right out from under him?" Oscar asked in a loud whisper.

Delanie reached out her hand to help Eli to his feet. Groaning, he accepted her offer, and she pulled him up. "Don't ever misjudge your opponent." She raised her eyebrow, tilting her chin upward. Turning, she faced the group of boys. "Can anyone play, or is it guys only?"

"Guys only," Eli answered, brushing the dirt off his sweats. He figured he'd cut her off before any of those awestruck teens could invite her into the game.

"But since you're tougher than most of the guys we know"—Miguel shot him a meaningful glance, his brown eyes glowing with mischief—"we can make an exception for you."

"Why, thank you." Delanie dazzled them with a smile that might possibly shame the sun. His little mob of junior high boys surrounded her like bees around a honeycomb, and they walked toward the court while he straggled behind completely forgotten. She joked with them, and they joked back, admiration written across each young face. Great. His little posse abandoned him for the first pretty girl to come along.

"Where do you guys play?" she asked.

"Peavine Elementary," Miguel said, "down on Grandview."

Delanie checked out the yellow school with bright, colorful doors—some blue, green, and red. It looked happy with vines growing up the side of the building, and to her surprise she saw no graffiti. She followed the guys around back to the playground where a full-size basketball court awaited them.

Oscar tossed the basketball to Delanie, and she tossed it to Eli. "Hope you don't mind a girl in the game." Her Caribbean-blue eyes mocked him. She knew he did mind, but she obviously didn't care.

"As long as you're not on my team." He threw the ball back to her—with force. She caught it, and from the slapping sound against her palms, he knew they had to sting, but she didn't even flinch.

Stopping at the edge of the court, Delanie asked, "So whose team am I on?"

"I'll take her," Miguel offered gallantly. She was shorter than most of the boys, so they all knew she was more of a liability than an asset.

"I'll take Eli." Oscar grinned, and Eli knew the chunky boy still pictured him sprawled out on the pavement and could barely contain his laughter. While Miguel and Oscar took turns choosing team members, Eli evaluated his opponent. She'd pulled her hair back into a ponytail, and in her navy tank top, shorts, and tennis shoes, she'd come to play. How did she know he'd be home or even where home was?

Okay, he grudgingly admitted, *she has a cop's nose. And she is spunky—definitely spunky.*

Each team gathered in a circle at opposite ends of the court, discussing strategy, but he only half-listened. Delanie Cooper had unquestionably earned an ounce of respect from him today—she was a fast thinker, quick and strong, and he wouldn't underestimate her again, nor would he lose his focus. He'd been thinking of her womanly wiles instead of keeping a clear head. Well, no more. No, sir. He'd pay no more attention to the smell of her, the touch of her, the sound of her, or anything else about her.

Both teams met center court, and Eli flipped a coin. Delanie called heads, and heads it was, so they had the basketball first. His team got into defensive positions while Miguel threw the ball to Delanie. She dribbled down court, weaving through his players. He planted himself between her and the basket. She collided into him, with more force than he expected from someone her size, and lost control of the ball.

Oscar grabbed the loose ball and passed it to Jorge, who dunked it, and they took the lead 2-0. Miguel threw the basketball back in, and Delanie carried it down court again, this time sinking the shot, making the score 2-2. The teams were evenly matched, and the game stayed close. Delanie played tough, and Eli grudgingly noted his admiration had moved up another notch. When they were all drenched with sweat and thoroughly exhausted, they called it quits. His team

15

managed to pull off a three-point victory.

"So now that we've shared a game of hoops, do I get an introduction to your friends?" Delanie asked, walking off the court. She took a gulp of water from the bottle he handed her, and he realized he'd already started taking care of her, watching out for her, even though he'd promised himself not to fall into that role.

"Sure. Guys, this is Delanie Cooper, better known as Coop the Snoop. Coop, the guys."

Delanie rolled her eyes and shook her head, but the smile she shined on him caused his heart to trip over itself. He shifted his gaze away from her. *I won't warm up to her. I will not!*

They all sat in the grass next to the court, chugging water, and each junior higher introduced himself to Delanie. Then they rehashed the best plays of the game. "Did you see the steal Eli made right out of Delanie's hands?"

"Yeah, that was some play, E. A clean lift—all ball." She was actually proud of him, and the thought made him feel warm inside.

He cocked his brow. "E?"

"Hey, if I'm Coop, you're E." She shrugged. "Take it or leave it, dude. It's either Delanie and Eli, Cooper and Logan, or Coop and E."

"Coop and E it is." Eli decided to get her riled. "You know, Coop, for a girl, you don't play half-bad." He stretched out on the grass, leaning on his right elbow.

She only laughed. "Thank you. And for a guy, you don't play too bad either—though my brothers would put you to shame."

"Brothers, huh? I knew you had one—Frank Jr."

"Yeah, since Frankie's on the force, I figured you knew him. He's the oldest. Brady is next, then Cody."

"And where do you fall in the lineup?"

She smiled and hung her head. "The baby."

"Three older brothers. Was the word *princess* used in regard to you?"

She blushed and played with a blade of grass. "Occasionally."

"Figures." Eli rose and grabbed his stuff. "Let's head back, guys." He had to keep the distance; they were getting too comfortable, too chummy. His little troop rose, as did Delanie.

"How do you know Eli?" Oscar asked her on the walk back to the apartment building.

"He's my new partner." Delanie glanced at Eli, but he gave no response.

"I figured you for a cop," Miguel said. "How many girls can take guys down unless they're cops?"

The whole herd started laughing. Eli shook his head and rolled his eyes. Nope, he wouldn't live down this humiliation for a long while. Junior high boys had memories a million miles long.

"Have you ever killed anybody?" Oscar wondered.

"Killing people isn't what the job is about. It's about protecting people, and I've protected a lot of people."

Eli thought her answer seemed trite. Of course the *princess* had never killed anybody. He hoped his life never depended on her doing that for him. He'd die for sure. Eli paused at the edge of the road next to his building, his resentment of her returning full force. "You guys head home for lunch and some family time. I want you each to volunteer to do a chore for your moms—an unrequested chore. I'll meet you at three in the clubhouse for a game of pool, but only if your home-work and chores are finished."

∞

Eli headed down the driveway toward the back of the complex. She stood on the curb, and he completely ignored her presence. Turning, he took a sidewalk toward the apartments.

"Eli, wait. Can we talk?" Today she'd caught a glimpse of the man he was, but she still hoped to break down some barriers between them.

He paused at his front door. "I have nothing to say." Opening the door, he faced her with one foot inside the apartment and the other on the outside mat. "Look, Delanie. Get this straight—I don't want to be your friend, your buddy, or even your partner. And I certainly don't ever want you showing up here again." His tone was even and matter-of-fact. "You got it?"

Delanie's spirits sank, but she wouldn't let him see the discouragement. Raising her chin a fraction, she said with determination, "With all my other partners—"

"I'm not all your other partners." He'd raised his volume a tad. "We're not having coffee. We're not having lunch. We're not having a conversation—not now, not ever!" He paused and shook his head. "What about this don't you get? I've been completely clear, haven't I?"

Delanie nodded. "Will you be at work tomorrow?" His words made her doubt he'd keep the job if it meant an assignment with her.

"I guess you'll have to wait and see." Eli slammed the door behind him.

Shoulders drooping, Delanie ambled to her car, kicking a pebble along the way. Climbing in, she buckled her seat belt and leaned her head against the bucket seat. "Lord, I feel so hurt. I've never had anyone so blatantly dislike me." The worst part was, she really wanted to be his friend. Closing her eyes, she sighed. No, the worst part was, she found him so attractive, so appealing—so manly.

"And he hates me." She'd hoped that someday he'd see God could rescue him from his lonely life, teach him about joy, lead him to peace. Not just because Joe wanted her to impact him for Christ, but also because he mattered to her.

She started her car and shifted into first. "Wonder what he'd do if I showed up for pool?" She laughed at the thought. He'd probably have her arrested for stalking him. "I'm going to make this guy like me if it's the last thing I do. People always like me." She let out the clutch, and the car rolled forward. He wouldn't be the first person to reject her friendship. Her pride wouldn't stand for that.

∞

The next morning Eli headed out the door early for his meeting with Sarge, where he'd get his next assignment. Hopping on his hog, he caught Virginia Street to downtown and took a left on Second. Parking his bike in the police lot, he caught sight of Delanie walking toward the two-story building. He didn't call out to her but avoided her presence as long as possible. She'd been on his mind all night—her smile, her warmth, her openness, even when he bordered on rude. Letting out a long, slow breath, he reminded himself that he didn't need her complicating his life. Besides, eventually every relationship ended in pain—they always did. He was living proof.

Eli took the narrow hall to Sarge's office. At least he'd be back on the streets, making a difference. He might be stuck with Delanie Cooper, but even having her as an albatross couldn't stop him from making arrests, busting dealers, and getting illegal substances off the street.

He rapped on the open door once. Delanie and Sarge looked up. "Eli, come in." Sarge rose and motioned him forward. Eli took the vinyl chair next to Delanie but never glanced in her direction. The scent of lavender, however, teased his nose with an awareness of her presence.

Sarge walked over and shut the door, handing them both a copy of the case file. Eli flipped it open. The words *Baby-Selling Ring* jumped off the page. He glanced at Sarge, who was studying him. Eli shut the folder, stood, and dropped it on the desk. "There must be some mistake. I'm assigned to the drug detail. You've got the wrong guy." Eli experienced a mixture of fear and anger—fear that they'd taken him off his regular unit and anger at their nerve.

"Delanie's the perfect cop for this assignment—"

"And she can have this assignment. I want to go back to the drug detail."

"Eli, sit down." Sarge used his no-nonsense tone. "Your old unit is full right now, and Delanie needs a partner. You, pal, need an assignment. It all works."

Eli dropped into the chair. "Not for me, it doesn't."

"I'm not fighting you on this one." Sarge leaned forward. "Are you in or out?"

"From what you said yesterday. . ." Eli stared at his fist in his lap. "I either accept this position and this partner, or I'm out of a job." He felt the urge to punch something. "I have a dad to support. I don't have a choice."

"Then will you try to remember that and stop butting heads with me at every turn?" Sarge handed the file back to Eli and cleared his throat. Then he put on his reading glasses and opened his copy of the case. "Delanie will pose as a pregnant teen, and you're the father of her child. She wants to keep the baby, but you're pressuring her into selling the child for money because you're out of work. Delanie's appearance makes her ideal. Not only do they have hope for a beautiful baby, but she can easily pass for a teen."

"Thanks a lot." Delanie spoke for the first time that morning.

"Someday you'll be happy—" Sarge began.

"You sound like my mother. Someday I'll be happy I look twelve when I'm actually twenty-eight."

Eli hadn't guessed she was that old. He'd have said twenty-four at the max, but Sarge hit the looks part dead-on. Delanie Cooper was one pretty lady. This morning she wore jeans that accentuated her small frame and a pink T-shirt that emphasized her slender waist. *Stop! You're thinking about her again.* Eli reopened the folder and focused on the task before him.

"Not twelve, but sixteen," Sarge assured her. "We'll set you up with a fake belly, maternity clothes, IDs. Both of your histories are in the folder." He held his hand up. "One thing." He looked at Eli. "You're a young couple who's in love, so you'll have to play the part. The animosity between you two must be gone. Just like in the drug world, Eli, you've got to be one hundred percent believable."

Great. Now we have to be lovey-dovey. The assignment got worse with every tick of the clock. If he didn't have this wall of hostility raised between them, how could he keep his distance? She'd already been popping up in his head; all he needed was her taking root in his heart. No, this news was not good at all.

"We've been working on this case for a while, to no avail. As you know, baby selling is still a misdemeanor in most states—fortunately no longer here. We've finally figured out we'll have to infiltrate the ring from the inside since we haven't been able to penetrate from the outside. Thus the need for you two. We believe a doctor and lawyer have teamed up on this venture and are making a fortune. We have several possible suspects, but nothing concrete. You two have a lot of work cut out for you."

"How do you even know the ring exists if you have so little evidence, and why are you suddenly willing to put two full-time cops on the job?" Eli asked.

"Murder. A young teen disappeared, and we treated it as a runaway. She was only thirteen years old. The information is in your packet." Sarge waved the folder in the air. "About four months later she placed a call to her mother saying she was pregnant and some people were giving her a lot of money for her baby. Problem was, she no longer wanted the money; she wanted to keep her baby. Before her mother could get any substantial information, she heard a ruckus, and the line went dead. The girl's body was discovered last week. From the autopsy we know she'd given birth just hours before her death."

Eli felt sick. A thirteen-year-old kid—not old enough to be a mom—certainly not old enough to die. He shook his head, and some of the pain from his brother's death punched him in the gut. Teen deaths because of crime—any crime—had to be stopped. He flipped through the file until he found her picture. Julie Johnson stared back at him with blue eyes and curly blond hair. He'd never forget her face.

Sarge and Delanie were talking, but he'd missed the gist of the conversation. "Sound okay to you, Eli?" Sarge asked.

Eli must have looked lost. Delanie said to him, "We'll go look over the file and come back this afternoon for the final briefing."

Eli nodded.

"How about if we head for Dreamer's? I haven't had my morning caffeine yet," she said.

Not into the popular coffeehouses, he was a simple guy who liked simple things like good old Folger's. "Whatever."

"Do you want to walk? It's easier than searching for parking."

He shrugged. They bid Sarge farewell and agreed to meet back in his office at three. In the meantime he and Delanie had a lot of work ahead of them.

She led the way down the drab hall and out into the morning sunshine. They walked in silence along the Raymond I. Smith Truckee River Walk. Following the waterway, they trekked the few blocks to the old red brick building housing Dreamer's Coffeehouse and Deli on the corner of Virginia and the river walk.

"I love the river—something about the sound of the water. . ." Stopping, she inhaled the fragrance of the flowers planted along the way. "The pastoral setting never fails to lift my mood."

Delanie ordered a hot latte, and he ordered plain coffee—black.

They found a corner table and spread out their files, what they could. The little round table didn't allow much room for spreading. He watched her thumb through the paperwork until she came to the girl's picture. She pulled it out and just stared for the longest time. He watched the emotions on her face; this case had become personal to her, too. Something about that young face in the photograph—the face that would never go to a prom, never get a driver's license, never grow old. . .

Delanie let out a long, slow breath and laid the picture on top of her paperwork. "Sometimes life isn't fair."

At least they agreed on something. "Seldom, if ever, is life fair."

Delanie studied him for a moment. He refocused on the case notes, not wishing to continue the conversation or the scrutiny.

Clearing her throat, Delaine said, "Joe thought the first thing we should do is choose names we'll both remember and respond to easily. I was thinking maybe Ethan for you, and I can still call you E, but it's your call."

"Ethan's fine."

"What about me?"

Eli shook his head, still not wanting to think about her.

"How about Coopet?" she asked with a grin. She must be trying to be silly to pull him out of his funk. "Or Coopetta?"

In spite of himself, he smiled. "You could be D, and I'll be E."

"Sure, and how about F for our last name?" She rolled her eyes, and they both chuckled. Laughter kept all cops sane, making the job bearable and releasing tension. Man, did she look beautiful when she laughed. He thought about what name might fit her, something fairly close to her own, something soft and feminine.

"How about Lanie?"

Her expression changed at his suggestion, but he couldn't quite read her. "Lanie?" she asked quietly.

"Lanie." This time he said it with absolute certainty.

Chapter 3

*L*anie. Pain squeezed Delanie's heart. At her insistence, everyone had stopped calling her Lanie when she was ten—right after Grandpa died. Hearing it now—after all those years—still brought a reaction. She'd been Grandpa's special girl, and Lanie was his special name for her. He'd started the trend, and soon the whole family followed his lead.

"Coop?" Eli's tone reflected his uncertainty. "If you don't like Lanie. . ." His brow creased.

She shook her head. He seemed so pleased with the idea; she didn't want to spoil what little progress they'd made. "Lanie's fine." Inhaling a deep breath, she pulled a highlighter from her purse and began to read the case file, avoiding his probing eyes, not wishing him to see the emotion the name evoked. They sat in silence, sipping their hot beverages, studying the notes, and occasionally commenting on something from the file.

A couple of hours later, Delanie stood, stretched, and turned her head to loosen the kinks in her neck. "I'm getting hungry. I don't eat breakfast, so by midmorning I'm always famished. Do you like Mexican food?"

Eli glanced from his paperwork to his watch, then up at her. "Sure, but at 10:00 a.m.?" His expression seemed to question her sanity.

"By the time we walk over there and order, and they cook everything, it'll be almost eleven." She tried to convince him of the common sense of her plan. "Eleven is lunchtime, right?"

"I suppose." He rose from his chair.

"Do you mind?" At his shrug Delanie scooped up her case notes and filed them back in the folder. He followed her lead. She grabbed her purse off the back of the chair and headed for the door, depositing her empty cup in the trash on the way out. Eli held the door for her.

"Ever been to Bertha Miranda's?" she asked.

"Down Mill?" Eli asked as he shot a basket with his cup, hitting the outdoor container dead center.

"Yep." Delanie raised her face to the warm Nevada sun, and they started their little jaunt toward one of Reno's older eating establishments.

"Never been there. I've heard the food's great, but the wait is always so long that I never bothered."

"Don't you know the best things in life are worth the wait?" She studied his profile—the strong jawline and chiseled cheekbone. He made no response to her comment, verbal or otherwise, so she continued, "Anyway, all your info is correct, which is why now is the perfect time to go. My family comes here often after church on Sundays. We make it a point to arrive early and then dash to a table when the doors open. So your job is to mow down anyone who gets in our way. My brothers have it down to a science."

"If I'm the mower, what's your job?"

"To apologize for your rude behavior."

Eli chuckled. Not quite a laugh, but a chuckle nonetheless. The sound quickened her heart. Maybe she was winning him over. They veered left at Mill.

"Now that you're Ethan and I'm Lanie, where do you think we should start? Obviously not with a doctor since I'm not actually pregnant. He might catch on rather quickly that we're phonies." Delanie laid her hand against her flat stomach, wondering what she'd look like with a protruding belly.

"I've been weighing our possibilities all morning, and I think we should start with a stakeout of the list of suspected lawyers' offices, figure out who's getting a lot of visits from pregnant teens. We'll pinpoint any expecting couples, follow them, and start up a conversation. You work on the women—I'll take the men."

Delanie nodded. "Ask pointed questions and share our story."

"Exactly."

They joined about fifteen or twenty other soon-to-be diners waiting out front for the restaurant to open. Both grew quiet, knowing it was inappropriate to discuss a case within earshot of others. Delanie had an idea and decided to proceed with their role-playing. They'd have to practice to be believable as a young couple expecting a child. She crossed her arms over her midsection. "How can you even consider giving up your own flesh and blood?"

A stunned expression crossed Eli's face before understanding settled in. "I don't have a job; we'll soon be homeless. How can you consider bringing a baby into this rotten situation?"

She thought about Julie Johnson losing not only her baby, but her life. Tears sprang to her eyes, which was exactly what she'd hoped for. Patting her stomach in a maternal way, she said, "Love is all a baby really needs."

"Lanie, what planet are you from? Babies also need diapers, formula, and a dry place to live." Eli's voice rose with each declaration.

By now the crowd had grown silent. Most eyes were on them. Tears rolled down Delanie's cheeks. She turned her back on Eli and crossed her arms again.

Unexpectedly Eli slipped his arms around her from behind and nuzzled the side of her neck with his scruffy chin. Thrill-chills shot through her all the way to her toes. "Don't cry, baby. It'll be okay." He spoke softly, tenderly. "We'll figure something out. Please don't cry." Her knees felt like noodles, and she leaned against him for support.

He turned her in his arms and planted a kiss on her lips. Her heart beat as if she'd jogged five miles at a quick pace. Dazed, Delanie couldn't believe this was happening or how much she enjoyed his arms and his kiss. She stood staring into his face, trying to discern the emotions she saw there, trying to discern her own emotions.

As quickly as he'd swept her into his arms, she backed away from him. "Our audience is gone." Delanie glanced around; she and Eli were the only two left waiting next to the rock wall. Everyone else had entered the restaurant through the double wooden doors. Her face grew warm.

She lowered her head and led the way into the restaurant, keeping her eyes on the floor tile. Luckily a table in the back remained open. Instead of taking her seat, she said, "Excuse me a moment." Not even glancing in Eli's direction, she quickly made her way to the restroom, hoping to compose herself. Once inside, Delanie leaned against the wall and covered her hot cheeks with her palms. *What's wrong with me? I cannot be attracted to him. I can't! But I am.* Staring in the mirror, she wished she could erase the "wide-eyed girl with stardust in her eyes" look.

∞

Eli sucked in a deep breath. When he'd decided to toy with Delanie, he hadn't realized the way it would affect him. Her innocence was obvious, and he knew she hailed from a staunch Christian family; so when he assumed her naive in the ways of a man and a woman, he'd been right. Her kiss was shy and uncertain. This girl wasn't worldly wise. The stunned expression etched on her face at the end of the kiss spoke volumes, and she couldn't get out of his arms fast enough.

What shocked him was his own response. He'd enjoyed holding her, but even more startling, he had the urge to hold her forever—and he wasn't a forever kind of guy. He shook his head to rid himself of the thought. *Delanie Cooper, I won't let you get to me.*

When she returned, he stood and pulled out the wooden chair with the padded seat. "You okay?"

"Fine." Her answer was short and clipped—her cheeks still flushed.

He took the chair to Delanie's right. Fairly certain their kiss had affected her even more than it had him, he decided he'd play it up and kiss her at every opportunity. Maybe then she'd ditch him and this job, and he could go back to his old unit, far away from her and those wide aquamarine eyes.

Taking her hand in his, he leaned over, kissed her cheek, and whispered in her ear, "Remember what Sarge said about being 100 percent believable as a young couple in love?"

Delanie nodded but remained tense. He smiled. His plan was working already.

"You're not playing your part very well," he mocked, placing a light kiss on her very kissable mouth.

She gave him a dirty look and picked up her menu. "I'm still mad at you for even suggesting we sell the baby." She pushed him away. "Don't act all ooey-gooey like that never happened."

The waitress arrived, and Delanie ordered the ground beef tacos. Eli followed her lead.

"Good job on the mad girlfriend role," Eli said softly.

"Let's talk about something else besides selling our baby, something more pleasant, or how about nothing at all?" Sarcasm laced her tone.

"Fine," Eli ground out. He needed to think anyway. Could he overdose Delanie on affection without risking himself? Every touch filled him with a longing for more. A longing for things he'd ages ago accepted he'd never have, never even wanted until now. Delanie Cooper made him wonder if his decision had been so easy because no woman had ever brought his senses to life the way she did.

The waitress set two plates in front of them, and they ate their lunch in silence. Delanie seemed to have as many uncertainties as he faced, though he was sure his touch had repulsed her—a much different response from his own.

After lunch they walked back to the police station not too far north of the restaurant. They found an empty interrogation room and spread out their files on a long table. Delanie settled in on one side, so Eli took the chair across from her.

"You think we should start with a stakeout?" She still hadn't made eye contact since the kiss.

Eli nodded, forcing her to look up.

"Tomorrow at nine?" She bit her bottom lip.

He nodded again, noting the vulnerability in her eyes.

Delanie flipped through the paperwork. "One of the suspects is in a downtown lawyers' office. Do you want to meet here or there?"

"Whatever," he said with a shrug.

Sarge rapped on the door once and joined them.

"How's the strategy coming?" He took the seat next to Delanie.

Eli filled him in on their plan of action.

"Sounds great. I knew the two of you would figure out something." Sarge pulled his cell phone out of his shirt pocket, hit a number on the face of the phone, and put the tiny thing to his ear. He made arrangements for a car to be delivered the next morning for Eli and Delanie to use during the case. Standing, he said, "At 0800. I'll see you then." He exited, leaving them alone.

Eli stared at Delanie. The reality of their situation hit him dead-on. Could she protect him if the need arose?

"What?" she asked. "Are you hoping if you stare long enough, I'll vanish?"

He ignored her remark. "Someone in this ring owns a gun and isn't afraid to use it."

"I know." Her expression grew solemn.

He rose and leaned over the table, taking an in-your-face stance. "Do you? Do you know? Can I count on you, Coop? This is a lot more than proving you can do whatever a guy can. Our lives are at stake. They killed at least one girl, and if we get too close, we might be their next target. Can you kill someone if you have to?"

Her face turned white. She closed her eyes and drew in a deep breath. Panic rose inside Eli until he thought it might choke the breath out of him.

"I can't be out there tomorrow with someone who's afraid. You need to get off this case right now!" Eli laid his right hand across his left shoulder. "I won't go out there with another coward."

Delanie rose and glared at him. "Your opinion of women is awfully low. Not all of us are cowards."

"I saw the fear, Delanie, written all over your face!" Eli was now yelling.

"I'm not afraid of my gun, nor am I afraid to use it," she assured him in a hushed tone.

"You can't deny the terror I saw with my own eyes."

"Yeah, I'm afraid, Eli." She hung her head for a quiet moment. When she raised it, he saw fire in her eyes. "Afraid I'll have to kill another person. Afraid someone else will die because I'm doing my job." Her voice cracked with emotion, and she turned away from him.

Is she saying she's already killed someone?

Before the words came out of his mouth, she was speaking again. This time there was no denying the pain woven through each word. "I've already killed someone, Eli—a nineteen-year-old kid in a convenience store robbery. He pointed a gun at the clerk, and I shot him." She sucked in a ragged breath and faced him. "Are you happy? Does that knowledge make you feel safer with me? Is that what you want—to know your partner has already shot and killed another human being?"

Sparks shot from her eyes. "I am not some women's libber trying to prove

I can do anything a man can do. I feel lucky to have been born in America—land of the free. I love this country. I love this city. What I do has nothing to do with proving anything. I just want to keep people safe. I want to keep another thirteen-year-old kid from living Julie Johnson's nightmare."

Delanie stuffed her paperwork into the folder. Her hand shook slightly. She looked him square in the eyes. "So don't you worry, Eli Logan. If I have to kill someone to keep you alive, I will. And I'll hate the fact every day for the rest of my life."

She grabbed her purse and threw it over her shoulder. At the door she turned to face him. "I think you're the one with the problem. You have some vendetta to prove that every female cop is incompetent. If I were a man, would you be having all these doubts? I think not! I'm sick of getting no respect because I'm a woman, because I'm small, because I'm the chief's daughter, or because I'm not ugly. I'm a good cop, Detective Logan, and if you don't believe it now, you will when we're finished with this case." She jerked the door open, then slammed it behind her.

For several seconds Eli could only stare at the door, trying to process everything she'd said. He shook his head, gathered his things, and headed down the hall to Sarge's office. The door stood ajar. Eli knocked once. Sarge glanced up from his paperwork.

"Why didn't you tell me?" Eli moved toward the green vinyl chair.

"Tell you what?" Sarge shuffled through the pile of papers.

"Why didn't you tell me Delanie had shot someone? Do you know what a fool I made of myself?"

Sarge shrugged. "I figured she'd tell you, if and when she wanted you to know." He pulled a manila envelope from one of his desk drawers. "Take these home and read them. I want them back in the morning."

Eli reached for the envelope.

"See you at eight—and close my door, will you?" Sarge dismissed him.

Eli did as he was told, heading back to the interrogation room he'd recently vacated. He dumped the contents of the envelope onto the folding table. Several newspaper articles spilled out—every one about Delanie Cooper and her heroic actions in the robbery. She'd received a citation from the department and was labeled a hero.

Great. Not only was she beautiful, appealing, and intelligent; now he also had to recognize her abilities as a cop. He didn't want to like her or respect her or admire her, but in two days she'd managed to make him guilty of all three.

And tomorrow her presence would wreak havoc on his already confused emotions.

Chapter 4

Shaking with anger, Delanie left Eli to draw his own conclusions. She practically ran to her car—escaping the man who caused her emotions to soar to heights and then drop to valleys she'd never known before. And all in the span of a few short hours.

She hopped into her little car, opened the sunroof, and hoped the wind would carry her woes away. Gulping deep breaths, she wanted to exhale the anger she'd allowed to overcome her. Taking the on-ramp, she shifted into fifth and merged onto I-80.

"I'm sorry, God." She blew out a noisy breath. "I can't remember the last time I've been that mad." But somehow she knew that the handful of times she'd been truly livid, work was always at the center. More precisely, someone questioning her ability as a cop. "How long will it take? I've been doing the job well for six years, yet no one believes I can."

Exiting at McCarran Boulevard, she followed a pickup until she hung a left at Mayberry Drive. A couple of blocks later she pulled into Mayberry Townhomes. She'd grown to love living alone. Well—almost alone. Hank, a retired police dog, and Junie B. Jones, a miniature beagle, resided with her. Or perhaps they allowed her to reside with them.

Thinking of her two buddies made her smile, and some of the anger dissipated. Delanie turned into her garage under the two-story town house and heard Junie's welcoming yelp. Junie and Hank would be waiting impatiently to greet her. She climbed the stairs inside her garage that led to her utility room. True to form, her dogs greeted her with wagging tails and leashes in their mouths as she entered the house. Dropping her purse on the washing machine, she knelt and scratched both dogs behind their ears. Hank rolled over on his back for a belly rub. Delanie grabbed both leashes and flung them over one shoulder.

"How did you two know it's time for our jog?" Delanie asked, starting toward the bedroom. Both of her furry roommates followed. She quickly changed her clothes, tied the laces of her running shoes, and snapped the two leashes onto the dog collars. Junie always made a game of the task, dancing and dodging her master as if she dreaded the daily jog. Once outside, Delanie did a few stretches, loosening her tight muscles. Today she needed the run more than most days and started at a quick pace, hoping to destress and decompress.

She always ran down South McCarran to Coughlin Ranch. The upscale housing community featured several jogging trails and nature walks, giving the impression of leaving "the biggest little city in the world" a million miles behind. While out there with her dogs and God, she could forget the casinos, the crime, and maybe even Eli. This was her time alone to focus on her Lord and the wonderful world He'd created.

At the end of her jog, Delanie followed her daily ritual of dropping by her parents' house. Her mom always gave her "granddogs" a biscuit and Delanie a glass of water. They'd visit for fifteen or twenty minutes while Marilyn Cooper started dinner. Some nights Delanie would stay and join them; but Tuesday nights she always ate with a group of her friends, and then they'd all go to the singles' Bible study together.

Delanie sat at the bar on the edge of her mother's kitchen, watching her peel carrots. "Mom, what makes one man's kiss so different from another's?"

"The shape and skill of his lips." Her brow was raised, and she wore a deadpan expression.

Delanie rolled her eyes at her mom's quick wit. "No, I mean the reaction we as women have inside."

Her mom laid down her peeler. "I'm no expert, but I think it's that old mystery called chemistry." She drew her brows together in an attempted stern look. "And whom have you been kissing?"

"Believe me, no one I want to be kissing, at least not the sane, down-to-earth side of me." Delanie took a sip of water before expounding. She filled her mom in on the events of the past two days. "But when he took me in his arms and his lips met mine, there was no place on earth I'd rather have been."

"Honey." Her mom's tone rang with parental concern. "Be careful. You're skating on thin ice."

Delanie nodded—that much she'd already figured out.

Her mother continued. "I don't believe in 'missionary dating,' going out with a guy to 'save his soul.' Only once in my life have I ever seen it work out. Most of the time it ends in heartache and sometimes disaster."

"I know." Delanie glanced at her watch. "I've got to run, Mom. I'm supposed to meet the girls in barely an hour." She jumped up, opened the sliding glass door, and whistled for her dogs. They'd been out back, playing with her parents' black lab, Rambo.

She kissed her mom's cheek and headed for the entry hall. "I'll be praying, honey!" her mom hollered as Delanie shut the front door.

An hour later, after taking a quick shower and feeding her dogs, Delanie pulled into Mayberry Landing—a casual galleria filled with boutiques. Because of its name, the place always reminded her of the Andy Griffith reruns she'd watched with her grandparents as a child, though much more upscale than his town had been. She parked in front of Walden's Coffeehouse. The quaint mini-mall also carried her far away from her job and downtown Reno.

Entering the wood-planked coffeehouse, she saw Jodi, Kristen, and Courtney already seated at their usual corner spot with their dinners in front of them. On her way to the table, she stopped at the counter and ordered a hot veggie wrap and a mocha ole to drink.

As she approached the table, she heard Courtney say, "He kissed me."

"Not you, too." Delanie sat in the last remaining chair. "Who kissed you?"

"Dr. Gorgeous," Kristen interjected. She shoved a long strand of chestnut hair behind her ear.

"Wait." Jodi pointed at Delanie. "You said, 'Not you, too.' Does that mean you were kissed today, as well?" She scrunched her forehead, her dark brows pulling together. "Spill."

Delanie decided to dodge the moment as long as possible, not even sure why she'd said anything. "Sounds like I arrived right in the middle of a kiss between Courtney and Dr. Gorgeous. Let her finish, and then I'll tell you my saga about me and Detective Dangerous."

"Detective Dangerous sounds simply dreamy, dahling." Courtney winked at Delanie. "But I'm certain he can't compete with my gorgeous doctor whose kiss sends me into orbit." Courtney used a corny accent, and they all laughed at her antics.

"Do tell us the tale of the gorgeous doctor and the nurse who's been swept off her feet by a single heart-stopping kiss." Kristen was always the romantic.

Courtney blushed. "Who said anything about a *single* kiss?"

"You kissed him more than once?" Amazement tinged Jodi's question. "How well do you know this guy?"

Kristen cocked her head. "Better than she did yesterday."

"Let's rewind," Delanie said. "I missed the beginning of this story, and I'm going to need a recap. So please, nobody say a word until I get back with my dinner." The guy who took her order had just called her name, and her food waited on the edge of the counter.

Delanie returned to the table and took a sip of her hot mocha, loving the soothing feel of the liquid sliding down her throat. Between her fast but hot shower and the warmth of her beverage, she'd finally relaxed some after her exchange with Eli a few hours prior.

"Do tell, Courtney, and start at the beginning." Courtney reminded Delanie of a model—tall, long, and lean. Her blond hair was always perfect, never a strand out of place, and her blue eyes resembled the sky on a clear day. Courtney never lacked for male attention.

"We have a new doc who just transferred into intensive care. He is such a hunk, and he's into me!" She made the statement as if it were a big surprise.

"Duh! They're always into you, Courtney," Jodi reminded her, shaking her shoulder-length brunette hair in exasperation.

Courtney daintily ran her hand over her sunshine-hued locks, and her beguiling smile showcased perfect teeth. "That is *so* not true. I've been trying for months to get Pastor Paul's attention. He never even notices me, so I'm moving on." It was an honest assessment. He seemed to be the one man on earth who was unaware of her, and his indifference made Courtney want him all the more.

Delanie asked, "How long has Dr. Gorgeous been on staff at St. Mary's?"

"He started yesterday." Courtney studied her napkin as she rolled it up into a tiny wad and avoided eye contact with any of her friends. She surely knew they'd disapprove. They'd been down this road with her before—numerous times. Men were Courtney's weakness, and no matter how many times she tried, she couldn't seem to remain objective or Christ-centered when a new guy strolled into her life.

Delanie held her tongue. How could she say a word about kissing a man she barely knew when she'd done that very thing earlier today? But honestly, she would have loved to give Courtney a good shake.

Jodi, however, had no qualms. "You made out with a man you've only known two days! What happened to the commitment we each made at the singles' conference last month? We all agreed to get to know men as friends *before* we let the physical aspect get in the way and confuse the issue." Jodi's brown eyes held a challenge as she glanced from Courtney to Delanie.

Delanie knew Jodi's message was directed at both her and Courtney. Guilt stabbed at Delanie's heart. She released a long, slow, audible breath. Eyeing each of her friends around the table, she knew they'd be disappointed in her, as well.

"And who kissed you?" Jodi's expression was confused. "I didn't even know you were dating."

"I'm not," Delanie mumbled, mentally preparing for her turn at the stake.

Kristen chimed in, "I just saw you at church on Sunday. You also met someone in two days?" She played with her large hoop earring.

"It was work—part of an undercover assignment." Delanie knew her justification sounded weak and pathetic.

Courtney said nothing. She'd spent an inordinate amount of time stirring her soup, not even glancing up. Her feelings were probably hurt; but truth be told, if this wasn't a repeated pattern, they'd all have been more supportive and less judgmental.

Two curious friends tossing out questions a mile a minute brought Delanie back to the present. She briefly gave them an overview of the past two days.

"So the kiss meant nothing to you—just an unpleasant job assignment?" Kristen raised her brows.

Delanie felt her face grow warm. "Therein lies the problem—it wasn't as unpleasant as I wish it had been."

Courtney made eye contact and smiled. "Boy, girlfriend, do I know what you mean. Heart-stopping, orbit-sending, incredible. I couldn't stop at just one—didn't even want to." Her face flushed with her excitement, and her gaze rested on Jodi, daring her to say another word.

Delanie shrugged. "Eli's kiss was amazing, but I don't want to kiss him, not ever again. He's not a Christian, and I can't risk falling for him. The attraction is already there, but I know I've got to be firm in my resolve. The pleasure of his kiss isn't worth risking my future. I want a husband like my dad—a guy sold out to the Lord—and I want a father like that for my kids."

Both Jodi and Kristen nodded in agreement.

Courtney spoke up. "But if he has feelings for you, maybe he'll start going to church, hear about God, and give his life to Jesus."

Delanie wondered at that moment if Dr. Gorgeous didn't follow Christ and Courtney was only justifying her own relationship.

"That never works." Jodi's statement was filled with certainty. "Look at all the kids from our days in the college group who made that decision. Many of them ended up compromising their beliefs and their convictions."

Courtney glared at Jodi. "You're always so sure of your walk, but maybe this time you're wrong." She raised her chin, daring any of them to question her wisdom. "He told me if I'd go out with him tonight, he'd come to church with me on Sunday."

Delanie's heart sank, and she had to speak up. "You know it's a risk at best. Don't you think Dr. Gorgeous is used to sleeping with his dates?"

"No. And you should know I won't do that!" Courtney's glare shifted to Delanie.

"Courtney," Kristen said, "he's a thirty-something-year-old man who lives in our modern world. In today's society it's more accepted and even expected by many. You know that—we all know that."

"Court." Jodi's sad eyes pleaded with Courtney to listen. "You've already come close a few times with Christian guys. If you're attracted to this doctor fellow, and he has the experience we suspect, how will you resist? He'll probably know just what he's doing and how to make a girl putty in his hands. I know you get mad at me for always telling it like it is, but I don't want you to fall. I don't want you to settle. I care about you."

Courtney rose. "I'm not arguing with you guys about this. I've made up my mind. I'm dating Tad, and I will not compromise my moral standards—not one bit!" She picked up her tea glass and soup bowl. "Now if you'll excuse me, I have a date with a gorgeous man, so I won't be at Bible study tonight."

As Delanie watched Courtney leave the coffee shop, she fought a huge urge to run after her, tackle her, and beg her not to go.

"No, he isn't affecting her decisions, not one bit. She hasn't missed Bible study in over a year, until tonight. . ." Kristen voiced what they were all thinking.

Delanie shook her head. "I need you guys to pray for me. I'm in the same predicament. Only it's my job assignment, so I have no option. Eli and I will be spending eight or more hours a day together, and I realize how vulnerable that makes me."

"So his kiss was pretty amazing, huh?"

Delanie smiled at Kristen. "You have no idea. When he slipped his arms around me, I felt like a bowl of jelly. At that moment every rational thought fled, and all I wanted was to kiss him. The only good thing is that I don't affect him at all—except maybe he feels disgust."

"So he won't be trying to date you?" Jodi asked.

Delanie chuckled. "When pigs fly—and believe me, I do see the blessing in that."

"That may be God's protection," Kristen agreed.

"I've decided to ask him to refrain from kissing me because of my religious convictions. We can play the loving couple without quite so much intimacy." Delanie raised her chin in determination. "There will be no more lip-locking with Detective Dangerous—absolutely none! I promise you guys that."

❦

Eli strapped on his helmet, sat astride his bike, and cranked the engine to life. Riding home, he couldn't get his mind off Delanie, her heroics, or the mayhem she inflicted on his emotions. Tuesday and Thursday nights he tutored his junior high posse, and he was running late. He attempted to focus on them and their educational needs, but Delanie kept sneaking into his thoughts. When he rode up to his apartment, the whole gang—all eight of them—were waiting for him in the parking lot. Removing his helmet, they loaded into his old, dingy-white, fifteen-passenger van—the one he'd bought just for toting them—and they headed for the nearby Burger House.

Oscar grabbed the other bucket seat in the front, and Miguel sat in the center of the seat right behind them. "So, Eli, how's that fine partner of yours?" Miguel asked in a teasing tone, and all of the boys chuckled.

Eli gave him "the look" through the rearview mirror, but he'd obviously lost his power of persuasion.

"She swept you off your feet again?" one of the boys from the very back hollered. The chuckles increased to loud laughter.

"Glad you boys can have fun with that whole incident." Eli knew their banter would be ongoing for the next few months, and he took no offense. He'd have done the same at their age.

"She's sure pretty," Oscar said in low tones for Eli's hearing only.

He smiled at the boy and nodded. "Too pretty. Girls like her get us boys into trouble."

"Whatcha mean?" Oscar asked.

Eli thought carefully about his answer. He didn't want his negative opinion to taint their young minds.

"She's the kind of girl to make a man think about marriage, and because of my job, I decided long ago that I'd never marry."

"But lots of cops are married." Oscar shot a hole in Eli's excuse.

"I know, but since I do undercover work, it's more dangerous. And I have my dad and you guys. My life doesn't have room for a wife." Only the empty ache in his heart belied his words.

When they arrived at the restaurant, Eli stepped to the end of the line, surrounded by his noisy band of boys. An obviously pregnant teen and a man in a suit were in another line, a couple of people ahead of where Eli stood, but they caught his eye. The hair on his neck stood on end. He studied them, straining to pick up bits of conversation. *If only these boys would be quiet.*

"How about if you guys go grab a couple of tables? I pretty much know what you want anyhow since your orders never change."

The rowdy group boisterously made their way to a spot in the corner. Eli focused on the odd couple in line, trying to figure out if the young woman was with her father or perhaps someone connected to the baby-selling ring. Tilting his head, he tried to catch their words, but the fast-food establishment was too loud, even with his boys across the restaurant.

After receiving their order, the man grabbed the bag in one hand and the girl's elbow with his other. As they passed Eli, he heard her say, "That's a lot of money." She wore a surprised but pleased expression. Eli resisted the urge to grab her from him then and there. For all he knew, they could be discussing her allowance, though he doubted it.

They exited out the side door. Eli darted to the back of the restaurant. "You guys stay put for two minutes." Eight pairs of startled eyes fixed on him, but he had no time to explain. He rushed for the door but caught no sign of the pair. He ran around the building to the other side. Still nothing. *How could they vanish into thin air?*

Chapter 5

Eli entered Sarge's office at seven forty-five the next morning, and there stood a very pregnant-appearing Delanie. He stopped short—the scene before him felt intimate, something he wanted no part of. She had her hands under the false belly, which only highlighted her "condition," but it was the yearning he felt that nearly sent him running. He thought he'd settled the issue of family long ago.

"Eli," Sarge said, "you're early."

He nodded, but his eyes hadn't left Delanie. At Sarge's greeting, her gaze rose and connected with his. She blushed, stood straighter, and let her hands fall to her sides.

"I came in early to get fitted with this thing." She patted the protruding bulge over her normally slender waist. "I wasn't sure how long it would take and didn't want you to have to wait."

Eli nodded again, grateful for her thoughtfulness.

Sarge shook some keys, and both Eli and Delanie refocused on the metal ring dangling before them. "An old beat-up Nova. You'll find it out in the fenced lot with the other police vehicles." He tossed the keys to Eli, where he still stood just inside the doorway. "Hit the road."

Eli's gaze returned to Delanie, and he knew Sarge was right. She was the perfect girl for the job. In her black capris, snug-fitting pink maternity T-shirt, and honey-hued locks hanging long and straight, she easily passed as a high school teen. Upon his scrutiny she tugged at the shirt, trying to loosen it across her midsection. "This isn't mine," she assured him. "I don't normally wear things this tight, but they thought I should look the part."

Once again he just nodded and waited for her to exit Sarge's office, then closed the door behind them. On the way out of the building, Delanie received a few wolf whistles and joking remarks from other cops in the hall.

She gave them a sidelong glance. "Grow up, boys." Her gaze returned to him. "Hey, E, I've been doing some checking. My friend Kristen is a paralegal, and she claims Peg's Diner on Sierra Street, just south of downtown, is a favorite hangout for many of Reno's attorneys. Do you want to start there? We can have breakfast, watch who comes and goes, formulate a plan."

Eli gave her a nod, held the door for her, and then led her to the beat-up black car. He opened the passenger door and waited while she struggled with her new protrusion to situate herself in the seat; then he shut the door. Once he turned the key, the engine roared to life.

"Nice pipes."

He glanced at Delanie, surprised she knew anything about mufflers.

She grinned at him. "What—girls can't like souped-up cars?"

He revved the engine. "The mechanics on this car are sure in better shape than the body." He let out the clutch, and they rolled forward toward the gate.

"Well, I'm relieved you don't have laryngitis," Delanie said.

"What?"

"That's the first thing you've said all morning. I thought maybe you'd lost your voice or the cat had your tongue."

Though he hadn't realized it, she was right. Not being one for idle chitchat, he'd have liked to keep it that way. Delanie, however. . .

He found a parallel parking spot along the street a couple of blocks from the restaurant. Digging in his pocket, he stuck a few quarters in the meter. Delanie had already exited the car and waited on the sidewalk. Remembering his self-made promise, he grabbed her hand in his, and they sauntered toward Peg's. Her small, warm hand reminded him he hadn't done this hand-holding thing since high school.

"Two, please," he informed Rosie, the hostess, as soon as they entered the building. He noted her curiosity as she gawked at Delanie's pregnant form. She led them to a small booth, and Eli didn't release his clasp on Delanie's hand until they arrived at their destination. Sliding into the seat proved difficult for Delanie. Her belly barely fit.

"You guys lucked out and just missed a big rush." Rosie handed each of them a menu. She directed her next comment at him. "You're running late today. The waitress will be around soon." She turned and walked away.

Delanie's forehead crinkled. "You're a regular here?"

Eli nodded, laid his menu aside, and flipped over the upside-down coffee cup. He was sure she'd have said more, but Sue ambled by just then with a pot in her hand and filled his cup with the rich, dark brew.

"Any for you?" she asked Delanie.

Laying her menu down, Delanie stroked her girth. "It's not good for the baby."

The waitress nodded and moved on.

Delanie checked out the restaurant. Eli had already noted several business professionals but saw no pregnant women dining with any of them.

"This is a fun place—all the colorful pictures on the walls," Delanie said with her normal enthusiasm.

Eli perused the light blue walls and shrugged. He'd never paid much attention before.

Another waitress took their orders, grabbing the menus as she left the table.

"You're really a gentleman at heart." Delanie squeezed lemon into her water.

He stared at her. Where had that come from?

"You open building doors and car doors. Not many men are that attentive these days. It's sweet."

Sweet? "My dad always did that for my mom." *Even in a drunken stupor.* "Comes second nature."

"You never speak of your family."

"Nope." *And I never will.*

Sue came by and refilled his cup. "It's good to finally see you here with someone." She smiled at Delanie. "We'd convinced ourselves the man was a hermit."

Delanie returned her smile and rubbed her tummy. "No. He's got me and the baby."

"Good for you," she said and winked at Eli.

"So you don't bring your women here?" Delanie whispered.

He shook his head. *Always fishing.*

"I've never been to this diner before," Delanie said, her gaze roving. Then she focused on him. "Are you married?"

"Nope."

"Me either."

As if he cared.

"Ever been?"

He stared into those tranquil eyes and debated answering. *Might as well. She probably won't let up until I do.* "Nope."

"Me neither."

The waitress set his usual in front of him and a spinach omelet in front of Delanie. She scrunched her nose at his *huevos rancheros.* "How can you eat that this early in the morning?"

"How can you talk so much this early in the morning?" he countered.

She grinned, apparently undaunted by his intended dig. Sometimes her beauty nearly stole his breath. Her skin glowed with peaches-and-cream perfection. The kiss from yesterday floated to the forefront of his mind, and he wanted to repeat it. No wonder he steered clear of all women; he obviously had no willpower whatsoever. Clearing his throat, he hoped to clear his thoughts, as well.

"My brother sometimes orders the same Mexican egg dish, but yours looks different." She pointed at his plate with her fork.

"It's served in a tortilla."

"And smothered in hot sauce," she noted.

Eli decided that since peace and quiet didn't appear to be an option, they might as well at least discuss work—a safer topic than his personal life. "I think I might have gotten a lead last night."

Delanie laid down her fork and leaned forward.

"I was at the Burger House up by where I live." She nodded, and he recounted the incident. "I had hoped to see them climb into a car so I could ID the vehicle, but they were nowhere to be seen. I searched both sides of the parking lot. The guys thought the girl went to their middle school a couple of years ago. Said she was in eighth when they were in sixth grade, so that would probably make her a sophomore. I thought I could get the police artist to sketch both her and the man with her. Might be our first lead."

Delanie chewed her lower lip, appearing deep in thought. "We could search all of the local attorney Web sites and see if we can find a picture that matches."

"Good plan. I also thought we'd visit Clayton Middle School and see if the principal or anyone else recognizes the girl."

"Okay." Delanie pushed away more than half of her breakfast. "I think I'll ditch this huge obstruction"—she looked down—"and put on my jeans. I don't know how women manage this."

Sue refilled Eli's coffee a third time. "You didn't like your omelet, honey?"

"No, it was delicious—just too much."

"You're eating for two now. You'd better pick it up a notch," she warned and cleared Delanie's plate. "And you—you never leave a scrap behind." She grabbed Eli's empty plate.

"How often do you come here?" Delanie asked, crawling out of the booth. He offered her a hand and pulled her to her feet.

"Hey, you never get up and fix me breakfast." Eli grabbed the check. "A man's got to eat."

Delanie's cheeks turned a pink shade. He wrapped his arm around her and nuzzled her ear while Rosie rang up their ticket. She eyed Delanie over her bifocals. "You'd best feed your man, honey. Otherwise somebody else will. Just ask my ex."

"Thanks. I'll remember that." Delanie glanced at him.

He leaned in and kissed her—slow, soft, sweet.

"Ahem." The hostess got their attention and held out Eli's change.

He grabbed Delanie's hand and led her out the door. Halfway to the car Eli said, "I finally figured out how to shut you up."

Delanie tugged on his arm and stopped. She faced him. "About that." Her voice was quiet and breathless.

He dropped her hand and lifted his to her cheek; cupping her face he kissed her again. Her arms slipped around his neck and his around her back. He drew her closer—as close as her newly acquired tummy would allow. He convinced himself he was only doing this to bug her—nothing in him actually wanted to kiss her. Nope—nothing at all.

"Stop!" She ran her fingers over her lips as if to erase the moment. "This isn't right. We can look like a couple without making out right here for all the world to see."

Eli grinned. He'd gotten to her. "I'm just following orders," he said innocently. Maybe she'd request another partner—he could only hope.

"I'll talk to Joe if I need to, but I don't think this assignment has to go against my religious convictions."

Eli chose to taunt her. "Don't tell me you're one of those virgins who wants her first kiss to happen at the altar. Too late for that now, baby."

Delanie put her hands on her hips. "For your information, I have kissed guys before. But what is wrong with being a virgin? In other societies it was considered a virtue, but in twenty-first-century America, it's looked down on. Why?"

Eli gave her his usual shrug. He honestly admired her for going against the grain, but of course he wouldn't tell her that. Someday some fortunate guy would be her first and only. Good for her. Lucky him.

∞

Delanie crossed her arms over her padded stomach. "I'm sorry you feel like my convictions are a joke. It's important to me, so if you can't refrain from kissing me—"

"Let me assure you, Delanie Cooper—you're not that hard to resist." He tilted his head in that cocky way of his. "I can refrain. Believe me, I can refrain."

His words verified what she'd thought all along. He found her repulsive, and the silly thing was, that fact bothered her. Swallowing hard, she asked, "Then will you?"

"No problem. You tell me where your lines are, and I won't cross them." Eli started moving toward the car.

"Fair enough." She outlined her boundaries—"Arm around my shoulder, holding hands, and maybe an occasional hug. Nothing more."

"Fine." He opened her car door.

"Good." Delanie relaxed, relieved to have that conversation over but also a little saddened by their spat. Would they ever be able to discuss things without childish quarrels?

They drove back to the police station in silence. While Eli met with the artist and worked on the sketches, Delanie ditched her belly and the maternity wear, then searched the Web and phone book for local attorneys fitting the description Eli provided. Not all lawyers had their pictures posted, so she knew her chances were slim. Someone into illegal activity normally didn't want his face plastered all over the Internet or yellow pages.

Eli joined her at the computer. "Any luck?"

She shook her head, taking the sketches he held out. "No, there was no one who resembled this guy." Then she studied the young girl's face. "She's so young."

"Too young to be a mom—that's for sure." Eli's shoulders slumped, and Delanie understood his burden for these young girls. "Before we head over to the middle school," Eli continued, "we should go for the hard-to-identify look—you know, hats and sunglasses. If you could stuff your hair in a cap. The more nondescript we are, the better."

Opening a locker, he handed Delanie a cap and grabbed one for himself.

"The Angels, huh?" She worked at stuffing her shoulder-length hair up into the cap. "Your favorite team?"

"Yep. Let's do it."

Delanie grabbed her sunglasses from her purse and an empty file folder from the file cabinet. She slipped the drawings inside. "Ready to roll."

Arriving at Clayton Middle, they followed signs to the office. "We'd like to see the principal, please," Eli requested.

"Do you have an appointment?" the secretary asked from her desk, not even coming to the counter where they stood.

"No, I'm sorry. We don't."

"But it *is* most important," Delanie tacked on.

Mrs. Simmons—as her name placard identified her—gawked at them over her bifocals. "Mr. McNally is a busy man." She refocused on her computer, typed a few keystrokes, and informed them, "He can see you a week from Friday."

Delanie glanced at Eli. He gave her an almost imperceptible nod. A thrill surged through her; she realized they'd made their first connection as partners. Simultaneously they both pulled out their badges.

"I think now is better," Eli told the staunch, follow-the-rules woman.

Her eyes grew large. "Yes, sir." She disappeared behind a door but returned quickly to summon them in.

Eli made the introductions, and they both shook the balding Mr. McNally's hand. "What can I do for you today?"

Delanie pulled out the sketch.

"We wondered if you could identify this young girl," Eli said. "A witness believes she attended school here a couple of years ago."

The principal took the sketch, studied it, and hit the button on the intercom perched on his desk.

"Yes, sir?" The voice of Mrs. Simmons echoed into the room.

"Hilda, could you come in here a moment?"

"Certainly, sir." In a matter of seconds, the school secretary entered the office.

Mr. McNally held up the sketch. "Isn't this that...?" He snapped his fingers, searching for a name. "Anderson, Alden—"

"I think it might be Brandi Alexander, sir. She's in high school now."

"Thank you, Hilda." He dismissed her with a wave of his hand.

"One moment." Delanie guessed the woman might be more likely to know the answer to her next question. She pulled out the second pencil drawing. "Is this her father?" She held it up so they could see.

They both moved in closer to study the picture. The principal shook his head. "I don't believe I've ever seen this man before." He glanced to Mrs. Simmons. "You?"

"No, and I don't think Brandi had a dad that was around. So many of the kids don't. I can't be sure, but I don't recall one."

Mr. McNally placed a call to the high school Brandi would have transferred to. He covered the mouthpiece with his hand and whispered, "She's enrolled there. Would you like me to let them know you're on the way?"

"Sure." Eli held the door open for Delanie. "And thank you."

They rushed to the car, Delanie's heart pounding with the anticipation of making headway in the case. This was when she loved being a cop the most, when the pieces of the puzzle started coming together. Would the case end today, and would Eli be out of her life so soon?

Chapter 6

"Well, so far this afternoon is a bust," Delanie said as they drove away from Brandi's neighborhood.

"Not completely," Eli corrected.

"Excuse me. Are you being optimistic?" She couldn't resist the jab.

"Never," he assured her. "But even though Brandi wasn't in school today, we know she's enrolled."

"Yeah, but she hasn't been there for the past two weeks."

"True, but we've got her address, and even though no one was home, we know where she lives," Eli reminded Delanie. "Plus the school secretary slipped us the address without forcing us to take the extra time to obtain a warrant."

"You're right." Delanie shifted in her seat, not missing her round belly one bit. "I just was so ready to solve the case today."

Eli chuckled. "You thought we'd go to the high school, interview her, she'd spill the beans, and we'd go make the arrest?"

Delanie rolled her eyes. "Not quite that cut-and-dried, but, yes, I'd hoped we'd be well on our way to closing this case." She stretched her neck, loosening a kink. "Where are we going now?" she asked when Eli turned in the opposite direction from the department.

"Thought we'd go hang out at that Burger House for a while—see who we might see." He glanced at her. "How long have you been a plainclothes detective?"

"Since Monday," Delanie said weakly. She studied the passing scenery, not wishing to witness Eli's reaction.

"Well then, you have a lot to learn. I'm guessing this case will take us at least three months, if not more."

She'd mentally prepared for him to mock her because this was her first undercover assignment, so she was surprised when he didn't. "You're kidding? Three months?" Even though she hated the fact that she became so angry yesterday, her little outburst must have paid off.

He shook his head, turning into the restaurant's parking lot. "Once we figure out who the culprit is, it could take months to flush them out. When people are making a lot of money doing illegal activity, they know how to cover their tracks."

Eli cut the engine. Once inside they ordered a late lunch, and then he led her straight to a table in the back corner. It was actually a large booth with a wraparound seat. "This way we can each see the doors and who uses them." He slid in until his back faced the front window of the building. She slid in the opposite side and sat at a ninety-degree angle to him.

"Amazing how much easier it is to occupy a booth without that big belly." Delanie laughed.

Eli jabbed his straw into his cup and took a long sip. "We can go over today's discoveries, and I also thought we should review the police report Julie Johnson's mom filed." Eli ran his hand through his dark hair.

"Sounds like a plan," Delanie agreed, unwrapping her fish sandwich. Eli certainly was talkative when the topic was work and not personal. Maybe she could slide in a few personal inquiries in the midst of their case conversation.

After taking a bite of his burger, Eli pulled a legal pad from his backpack and made three columns. At the top he labeled them KNOW, SUSPECT, and To Do. "What do we know for sure?"

Delanie set her cup down. "Julie Johnson is dead."

"Brandi is pregnant," Eli added. He jotted the facts in a scribbled form Delanie wondered if she could ever decipher. "She has a single mom and no siblings."

"Her neighbor believes she plans to give the baby up for adoption."

"I'll put that under 'SUSPECT' because we didn't hear it from Brandi herself." They continued recalling info and categorizing it as they finished lunch.

One of the restaurant employees was cleaning the tables after the lunch rush. She stopped at their table. "I've never seen you in here without them boys before." Though she spoke to Eli, her gaze never left Delanie, inquisitiveness written all over her face. She moved on to the table next to theirs and cleared the trash.

"You must come in here often." Delanie kept her voice low.

"Couple of times a week. You've heard the way to a man's heart is through his stomach?"

Delanie nodded.

"Junior high boys aren't any different. I feed them in hopes of gaining their loyalty."

"Loyalty?" Delanie thought the statement seemed odd.

Eli wadded up the wrapper from his burger. "If they feel loyalty to me and to our little group, feel like they have a place to belong, they'll be less likely to join a gang. Everybody needs a sense of belonging, a sense of fitting in and importance. We all need to know there are people who care."

Delanie wondered what people Eli had. "So in a sense, you've become family to those boys."

Eli nodded. "And them to each other. Sadly, most come from single-parent families where their mom or dad is working long hours, sometimes two jobs, just to put food on the table. They don't have much left to invest in their kids."

Eli, you're a good man. "So you do it for them?"

"Not in place of, but I try to come alongside the parents."

"Why?"

He shrugged. "Why not?"

"Don't get me wrong. I think what you're doing is wonderful. I'm involved in a youth program—Cops-N-Kidz. Maybe you've heard of it?"

Eli nodded.

"It's a joint venture between my church and Cops for Christ. A big warehouse downtown was donated to us, so we've refurbished it and made a cool place for kids to hang. You're welcome to bring your crew by anytime."

"I don't think so. We're pretty busy." He blew off her invitation.

She studied his blue-green eyes that changed with his mood and what he wore. Today his navy T-shirt made them look totally blue, not a speck of green to be found.

"So what keeps you guys busy?" She tried to sound offhanded, uninterested, but she still wanted more information on this enigma of a man.

"How did this conversation get to be about me?" he asked.

Delanie shrugged. Even though he'd deny it, she sensed a change in Eli. "Just curious about your little gang and how you come alongside the parents. At CNK we rarely see a parent, and I'd like to change that. Thought you could offer some suggestions."

"Still Coop the Snoop, I see." He made the statement with a slight grin, though, so she pushed for more information.

"For a good cause," she reminded him. "How did you get started in this endeavor? Was it hard to gain the parents' trust?"

∞

Eli didn't jump right in with answers but pondered her questions. He studied her earnest expression. Her petite appearance camouflaged a much tougher woman than people would guess. He'd learned that lesson and wouldn't forget anytime soon.

As he debated how much to share, weariness settled over him. He was sick of dodging the truth, hiding the ugliness of his past, and closing up to anyone interested enough to ask. Delanie's openness caused him to wish for the same freedom.

"I grew up much the way they are. My mother left when I was twelve, so it was just my old man and me. He was a functioning alcoholic. Now he's no longer functioning—spends his days in an alcoholic haze. Anyway, often days would go by, and I'd never see him. He'd leave for work before I was up and stumble in long after I'd hit the sack. It was a lonely existence. So when my dad and I moved into the complex seven years ago and I saw all these young boys with the same kind of life I'd known, I decided to invest."

Compassion filled Delanie's expression, not pity. He appreciated that. Her crescent eyes shone with admiration, and that was enough to keep his story rolling. He'd never had a woman gaze at him with the respect he saw on her face. Man, did that make him feel ten feet tall.

"I resolved to fill whatever gaps I could in these kids' lives. I'm their friend, their greatest fan, and their teacher. I tutor them twice a week, take them to games at the college—"

"Feed them burgers, shoot hoops with them. Sounds like you do all the things my dad did for us."

A pang of longing hit him. "Then you were a lucky little girl." Her childhood contrasted starkly with his.

"I was." Her expression reflected a contentment he'd never known. "But how do you do it? I don't even think I could remember junior high math, let alone teach someone else."

"I couldn't either—had to take a couple of refresher courses at the junior college in order to bring my long-forgotten skills up to speed."

"You did that? Just for them?" She'd tipped her head to the side a bit, and her voice rang with approval, as if he'd made the greatest sacrifice of all time. "You're the most giving person I've ever known."

Her smile reached all the way to her eyes and all the way to his heart—it danced to her praise. He'd never received many accolades and had to admit it was nice.

"Maybe my motives are selfish. All I know is I'm determined to do everything in my power to keep these boys in school, out of gangs, and off drugs. It's their only hope for a halfway decent life. My deepest desire is for them to graduate from high school and make something of their lives."

"They have a much better chance with you involved."

Eli smiled. He'd never shared those thoughts with another living soul. Something about her made a man want to be better than he was, do more than he thought he could. *I'm falling for her.* The realization scared the socks off him. Nothing could come of the unfortunate boy from the wrong side of town and the chief's daughter. Besides, he was a lifelong, card-carrying member of the "I'll be single forever" club. *Time for us to get back on track. Time for me to get back on track and remember my plans and goals. No women, not now, not ever—too much pain, too little return.*

"We have work to do." He rummaged through his backpack and dug out the copy of the report filed by Mrs. Johnson. Delanie followed suit.

"Julie Johnson was reported as a runaway in April." He read the file in a low tone. "Four months later, in August, she placed a call to her mother. During the conversation she revealed being eight months' pregnant. Last week her body was discovered, and the autopsy revealed she'd given birth hours before someone strangled her and placed her in a shallow grave not too far east of town." He paused, taking a deep breath. "I never thought I'd say this, but in many ways this assignment is more tragic than the drug unit." His gaze locked with Delanie's. "There I dealt with criminal masterminds selling drugs but wasn't face-to-face with death. I mean, murder happens, people OD—but my main job was just to set people up, bust them, and ship them to prison." He shook his head and knew he'd never get over this young girl losing her life because a greedy person sold the child she carried inside. Human trafficking.

Delanie squeezed his hand. "That's why we're cops, right?" She picked up the report. "Here are the bits of conversation Mrs. Johnson remembers." Delanie started reading. "When she answered her phone in the middle of the afternoon, her daughter said, 'Mom, I'm sorry.' Mrs. Johnson remembers the relief that washed over her, knowing Julie was alive. She asked if her daughter was okay. Julie was hard to understand because she was not only crying but also talking very fast and very soft. Her mother struggled to distinguish her actual words." Delanie took a sip of her diet soda.

Eli continued. "Julie said she was eight months' pregnant and had been offered a lot of money for her baby, which of course sounded wonderful to a thirteen-year-old girl. After feeling the baby move and grow inside of her, she'd changed her mind. Mrs. Johnson asked where she was and who was going to give her the money. She thought Julie said 'the doctor' but didn't name a specific person. Suddenly she heard Julie scream, some muffled wrestling-type sounds, and the phone went dead. Mrs. Johnson has caller ID, but the call came from a private name, private number. She immediately called the police in hysterics; they were able to have the call traced, but it came from a prepaid cell phone."

"Every end is a dead end." Delanie rested her face in her hands. "A young girl wondering if she was pregnant wouldn't go to a doctor."

"You're right," Eli agreed. "She'd go to the corner drugstore, buy a pregnancy test, and find out for herself."

Delanie nodded. "Exactly."

47

"There has to be a source enlightening young pregnant girls about earning a lot of money by having their baby. I mean, if they're already pregnant, why not?"

"Turns a negative into a positive, or so it would seem."

"We've got the bait." Eli focused on Delanie. "At least when you're wearing your disguise."

"Now we just need someone to bite."

"Our hope is that Brandi will." He pictured the young teen he'd seen in this very spot just the night before.

"If we can find her."

"Why don't I pay a visit to her house about 7:00 a.m. tomorrow? Maybe at that time both she and her mom will be home." Eli started repacking his strewn paperwork into an unzipped pocket on his backpack. "You can wait in the car so she doesn't see you. I'll be wired, and you'll hear everything. Then if the direct approach doesn't work, we'll plant you in her path as plan B."

"Why risk the direct approach? Why not start with me?"

He slid out of the booth. "Plan B can take weeks, if not months." He watched her gather her things. "It takes time to build a relationship and glean information, but sometimes the up-front method can reap immediate results." He automatically offered his hand as she slipped out from her side of the table. Something had changed between them this afternoon, and try as he might, he hadn't been able to resist opening up to her.

She glanced at the plain watch wrapped around her slender wrist. "My dogs are going to hate you for disrupting their run."

"Dogs, huh?"

"Hank and Junie." On the drive back to the station, she filled him in on their antics and their need for a daily jog.

When he dropped her off at her car, he said, "Give Hank and Junie my apologies."

She turned slightly in her seat to face him. "I will."

The air crackled between them. He had a sudden urge to kiss her. Her eyes told him she had the same urge. He cleared his throat. "Well, see ya."

"Yeah, first thing in the morning."

He waited until she was safely in her car before driving the Nova back into the fenced lot.

You're taking care of her, a little voice in his head accused. "Shut up."

Chapter 7

At Delanie's request Eli parked as close as possible to the Alexander home without the car actually being in clear view of the windows and doors. They were about five doors down and across the street. Her stomach knotted, thinking about sending her partner out alone with little to no backup. She wondered if she'd feel apprehensive with just any old partner or if she felt this way because it was Eli—the man who'd already become dear to her. The guy she prayed for night and day.

"Eli?"

"Huh?" He didn't look up but reholstered his gun. He'd finished checking the chamber.

"Be careful." Was that her voice, fearful and apprehensive? She knew she was overreacting and being silly but couldn't help herself.

He glanced in her direction. "I will. I'm wired for sound, so you'll know everything that's going down. Plus with these"—he held up the binoculars—"you can see pretty well."

Against her better judgment, she reached out and squeezed his hand. "I'll be praying."

Handing her the binoculars, he said, "You do that." Sending her a crooked smile, he was on his way. She focused the binoculars and watched him walk to the third house and cross the street.

The neighborhood was run-down—trash in front yards, old cars with parts lying loose on the ground surrounding them, and weeds growing knee-high. When she heard Eli's knock on the front door, her heart doubled its speed. She focused on Eli.

"Lord," she whispered, "give us wisdom and keep us safe, especially Eli."

"Whoa!" Delanie reacted to the scantily clad woman who opened the door; her audacity surprised Delanie.

"Hello there. What can I do for you?" The woman's voice purred, and even from where the car was parked, Delanie could tell her body language was flirtatious. Jealousy pounced on her like a mountain lion on its prey.

"Are you Mrs. Alexander?" Eli's voice was no-nonsense, and relief washed over Delanie.

"Honey, I haven't been Mrs. Anybody in years. The better question, who are you?"

Eli pulled out his badge. "Eli Logan. I'm a detective with Reno PD. I'm actually here to see your daughter, Brandi."

"Oh man, what's she done now? Not more shoplifting. Brandi, you get down here right now!" She screamed so loudly the sound hurt Delanie's ear.

The mother, whatever her name was, disappeared into the house. Eli waited on the porch. A few minutes later Brandi was shoved out the door. She wore a knit tank top that no longer covered her protruding belly or met her plaid pajama bottoms. With eyes barely open she said, "I didn't do anything."

"I'm not here because you did," Eli assured her. "I wanted to talk to you about your baby."

Even through the binoculars Delanie saw a mask slip over Brandi's face, and her expression went from sleepy to alert and guarded. Brandi laid her arm and hand across the unborn child. "What about my baby?"

"I understand the child is up for adoption."

Her eyes squinted against the rising sun. "No. You heard wrong."

"I'm not feeding another mouth. I already told you that!" Though Delanie couldn't see Brandi's mother, she must have been just inside the front door.

Brandi swung around. "Everything is taken care of."

"How is everything taken care of?" Eli asked.

Brandi faced him, arms folded over her chest. "I haven't done anything illegal, so I don't think it's any of your business."

"Baby selling is illegal."

She glared at Eli but made no response.

"You are selling the baby, right?"

She made a little snorting noise. "I am not selling my baby. For your information, a nice couple is adopting it."

"Are you being financially compensated in any way?" Eli's voice was compassionate and caring, not harsh and demanding as some cops often were. Every day he moved a little deeper into her heart, and Delanie knew she wouldn't leave this case unscathed.

Brandi fidgeted with the drawstring on her PJs, ignoring Eli.

"If you're getting money for that baby, I'd better know about it." Her mom was yelling again.

This poor kid had no one on her team who cared about her. She'd be easy prey for any compassionate person, even just a doctor and a lawyer pretending to be compassionate. She might not be savvy enough to know they weren't really on her team.

"Brandi, just give me a name, and you'll never see me again."

"George." Her tone was laced with sarcasm. "The baby's name is George." She turned to go back into the house.

"Wait." He grabbed her arm to stop her forward movement. "Another girl, even younger than you, was murdered just after the birth of her baby. These are not nice people."

She glared at the hand holding her arm.

Eli released her, and she disappeared into the house. He handed her mother his card, though all Delanie could see was her arm. "This is serious, not to mention illegal. Please talk to her and call me. All I need is the name of the doctor or lawyer she's dealing with."

The door shut, and Eli let out a long, deep breath. His head drooped, and several seconds later he turned and moved toward the car. She wished she could comfort him but knew she must keep her distance, so neither spoke when he hopped into the car.

They drove to the police station, and Delanie followed Eli to Joe's office. He rapped once on the half-closed door, and Joe hollered, "Yeah?"

Eli pushed the door open and stood back to let Delanie enter first. They each plopped into a green vinyl chair.

"What's up?" Joe pushed aside his paperwork and focused on them.

They reviewed the case notes with him, and Delanie asked both men, "So what's next?"

"Let's put a twenty-four-hour tail on her for the next couple of weeks. Can you guys cover twelve?"

Eli nodded.

Delanie hesitated. *There goes my life. I'll have to see if Hank and Junie can stay at Mom and Dad's during the day.*

"Delanie?" Joe raised his brows.

"Sure." Though she felt far from sure. She and Eli together twelve hours a day, seven days a week, crammed into a car for most of it, held zero appeal.

"Which twelve do you want?" Joe asked, his gaze flitting from one to the other.

"Nine to nine—the daylight shift," Eli answered.

There go evenings.

"That okay with you, Delanie?" Joe focused his full attention on her.

"I was hoping more like six to six. That way we'd still have our evenings."

Joe's gaze returned to Eli.

"The reason I thought nine is because the girl was still sound asleep at seven this morning. We'd be sitting for several hours doing nothing. Plus I'd like to get a pulse on her evening activity."

"All good points. Delanie, why six?" Joe asked.

"The youth center. I'm scheduled there three evenings a week."

Eli gave her a pointed stare. "Maybe your life is better suited for the regular hours a patrol car provides."

"Still hoping to rid yourself of me?" She returned his look with one just as pointed, then looked at Joe. "Nine to nine will be fine." She smiled sweetly at Eli. *You're not winning that easily.*

"Why don't you both take the rest of today off? We'll start the stakeout at nine tomorrow morning. I'm going to issue you a different car in case they spotted the Nova. Eli, if you want to hang around, I'll send you home with it today. Then you can just pick up Delanie each morning and drop her at the end of the day. Save you both the extra time of coming here."

Delanie wrote out the directions to her place for Eli before she left. Eli said he'd turn in the equipment they'd used today.

What do I do with a day off in the middle of the week? Delanie exited the police station and headed for her car. Feeling restless and needing to process everything going on inside her, she glanced at her watch. Barely midmorning. Jodi would be tied up with her first graders for several more hours. Courtney was pulling a twelve-hour shift at the hospital. Kristen might be able to catch an early lunch. She pushed the number 8 on her cell phone, and the call went to Kristen's cell.

"Hey, D, you don't normally call me in the middle of the day. Everything okay?"

"You want to grab an early lunch? I'm free for the rest of the day, and then life as I know it will end for two weeks."

"That sounds like enough enticement to get me to drop everything. Where?"

"Where else?"

Kristen laughed. "Bertha's. I'll be there in about ten minutes."

Delanie decided to walk, clear her head, and grab some fresh air. She'd probably get there about the same time as Kristen.

The host led her to a small booth with a red tablecloth and brown vinyl seats. She faced the lone rock wall inside the place. All of the others were wood paneled. Kristen joined her. Neither even bothered with the menus. They both ordered their old standbys and would share.

"So what's up, girlfriend, and why are you disappearing for two weeks?" One of Kristen's arched brows rose.

"Eli and I will be doing surveillance for the next fourteen days—nine to nine."

"There goes your life."

"Yep, and possibly my sanity." Delanie sipped her iced tea the waiter had just dropped off.

"Sanity?" Kristen's brow wrinkled.

"I cannot tell you how attracted I am to this man. I think I'm falling in love with him. I mean, is that even possible in such a short amount of time?"

"You're asking the wrong girl. I'm still waiting, so I don't even know what falling feels like."

"Me either, having never done it myself, but he is always popping up in my thoughts."

"Always on my mind—sounds like a country western song my dad used to like." Then she proceeded to sing the chorus.

Kristen could always make her laugh. "He is always on my mind. I fall asleep praying for him. I wake up thinking about him. When he smiles, my heart does this little flutter thing."

"You sure it's not a heart attack?" Kristen quipped.

The waiter delivered their food, and they did their usual swapping. After praying, Kristen said, "I'm sorry, D. I know this is hard for you, but laughter is good medicine. I'll be good. Pinkie promise." She held up her pinkie like they did as kids. "Finish your story."

"He's just this incredible guy with character and integrity and everything I'd want in a man—everything except Christ. Sad to say, but he's better than most Christian guys."

Kristen's face showed concern. "What are you going to do?"

"Nothing. What can I do?" She took a bite of her taco. "But for the first time in my life, I understand how easy it would be to fall for an unbeliever. I've always been all smug, thinking it could never happen to me. But it could. It is."

"I guess it's not whether it happens, but what you do when it happens that matters." Kristen's eyes held compassion, and her words held truth.

"Yeah. I'm learning it's easy to have the answers until the rubber of life meets the road of faith. Anyway, pray that I'll stand firm. Some days I just want to chuck all my ideals and grab hold of life, but I know in the long run the cost would be too high. I don't want to rob myself of God's best." Delanie sighed. "Enough about me. How are you?"

"I'm fine. Status quo and all."

"I'll miss not seeing you guys at the youth center, at church, at Bible study."

"It'll be weird, that's for sure."

"I'm also worried about all that intense time with Eli, so don't forget to pray for me."

"I will. Every day." She held up her pinkie again. "Promise." They both chuckled.

"I have another favor. . . ."

Kristen glanced up from her food.

"Can you get me a list of lawyers who do adoptions?"

Kristen nodded. "Sure—no problem."

"Can you also do a little fishing? See if any of the partners in your firm have heard of anyone arranging—shall we say—some very high-priced adoptions."

"Ooh, intrigue, mystery—I love it. I'll see what I can find."

"Discreetly." Delanie felt the need to tack that on.

"Are you saying I lack discretion?" Kristen feigned a hurt expression.

"You're funny, you're direct, but sometimes. . ."

"I know, I know—a bull in a china shop. I've heard that one before." Kristen wasn't afraid to laugh at herself either—a great quality.

"One more request," Delanie said while searching through her wallet for a tip. "This is really out there, but can you make me a list of all the attorneys with George in their names? First, last, middle—doesn't matter."

"George, huh?" Kristen frowned and shrugged. "Okay."

"Unless you come across pertinent info, I'll just get all this from you when my two weeks of torture end." Delanie laughed and slipped from the booth. "We won't be checking out attorneys until then."

After paying their bills, they hugged and said their good-byes.

∞

Eli suffered through being in Delanie's presence day in and day out. She'd been quiet and withdrawn—said very little and asked no questions. He wasn't sure which was worse—the energetic, talkative Delanie or this one. He was thankful their two weeks were almost over. One more day after today. The whole stakeout had been a complete waste of time.

The kid was a couch potato to the max. They'd tailed her to the mall a couple of times, but other than that, she watched TV and played video games. He knew that from the bug Sarge had planted. He'd obtained a warrant, and while Delanie and Eli trailed Brandi last week, Sarge sent a crew in to do the job.

Today was no different. Here they sat watching, waiting, bored to tears. He missed his junior high brood. This assignment certainly wasn't worth giving up his time with them.

At Sarge's request Delanie had worn her pregnant teen getup the last couple of days, in case Brandi hit the mall again. Delanie didn't complain, but he knew from watching her that the bulky thing was uncomfortable and probably hot.

She'd laid her seat back and grabbed a few minutes of shut-eye. They took turns with the afternoon siesta. For a little thing, she was tough as nails. She'd earned his respect in so many ways, but most of all for her performance as a cop. And she read him like a book. He hadn't had a partner he'd been this in sync with since Gus, and that was more than five years ago.

She opened her eyes and caught him gawking. When she smiled up at him, he nearly forgot to breathe.

"Welcome back to the wonderful and exciting life of an undercover cop." He had to say something, or they would have gaped at each other forever. Sometimes when he stared into her eyes, he was certain she was crazy about him, but her actions never supported his theory. Not that he cared anyway. Things were better off this way.

She pulled the lever on the side of her seat to return it to the upright position. "Who knew what I'd been missing all these years?" she joked. "Eighty-four hours a week in a car. It's like being back on patrol, but we never move."

Eli laughed.

"She's coming out!" Delanie pointed to the house.

"I'll follow on foot. You hang back in the car." Eli raised his pant leg and checked his pistol. "Our wire should work for about a block or two, so you'll have to stay fairly close."

Delanie nodded and went around the car to the driver's seat.

"Be careful and watch your back." Eli closed the car door and started a casual stroll down the street. As he rounded the corner at the end of the block, he heard Delanie start the car and glimpsed her rolling forward. Eli kept his eye on Delanie about a half block back, and Brandi was about the same distance ahead.

As expected, Brandi led them to the mall. Eli kept her in sight while Delanie parked the car. He instructed Delanie where to enter the mall so she'd be in Brandi's path. Brandi's first stop was the food court, and Delanie stepped into line right behind her. *This couldn't have worked out better.* Eli settled at a table in the back corner.

"So when are you due?" Delanie asked in a casual tone.

Brandi turned. "You scared me. I didn't know anyone was behind me."

"Sorry." He couldn't see Delanie's face, but he imagined her warm smile winning Brandi's trust. "This is my first baby, and I have a million questions."

"Me, too!" Brandi said.

"Next!" the man behind the counter yelled.

Brandi moved forward and ordered.

"Get her to lunch with you," Eli spoke softly. Delanie gave a slight nod, and he knew her receptor was working.

"Next."

Delanie ended up at the register beside Brandi. "Hey, are you here by yourself?"

"Why?" The one word was riddled with suspicion.

"I just hate to eat alone. Don't worry—I'm not an ax murderer or anything. I just thought if you were here by yourself, too, we could talk about babies and pregnancy and stretch marks." Delanie paid for her order. "It's okay if you don't want to." She raised her left shoulder in a *whatever* gesture.

Brandi picked up the tray with her order on it. "Sure, I guess. I'll grab us a table over that way." She pointed in Eli's direction, and he quickly raised the newspaper he'd carried in—just in case. He couldn't risk her seeing him. She'd flee for sure.

"Her back is toward you," Delanie said softly into her lapel.

He lowered the paper just enough to keep an eye on things. His gaze connected with Delanie's for a brief second as she set her tray on the table. This being her first undercover assignment, she handled herself well, like a pro. She was relaxed and natural. He supposed he shouldn't have been surprised; everything about her was exceptional.

"Do you have stretch marks?" Delanie made a disgusted face, and Eli smiled. Brandi only nodded.

"Man, I have like two hundred of them." Delanie looked around. "Are you expecting someone?" She crinkled her nose the way she often did when she asked a question.

"No, why?"

Delanie shrugged. "I don't know. Your eyes are darting around like you're searching for someone."

"Good girl!" Eli whispered. "Thanks for the tip. I'll keep my eyes peeled." Delanie had taken a bite of her burger when he started talking. She was a quick thinker. That way she had a natural break in conversation with Brandi and could focus on his words.

"So when are you due?" Delanie asked between mouthfuls.

"I'm not really sure."

Eli wished he could see Brandi's face—easier to read a person.

"So I guess you don't know the sex of the baby, then?"

"I don't really want to talk about babies." She rose. "I gotta go." She left her barely touched lunch behind and rushed from the food court.

Delanie turned to watch Brandi depart. Eli scanned the area, but no one was following Brandi as far as he could tell. "Stay put," he told Delanie. She kept eating as if nothing had happened. He carried his paper casually to the trash. While facing the can, he said, "I'll see if I can find her."

Chapter 8

The following morning Delanie tied the laces on her running shoes. She'd started jogging with her dogs before work and then leaving them at her parents' for the day. Twelve hours was too long without a puppy potty break. Her parents had a doggie door, so her pets were free to roam in and out.

"How does someone just disappear?" Delanie asked Hank as she hooked his leash to his collar. They'd lost Brandi, and Joe was not happy. She still hadn't shown up at home when they left at the end of their twelve. Delanie worried about her and prayed for her all night. The girl was afraid. Delanie knew in her gut that someone had threatened Brandi.

"Junie, I'm in no mood to chase you around," Delanie informed the beagle when she dodged Delanie and dove under the bed.

The doorbell rang. Delanie glanced at her watch. Her gut tightened. Nobody came this early with good news. She ran downstairs, checking her peephole before throwing open the door.

"Eli! We're on duty early. . . ." His expression silenced her.

"Mind if I come in?"

She stepped aside, her heart pounding. Closing the front door, she leaned against it for support. "What's wrong?" Fear lodged itself in her throat, and she barely got the words out.

"Brandi's dead."

She buried her face in her hands. "No!" Lifting her head and focusing on Eli, she begged, "Please tell me it's not true. Please." Tears streamed down her face, and his face grew hazy.

He took a step toward her. Hank growled.

"Hank, settle." At her command he lay next to his mistress, eyes on Eli, ears pointed straight ahead.

Eli pulled her into his arms. She buried her face in his chest and wept for a girl she barely knew; yet it felt very personal. He held her and stroked her hair, offering comfort.

"Is this our fault?" She raised her head and sniffed. "Did we carelessly endanger her just to close a case?"

Eli's eyes glistened. He swallowed hard. "We followed orders, Delanie."

Using his thumbs, he wiped the tears from her cheeks, then rested his forehead against hers.

Junie barked, and they both jumped. "We were just about to take our daily jog." Delanie glanced at the dancing beagle. "I think she resents your intrusion."

"Mind if I go with you?" He was in jeans and a T-shirt, but at least he had on his running shoes.

"If you want." Was he or Joe worrying about her safety?

He nodded. "I've got my workout clothes in the car. I usually hit the gym before I pick you up in the mornings. I'll just be a minute."

While he was gathering his clothes, Delanie went into the downstairs powder room and splashed water on her face. Had she made a mistake changing assignments? More important, had she made a mistake approaching Brandi at the mall?

"I don't think I'm cut out for undercover work," she said when Eli reentered her town house.

He sent her a compassionate smile, his eyes bearing sorrow. "Sometimes—like today—I know I'm not." He touched her cheek for a second, then closed the bathroom door.

Delanie caught her breath and rubbed her fingers where his had just been. *I've got to be careful. He's doubly dangerous when he's nice.* She grabbed Junie and snapped her leash in place. Moments later the four of them were out in the crisp autumn air. Eli tried to take Hank's leash, but the German shepherd wanted no part of that. Junie, however, had no qualms, so he jogged with the little dog running beside him.

Delanie set the pace and led the way. Eli had no problem matching her step for step, and at the end of the five miles, he seemed to barely break a sweat.

"I need to drop the dogs off at my mom's before work," she said, breathing hard. She halted when reality hit her. "We're not on stakeout today, are we?"

"Sarge told us to take the day off since it's Friday, but on Monday he wants us to find the guy responsible for this."

"A three-day weekend? I feel at a loss to know what to do with myself." She stretched her legs while they stood on the corner of her parents' street. "I may have to go sit in my car for a few hours just to survive."

He grinned at her joke, and her stomach flitted and fluttered. He sure was cute when he smiled, even with hair that needed a trim and a face that needed a shave.

"My parents live down this way." She pointed. "My mom's expecting me, so if you want to head back to your car. . ."

He shrugged. "I'll go with you." He headed in the direction she'd pointed.

Delanie grabbed his arm, pulling him to a stop. "Eli, am I in danger?"

"Sarge doesn't want you to be alone until we know for sure." They started walking again.

"So you're stuck spending your day off babysitting me?"

"Hey, you're the one who wanted to hang, get to know each other better," Eli reminded her. "You finally got your wish."

"I changed my mind," she informed him—half joking, half deadly serious.

"Gee, thanks." He wore a hurt expression.

But she knew just what they'd do; she'd take him to the youth center. Once he saw how great it was, maybe he'd realize it was the perfect place for his guys to hang out. Then they'd all hear the Word taught, even Eli. Could be a win-win situation—at least that was the hope of her heart.

∞

"Here we are." Delanie led him up the hill at the end of the cul-de-sac to a beige two-story with white trim. This was how he'd imagined her growing up—the perfect well-manicured neighborhood with quiet, tree-lined streets. Following the sidewalk up to the front door, Delanie pulled a key off a chain around her neck. She unlocked the door while Hank and Junie did some sort of happy dance; apparently they enjoyed their visits here.

"Mom?" she called.

Her dad came out of his office, just to the left of the front door. He was tall, in good shape, and toted a full head of silver hair. "Morning, honey." He hugged Delanie and kissed her check.

"Detective Logan." He held out his hand, welcoming Eli.

"Chief Cooper." Eli bobbed his head once.

"I heard about the girl who was murdered last night. I'm sorry." His expression held concern. "Any leads?"

"No, sir."

"It's always harder when it's a kid that dies." He shook his head.

"Where's Mom?" Delanie glanced toward the stairs.

"She had an early meeting this morning. I'm on my way out." He again kissed Delanie's cheek and patted Eli's shoulder. "Lock up on your way out."

"'Bye," Eli and Delanie said in unison.

While Delanie put the dogs out back, Eli's gaze roamed the great room. It was warm, peaceful, inviting—everything his place wasn't growing up. Another reminder Delanie Cooper was out of his league, which didn't matter, because he wasn't looking anyway, he told himself again.

On the walk back to her house, Delanie wanted to stop at Walden's for a mocha ole, and they decided to grab breakfast. Being with her felt natural, and their conversation was comfortable. Frankly, it caught him by surprise. He asked about her job on the force, what she'd done so far and who her partners had been, and he shared the same information with her.

Eli checked her town house thoroughly before leaving her safely locked inside—doors and windows secure—then he ran home, showered, and changed. Her home was cozy—a lot of plants, a lot of candles, but not too girly. Nothing fluffy or ruffled. Her taste was simple. He liked it. A man could live there contentedly.

What am I thinking? He caught himself again. Entering his apartment, he was hit with dark, drab, and undecorated. He realized that though his place was clean and tidy, he was ready for more of a home. On his way to the shower he checked on his dad. He was still passed out in his bedroom, fully clothed, shoes and all, lying on top of the covers. Eli shook his head, wishing there was a way to save his dad from this life he'd chosen. But Eli had tried numerous times and in numerous ways. As the old saying went, you can lead a horse to water, but you can't make him drink—or stop drinking, as the case may be. Eli threw a light blanket over him and shut the door.

When he picked up Delanie, she told him she had two things she planned to accomplish today. The first, meet her friend Kristen for coffee and information. The second, go by the youth center and do some cleaning. Since he was curious about the youth center, her plans suited him just fine.

They met Kristen at a café near her office and shared a quick cup of coffee. He noticed her scrutinizing him when she thought he wasn't paying attention. *Wonder what Delanie's said about me.* She handed Delanie a manila envelope on her way out, apologizing for the rush, but she was working on a case that went to trial next week.

Delanie perused the information from Kristen while he drove to the center, not far from downtown in a warehouse district. The old brick building didn't look like anything special on the outside, but the inside impressed him—it was definitely teen-friendly.

"Want a tour?" Delanie asked.

"Sure."

She flipped on the lights. The high small windows kept the building only dimly lit. Now it was bright, and Eli marveled at all they'd done. "This is quite the place." The walls were painted in loud primary colors, and they'd clustered areas together, giving a warm sense rather than a large warehouse feel.

Delanie smiled. "All done with many loving donations and tons of hard work. You should hear the noise level in the evenings and on weekends."

His gaze traversed the huge room. "I bet."

"Except for the kitchen, bathrooms, library, and movie room, everything is in this main area. We figured without walls it would be easier to keep an eye on everything going on."

The entrance was at the center of the building's facade. Off to his left were a couple of pool tables, foosball, Ping-Pong, and several dartboards. "Impressive." Delanie led him to the right, past several couches set in groupings with chairs and love seats surrounding TVs.

"Those are for video games. We closely monitor the games and are selective with what they can play. Now several companies are producing Christian versions of video games, which makes us even happier."

"So everything was donated? It's really pretty nice stuff."

"I know. Isn't it great? A lot of retailers got on board and gave us brand-new stuff. It was so much more than we imagined or hoped for. We sort of expected outdated electronic equipment and old, worn-out plaid couches."

"And what's wrong with worn plaid couches?" Eli joked. "You could be describing my place."

"Nothing is wrong with them," she assured him. "We gladly would have accepted anything and been thrilled to receive it, but my point was, God always gives so much more."

They'd been working together almost a month, and this was her first mention of God. Eli had expected it long before now. "And sometimes He gives so much less."

"What do you mean?" Though she attempted to sound nonchalant, the shocked expression she wore spoke volumes.

"He doesn't come through for everybody. That's all I'm saying."

Delanie paused and seemed to choose her words with care. "Maybe it looks that way—"

"No, Delanie, it *is* that way."

∞

Her heart actually hurt as he slung unfounded accusations of her loving heavenly Father. She sent up a quick prayer, asking God to heal his hurt and disillusionment. Should she argue God's cause or simply agree to disagree? "I'm sorry you feel that way, but if you'd just get to know Him, you'd discover He's a good and loving God."

"How good is a God who ignores the pleas of a twelve-year-old boy, begging for his brother's life? How good is a God who allows that same kid's mother to leave the day after his brother's funeral? How good is a God who lets some doctor cut open a fifteen-year-old girl, steal her baby, and leave her in a back alley to bleed to death?" His jaw and fists were clenched, and his eyes glistened with tears he seemed determined to keep at bay. And his intense pain became hers.

This morning he'd comforted her, and this afternoon her prayer was to do the same for him. She wrapped her arms around his waist and laid her head against his chest. "I'm sorry, Eli. So sorry." At first he remained stiff, arms at his side, but finally he hugged her back. His silent tears ran down his face, and she felt them drop onto her head.

I love this man, and he hates my Lord. Delanie wept for him, for Brandi, and for the "them" that could never be. Eli held her for a long time.

When Eli took her home late that evening, he rechecked her apartment. On his way out the door, he kissed her cheek. "Thanks for everything. See ya Monday."

Locking the door behind him, she wondered what he'd thought of the youth center as it filled up with teens earlier this evening. He'd shot pool with some of the guys and even listened attentively when a couple of ex–gang members shared their testimonies. She prayed for a seed to be planted.

∞

Eli planned to spend his entire Saturday with his junior high buddies. It had been two long weeks since they'd had more than fifteen minutes together. When he awoke to the sound and smell of rain, he felt cheated.

He padded around his now noticeably dingy apartment for a couple of hours, doing chores and fixing his dad and him some breakfast. They shared idle conversation over a cup of coffee and scrambled eggs. Then Eli switched gears.

"Dad, have you thought any more about trying another rehab?" Just looking at his dad made Eli's heart ache. He seemed much older than his fifty-five years. A life wasted. Alcohol was his drug of choice so he could stop feeling.

"I've tried. Why waste the money? I am what I am." His bloodshot eyes held deep sadness.

"No, Dad, this isn't who you are. I remember—"

"That man is gone. He died a long time ago." His dad rose and headed into the living room, switching on the tube and effectively ending any further conversation.

The boys showed up one by one. By eleven o'clock, seven middle schoolers, his dad, and he were sharing one plaid couch, a matching easy chair, and most of the floor space, all attempting to focus on a football game playing on a TV the size of an old record album.

The youth center popped into his head for about the tenth time. It had to be better than this, but he knew if he took them once, they'd want to go back all the time. Was he willing to listen to the God-thing for their sakes? *Ah. . .why not? It would beat this scenario.*

Eli instructed the boys to go tell their moms they'd be with him the rest of the day. He'd have them home by nine and would escort them to their doors.

Their excitement was worth his personal discomfort. *Hope I don't live to regret this day.*

Arriving at the center, his brood nearly charged the door. Once inside, they headed in fifty directions. They were like kids turned loose in a candy store.

He searched the room for Delanie, a little embarrassed to be there after his uncharacteristic emotional tirade yesterday. He spotted her over by the tables and chairs near the kitchen, talking to a rookie he'd seen at the station a couple of times.

Her gaze connected with his, and she sent a welcoming smile his way. His heart did a little dance, and a moment later she headed toward him.

"Hey, you, I'm so glad you came. Did you bring the guys?"

"Seven of them."

About that time Oscar and Miguel approached. "Hi, Delanie," they said in unison. Both wore face-splitting grins, and admiration was written all over their boyish faces.

Delanie welcomed them. "If you'll excuse us," she said to Eli, "I have two important guests I'd like to show around and introduce to a few people." She made their day. Lately, just seeing her made his. He shook his head, trying to rid himself of the unwelcome thought.

Eli saw her dad playing foosball, Sarge standing over near the video games, and her brother Frank Jr. playing a board game at the far end of the room. Several other cops were scattered around the room, and they all wore bright green T-shirts that said "Cops-N-Kidz" in huge letters on their backs. Delanie carried one and was headed toward him.

"Where are Oscar and Miguel?"

"I lost them in the media room. The Star Wars trilogy is playing today."

"We won't see them again for hours." He reached for the lime green shirt. "Where can I help?" Eli glanced around, but all of the areas appeared well monitored.

Delanie scrunched her nose. "How good of a sport are you?"

"Depends. Why?"

"We're short in the kitchen today. Two people called in sick."

Eli groaned. "The kitchen? You mean no video games, no *Star Wars*?"

"That's what I mean. You in or not?"

"I suppose." He let out a long sigh as if the assignment was more than he could bear. Then he winked. "I take it I'm supposed to put this on?" He held up the bright shirt.

"Yeah, makes it easy for the kids to spot a leader if they need one."

"Green's *not* my color," he joked, heading for the restroom to change. "I'll meet you in the kitchen in five."

The place was bright and cheery, and even with all of the commotion and noise, Eli sensed a peace there. And Delanie. . . Things were changing between them. He'd lost his hostile edge. It felt as if they were on the cusp of friendship. He hadn't had a friend in a very long time.

A couple of minutes later, he joined Delanie in the kitchen. She introduced him to her mother and her sister-in-law, Sunnie. After everyone was served hot dogs, hamburgers, french fries, and baked beans, Chief Cooper said it was his turn to share the message.

Someone dragged out a little mock stage that put him a couple of feet higher, along with a metal music stand. "I hate standing on this thing." He hooked a little mic on the neck of his T-shirt and clipped the box to the back of his jeans. "But it makes it easier for everybody to see me, and it makes me feel taller." He picked up the metal stand and moved it all the way to the edge. "I don't need this thing. I'm not going to use any notes," he informed the guy who'd carried it out.

This was the part Eli dreaded, where they'd try to cram Jesus down everyone's throat. He searched for an escape route, but there was none to be had. *I wonder how they'll try to guilt us all into this.*

Chapter 9

I want to speak on the sovereignty of God," Chief Cooper began. "Being a cop, I have to tell you I often wonder, why do bad things happen to good people? And I also question, why do good things happen to bad people? Doesn't make much sense to me—does it to you?"

None at all, Eli agreed.

"I see the single mother working two jobs just so her kids can eat and live in a rat-infested apartment complex. Meanwhile, the drug lord resides across town in a mansion with servants and enough money to buy anything he could ever want. Where's God? Where's fair?"

Eli noted that all of his brood sat together in a clump at one table. They were in front of him, so he couldn't see their faces, but they, like everyone in the room, were still and attentive. That said a lot for Chief Cooper's speaking skills.

"I don't know about you, but that used to bug me—a lot—until I settled the whole thing with God through studying His Word. I'll tell you what I discovered. . . ."

Eli realized Delanie must have mentioned the "Where was God?" questions Eli had shouted at her yesterday; otherwise, why would her dad broach the subject? *Should have known not to trust her.* He glanced over at her, but her attention was solely on her dad, admiration highlighting her expression.

Eli refocused on Chief Cooper.

"God did create a perfect world for us to live in. The whole account is in the early part of the book of Genesis—if you care to, read it yourself later. There was no sickness, no death, no sorrow, no shame. Then Adam and Eve disobeyed God, choosing to consume the fruit He'd told them to leave alone. How many times do we do the exact opposite of what a parent or teacher asks? I know I had that tendency, especially when I was younger.

"But by sinning, disobeying, doing wrong, Adam and Eve ushered evil into the perfect world God provided. Along with their action came sickness, death, and every form of wickedness. So now because of man's choices, not because of God's lack of provision, we live in a fallen and imperfect world."

Chief Cooper moved around as he spoke, looking into each face. "With

65

cancer, killing—the list goes on and on. But the Bible says it's temporary. Do you know why?"

Some nodded yes, some no. Eli knew why. Jesus. He'd gone to church as a kid, even asked Jesus into his heart. But if a *loving* God didn't care about a twelve-year-old boy, Eli didn't need Him. Anger surged through him.

"If God gave His very own, one and only Son to die in your place, there's nothing He wouldn't do for you. Absolutely nothing."

Except save my brother's life. Make my mother stay when I needed her so much. Eli swallowed, trying to dislodge the lump in his throat.

"Now I'm certain some of you are doubting my words. I see it on your faces. You're thinking, *If what the chief is saying is true, why did my grandpa die or my parents divorce or my mom get beat up?* I guarantee you, none of that is God's will, but every man, woman, and child on the planet has a free will. Each person chooses for himself what his actions and reactions will be. Like the law of gravity—if you drop something from a second-story window, it will splat to the ground. God could override that law of nature but doesn't. You touch a hot stove—you will get burned."

You take too many drugs—you die.

"Bad things happen. Not because God wills them, but because we or other people choose them."

Ronny chose to take more drugs than was medically possible for him to survive. Maybe it wasn't God's fault. The thought was new to him. He felt the words chiseling away inside his chest, chipping down the walls he'd placed around his heart. Chief Cooper asked everyone to bow his or her head; then he said a prayer, but Eli didn't hear. He was too busy with his own. *God, if You're real, and if what Chief Cooper says is true, show me. Please show me.*

Eli wanted to believe, wanted what he saw in Delanie. Was it possible?

He and his posse headed outside after the message to shoot some hoops. The rain had stopped, though it was still cloudy and windy. Several other guys joined them. Eli avoided Delanie the rest of the day, lest she want to play twenty questions about her dad's talk.

At eight he rounded up his crew, and they said good-bye. Amid their protests they loaded into the van and headed toward home. Once the van was rolling, Oscar asked, "Hey, Eli, what you thinkin' 'bout that Jesus dude?"

He'd been thinking a lot about Him all afternoon but wasn't sure what to say to the boy. Eli's head was mixed up; he didn't want to confuse the kid, as well.

"He sounds like a good guy."

"You ever heard of Him before?" one of the boys in the very back hollered.

" 'Course," Miguel answered. "My grandma has pictures of Him in her house. We go to Mass."

"You heard of Him, Eli?" Oscar asked.

"Yeah, I went to Sunday school as a kid."

Eli listened but didn't say much. What *was* he thinking about that Jesus dude? He had no idea, but for the first time in almost twenty years, he was thinking about Him. He wished he could go home and ask his dad, but he rarely saw him. He spent about twelve hours a day at the bar and the rest sleeping it off. Sometimes, like now, Eli ached for someone to talk to. They used to go to church as a family. Why did they quit, and what did his dad believe about God?

∞

Delanie and Eli fell into a comfortable routine. During the week they began their stakeout of various lawyers, and on weekends they spent their time at the youth center. Delanie was dying to know what Eli thought about the various messages and testimonies he'd heard, but she refused to allow herself to pry. If and when he chose to share with her, she'd love to listen, but it really was between him and God.

Delanie pulled up in front of Walden's. She'd been surprised when Courtney called and wanted to get together. Courtney had all but disappeared the past three months or so.

"Hey, Court." Delanie made a beeline for the table and gave her old friend a big hug. "I've missed you, girl. How have you been?"

Courtney literally glowed. "Wonderful." She held out her left hand and flashed a large diamond under Delanie's nose. "I'm engaged."

Delanie so wanted to be happy for her, but how could she be? Her heart weighed heavy in her chest. "Wow, so you are." *Lord, help me know what to say.* "This is quick. Are you sure?"

"Three months is long enough to know." Courtney's tone was defensive. "Truly, it was love at first sight."

Delanie thought of her own timeline with Eli. Yes, three months was enough time to know. Only she and Eli wouldn't have a fairy-tale ending. There'd be no happily ever after. She doubted Courtney would have that experience either, even if she married the guy. They could never truly be one in the spiritual aspect. Blessing follows obedience, just as havoc often marks disobedience. She wished she could make Courtney see that principle.

"So when's the big day?" Delanie hoped Courtney would wait at least a year. She'd read it takes a full twelve months to begin to see each facet of a personality.

"We're talking spring, maybe April."

Delanie bit her lip. "You won't have known him long, less than a year."

"True. About eight months, though, and when you're in love, what does it matter?"

Delanie considered giving her the whole list of reasons to wait but chose not to waste her breath.

"Anyway." Courtney laid her hand on Delanie's arm. "Will you be my maid of honor?"

Delanie smiled, touched that Courtney felt so close to her, and then panic hit her. Would it be wrong to stand up for her friend when she didn't agree with her decision? Or did a true friend shut up and mind her own business?

"You are my oldest and dearest friend." Courtney must have assumed Delanie's smile meant acceptance. "We've known each other since what?"

"Third grade."

"And third grade was about twenty years ago. Over two-thirds of our lives."

Delanie nodded. Even way back when, Courtney never had a hair out of place and always had boys on her mind.

"I never thought I'd be the first one of our group to marry!" Courtney was positively giddy. She stared at her ring. "Can you believe it, D? I'm getting married, and you're going to be my maid of honor!"

No, frankly, she couldn't believe it. This was all happening way too fast, for Courtney and for her. She didn't even know if she wanted the maid of honor position.

"Now tell me about you and the detective fellow. Are you going to race me to the altar?"

Had Courtney not heard a thing she'd said a few months ago? "I told you, I won't date an unbeliever." Delanie's words sounded harsher than she'd intended.

"Tad goes to church with me every Sunday." Courtney refolded her napkin so the crease was exactly in the center.

"You know that doesn't make him a Christian. You're still unequally yoked." Delanie wished she were better at speaking the truth in love; for some reason she always ended up sounding self-righteous.

"He's not now, but he will be. You just watch and see." Irritation wove itself through Courtney's words.

"I hope so—for your sake, I really do."

Jodi and Kristen joined them at the table, and Courtney went through the whole story all over again. Neither of them seemed thrilled either but tried to simulate excitement. Their mouths nearly fell open when Courtney announced Delanie would be her maid of honor. Then she asked them to be her two bridesmaids. They, too, agreed, though Delanie sensed the same uncertainty in them that she wrestled with.

Jodi and Kristen returned to the table with their coffees in tow when Courtney rose. "Hey," she said, glancing at her watch. "I've got to run. I'm having dinner with Tad." She slipped her purse strap over her shoulder. "Thanks for being in my wedding. We'll get together later and pick dresses and all that fun stuff." She hugged each of them and was gone.

Jodi and Kristen were both wide-eyed, mirroring what Delanie felt.

"What just happened here?" Kristen frowned.

Jodi shook her head. "Did Courtney, or did Courtney not, invite all of us to join her for dinner?"

Delanie laughed. "Apparently Dr. Dreamboat must take precedence."

"They're getting married." Jodi's tone sounded as if someone had died.

"I know, and instead of rejoicing with her, we're all saddened by her big announcement." Delanie sipped her mocha.

"What should we do?" Kristen asked.

"I wish I knew." Delanie let out a long sigh. "Last time we got together, I explained why it wasn't a good idea and told her why I can't let my attraction to Eli get out of hand."

"Speaking of. . ." Kristen raised her brow. "He is pretty cute, in a rugged-looking actor sort of way."

"You've seen him?" Jodi asked. Then her accusing glare settled on Delanie.

"Kristen got some information for our case, so we grabbed a quick latte."

"So what does he look like?" Jodi quizzed Kristen.

"Not Delanie's type—that's for sure."

"What is my type?"

"Clean-cut, short hair, well dressed. Everything Eli isn't." Kristen recited the list Delanie once thought described her kind of man.

"You make him sound like a bum off the street." Her hackles rose.

Jodi patted Delanie's hand. "A little defensive, aren't we?"

"No, no." Kristen held up her hand like a crossing guard. "I didn't mean it to sound negative. The guy is very good-looking. His hair isn't long like the hippie look, and he's not toting a ponytail or anything, but it's not that close-cropped look you usually go for—he's sort of shaggy around the edges."

"Like Tom at church?" Jodi asked.

"Exactly. And Eli isn't clean-shaven either." Kristen glanced at Delanie. "Not that that's a bad thing."

"Another Delanie requirement, though," Jodi reminded her. "Does he have a beard? Because you hate beards."

"No beard," Kristen assured Jodi. "Just scruffy. You know that shaved-two-days-ago look?"

"I would think kissing a guy like that could be rough on the face." Jodi rubbed her fingers across her chin and waggled her eyebrows at Delanie.

"You guys make me sound like a stern taskmaster. No wonder I'm still single at twenty-eight," Delanie joked. Then she grew serious. "I've fallen in love with him."

"For real?" Kristen asked.

"Wow." Jodi's brown eyes reflected a million questions.

"Don't worry. I'm not following in Courtney's footsteps, but it happened nonetheless. One thing I've learned—it's easy to have all the answers until you're faced with the questions."

"What about him? What's he feeling?" Jodi asked.

Delanie smiled, and her heart responded, as it always did, with a warm feeling when she let her thoughts wander to Eli. "He's gone from open hostility toward me to a cozy friendship. Sometimes when he looks at me, I see all the unnamed emotions I'm wrestling with, but he guards them closely, just as I do."

"This must be really hard. I'm so sad for you."

Jodi's compassionate response brought unexpected tears. "Me, too." Delanie dabbed at her eyes with her napkin. "I've waited my whole life for the moment I'd fall in love." She could no longer stop the tears. "And my heart betrayed me, falling for a guy I can never have."

Jodi held one of Delanie's hands and gave a little squeeze. "It's breaking my heart to see you go through this." Her eyes were teary, as well.

"Do you think this is some kind of test? Kind of like Job. Maybe God's saying, 'I know Delanie will stand in obedience no matter what's thrown her way.'" Kristen sniffed.

Delanie dried her cheeks and smiled at her dearest friends in all the world. "I don't know. Maybe I'm just in the wrong place at the wrong time. But I'll tell you what I do know—I know why my mom says Christians must be very careful about opening their hearts to non-Christians of the opposite sex. She calls it missionary dating and says it dangerous. For the first time I really understand why. The better I get to know Eli and the more I pray for him, the deeper my feelings run."

"Mother knows best," Kristen quipped.

"The sad thing is, for you, this whole trip down lovers' lane has been completely innocent." Jodi released her hand.

"Yeah. It's not like you chose to date a guy who you knew didn't know God. Work has forced you two into this relationship."

"True. But it's also opened my eyes to so much. It's easy to be self-righteous when you've never faced the temptation. If I've said it once, I've said it a million times: *I would never fall in love with someone who didn't love God as much as I do.*

Not only am I in love with Eli, but he doesn't love God at all. As a matter of fact, he's antagonistic toward Him."

"That's got to be hard, especially since you have to be around him so much." Kristen toyed with her empty cup.

"I can't imagine how difficult it is for women married to guys like him." Delanie rubbed the back of her neck.

"Nor can I envision how hard Courtney's life could end up being. Why doesn't she see it?" Kristen's words were laced with discouragement.

Delanie thought about Courtney's situation. "I'm not sure any of us can see it when it's our own sin."

"You're probably right," Kristen agreed. "But if it's ever me, slap me upside the head, tie me in a closet, whatever it takes."

"Courtney's mistake was saying yes to that first invitation." Jodi looked from one to the other. "Temptation comes in just the right package whether it's a man or whatever would float our boat."

"My mom always says anything that takes our eyes off God and steals our passion can turn into sin—no matter how good or innocent the thing is. If it controls us in any way, we'll end up in trouble." Delanie was only now beginning to appreciate her mother's wisdom.

"So what do we do about Courtney?" Kristen brought the conversation full circle.

"I'm not sure there's much we can do, except pray." Delanie popped the lid off her empty cup and stuffed her napkin inside.

"Why is it that prayer sometimes feels like a passive approach, when truly it's the most aggressive approach?" Jodi tended to challenge their thinking at times. "Only God can change Courtney. We can talk until we lose our voices."

"That's the truth. I've tried to get her to think and share with her my own struggles regarding Eli, but I believe she's determined to have her own way. She's convinced herself she can have the good doctor and God, too."

"And she can." Jodi's statement surprised Delanie. "But she'll never experience the fullness God intended. I think it'll be difficult to give her whole life to God when part of it will always be tugged in another direction."

"And it'll be hard to give her whole self to her husband when he's missing the spiritual component," Kristen added.

"I feel like I need to stop the impending disaster, but as we said, only God can." Delanie shrugged her shoulders. "Let's commit to pray daily for Courtney, for Tad's salvation, and for wisdom to know if God would have us intervene in any way."

"And we'll pray for you, too," Jodi promised.

71

"Yeah, you're not out of the woods yet. Now let's get dinner. I'm starved." Kristen grinned.

Delanie felt better having finally unloaded her struggles on her friends. She'd thought if she refrained from voicing the feelings blooming within, they'd dissipate. Unfortunately, that wasn't the case. They were like weeds, growing bigger and stronger each day.

∞

When Eli arrived at the youth center that evening, Delanie wasn't there. Her brother said she'd taken the night off, and disappointment hit him square-on. The two reasons he came here were time with the guys and more time with Delanie—a fact he hadn't acknowledged until now.

Not in the mood to talk, he grabbed a basketball and headed out back to the court. Nobody was there—which suited him just fine. The chill in the air was his ally, keeping others inside.

He shot the ball, missed it, chased it down—all the while his mind on Delanie. What should he do with these feelings clamoring around inside him? He'd never even expected to like her, let alone fall in love with her. In fact, he'd never planned to fall for anyone, not ever again. He knew women couldn't be trusted in the long haul, but somehow he couldn't quite believe that about Delanie. She was so different from anyone he'd ever known, so full of life and joy.

Something was different about most of the Christian people he'd gotten to know here at the center. The place had a calmness and a peace he sensed whenever he was there, as did the people. No one was perfect, as most were quick to admit, but all seemed centered, selfless, and crazy about God. Their outlook on life seemed foreign to him yet appealing, as well.

He dribbled the ball, pondering his unanswered questions. Were his decisions about women and God made too prematurely, before he had the answers? He shot and missed again, his focus gone. *God, are You real? Is what I'm feeling for Delanie real? And are both of you worthy of my trust, or will it be another hard lesson in the letdowns of life?*

Chapter 10

From your reports and surveillance observations, we all agree the attorney has to be George Benavides." Sarge looked from Eli to Delanie and back again.

Eli nodded. His cop's instinct was certain.

"We haven't been able to get information from any of his clients, so it's time to try a different tack and take a more aggressive stance. We're sending Delanie in undercover."

Eli's heart stopped beating for a split second. Fear clenched his gut. "You mean both of us, right?"

Sarge shook his head. "I mean Delanie—alone. We're hoping he'll feel safer and less threatened by a single, desperate, pregnant female. Word has to have gotten back to him that we're nosing around."

"I don't think that's such a good idea." Eli didn't care for the plan and certainly didn't want Delanie put in any danger.

Delanie sat up straighter. "You still doubt my abilities as a cop?" Her question held disbelief. "Come on, Eli. When are you going to believe I can handle myself out there?" She rose from the vinyl chair and walked to the window.

"She'll be wired. I'll keep you as close as possible, only seconds away. We're checking into the office one door down the hall. It appears to be vacant. We'll have several officers in the building, ready to respond, should the need arise."

Eli nodded. He knew he was overreacting, but Delanie mattered to him—too much. Definitely much more than a partner should.

The phone rang. Sarge answered, then excused himself momentarily, leaving them alone.

Delanie glared at him from her spot by the window, arms crossed over her chest. "I can't believe after working together almost four months we're back to square one."

He fought the urge to take her into his arms and tell her he couldn't bear to lose another person, especially her. Instead, he joined her by the window.

"I have no doubt you're a good cop, far better than most I've seen."

Her expression softened when he acknowledged her abilities as a police officer. "What is your deal, then?"

What could he say? She wouldn't let up until he gave her some sort of answer. He cleared his throat. "I care about you."

Her face became guarded.

Maybe he'd misread her, because he thought she at least considered him a friend. "I don't make friends easily or lightly. Since you're one of the very few I have..." *The only one I have.*

Her face relaxed, and she smiled, sending his heart sailing.

"I only want you safe."

"Thank you." Her voice sounded croaky. "For counting me as a friend. I feel the same about you. And thanks for acknowledging that I'm a good cop. That means more than you know and rarely happens around here."

"Don't let it go to your head." He smiled, hoping to lighten things up. The mood was getting far too sappy for his comfort.

Sarge reentered the office, stopping just inside the doorway. His head tipped a tad to the side, and his gaze bounced from one to the other. "Things okay in here?"

"Fine," they both answered, sounding like kids caught with their hands in the cookie jar.

Sarge raised his brows, nodded, and took his chair behind the desk. "This is the way we'll play this out." He began detailing the plan. Delanie and Eli returned to the chairs, both listening to their instructions. Eli still hated sending her in alone.

"Delanie, if you want to head downstairs, they'll get you wired and ready to roll. I'll go over the building plans with Eli."

"Sure." She headed out the door.

"Something going on between you two?"

Eli shook his head. *Only in my heart.*

"The scene I walked in on looked pretty intimate."

"How? We were standing together by the window—nothing more."

"Maybe it was the rapturous expression on each of your faces, the air crackling with emotion, that misled me."

Eli's heart took flight. Based on Sarge's observations, maybe Delanie's feelings ran deeper than she was willing to admit....

"So why do you object to her going in alone?" Sarge pressed.

Eli rubbed the back of his neck, trying to work out a knot. "I don't want to take any unnecessary risks—with her or with me."

"That's your story?"

"Yep."

"You know department policy. You two can't work together and be involved.

I'd have to transfer one of you to another unit."

Eli knew. He also knew he'd failed to convince Sarge, but other than unspoken attraction, nothing was going on between them.

Sarge went over the blueprints with Eli, showing him where the two other cops would be. They'd all be connected to Delanie's wire, just as Eli would. An officer had confirmed that the space across the hall was vacant, so they'd secured permission to use it. Eli needed to dress the part of a businessman in case he ran into anyone in the hall. "Don't want to raise suspicions."

"Will you let Delanie know I ran home to change?"

Sarge nodded.

"Tell her I'll meet her back here at noon."

∞

Joe had to leave for a lunch appointment, so Delanie waited in his empty office for Eli. All sorts of emotions swirled through her—excitement and anticipation over their assignment this afternoon, and tenderness over Eli's declarations. For a moment she'd feared he was going to proclaim his love or something awful like that. If he did, she'd have to reject him, and hurting Eli would just kill her. Looking back, she knew that was a crazy notion. She did, however, feel blessed that he counted her among his friends.

"Delanie? You awake?" Eli startled her.

"Sorry. Daydreaming." When she turned away from the window to walk out the door, she stopped midstride, and her heart shifted into overdrive. Eli had gotten his hair cut, had shaved, and wore a gray business suit. "Wow. You clean up nice."

He struck a model-type pose. "You like?"

She nodded. His new look only increased the attraction.

"Sarge said I needed to dress the part."

"And dress the part you did. I hardly recognized you."

Eli held the door open for her, made his way around the car, and climbed in. He turned the key; the engine roared to life.

Eli pulled into traffic while Delanie updated him. "I tried to make an appointment to see the lawyer, but his receptionist informed me he doesn't do adoptions, which I find interesting since a large percentage of the clientele we watched coming and going while staking out his office were indeed pregnant. Anyway, then it hit me: He isn't on the adoption list, but the 'George list.' I think Brandi tried to help without helping, if you know what I mean."

Eli pondered that idea. "It never occurred to me that George was a clue. Good work, Detective." His smile told her how proud he was of her. "What is plan B?"

"Sarge said grab lunch, look over the blueprints he gave you, and you can fill me in on that end of things. At three, when the attorney's office reopens after lunch and court, he wants me to be there—upset, crying, I hope, and insisting that my friend told me to come. Do you think I should use Brandi's name? Or just pick a really common name and hope it rings true with him?"

Delanie looked up from her notes and discovered he'd brought her to Bertha's for lunch. "You're scoring all sorts of points with me today," she joked as he opened her car door and helped her out. "You compliment my ability as a cop, bring me to my favorite restaurant, and promote me to your friend list." She dared not also mention how attractive she found him in his new getup.

While they waited for a table, they talked about the youth center and how much his group of junior highers loved being there. "What about you? You've never told me what you think of the place."

He shrugged. "It's okay." The subject seemed to make him uncomfortable.

Delanie nodded.

"I mean, it's a great place for the guys, and I appreciate everyone welcoming them and making us all feel right at home. Don't get me wrong—I'm grateful."

"Do you miss having more time—just you and them?"

"I do."

The host called them and led them down a few steps to the back of the room and a little booth for two.

Eli looked up. "I hadn't noticed this before." The ceiling on this part of the restaurant wasn't wood like the rest, but Plexiglas.

"It's kind of weird being inside yet seeing the sky overhead, isn't it? I think my dad said they added this part later. See the half wall with the large pots on it? That used to be the outside wall. My favorite time to come, though, is in the summer when they open their outdoor patio and you can eat outside in the shade of a big tree."

"You're an outdoor girl at heart, aren't you?"

Delanie nodded. "One reason I chose this job."

"Do you hunt?"

"I have with my dad." She scrunched her face. "I don't enjoy the blood-and-guts part of it. Fishing's the same way. I don't mind the catching part but hate the cleaning part. How about you?"

"I do love any outdoor sport, and I like spectator sports, as well. I'm a huge Angels fan."

"So I noticed by your caps and attire." She winked at him.

"Guess I'm not the classiest guy around, huh?"

"I think you're pretty classy, at least in the ways that matter. Any single guy who dedicates his life to a group of neighborhood kids is the classiest."

The smile he shined on her jump-started her heart.

The waiter arrived with hot plates of food, interrupting the moment.

Delanie took a bite of her enchiladas. "Do you think I should mention Brandi's name when I get to the lawyer's office," she asked again, "or will that draw suspicion?"

"I'm not sure, but let's err on the side of safe rather than sorry. I'm afraid mentioning Brandi's name might increase wariness. What's a fairly common girl's name?"

"Amanda, Melissa. I don't know. Maybe I'll try not to mention a name but just refer to 'my friend.'"

They ate lunch and chitchatted. Delanie loved their easy conversations. If not for her attraction, she'd love to work with Eli forever; but as things stood, she'd decided that when the case closed, she'd request a new assignment. Sarge would understand.

Eli paid the bill. Their short drive to the bank building was quiet. She was planning what to say, and Eli was engrossed in thought, as well.

∞

Eli had never experienced so much apprehension about an undercover assignment before. He hated Sarge's plan and wished he had tried harder to dissuade him. His feelings for Delanie were messing with his mind and impairing his judgment as a cop. This was the first case ever where he wasn't willing to get the guy whatever the cost. He could barely stand the thought of her going in alone.

The irony of the situation was that when they started this case, he worried about Delanie's ability to handle things, but now he was the one struggling to keep a cool head and stay unemotional about her safety on the case. If there was a God, He must have a sense of humor.

"I'm going to park in this garage, which is a couple of blocks away. Right outside the garage is a bus stop where you can wait while we get set up."

Eli drove all the way to the roof of the garage. Only three cars were up there—all empty—and not a soul to be seen. He pulled into a spot, gave Delanie last-minute instructions, and got out to walk her to the elevator.

He struggled to let her go through with the plan. He couldn't bear the thought of something happening to her, and he knew these people weren't afraid of murder.

Delanie reached for the elevator button, and he grabbed her hand. "Wait."

Her brows drew together as she studied him. "What?"

I'm in love with her, totally and completely. Fully acknowledging all of the feelings floating around in his heart caused Eli to throw caution to the wind. He pulled her into his arms and watched several emotions play across her features. The first was surprise, but as his lips found hers, he saw the same longing he felt.

He pulled her close, which wasn't close enough at all with her fake tummy between them. As the kiss deepened, he wondered how it had taken him so long to recognize the love between them. She felt it, too; he was sure of it.

When the kiss ended, he held her tight for several seconds and whispered her name.

She pushed out of his arms. Her expression reminded him of a deer in headlights—dazed and confused. "What are we doing?"

"I have feelings for you, and I wanted—"

"Don't!" She backed up a couple of steps, just out of his reach. "Don't have feelings for me." She pushed the elevator button and turned accusing eyes on him. "I asked you not to *ever* kiss me again." Her voice grew demanding. "Now I'm telling you—never again! You got it?" She pointed her index finger at him.

The elevator doors opened, and she stepped inside. He blocked the doors from sliding shut. "I read you loud and clear." The truth was, he'd completely misread her. "Turn on your body pack so we can make sure our gear is working." They both reached behind them and slid the little buttons over. "Testing."

Delanie nodded that his voice had come over the wire. "Testing," she said in a shaky voice.

"We're good." Eli walked away, and the elevator whisked Delanie off.

He wondered how he'd so utterly misinterpreted her. He leaned against the car to catch his breath and regroup. Though his feelings ran deep, hers obviously didn't. He shook his head, struggling to reconcile her words with the tender looks she sometimes gave him and the kiss they'd shared moments before with this end result. He climbed in the car, slamming the door. Now he remembered why he'd avoided women—none of them made a bit of sense.

∞

Delanie couldn't chase away the memory of the hurt expression she'd brought to Eli's face. It broke her heart to treat him so callously, but she didn't know what else to do.

Exiting the elevator, she took a seat on the bench at the bus stop. She couldn't very well tell him she had feelings for him, too, but because of her relationship with God, she'd have to ignore those emotions. He already hated God enough without her adding more ammunition. Then he'd not only blame God for his brother's death and his mother's leaving, but blame God for their failed relationship, too.

She also couldn't risk telling him the truth in case he decided to become a Christian just so they could start dating. Nope, that was never a good idea. A true conversion had to happen between a man and God, not with the motive of a woman behind it.

The one plus from this mess—Delanie would have no trouble crying in the lawyer's office. She was on the verge now.

A bus pulled up, and the door opened. Shaking her head, she waved it on.

"Then get off my bench, lady," the driver yelled. He shut his door and drove off, leaving Delanie to choke on the bus's exhaust. She rose and started walking toward the bank building.

Eli pulled out of the garage and passed her. "Don't enter the building until you're told." His voice had a hard edge to it. "Copy?"

"Copy." She wanted to find a quiet corner somewhere and bawl her eyes out, but three other guys heard everything she did, so she'd have to be tough and save the tears for later. *Buck up, little buckaroo.*

She walked to Dreamer's and ordered an iced blended mocha. The other two cops teased her and complained about sitting in a hot stairwell while she lived the good life. Eli, however, said nary a word.

Delanie grabbed a table outside and watched the river rush by, wishing she could follow it somewhere far away from heartbreak. Even worse than her own sorrow was knowing she'd hurt Eli. He'd opened his heart for the first time in a long time and offered not only his friendship, but more, and because of circumstances beyond her control, she cruelly shoved the deal back in his face. She knew instinctively they'd no longer share the lighthearted relationship she'd come to love. Eli would shut her out, and their tenuous buds of friendship would not survive today.

Lord, please heal his hurts and touch him with Your love. Send someone who'll adore him and then draw them both to You. Delanie wiped a silent tear from her cheek.

"Cooper, we're in place. Keep us apprised of your approach." Eli was all business.

Digging through her purse, Delanie said, "I'm leaving the river walk. ETA at the front door in two minutes." Once she finished talking, she closed her oversized handbag. Rummaging through it provided a good distraction for conversing without anyone's being able to tell.

She entered the building and pressed the elevator button. She was the only one in it, so she freely said, "Approaching the third floor."

"Copy," echoed in her ear three times.

"This will be my last update, so unless I say different, assume all is going according to plan." Delanie grabbed a stick of gum from her purse. "Excuse the chomping, but I'm role-playing."

She stuffed the gum in her mouth, exited the elevator, and found suite 314.

Delanie's heart pounded. She stopped by the restroom to inspect her appearance. Yep, she looked the part of a pregnant teen. She said a quick prayer and sauntered through the office door and up to the receptionist, requesting to speak to George Benavides.

"Do you have an appointment?"

Delanie chomped, shaking her head back and forth.

"I'm sorry. Without an appointment he can't see you."

Delanie pictured Eli's face when she pushed him away and rejected his offering of something more. This time she could let the tears fall, and fall they did.

"I tried to make an appointment, but you wouldn't let me." She spoke loudly to draw the attention and, she hoped, sympathy of the onlookers.

"Miss, please calm down." The receptionist spoke in a quiet, calm tone. "Mr. Benavides doesn't handle adoptions. Isn't that why you're here? I explained that to you on the phone when you called earlier."

Delanie cried harder, for Brandi, for Julie, for Eli. "He does. I know he does. A girl I met on the bus told me he'd help me find a wonderful home for my baby. Another girl I met in the mall told me the same thing." Delanie sobbed. "Why are you lying to me?"

Two security guards entered the office. The receptionist must have pushed some sort of button to summon them. Delanie hadn't counted on that.

"Please show this young lady out and see that she doesn't return."

The men each took an arm and escorted her all the way to the front door of the building. "You'd best heed our warning, miss. Don't come back, or we'll handle you more severely next time."

Delanie nodded.

"Head to the garage," Eli's voice boomed through her earpiece. "I'm in section 4B. I'll meet you at the car."

All of the emotion of the day wore on her. She wanted to go home, soak in a hot tub, and shed a few tears. Oh, how she wished she could unbreak a couple of hearts.

Chapter 11

Delanie was already waiting when he got to the car. She looked a mess, her face red and blotchy, her eyes swollen. She didn't say a word, which was fine by him. He'd foolishly thought she cared. He'd obviously failed to learn his lesson well enough, but this would be the last time he'd ever open himself to anyone.

He pushed the number 3 on his cell phone and unlocked her door.

"Eli, how'd things come down?" Sarge asked.

Eli recounted the afternoon.

"You two head home. We'll put our heads together and devise a new plan in the morning."

"Will do." Eli shut his phone and slipped it into the pocket inside his suit jacket. When he pulled to a stop in front of Delanie's place, he relayed what Sarge had said.

She nodded. "I think I'll drive myself in to work tomorrow morning. I've got some errands and stuff. . ."

Relieved, he agreed. "Yeah, that's probably better."

She opened her door.

"Delanie?"

She paused.

He hated to ask but had to know.

"Are you going to the center tonight?"

"No. I think I'm going to take a break for a while."

Good. "When you decide to go, if you'll give me the heads-up, I'll stay out of your hair."

She inclined her head in acknowledgment. "Bye, Eli." Her words sounded so final, and his heart hurt with the loss. *What went wrong?* He didn't have a clue.

He was relieved she planned to take a break from Cops-N-Kidz. The guys loved going there, and frankly, so did he. Some unknown something inside him craved more of what he found there—the joy, the peace, even the messages that uplifted instead of condemned. His brood felt the same way, and they often ended up there four or five times a week. Tonight was no different. The vote was unanimous, and they loaded up the van and headed over, stopping at the

Burger House on the way.

Sarge delivered tonight's message, and his words were powerful. He spoke about God's amazing, immeasurable, unconditional love for each person in the room. "No matter what you look like, how unlovable you feel, God adores each one of you. The Bible calls us—all people everywhere—the apple of God's eye!"

Eli felt a tug on his heartstrings but chalked it up to a long day and Delanie's rejection.

At the end Sarge invited people forward to receive Christ. Oscar and Jose both responded to the invitation. Eli envied their childlike faith, wishing it were that easy as an adult to simply believe.

The following morning Eli made his way to Sarge's office, wishing he didn't have to face Delanie after his foolish proclamation yesterday. Talk about a man with regrets.

Yet there she was in the midst of a serious conversation with Sarge. Were they talking about him?

When Delanie saw him, she smiled, one of those ear-to-ear jobs that lit her whole face. "Sarge said Oscar and Jose accepted Christ last night! That's so wonderful!" She bubbled over with excitement.

So that was what they'd been talking about. Probably wondering when he'd take the plunge. He decided a change of topic was in order. "Anybody come up with a plan yet?"

"We need to get an undercover worker into the office." Sarge focused on him. "Any ideas?"

"It would have to be entry level." Eli took the seat next to Delanie. "Cleaning service? Night security for the whole building?"

"What about the receptionist?" Delanie paced to the window. "The person who has direct access to all files."

Sarge nodded. "Could work."

Skeptical, Eli reminded them, "That lady was no-nonsense and pretty hard-nosed. I'm not sure she'd roll over easily."

"Let's check the angles." Sarge grabbed a pen and jotted as he spoke. "Eli, you check out the building, both security and cleaning. Who does it, what sort of access they have to files, and the like."

Pointing his pen at Delanie, he continued, "Find out everything there is to know about the receptionist. We'll meet back here tomorrow morning and make the best plan with all the info available. Agreed?"

A day without Delanie—he'd more than agree.

The next morning Eli and Delanie met in Sarge's office. He was there first. She blamed the line at the coffee shop for holding her up.

"So what did you discover?" Sarge gazed in Eli's direction.

"The janitorial service cleans the building every Saturday."

"That's out. We'd stall the case for another week." His eyes shifted. "Delanie?"

"The receptionist, Lisa Konica, is a single mom with two teenage boys. Both have had minor scrimmages with the law. She needs her job. I think she's the way for us to go." She glanced at Eli, looking as if she expected an argument.

"What's your plan?" Sarge asked.

Delanie shared her idea.

"You have anything better?"

Eli shook his head. "The night guard wouldn't necessarily have access to files."

"All right, then. You two head out and conquer the world. Get the warrants and paperwork in place. I'll arrange for a temp to step in this afternoon. I know the perfect policewoman for the job. Name's Mildred. She'll whip their office into shape in no time."

"We'll get it all done before noon," Eli promised.

They took care of all of the arrangements and at noon were waiting outside the bank building to tail the receptionist. Other than the frosty silence, she and Eli were still simpatico. They worked well together. And other than the empty ache in her heart and the sadness in his eyes, she could almost pretend life was status quo.

"She's leaving the building," announced an officer planted near the elevator on the third floor. Eli glanced at Delanie, and she gave him a nod, letting him know her earpiece worked and she'd heard.

Another announcement came from the cop planted on the first floor. Eli had parked near the receptionist's car, and they'd trail her off the property in case those security goons were anywhere near the site.

The plan was flowing perfectly. Lisa Konica climbed into her car and drove out. Eli followed at a respectable distance.

"Target en route. Thanks, guys," Delanie said into the radio.

"Over and out, then."

"Wonder where she'll go for lunch."

Eli didn't respond to her ponderings other than giving a shrug.

The woman drove toward Delanie's part of town, turning into Plum Tree Plaza.

"I'll bet she's going to Emerald City."

∞

Eli glanced up at the sign. EMERALD CITY ESPRESSO & TEA CAFÉ. No surprise that Delanie knew about this place. Any spot in Reno that sold designer coffee, she had a handle on.

The receptionist entered the restaurant with her purse and a book. "Let's give her space—let her order and settle in. Then we'll join her."

"Okay."

They waited a few minutes to walk in, then got in line to order at the counter. Delanie wore a cap and had her hair up. Without the belly and her trademark hair, they figured the woman wouldn't recognize her until they approached.

Eli perused the whiteboard with the menu printed on it. They had soups, salads, sandwiches, quiches, and pastries. Girl food, if you asked him. Delanie would call this place quaint; he, however, thought it was just plain weird, yuppified to the max.

The one nice touch was a fireplace with a roaring fire. Perhaps Ms. Konica would grab one of those plush couches near the fire.

Once she ordered, she settled in a cozy chair in the corner and opened her book. He and Delanie ordered drinks and sat in a chair on each side of the unsuspecting receptionist.

"Excuse me." Delanie removed her hat, her silky locks falling over her shoulders.

"You! Get out of here right now, or I'm calling the police," Ms. Konica hissed.

"At your service." Eli whipped out his badge. Delanie followed his lead.

Ms. Konica swallowed hard and laid down her book. "What is this about?"

"Your employer." Delanie leaned forward. "What can you tell us about his activities?"

"Look." She paused when the waitress brought her salad. "Thank you." Ms. Konica set the salad aside on the coffee table. "I do my job, nothing more, nothing less, and I don't get involved in the clients' personal dealings."

"Are you familiar with the term *accessory*?" Eli asked.

She glared at him. "I work for an attorney; of course I know and understand legal terms." She acted calm, but her quivering voice belied her demeanor.

"You give us what we need, and we'll keep you out of what comes down." Eli leaned toward her.

Her eyes filled with tears. "I'm a single mother, and I'm all my boys have." She sniffed. "Their dad's been MIA for years. They need me."

Delanie patted the woman's hand. "We know that, and we want to keep you out of this. There are several ways this can play out—the choice is yours. You can give us the information we seek about the baby-selling ring, or we can charge you and run you in."

Terror filled Ms. Konica's face, and Eli knew she was aware of more than she'd admitted to knowing.

Delanie continued. "You go back to work this afternoon, and we gather the needed evidence to make the bust. Choice two, you call in this afternoon with a long-term excuse—mother with cancer, death in the family far away in another state. Offer to set up a temp. We send in an undercover policewoman. In the meantime, you and your boys are taken to a safe house and kept under twenty-four-hour surveillance until this is over. It's your call."

Ms. Konica buried her face in her hands.

"I know this is tough." Eli's patience wore thin. "But you should have resigned the minute you knew your boss was involved in anything even slightly shady, let alone a class B felony."

She raised her head and glared at Eli. "That's easy for you to say. Do you have two kids to feed and no one in the world to depend on except yourself?" She spat out the words. "Mr. Benavides pays me very well."

Delanie also glared at Eli. "I'm sure what Detective Logan is trying to say is that, unfortunately, you're in a difficult position, which results from working for a man who isn't honest."

Ms. Konica nodded her head. "Can you send us to Kansas? My mother is there, and her health is failing."

Delanie glanced at Eli. He deemed her far too compassionate. "We'll see what we can do. Meanwhile, call your boss," Eli instructed.

She pulled out her cell phone, searched her phone book, and found her boss's cell number. Her hand was unsteady. She hit TALK and put the phone to her ear. "Mr. B., it's Lisa. My mom's health is failing, and I need to catch a flight to Kansas this afternoon. I'm having a temp sent in." She paused. "Thank you, sir. I'm not sure how long I'll be gone. I'll keep in touch." Her breathing was hiccuppy, indicating she'd been crying. Everything about the call rang genuine.

"Delanie, why don't you visit with Ms. Konica while I call Sarge?"

Delanie nodded and encouraged the woman to eat her lunch.

Eli stepped outside. "Sarge, Eli. Send Mildred in."

"Good job." Sarge's voice boomed over the cell phone.

"Thanks. Delanie wants to know if we can send Ms. Konica and her boys to Kansas."

"Not yet. After it goes down, we'll talk. Right now I want to keep an eye on her. Make certain she doesn't decide to alert her boss."

"Got it." Frankly, Eli didn't feel the woman deserved any special favors.

"We'll get Mildred in there and have you and Delanie posted in the office you used the other day. She'll be wired, and her code word will be *blue*. You hear 'blue'—you move."

"Yes, sir."

"I'll meet you there this afternoon, and we'll get set up. I've got warrants for video feed and bugs. The whole crew will be there at two, ready to go."

"See you at two."

Eli returned to the café. Ms. Konica was finishing her salad. Two plainclothes officers showed up to escort her to pick up the boys and get them settled.

Eli recapped his phone conversation with Sarge on his and Delanie's drive back. He dropped her off to change into a business suit, then ran home to do the same. When he picked her up not thirty minutes later, they headed back to the bank building.

The afternoon bustled with activity. Luckily George Benavides had court, leaving them open access to the office for a couple of hours.

Sarge brought Mildred over for a quick introduction. Eli wasn't sure what he expected, but a chubby, fiftysomething with attitude wasn't it.

"So you two young things got my back, right?"

"Right," Eli affirmed.

Delanie echoed his answer.

"Okay, enough niceties. I've got to get over there and on the phone with Lisa Konica so I can pick her brain and learn the ropes. I gotta do this job well so old Georgie will keep me around." Mildred smiled and was gone.

By four, everything was in place. Eli and Delanie could watch the office from the monitors across the hall, seeing and hearing everything in the waiting room. They'd placed bugs in the attorney's office, as well.

"Anyone asks," Sarge informed Delanie and Eli, "you're private investigators, recently leaving a bigger firm and starting your own."

Both nodded.

"Mildred's hours are eight to five, so yours will run seven thirty to five thirty. No need to come in to the station; just be here every morning with your lunch in tow. The less attention you draw to yourselves, the better, so lay low."

"Got it." Eli saluted Sarge.

"Mildred will keep her wire on until she's safely in her car. Her safety is priority one; catching the crooks is number two."

Sarge looked both Eli and Delanie up and down. "I hardly recognize you two. No need for the executive attire if you're both private eyes; so come to work tomorrow looking less like lawyers and more like MacGyver."

Eli laughed. "I'd rather look like him any day than wear these duds." He pointed at the only suit he owned.

Sarge left, and Eli and Delanie hung out watching monitors. George Benavides returned and greeted Mildred.

"He seems pleased," Delanie said, watching their interaction on her screen.

"Yeah, what a great decoy. Who'd ever guess she's one of us?"

Delanie glanced at Eli. "Do you think he was suspicious?"

"I think anyone in his boat would have to be—all the time. That's a rotten way to live, always looking over your shoulder." Eli's own words convicted him. That was exactly how he lived—never trusting, never opening up, keeping himself closed off from anyone over fourteen, always looking over his shoulder for the next raw deal to hit his life. His heart pounded faster at the discovery.

He and Delanie waited in silence until both George and Mildred left the office. They exited together and walked to the garage. On the way George asked her about her family, how long she'd lived in Reno, those sorts of things.

"She's perfect," Delanie said in awe.

Mildred was a natural, so calm, so real, so unassuming. She bid "Georgie" good-bye at the elevator. They could hear the heels of her pumps clicking against the cement. Once Mildred was inside her car, they heard the buzzer, the engine turn over, and the seat belt click shut.

"Sitting duck safely in her car," Mildred quipped. "Until tomorrow, over and out."

"That's our cue." Eli removed his headphones and shut down his computer. "Ready?"

He drove back to the department so Delanie could pick up her car and he, his bike.

"I'll meet you in our new office in the morning. 'Night, Eli." Delanie exited her side of the car before he had a chance to get out and open her door.

"See ya."

He decided to go straight to the youth center. Tonight was labeled family night, so all of the guys stayed home, helped with chores, played games, whatever. He was teaching them to initiate relationships and make things happen within their families. He recognized the irony in that but wanted them to have better memories than he did as a boy.

When Eli entered the center, he spotted Chief Cooper. Eli sauntered over to him, hoping to appear casual. Inside, a million questions rolled around. "I was hoping you'd be here. Can we talk?"

"You bet." The chief shook his hand. "I haven't taken the time to tell you how good it is to have you and your brood here so often."

So he'd noticed.

"Let's go in the office. We can shut the door and have some privacy."

Eli had never been in the office. It contained a desk and two upholstered chairs. The chief settled in one and motioned for Eli to do the same.

"What's on your mind, son?"

Chapter 12

Eli sat in one of the wingback chairs facing the chief. "I had some questions regarding your message a few weeks ago—why bad things happen to good people and vice versa."

"I'll do my best to answer."

"I assume Delanie already told you my story and my struggles with God."

The chief had a blank expression. "No. The only thing she's shared with me is your expertise as a cop and how much she's enjoyed working with you."

Though he fought it, the revelation touched his heart with that warm, fuzzy Delanie feeling. "I just assumed you taught that lesson because I'd shared those same questions with your daughter the day before."

Chief Cooper smiled. "Purely a God-thing, son. I had no idea you struggled with those issues, but God knew. Maybe He's beckoning you to Himself. Did He use me to answer some of your questions?"

"God knew. Maybe He's beckoning you. . ." The words reverberated through his head and his heart. *You're proving to me that You're real, aren't You?* "You answered some of my questions, but now I have even more." Eli filled him in on the details of his background—the ugly truths of his life.

The chief's compassionate eyes matched his daughter's exactly. "I'm sorry, son. No boy of twelve should have to deal with those kinds of things. I'd stake my life on the fact that God's heart was as broken as yours. I believe His perfect plan for twelve-year-old boys would be flying kites and playing with puppies, not drugs, funerals, and missing mothers."

His words brought tears to Eli's eyes but also comfort to his heart. "If what you said is true, that bad things happen because of man's sinful choices and not because God wills them, can God forgive me for all the things I've said against Him?"

"He can, and He will. All you have to do is ask. Have you heard the story of the prodigal son?"

Eli shook his head. "I don't think so, not that I can remember, anyway."

Chief Cooper proceeded to recite the story of a boy who'd taken his inheritance, left home, and squandered it on parties and friends. "When he had nothing left and hunger forced him to eat with the pigs, he decided to return home, if only as a hired hand, and beg for his father's mercy."

Eli didn't exactly understand what was happening, but he felt different inside. His heart had softened somehow over the last couple of months as he'd spent time here at the youth center—softened toward God. He no longer felt angry with Him, no longer blamed Him for all of the rotten stuff in his life.

The chief's voice had grown softer and a bit raspy. "While the boy was still a long way off, the father ran to him. He threw a party in his son's honor. 'My son was lost and now he's found.'" He swallowed hard. "I've been that boy, Eli. I chose what I thought was the good life." He cleared his throat. "The good life isn't women and parties. The good life is the joy and peace that come from walking in obedience and living for the Lord. And just as He did for me, He's waiting to welcome you home."

Eli could barely breathe past the wall of tears lodged in his throat. "How?" He could scarcely get anything else out. "How do I find my way home?" A single tear rolled down his cheek.

"Just talk to God like you're talking to me. Tell Him you want to accept His forgiveness for. . .name a few things that come to mind. Tell Him you want to come home."

Eli nodded.

"Would you like a few minutes alone with God?"

Again he bobbed his head, unable to speak. His throat burned.

"I'll give you about thirty minutes, and then I'll come back and we can pray together." The chief grabbed a Bible off the desk and flipped through it. He handed it open to Eli and pointed to a passage. "Here's the story if you want to read it for yourself." He quietly shut the door on his way out.

Eli hung his head and cried as he hadn't cried since Ronny's funeral. He listed the sins that came to mind in his conversation with God and asked Him to forgive them. Just as he couldn't see the wind but often felt its presence, he knew God was right there, and he experienced His love.

After he finished praying for himself and his dad, he reread the story in Luke 15. Eli understood not being worthy to be called God's son, but he also knew that because of Jesus' death on the cross, he was indeed worthy. As he read in verse twenty-four, "This my son was dead, and is alive again; he was lost, and is found." Eli knew he'd been found, and he, too, felt like celebrating.

The person he'd most like to celebrate with was Delanie, but that wouldn't work. He asked God to help him forgive his brother, his mom, his dad, and all of the other people who'd hurt and disappointed him along the way. He longed to find freedom from yesterday and freedom from his feelings for Delanie.

Chief Cooper returned and hugged Eli and then prayed for him, asking God to grow Eli into a man of the Word, a man of prayer, and a man of integrity like Daniel. After his prayer he presented Eli with a brand-new Bible. "Start with John. And remember life is going to happen—the good, the bad, and the ugly—and through it all, God's provisions can be seen if we look for them."

"I'll remember that, sir."

The chief stopped, his hand on the door handle. "And when you're ready, I'd like you to share your testimony. Who knows? It might be just what someone else needs to hear."

Eli grinned. He felt a hundred pounds lighter. "Will you give me a couple of weeks?"

"Done."

"And, sir, will you not tell Delanie? I'd like to surprise her when I share my story." He knew he should apologize to her for crossing the line the other day.

"Deal. And welcome to the family." The chief held out his right hand.

Welcome to the family?

"The family of God."

"Oh."

"You're now my brother in Christ."

"Got it."

∞

The next morning Delanie arrived a few minutes late. Upon unlocking the office door, she found Eli humming. Humming! *What in the world?*

"Good morning." His greeting was exuberant.

" 'Morning," she said, still bleary-eyed.

"Before Mildred arrives and we have to focus solely on her, I wanted to apologize to you."

Delanie nearly dropped her coffee. She set it on the desk and slipped her purse off her shoulder. "To me? For what?"

"I'm sorry about the other day, and it won't *ever* happen again. I was out of line."

"I'm sorry, too, Eli. I way overreacted." She forced her feet to remain planted, wanting nothing more than to run into his arms.

"Then let's forget it, okay?"

"Done." She settled at her desk, pondering what had just taken place. She booted up her computer, contemplating the change in Eli. He'd apologized, and he wasn't the apologizing type. *What gives?*

Soon both she and Eli stared into the video feed of George's empty waiting room. She laughed. "Wonder what he'd think of his nickname *Georgie*."

Eli chuckled.

Delanie sipped her coffee and waited, waited and wondered, wondered about the change in Eli.

Mildred arrived at the office about ten minutes before eight, and she, too, hummed in the morning. Delanie wondered if she'd missed out on some phenomenon that was going around. She had zero desire to hum in the morning.

A couple of hours later, a pregnant teen and her parents entered the office across the hall. Delanie glanced at Eli and he at her.

Mildred greeted them. "I'm new, so you'll have to bear with me. Is this your first visit?"

"Yes," the man answered. "Dr. Barnes sent us."

"Dr. Barnes, huh?" Mildred searched the desk. "Oh, here it is. I'll need you to fill out this intake form, and Mr. Benavides will be with you shortly."

The gentleman took the form and returned to the seat next to his wife.

Delanie already had the phone book open. "Dr. George Barnes," she whispered. "An ob-gyn."

"Why are you whispering?" Eli asked.

She laughed. "So they don't hear me. Guess that can't happen, can it?"

"Not likely."

Eli took the phone book and found the listing. "Now the question is, how do all these young girls get connected with this doctor?"

"Another missing piece of the puzzle."

When the attorney took the clients back to his office, Mildred searched some files. Every time she found another patient of Dr. Barnes, she gave a thumbs-up. Eli kept track of Mildred's signals while Delanie listened in on the conversation back in George's private office, jotting down a few notes as they conversed.

"I think I may have found our link," she whispered. She handed Eli a piece of paper with the name of a school guidance counselor scribbled across it.

Eli acknowledged her lead and refocused on the monitor. "Shut the file cabinet." Eli coached Mildred, though she couldn't hear him. "They're coming. Mildred, they. . .are. . .coming."

Mildred must have heard them coming down the hall, because she quietly closed the cabinet and whipped out a feather duster. She smiled at George as he escorted his new clients to the door.

"You are good, woman," Eli praised her. "You are good! Quick thinker, that Mildred."

"Are there any tasks you'd like done while I'm here?" Mildred asked George when the clients left. "I thought I'd dust, but is there any typing, filing, or anything else you need?"

"No, but thanks."

"Am I doing the job all right? I'm hoping for a good reference from you to the temp agency, so I want to be certain you're pleased."

"You're doing fine." He appeared distracted. "I have a luncheon appointment. I'll be back later."

"Yes, sir."

He left the office.

"What did you learn from eavesdropping on the meeting with George?" Eli questioned.

"I'll play it back for you." Delanie hit a couple of keys on her computer and replayed the tape from a few minutes before.

A very compassionate George Benavides explained the adoption process to the family. There was no mention of money. The only headway was a doctor's name. The same referral name found in fifteen other files.

Eli phoned and updated Sarge.

Delanie spent a long afternoon watching Mildred dig through files and listening to her hum. Eli said he'd plant himself in the lobby so he could warn her when George returned. The day dragged on much as their time did watching Brandi.

Delanie phoned Joe. "How late will you be there tonight?"

"Sixish. Why?"

"I just wanted to drop in and have a chat."

"Alone?"

"Alone. I won't make it until 5:45 or so."

"I'll be here."

The day ended uneventfully, and Delanie headed straight for the department. Upon entering Joe's office, she pushed his door shut.

"One of those kinds of talks, huh?" Joe raised his eyebrow.

Delanie sat on the edge of the padded chair. "When this case ends, and it may soon, I need a new partner."

"Eli getting to you?"

"Not in the way you might think."

Joe frowned. "I'm not following."

"I'm in love with him."

"I thought so!" His face lit up, and he slapped his knee.

How could he possibly be excited?

"Not a good idea for two lovebirds to work together." He resembled the cat who swallowed the little yellow bird.

"I cannot be in love with Eli. You know what the Bible says about being unequally yoked." The sadness weighing down her heart made it feel heavy in her chest.

"I hadn't thought that far ahead." Joe rubbed his forehead with the tips of his fingers. "I guess I'd hoped, with all the time he was spending with God's people, hearing God's Word, a seed would have sprouted."

"Me, too." Delanie sighed.

"After this assignment we'll figure out something. Hey, I already called Eli, but in the morning I need you two in here instead of the bank building. I got someone else to cover Mildred. You and Eli have a doctor's appointment."

"But I'm not really pregnant. Don't you think he may figure that out?"

Joe winked. "I've got a plan, but"—he glanced at his watch—"I'm late. I'll fill you in tomorrow." He grabbed his jacket off the back of his chair and was gone.

Delanie both dreaded and ached for this case to end. The sooner the better. Maybe then her heart could start to heal. Maybe Eli's would, too.

∞

Eli arranged to meet with Sarge a half hour before Delanie's arrival time. When Eli got there, he closed the door. Sarge raised his brows but said nothing.

"When this case ends, I need a new partner."

"I thought by now you'd have figured out she's a decent cop."

"She's better than decent," Eli corrected.

"What, then? Are you still on your 'I won't work with a woman' kick?"

"Not completely, but I'd still prefer my next partner to be a man. I believe Delanie is the exception rather than the rule."

"So you respect her as a cop. What's the problem, then?"

"It's complicated," Eli said hesitantly. He'd humiliated himself enough for one lifetime and didn't want to relive it for another human being.

Sarge said nothing but gave Eli the eye as his dad used to years ago.

"All right. I'm in love with her—but it won't work. Are you satisfied?"

"When the case closes, I'll see who's available."

Not a firm promise, Eli noted. "I'd like to put in for the drug detail again." Sarge nodded.

There was a single rap on the door. "Yo!" Sarge hollered.

Delanie entered. She glanced from one to the other. Her eyes filled with questions, such as why she'd been left out of this powwow.

Neither offered her an explanation.

A second later a pregnant woman entered. She could have been Delanie's sister—small, blond, but not nearly as pretty.

"Delanie, Eli, meet Suzy Jones, aka Lanie Lucas—for today." Delanie's gaze met his. "Eli and Lanie have a doctor's appointment in"—he checked his watch—"two hours. Turns out old Doc Barnes had a cancellation today. Delanie, you and I will attend the appointment from the parking lot, via earpiece. We can only wire Eli for obvious reasons. During the doctor's exam he might stumble across the equipment."

"Wait." Eli didn't care for the sound of this. "I'm going in with her for an examination?"

"Where's cool, calm Eli?" Delanie teased.

"We have it all figured out, and Suzy's husband gave his blessing," Sarge assured them. "It will be aboveboard. The appointment is for a consultation, so there shouldn't be an exam; but in case there is, Eli will play the squeamish boyfriend and station himself at Suzy's head. Should anything get personal, he can turn away and close his eyes."

Eli arched his brow. "And Mr. Jones isn't going to hunt me down later?" He wasn't liking this one bit.

"No, he's very mild-mannered. Anything for the force, you know." Suzy patted her slightly protruding tummy.

"How far along are you?" Delanie asked.

Eli heard a tinge of longing in her question.

"Five months. We just found out it's a little girl, which is what we hoped for. We already have a two-year-old son."

"Nice." Delanie smiled.

Eli left them to their chitchat and ran down to get a body pack. He brought back the earpieces for Sarge and Delanie.

"Let's get this show on the road." Sarge headed for the door. He led them to an SUV parked in the police lot.

∞

Delanie sat in the back with Suzy, and they talked about having a police job with a husband and kids. When Suzy and Eli went into the office building, Delanie joined Sarge in the front, claiming the passenger seat.

They listened to Eli and Suzy as they signed in and filled out forms. Since it had been discussed beforehand, Delanie knew the couple would write that Eli was unemployed and Lanie worked at the Burger House. They would check the no-insurance box. And Eli would pay with cash. Joe had every detail covered. He always did.

"Lanie Lucas," a pleasant voice called out. Delanie heard shuffling, and then the voice said, "I'll show you into the doctor's private office, where he does consults."

Delanie heard the sound of shoes against a tile floor. The same voice said, "He'll be in shortly." And then nothing. Dead silence.

After what seemed like forever, she heard a brief knock and the squeak of a door. "Lanie Lucas, I'm Dr. Barnes."

"This is my boyfriend, Ethan Farnsworth."

"Mr. Farnsworth."

Delanie could easily picture Eli's expressions.

"I see you two aren't in great financial shape to pay for this pregnancy."

"No, sir." Suzy came across as timid and unsure. "My parents aren't exactly thrilled, either. They kicked me out, so we can't count on their help."

"Have you considered adoption?"

"Bingo!" Joe said.

"Well..." Suzy hesitated.

"That's what I think we should do." Eli spoke up.

"You know," the doctor continued, "you can often ask for the baby's expenses to be covered by the adoptive parents, things like the doctor and hospital bill."

"How?" Suzy played the role well.

"I know a lawyer." There was a pause. "Here's his card. I'd recommend you meet with him and weigh your options."

"If we meet with him, are we committed to adoption?"

"Good job, Suze." Joe gave Delanie a thumbs-up.

"Not at all," the doctor assured her in a good-old-boy voice. "You're just checking out the possibilities, nothing more."

"I think I'd like that. At least, like the doctor said, we'd know what our choices are."

Eli's voice brought with it a pang of regret for Delanie. *How I wish we had choices.*

"Do we just call the number on this card?" he asked.

"No. The appointment has to be made through our office. He doesn't take walk-ins. If you'd like, I can have my receptionist set it up for you."

So that's how it works.

"Sure," Eli agreed.

"I don't know." Suzy was holding back.

Delanie thought they did a good job of sounding conflicted, like a true couple might.

"Remember—it's only to see what opportunities are out there for both you and your child," the doctor reminded her in a caring tone.

"Smooth, very smooth." Joe shook his head in disgust.

"Excuse me. I'll be but a moment." They heard the click of a door, so Delanie assumed the doctor had left.

The office was silent while he was gone.

"I wish they'd argue like a real couple might, in case the place is bugged, which it probably is," Joe commented amid the silence.

The door squeaked. "Mr. Benavides has an opening tomorrow morning. Why don't you at least pay him a visit and hear what he has to say?" The man's solicitous tone grated on Delanie. "He's expecting you both, and please take your picture ID."

"We're in!" Joe yelled and high-fived Delanie. "Finally."

Chapter 13

Delanie finished her jog and was walking her final mile to cool down. Today marked the beginning of the end. As they neared the finish line on the case, and she closed in on the termination of her partnership with Eli, she dealt with a plethora of emotions—anxiety, fear, regret, sorrow.

"God, don't let this heartache be wasted. Use it to reveal more of Yourself and to refine me. More of You, less of me." That was the constant cry of her heart, but she had such a long way to go.

Arriving at her town house, she fed her dogs and hopped in the shower. Tonight she and Courtney were meeting for dinner. Courtney thought they were discussing wedding details, but in truth Delanie planned an ambush. She'd invited a friend from high school to join them, a friend who'd married an unbeliever. She couldn't just roll over without at least trying. When Courtney was fully informed and still chose Tad, that would be her business, but Delanie decided she needed all of the facts and felt God nudging her to supply them.

She met Courtney at a restaurant in Sparks, one they hadn't been to before. She'd picked up Mickie on the way. Courtney was already seated when they arrived. Her surprise was evident when the two of them showed up.

"Courtney, this is an old friend from high school, Mickie Jordan, now Mickie Banks."

Courtney hugged Delanie and sent Mickie a smile. "I remember you." She slid back into the circular booth. "You were one of Delanie's brainy friends."

"Guilty as charged. We were on the debate team together." Mickie adjusted her glasses.

Delanie slid into the booth first, and Mickie followed.

"Are you a wedding planner?" Courtney tried to piece the puzzle together.

Mickie giggled. "No. Sadly, I have no right brain at all. Wedding planning would debilitate me. I could never do something so creative, though I wish I could."

"Mickie is a chemical engineer." Delanie placed her napkin in her lap.

"Oh?" The question mark in Courtney's tone grew. Her gaze settled on Delanie; she obviously expected an explanation.

Delanie picked up her menu. "Let's order. I'm starving." She wanted to wait until after the waiter came, figuring Courtney would be less likely to leave if she had food on the way.

They perused the menus in silence, and when the waiter returned, they each placed their order.

"Courtney, the reason I brought Mickie tonight has nothing to do with your wedding and everything to do with your groom." Delanie paused to let the information sink in.

"What?" Courtney's gaze shifted to Mickie. "Do you know Tad?"

"No, but I'm married to a guy just like him—a guy who doesn't know God in a personal way."

Anger settled over Courtney's features, and her face reddened. Glaring at Delanie, she said, "I don't appreciate your interference. It's none of your business."

Delanie wasn't sure whether Courtney would stick around or not. Her posture indicated flight. "Courtney, please, please hear us out. I will never bring it up again, if only you will sit through this dinner with an open mind and open ears."

"Why should I?" The pulse in the side of Courtney's neck popped in and out.

"You told me I'm your oldest and dearest friend. If that's true, then you know how much I love you."

Courtney's expression softened the tiniest bit.

Delanie inhaled a deep breath. "You say this is none of my business, but as your friend and your sister in the Lord, I have to, at the very least, arm you with all the facts. I *have* to be certain you understand the reality of saying 'I do' to a man who doesn't share your faith."

"Fair enough." Courtney rearranged her silverware. "I'll listen if you promise this is the end of your crusade. From this day forward you'll accept my decision and be happy for me. You're my maid of honor, and the least you can do is share in my excitement."

Courtney was right. Delanie never should have accepted the position when she was so convinced of the wrongness of Courtney's choice. *Too late to turn back now.* "I promise." If Courtney plowed ahead, she wasn't sure how she'd feign happiness, let alone excitement, but she would do her best. Nobody wanted a dour maid of honor.

"Okay." Courtney accepted her iced tea from the waiter.

Then he placed a glass of ice water in front of Delanie and a diet soda next to Mickie's silverware.

Delanie glanced at Mickie. "You're on."

Mickie smiled at Courtney. "I'm not here to talk you out of anything. As Delanie said, she wants you to make an informed decision, so I'll share bits and pieces of my life with you. Feel free to ask me anything. I'm going to bare my soul and be honest."

Courtney nodded, squeezing lemon into her tea.

"Just so you understand, I'm crazy about my husband. He's a great guy— kind, thoughtful, generous to a fault. We have two little boys, and he's a great dad, but who will teach my little guys to be godly husbands and fathers? Who is their role model to show them what a godly man looks like?"

Mickie paused, dabbing at the corner of her eye with a napkin. "Don't get me wrong. He teaches them many wonderful things, like work ethic and integrity, but what are the chances my boys will carry their Christianity into adulthood? The hero of their lives models the message that church is for women and kids. Real men don't need God. It's hard enough to raise godly kids with two parents who love the Lord. The odds decrease by at least 50 percent with only one parent, especially if it's not a parent of the same sex."

Courtney listened, but Delanie thought her posture was defensive. This all felt so futile.

"Courtney, I know you don't want to hear this, but at least think about what I'm saying. It can be a lonely life. There's this huge emptiness."

The waiter brought their salads.

"I hear what you're saying, but Tad does go to church. I'm sure it's just a matter of time. . ." Courtney stirred her tea.

"I meet with a group of women in the same boat. A lot of their husbands went to church for a while and then grew tired of it. Now those women go alone."

Delanie spoke up. "Courtney, most men will do anything in the wooing process, but when the honeymoon is over and reality settles in, people change."

"She's right," Mickie said. "I'm reading a book titled *Spiritually Single*. Why don't you at least read it before the wedding? The author is crazy about her husband, but she faced a long and lonely trek for many years. It will give you an idea of what you might face in the days and years ahead."

"I'll think about it." Courtney studied Mickie. "Tell me something—would you marry him all over again?"

Mickie sighed. "That's a really hard question. I love him. We have history and children. Do I relish the spiritual loneliness? No. Do I love the man? With all my heart. If I knew then what I know now, I'd never have said yes to the first date."

"But I already said yes—to the first date, to falling in love, and to his proposal. I think I'm in too deep to turn back now."

Now it was Courtney's turn to dab her eyes. Delanie joined her.

"It's not too late until you've signed the license." Mickie gave Courtney's hand a squeeze.

"Sometimes I am afraid." Courtney's gaze shifted from one to the other. "And I wonder if I'm making the biggest mistake of my life, but it's too late." Courtney paused and swallowed hard. "I've given too much of myself, my heart and other things that I can't get back. I won't change my mind now."

A deep sorrow settled over Delanie. She'd tried and failed. For better or for worse, Courtney would yoke herself to Tad.

Mickie also seemed to sense the futility of their mission. She said nothing more. They shifted into small talk and finished their meal. Delanie prayed she could keep her promise. Her emotions were at the opposite end of the spectrum from happy and excited. Even worse, she sensed Courtney's were, as well.

∞

"Months of hard work are coming to an end," Eli announced in Sarge's office the next morning.

"It feels good, doesn't it?" Sarge glanced up from the folder of paperwork. "This is what we live for—the bust. Beating criminals at their own game and sending men who think they're above the law up the river for a very long time."

"You sound positively thrilled." Delanie grinned.

"I am. I hate people who think they can do as they please with no personal cost. These men have gotten very rich preying on young girls and poor families. Nothing will make me happier than seeing them behind bars. Adding murder to the mix only increases the length of their stay."

Delanie sighed. "If only it were that easy, that cut-and-dried. Sadly, we all know this is just the beginning."

"Now we hope for a jury to see things our way." Eli finished cleaning his gun and returned it to the holster under his pant leg. Then he retrieved the pistol from under his arm. His heart beat faster in anticipation. He, like Sarge, lived for this moment. The bust made the hours of boring stakeouts worth it.

He no longer feared being partnered with Delanie, not in light of her skill and ability on the job. He did, however, fear the damage she'd done to his heart. He knew she wanted another partner as much as he did, so if they made an arrest today, this could end up being their last day together.

The thought brought mixed feelings—sorrow and relief. Nevertheless, he'd see her around. She wouldn't avoid the youth center forever, though a part of him wished she would. He was sure running into her in the future would be a mixed bag.

What he dreaded was the day he ran into her with another guy or the day he heard she was marrying someone else. Eli sighed and checked his chamber. *Time heals all wounds.* Eli knew from personal experience God healed better than time did. He'd made more progress in the past week than in the past two decades.

Smiling, he wondered how Delanie might react when she finally heard his testimony. Her dad promised he'd get her to the center on Saturday. For some reason it was important to Eli that she hear his story, that she know her prayers made a difference. If not for Delanie, he doubted he ever would have given God a second chance. He supposed his unrequited love was worth that.

"Everything's in order." Sarge fanned through the stack of forms one last time. "The warrants are secured." He stood the pile on end and tapped it against his desk, aligning the edges just so. "Months of tailing pregnant girls, attempting interviews with possible adoptive couples, and staking out law firm after law firm ends in this." Sarge waved the folder filled with the evidence, case notes, and legal documents they'd collected. "Soon this will all be passed to the DA, and whether he wins or loses has a lot to do with how well we did our job and the written substantiation we provide. Once we tie them to the baby-selling ring, we're hoping their own files will tie them to the murder victims."

Eli admired Sarge's work ethic; he wanted everything done right and well. He didn't just want the arrest; he went after the conviction.

"The sad thing about that file folder—it's only paper." Delanie's gloomy gaze connected with Eli's. "We've met the people and seen how their lives were affected. Brandi wasn't just a death certificate, a picture, or an autopsy report; she was a flesh-and-blood person who mattered to somebody. And her baby mattered. My hope is that the doctor and the lawyer who run this baby-selling ring are both prosecuted to the full extent of the law."

"We're all on the same page," Sarge assured her. "You're preaching to the choir."

Eli glanced at his watch. "It's about time to roll." He and Delanie both had their wires on, and with her fake belly, they looked very much the part of young expectant parents. A part he'd never play in real life...

Sarge stationed a couple of men across the hall, just in case, though nobody expected more than a routine arrest. "You two be careful. Play it cool, but play it safe."

They both gave Sarge a nod and headed for the car. Eli drove the few blocks to downtown, pulling into the parking garage. Before leaving the car, they double-checked all of their equipment, including their guns. This time there would be no tender scene, no crazy unreturned proclamations—just two cops doing their jobs.

Delanie was quiet and kept clasping and unclasping her hands. Eli figured their nervousness would work to their advantage, which wouldn't be the case in a drug deal. He assumed a young couple considering selling their baby might be a little uneasy.

He held open the door, and Delanie waddled through. She always walked funny with the big belly strapped to her. He'd bet she sure would be cute pregnant. The second he caught the direction of his thoughts, he refocused on the case.

The elevator doors opened, and they stepped inside. Delanie closed her eyes, and he assumed she was praying. He shot up a quick prayer himself. He'd been in much more dangerous situations than this. No one in their right mind would resist arrest in an office complex, filled with people, in broad daylight. Old Georgie's chances would be much greater if he hired a good attorney rather than put up a fight.

They left the elevator and strolled down the hall to the correct office. At least he knew he could count on Delanie—that felt good.

He opened the office door, and she entered first. She approached Mildred's desk. "We're here for our appointment. Lanie Lucas and Ethan—"

"Yes, your paperwork was faxed over this morning." No one would ever guess Mildred knew them or they her. There were no conspiratorial glances or words exchanged with hidden meaning.

Delanie picked up a magazine and took the chair next to Eli's. "I'm not sure this is the right choice," she whispered.

Eli caught a glimpse of a man at the edge of the doorway. They'd put on a good show for him. "Lanie, I don't know what else to do. I have no job. Your parents kicked you out. My old lady isn't going to let us live with her forever."

"But this is our baby." She laid her hand over her padded protrusion. "This is you and me—a consummation of our love. How can you just give our child to a stranger?"

"Love is doing the selfless thing. We have the opportunity to give this baby more—so much more—by letting a wealthy family adopt it and raise it."

"He's not an it!" Delanie raised her voice. "He's a baby. I hate when you do that."

The shoes Eli had seen on the man in the hall stepped around the corner. "Lanie Lucas and Ethan Farnsworth?"

"Yes," they answered in unison.

The man in the expensive suit held out his hand. "I'm George Benavides." Eli shook the guy's hand. "Would you please follow me back to my private office?"

Not as private as you think, buddy. We've got people listening.

Georgie led them and once inside waved his hand toward two leather chairs facing his desk. The desk was fashioned from dark wood, a beautiful piece of furniture—large and masculine.

"Dr. Barnes said you'd like to hear the options. Of course, please understand you're under no obligation. I'm only here to present to you other alternatives than raising your own child. Why might adoption appeal to you?" He raised his brows, his gaze bouncing back and forth from him to Delanie.

Eli knew the guy had already heard the list of reasons he'd verbalized to Delanie while they waited in the reception area. He'd been eavesdropping, but to appease the man, Eli recited them again.

"You make some good points. A few other considerations"—his gaze focused on Delanie—"the child's education. People who spend thousands of dollars on a baby aren't likely to settle for public school. These are highly intelligent individuals, and for any offspring of theirs to receive less than a college degree is unheard of. You get to choose the parents you want for your little one." He laid out several résumés of couples waiting for a baby. "These are all wealthy professionals, and your infant would have the best of everything."

"But would a stranger love our newborn the way we would?" Delanie understood a mother's heart.

Georgie put on his most compassionate face and patted her hand. "Sometimes more, dear, sometimes more. Think of their heartbreak. Many have struggled to produce an heir for over a decade. Sometimes the longer a person waits and the more they want something, the more likely they are to appreciate the culmination of their dreams."

Delanie bit her bottom lip and picked up one of the résumés.

"Dr. Barnes said all our expenses would be covered." She raised her gaze from the paperwork.

He nodded. "That's true. Though it's illegal to sell a child, it is acceptable to cover the medical expenses accrued."

What game did Georgie-boy play? Maybe he kept the proceeds for himself. Eli decided to push. Without an offer of money, they had nothing.

"A guy down at the bar—"

"What bar?" Not a trusting soul, this Georgie-boy.

Eli rattled off the name of a corner joint not far from his place. "Anyway, he said his sister and brother-in-law made twenty thousand dollars for their baby. Said he could hook me up."

"As I said, that is illegal."

Eli nodded and looked the guy over. "I promised Lanie here that if we gave up the baby, we'd have some dough to start fresh, buy her some nice things." He rose. "I think I'll see if Jose can hook us up with the guy his sister used."

George studied them. Delanie rose, glancing from him to Eli. He reached for her hand, and they took their first step toward the door.

"Wait."

They paused.

"Twenty thousand?"

Eli nodded but didn't return to his chair.

Delanie whispered, "This isn't working out. I think it's a sign we should keep the baby."

"Please take your seats for another moment." George motioned them back. They complied.

"Are you willing to sign a contract today if I can get you twenty thousand dollars?"

Eli was quick to agree. Delanie held out.

George pulled a contract from his drawer. "I'll get you the twenty thousand if you agree to silence. Baby selling is a class B felony—enough to get you a lengthy stay in the pen."

How clever of him to manipulate the parents into shouldering the blame. No wonder they couldn't find a single person to rat him out. He had them convinced that they did the crime and they'd do the time. Somehow he managed to come off seeming like the hero.

Delanie looked at Eli. "That's a lot of money."

"It is, baby; it is. We could get a place to live, a decent set of wheels..."

Delanie pulled her lips together in a tight line and cradled her belly. A tiny tear escaped the corner of her eye.

"How about twenty-five thousand?" George dangled a bigger carrot.

Her mouth dropped open. She glanced at Eli, and he gave her a nod. She stared down at her stomach. Sucking in a big breath, she said, "Okay." She turned her attention to George. "We'll do it."

The attorney filled in the blanks with an ink pen on a premade form. Interesting that a guy who didn't regularly pay people for babies had a contract all drawn up and ready to sign.

While Eli examined the contract, he noticed George scrutinizing Delanie for about the tenth time.

"You look very familiar to me." George drew his brows together. "I never forget a face. Are you friends with one of my kids?"

Delanie shook her head. "I don't think so."

"Where do you go to high school?" he demanded.

Delanie froze, and Eli knew she'd forgotten the name of the school they'd discussed. His heart beat faster. *Say something, Delanie; say anything.* Though only seconds ticked by, for Eli it felt like days.

She named the high school she'd graduated from.

Eli watched the attorney's demeanor and expression change. Somehow he knew. He knew!

He grabbed the signed contract with Eli's still damp signature. "If you'll excuse me, I'll have Mildred make copies."

Eli grabbed Delanie's hand and squeezed. When she made eye contact, he mouthed the words *"He knows."*

Chapter 14

Mildred shouted from the hall. "He left! He left the office!"

Eli and Delanie were on their feet and at a dead run. They paused in the hall. He looked left. She took off full speed to the right. Eli followed, and the two officers in the faux office across the hall were dead on his heels.

Delanie tugged open the stairwell door. She was fast; he'd only now caught up to her.

"Did you see him take the stairs?" Eli shouted.

"Yes."

He paused. "You guys go up. We'll go down."

Delanie was already at the bottom of the first half of the flight of stairs. She rounded a corner, and he lost sight of her. Panic spurred him to move even faster. *God, keep her safe.* When he got to the second floor she was still about a quarter of a flight ahead of him.

When she disappeared around the next bend, he heard her yell, "Freeze!" And his heart did just that. Fear for her safety fell over him like a blanket, nearly suffocating him. Circling the next turn, he almost collided with Delanie. He was thankful he didn't. He'd have knocked her gun out of her hand, and they'd have been at George's mercy. As it was now, all three of them held weapons. He and Delanie had the advantage because there were two of them.

Eli decided to stall until their backup arrived. It could take them awhile to follow the stairwell to the roof and back down again once they discovered their assailant went the other direction. "What tipped you off, George?" Eli was surprised by how calm his voice sounded, because inside him was turbulence.

"Her." He took a step backward and moved down one stair.

Eli followed suit, feeling better with Delanie behind him.

"Don't come any closer." George raised his gun.

"George, you're fighting a lost cause. Other patrolmen are on their way. You don't stand a chance." The man had a wild look in his eyes, one Eli had seen before. George wasn't in a surrendering mood. Eli took another step, and Delanie did the same. She stood one step higher and to his right. Her gun was level with his ear.

"Don't move again." George was panicked. He had that fight-or-flight expression. "I'll shoot her if either of you moves again."

Dear God, please, no. "We won't move, George. Will we, Cooper?"

"No." Her breathing was rapid.

He heard the other officers running down the stairs. How he wished they were apprised of the situation. He braced himself for a possible crash when they rounded the corner.

"George!" Eli yelled. "Give yourself up."

The running stopped. A stairwell door opened and shut. *They heard me.* They'd get to the first floor and come in from behind.

George raised his gun. "I won't go down alone."

Eli stepped in front of Delanie, but she shifted to the other side of the stairwell. Not what he'd intended.

The door behind George creaked, and Eli's gaze shifted for a mere second from the assailant to their backup. Delanie leapt in front of him. She yelled, "No!" Her gun fired at the same time he saw a flash from George's. The noise from the two shots echoed through the stairwell with deafening certainty. One of the bullets ricocheted off the metal stair rail. Delanie fell back against him. George crumpled to the ground.

Eli lowered himself onto the stair, gently cradling Delanie. His left hand that lay just under her rib cage was wet and gooey, covered in her blood. "Oh, dear God, please help her."

"Officer down! I repeat, officer down." One of the two patrolmen knelt over George's still form. The other yelled into his radio. "Shots fired! Send an ambulance! Now!"

Eli sat very still, trying to support her without moving. She was losing blood at a steady rate.

"Please don't die," he whispered. It took all his willpower not to sob.

Delanie opened her dazed eyes. "I'm. . .sorry. So. . .very. . .sorry."

"Shh." He caressed her cheek. "You have nothing to be sorry for. You're the bravest person I've ever known."

She moved her head to the side. "My. . .fault. Sorry."

Breathing seemed increasingly difficult for Delanie. "Where are the paramedics?" Eli asked in a loud whisper.

"On their way," the other officer promised. He had joined Eli and was leaning over Delanie.

"Hang tough, Delanie. They're almost here. You'll be fine." How Eli wished he truly believed his own words.

"Forgive. . .me?" Her eyes were glazed over. "Let. . .you. . .down."

"No." He fought the tears. He must be brave for her.

"E?" She gasped for breath.

"I'm right here." He stroked her hair.

"Love. . .you. . .t. . ." Her body went limp in his arms.

"Get somebody here now!" *Dear God, please don't let her die. Please.*

The paramedics ran up the stairs, carrying a gurney. Eli moved out of their way.

"She's in respiratory arrest with a weak and thready pulse."

The words nearly stopped Eli's heart.

"Bag her."

They slipped a mask over Delanie's face and squeezed an air bag, letting the air flow in and out. The paramedic literally breathed for her with his hands.

"Let's go. We need to get her in."

"Will she be all right?" *Please say yes.*

"It's touch and go. She's lost a lot of blood." They carefully lifted her to the stretcher. "We've got to get her to the ER. She needs a chest tube inserted." They strapped her down and wheeled her out. Eli followed until Sarge grabbed his arm.

"Come with me. They're taking her to St. Mary's. I'll give you a ride."

The ambulance shot out from the drive in front of the building, the siren screeching.

"She may not make it." Tears ran down Eli's cheeks. "They said touch and go."

Sarge put his big hand on Eli's shoulder. "Pray. It's our best option."

Never has been for me. He hated feeling that way. Then he echoed a prayer he'd read recently in his Bible. *Lord, help my unbelief.*

"She said she loved me. Do you think she meant it?" Eli watched the ambulance until it disappeared from his sight.

"She did," Sarge assured him without hesitation. "I can guarantee she did."

When they arrived at the ER, Chief Cooper was already there, his face ashen. Eli wondered if her dad would hate him for not protecting Delanie better.

"Eli, Joe." Chief Cooper came over and gave both men a hug. "They've taken her in to insert two chest tubes. I got here before the ambulance arrived. I caught a glimpse of her. She looks bad." His shoulders sagged. "What they know at this point is that she has hemothorax and pneumothorax, both the result of a collapsed lung."

"What does that mean?" Sarge asked.

"She has blood and air in her chest cavity due to the bullet wound and the nonfunctioning lung. The chest tubes will reinflate the lung. Once that's done and she stabilizes, they'll take her to surgery and remove the bullet."

Marilyn Cooper, a woman not much bigger than her daughter, rushed through the sliding doors and straight into the chief's arms. Once in his embrace, she wept uncontrollably.

Eli decided to give them some space. "I think I'll find the chapel."

"I'll join you." Sarge followed.

"I'm terrified she's going to die." He whispered his greatest fear as they followed the signs to the hospital chapel.

"Me, too." Sarge's voice broke. "It's this way." He veered right. "I was here almost a year ago, praying for you while you were in surgery."

The news touched Eli. "Thank you." He patted the big guy's back. Then his thoughts returned to Delanie. "I was so wrong about her." He settled into one of the blue padded chairs and rested his head in his hands. "I was afraid I'd have to take a bullet for her. I never guessed she'd take one for me."

"What happened?"

Eli focused on the stained-glass window at the front of the room. "She was behind me on the steps. When she saw him aim the gun, she jumped in front of me and fired."

"Sounds intentional."

"She was protecting me." He stood, running his hands through his hair. "I should have been the one protecting her. Then she apologized for letting me down, but the entire fault is mine. When I heard the door open, I shifted my gaze for a split second. He'd have shot me, and I never would have seen it coming." He returned to his chair. "Maybe if I hadn't been so hard on her in the beginning, she wouldn't have felt the need to prove herself."

"Eli, sometimes heroics are instinctual. This isn't the first time Delanie's risked her life for the job. Probably would have been her gut reaction no matter how you treated her early on."

"You think?" He wanted to grab hold of that idea and believe it with all his heart.

"I know, and I also know she thought you were pretty terrific."

Eli didn't feel terrific. All he knew was, given the chance, he'd go back and do it all differently, everything except loving her.

"Why do you believe that when Delanie said she loved me she meant it?"

"When people face death, that's when they are the most honest."

Eli supposed Sarge was right. They spent some time in prayer together. It was Eli's first time to pray aloud in front of another person, but it came much easier than he thought it would.

When they finished, Sarge gazed at him through squinted eyes. "I didn't realize you'd become a man of faith."

"Just happened last week. I haven't even told Delanie yet—wanted to surprise her. The chief asked me to share my story at the center tomorrow. Now she may never know. . . ."

"She'll know, Eli. Whatever happens, she'll know." Sarge rose. "Let's go see if there's an update."

The prayer time calmed Eli. In the midst of it he'd come to terms with God's right to choose Delanie's future. He concluded that whatever happened, he'd survive it with God. This time he'd fight for his faith, not walk away from it. But his continual plea was a second chance to share his newfound faith with Delanie. The changes brewing within sometimes surprised him.

Back in the ER waiting room, Delanie's family huddled together in a cluster of chairs, talking in soft tones. Eli hung back, feeling like an intruder. Sarge moved in and took a seat next to her brother Cody. "Any word?"

The chief searched the area and, when he spotted Eli, motioned for him to join them. He took the chair next to Chief Cooper. Eli had met the whole family at one time or another at the center. They all welcomed him now with compassionate looks or nods. No one seemed to blame him—no one except himself. Delanie had a great team rooting for her.

"Delanie is in surgery. God was with our girl today." The chief's voice was deep and raspy. "They say the bullet must have ricocheted rather than a dead-on shot and then entered low in her chest, hit and broke a rib before lodging against a posterior rib, just above her diaphragm. It's the best-case scenario for a gunshot to the chest. That was God's protection. The doctor said if she'd been one step lower, chances are the bullet would have hit her heart for sure."

Eli liked the way this family looked at life. He'd learned much from the whole brood. Before, instead of seeing the blessing, he'd have been mad that God let it happen. Through the teaching and testimonies at the center, he'd learned that what he'd wanted before was a fairy godmother as opposed to a sovereign Lord. He'd wanted to call the shots and wanted God to do the work, his way.

When the doctor came out a couple of hours later, everyone jumped up and surrounded him.

"We got the bullet and stopped the bleeding. No major vessels were hit. Your daughter must have a guardian angel, because the damage was minimal, considering."

God again! Eli decided their thinking was contagious, and he'd caught it.

"Don't get me wrong—she's still listed in critical condition." The doctor looked around at the group that had gathered. "But from a medical standpoint, the fact that she's alive is amazing."

The doctor's words gave Eli hope.

"You may go back two at a time. But let me warn you—she's hooked up to a lot of monitors and machines. Don't let them frighten you. She's yet to regain consciousness, so don't expect a personal greeting. One last thing—she lost a lot of blood and is white as a ghost. Expect it—it's normal at this point."

The doctor led Delanie's parents into the intensive care unit. Eli realized he probably wouldn't get to go back. The sign said immediate family only; he should just pack it up and go home, but he couldn't bear to leave. Somehow he felt closer to her here.

About fifteen minutes later, her parents returned. They filled everyone in on how she looked and reiterated what they should all expect.

Eli still wrestled with what he should do. Should he stay? Should he go? He really didn't belong here. He wasn't family, and as of late he and Delanie weren't even friends.

He approached the chief. "I, uh. . .should go."

"Don't you at least want to see her first?" The chief's brows shot up.

Eli pointed. "The sign says immediate family only."

Her dad smiled and placed his hand on Eli's shoulder. "You are family. You're my spiritual son, and we're all brothers and sisters in the Lord. But more than that, Delanie would want you here. You're her partner and her friend." He gave Eli's shoulder a squeeze. "I thought Cody and Brady could go in next, then you and Sarge."

"Thank you." Surprised by how much the small gesture touched him, he felt as if he finally belonged somewhere, and belonging was a good feeling.

At the top of the next hour, her brothers went in for their short time with Delanie.

When they returned, Chief Cooper gathered everyone in a huddle. "I thought after we've each seen her for a few minutes we could take shifts sitting with her." He'd slipped into his cop persona, taking charge and having a plan. "Since there are eight of us, maybe each of us could take a three-hour segment over the next twenty-four-hour period. Of course we can only sit with her for the fifteen-minute stint at the start of each hour." Her dad glanced at Eli. "But only if each of you wants to—feel absolutely no obligation." All of them agreed they wanted their names added to the roster. Eli took the 3:00 to 6:00 a.m. time slot, leaving the better hours for her family.

A couple of hours later, he and Sarge finally got their turn and went back to Delanie's room. Eli stopped in the doorway, unprepared to see her so vulnerable. She lay there so small and fragile among all of the tubes and machines. Her skin tone gave the white sheets competition as to which was paler.

Sarge picked the chair on the far side of the bed. He laid his hand on

Delanie's and hung his head. Eli knew he was praying

Gaining a new sense of purpose, Eli settled in the other chair on the opposite side of her bed. Resting his forehead against the rail of her bed, he carefully laid his hand on her arm. Her skin was cool against his fingers. He, too, beseeched God on Delanie's behalf.

A little beep on Sarge's watch indicated their time was over, and he rose and stretched. The day had now worn into evening, but Eli wasn't ready to leave yet. "Do you mind if I take an extra minute with her?"

"Go ahead. I'll be in the waiting room."

Eli stood next to her head and leaned in near her ear. "Delanie," he whispered in a shaky voice. "I've invited Jesus to be part of my life. I wanted to surprise you tomorrow with my testimony, but they say you'll be busy tomorrow. So I absolutely had to tell you—I know your Jesus." He longed to say so much more, but the last time he'd bared his feelings to her, she hadn't wanted to hear.

He touched her cheek with the tips of his fingers and decided he'd say it anyway. She'd never know. "I love you, Delanie Cooper." His tears returned. One dropped onto her pillow. He bent over and kissed her cheek. "And I know you don't feel the same way about me, but I needed to say it out loud, just this one time. My life has radically changed—thanks to God and you." He forced himself to walk away, but just before he did, he kissed the tips of his fingers and tenderly touched her lips.

When Eli returned to the waiting room, Delanie's brothers talked him into a game of Battleship. Eli was grateful he'd been invited right into the midst of things. He'd take whatever they gave him, hungry for this type of connection and acceptance.

When the game ended, Eli was tired. He tried to get comfortable in the vinyl padded chairs to grab a catnap, but it wasn't happening. Many of the guys on the force came by, as well as the volunteers from the center and many people from the Coopers' church.

People cared about this family. A woman named Valerie carried in a hot meal. Guys from Brady's paramedic unit brought sleeping bags and pillows. Eli was awed by all of the activity. He was seeing firsthand how the body of Christ functioned when one of its members was in crisis.

Eli, Cody, and Brady each grabbed a sleeping bag from the pile in the corner and unrolled them against a wall, out of the way. It felt good to stretch out his exhausted body. He hadn't realized how tired or hungry he'd been until these good people showed up with precisely what he needed.

The mood had lightened some. Clusters of folks chatted quietly. Eli shut his eyes, convinced he'd never sleep in the controlled chaos, but he did catch a few winks. When he awoke, the waiting room had emptied out. He still had several hours until his shift with Delanie. Her family and another, whose grandfather had undergone a heart attack, had taken over the alcove designated as the ICU waiting room.

Eli paced, went to the chapel for a while, then headed to the cafeteria for coffee. Time dragged. Finally, 3:00 a.m. rolled around. He headed for the double doors of the unit and made a beeline to the third door on the right. He thought Delanie's color had improved slightly.

A nurse came in and checked one of the machines, pushed a couple of buttons, and wrote something on Delanie's chart. Eli settled into the same chair he had before. Less medical equipment was on that side. He carefully slid her limp hand into his and talked to her for the next fifteen minutes. The doctor said touch and familiar voices were an important part of recovery.

They all rotated shifts over the next day and a half. As her vitals stabilized, family members began to leave for showers and sleep. Eli had gone home for a few hours to clean up and sleep in a real bed. Just as he finished his shower, his cell phone rang. His heart dropped as he read the name across the face of his phone. It was Brady.

"Hey." Eli's heart pounded hard against his ribs.

"She's awake!" Brady's voice danced over the line.

Chapter 15

Thank You, Lord. Thank You!" Eli's eyes misted.

"She's asking for you."

"For me?" Someone must have misunderstood what she said.

"Yeah, man, for you." Brady chuckled over the line.

Eli's heart took flight. "I'll be right there."

"She's awake, Dad!" He grabbed hold of his dad—who'd just sauntered into the kitchen for a bite to eat before heading back to his favorite stool at the corner pub just blocks away—and hugged him as he hadn't done in years. "She's awake!"

When he arrived at the hospital not fifteen minutes later, his hair was still wet. He'd grabbed a shirt and his soccer sandals and run out of the house, forgetting the need for incidentals like warm shoes and a jacket.

Parking his car, he ran to the front entrance and took the stairs two at a time, not having the patience to wait on the elevator.

Chief Cooper was in the hall, beaming. "She seems fine. They'll do further testing on her cognitive skills, but I don't think they'll find a problem. Our God is an awesome God!"

"That He is. Is it all right if I go on in?"

The chief slapped him on the back. "Absolutely."

Eli stopped in the doorway. They had rolled the head of her bed up some so she was halfway between lying and sitting. Her eyes were closed, and though still pale, she had much more color than yesterday morning. The doc had said the transfusion would do that. His heart felt as though it might burst at the seams; he was so full of love for her.

Standing there, he suddenly felt shy. He'd said a lot of things to her since the shooting. What if she remembered? His face grew warm at the thought.

She opened her eyes, and he was certain they brightened when she saw him. "Eli, you came." Her voice was soft and weak.

He moved to her bed. "Of course I came."

"I'm so sorry I botched the case. How did I blow our cover?"

"Turns out they were only targeting a couple of the poorer high schools in the city. Dr. Barnes had met with a few of the guidance counselors, generously

115

offering his free prenatal care to pregnant teens desiring to keep their babies or those planning to put them up for adoption. None of the high school employees knew what he was really up to."

"The baby-selling charges are rock solid and should be an easy conviction. The murder charges may be harder to prove, but the DA is hoping, with the help of DNA and both guys' files, to build a solid case."

Delanie moved her head in a rather weak and pathetic nod. "So when I named my high school. . ."

"He'd also seen the newspaper article about your heroics several years ago. The one with your picture—says he never forgets a face. When you named your high school, it all came together for him."

"So George isn't dead?"

"No."

∽

"I'm glad." Remembering the horrific emotions she'd dealt with after the last shooting, she was thankful to avoid that again. "I'm sorry, Eli. I nearly got one or both of us killed. My pride in my ability as a cop had a hole shot right through it."

He smiled at her pun. "It was my fault. I took my eyes off him."

"Please don't blame yourself. Guess I'm another female partner you'll say good riddance to."

He swallowed hard and shook his head. "Sarge put me back on drug detail, after a week of forced vacation. He insists I need the R & R."

A part of her wanted to cry at his news. "So the days of the dynamic duo are over. I don't guess I'll be on active duty anytime soon."

"Probably not." His mood was solemn.

Delanie's eyes filled with tears. "So this is good-bye?"

"I'll see you around." He attempted to be chipper but fell flat. "I have so many things I want to say to you." His gaze shifted to the floor. "I'm sorry I was such a jerk to you in the beginning. I was wrong about you." He raised his gaze to meet hers. "You're a great cop—one of the best partners I've ever had."

"Right up there with Gus?"

"Yep." He smiled. "Seriously, I can't begin to list what your friendship has meant to me." His voice cracked. "And the ways God has used you in my life."

"God? Did you say God?" *Dare I hope?*

"I did say God. Your dad prayed with me last week. This prodigal quit running and found his way home."

"Oh, Eli." He blurred in her vision as her eyes teared up. She held out her hand to him, and he took it. "Last week? Why didn't you tell me?"

"I planned to this morning at the center. Your dad scheduled me to share my testimony, only you were a no-show."

"Sorry about that." She drank in every detail of his face. "I can't tell you how happy I am."

"You have a funny way of showing it." Eli pulled a tissue from the box with his free hand and dried her cheeks.

"You *are* the sweetest man." The words came out husky-sounding. Dare she tell him how she felt? Her heart raced. What if he'd changed his mind? Life was precarious at best. She had no idea what even the next minute held, so she decided not to waste it.

"Eli." She moistened her dry lips. "I love you."

∞

The words warmed his heart. "I know." He'd figured out that much about being a Christian. They all loved each other in the Lord. "I love you, too." *More than you'll ever know.* "Even though we'll probably lose touch after time"—*After you fall for some other guy*—"I'll always consider you one of my dearest friends."

"Thank you." Her smile was weak, and he knew she needed rest. "But—"

"I've worn you out and had better go—"

She tightened her grip on his hand. "Eli, stop talking." Her eyes gazed into his. "I'm *in* love with you."

He replayed her words, and his chest filled with a warm puddle in the spot previously occupied by his heart. "But I thought—"

"Don't think." She stroked his hand and smiled. "I fell in love with you hard and fast, starting the very first day."

"You mean when I was Mr. Charming? How could you have fallen for me then?"

"Seeing you with the guys from your hood blew your hard-edged image away, clinching it for me."

"Then why—"

She explained her reasons and why she didn't feel at liberty to reveal her heart to him.

"I understand." He ran his thumb across her cheek.

"So—what about you?" At his perplexed expression, she continued, "Do you still have feelings for me?"

"So many—respect, admiration, but love is at the very top of the list. I love you, Delanie Cooper."

"And I love you, Eli Logan." She tugged him closer. "Now will you kiss me, already?"

And he did. The first of a lifetime's worth.

Epilogue

A year had passed since Eli had made things right with God. To commemorate his one-year birthday as a Christ follower, he would marry the love of his life.

Delanie wanted to wait a year, make sure they knew the ugly side of each other. The truth was, he hadn't found an ugly side to her, but she insisted there was one. He had yet to see it, though. Of course, love was said to be blind. And he was glad of that, because she seemed quite clueless to his flaws, as well.

Eli followed the minister up on the platform. Sarge stood next to him as his best man. He was the perfect choice; after all, he'd paired them together in the first place. As Eli stood before a church filled with people who loved them and people they loved, he anticipated his beautiful bride walking down the aisle toward him. He smiled at his dad on the first row and at each of his now high school crew lining the entire family pew.

Eli shot off a prayer for his dad. He'd finally agreed to try a rehab the chief had recommended—a Christian-based one. Eli knew firsthand God could change people from the inside out, even when several other programs had failed. They'd also train him to live on his own again. He'd stay at the old apartment, and Eli would move in with Delanie, Hank, and Junie. Of course he'd be at his dad's often, keeping an eye on him and his boys. As hard as it was to watch him continue his battle with alcoholism, Eli knew he had to give up worrying about his dad and trust that God was in control. And he'd learned that God really was in control, even when life seemed to spin out of control.

The music began, and Frank Jr. escorted his mother down the aisle. A tinge of regret hit Eli as he thought of his own mom. As a cop, he could probably track her down, but she apparently didn't want to be found. He'd forgiven her for disappearing, and now he prayed regularly for her. Maybe someday. . .

Mason and Summer, Delanie's nephew and niece, started down the aisle. Courtney and Brady followed them. Next were Jodi and Cody, and behind them were Kristen and Frankie. Delanie couldn't choose one from among her friends, so she'd asked Sunnie, Frankie's wife, to be her matron of honor. She put the others in alphabetical order, avoiding any sort of favoritism. That was his Delanie.

As he watched them coming toward him, he noted a sadness in Courtney's eyes and a droop to her shoulders. Tad couldn't make it today. Duty called at the hospital. He'd all but quit coming to church, and their wedded bliss had already vanished. Courtney never voiced it, but both he and Delanie believed she'd grown to regret her decision. They both prayed for them regularly. If God could soften Eli, He could soften anyone.

When Sunnie reached the stage, the music changed. The "Bridal March" began. Eli's heart shifted into high gear. Delanie moved toward him on the arm of her dad. Their gazes locked. All praise and thanks to God, she'd fully recovered. As she glided closer, he knew one lifetime with her would never be enough.

"Who gives this woman?" the pastor asked when they reached the front of the church.

"Her mother and I." In many ways Frank Cooper had become the dad to Eli that his real father had never been able to be.

"I love you, Daddy." Eli heard her whispered words.

"And I love you." He turned her veil back, kissing her cheek. "Both of you." He hugged Eli and whispered, "I'm so glad her heart found you and yours found Christ."

"Me, too." Eli had grown to love her whole wonderful family. They'd welcomed him and become all he'd ached for as a child. Not only had they embraced him, but they'd also done the same with his group of guys, including them in their gatherings.

Delanie's father placed her hand in Eli's and took his seat on the pew next to her mother. And today Delanie, this woman he cherished more than life itself, would become his wife. God had freed him from the pain of yesterday, and his tomorrows had never looked brighter.

ONLY TODAY

Prologue

Kendall Brooks rose before dawn, not a difficult task since she'd barely slept. Somewhere in the midst of her sleepless frustration, she had decided to spend her last day in Mexico alone with her bike, her thoughts, and her God. As she slipped into her blue and yellow riding gear, she convinced herself that she wasn't avoiding anyone. She was just spending her final day enjoying her favorite pastime—solo. Shoving her thick dark mane of hair into a ponytail at the base of her neck, she tiptoed through the house, scribbling a quick note for her mom and laying it on the kitchen counter.

Holding her breath, she exited through the back door, praying the squeaking didn't arouse one or both of her parents. They, of course, hoped she'd spend the day with them and Javier, but Kendall couldn't force herself to comply. She had to get away.

Lifting her bike from the porch, she straddled it, buckled her helmet in place, and pedaled away fast, skipping her usual memorized preride checklist. Off to the east, the sun's first rays lit the dark sky with tiny traces of orange. Kendall arrived at the bus depot and purchased her ticket, catching a ride north from her home village of Teotitlán. Strapping her bike to the rack on the front of the bus, she boarded and rode the twenty-five miles to Benito Juárez. Out the window, she watched rich orange hues explode across the horizon. *Breathtaking. Lord, Your creation is simply amazing.* One of her favorite things about Mexico was the sunrises, and this one didn't disappoint.

After an hour of jolts and jostles, the bus pulled into Kendall's destination. Unloading her bike, she rode to her favorite restaurant for breakfast. This small community of six or seven hundred people made their living growing flowers and selling them at the market in Oaxaca, so tourism played an important role in their economic survival. The tiny town boasted three diners, one having the highest elevation of all the restaurants in the Sierra Norte mountain range. Kendall parked her bike in front of the small establishment and settled at a cozy table in the corner.

"*Gunaa huiini Brooks!*" the waitress greeted in her native Zapotec. "*Ra riaa stibe binni lidxi? Stibe xombre?*"

Where is your family? Your man? Kendall's brain automatically translated the questions into English before she answered that they were still sleeping. Most people in the eight villages making up the Pueblos Mancomunados of the Sierra Norte mountains in Oaxaca knew the Brooks family, so Kendall wasn't surprised by the personal questions. They'd been missionaries in the area all but two of her twenty-six years. She'd grown up here among the Zapotec people, spoke their language, played with their children, and knew many of them personally.

Kendall attempted a casual smile, hoping to sound and look normal, though inside she felt anything but. She'd trapped herself into a life that wasn't hers, a dream she didn't dream, and now it was too late to escape. Promises had been made, deals sealed, and she no longer controlled her own destiny. The worst part— she wasn't sure God did, either.

"Dxita bere ranchu." Kendall ordered eggs Mexican-style, served with beans, chilies, and cheese. She toyed with her spoon, avoiding curious eyes.

"Candaana, ya?"

Kendall nodded. She was hungry and would need the energy riding to El Mirador—the high peak.

The waitress smiled and retreated to the kitchen.

Kendall pondered her ride and the view at the end. As a silly romantic girl, she'd dreamed of a man proposing to her up there as they gazed out over the vista. She wondered what it would be like visiting that spot with a man she truly loved. Having never been in love, she could only imagine. She glanced down at the slip of gold circling a long chain dangling from her neck. She never wore the ring on her finger. Javier seemed satisfied with it hanging somewhere near her heart. Now she would never ride to the summit with someone she'd fallen in love with, for her chance at that was forever gone.

Kendall said a quick prayer, ate her spicy breakfast, and contemplated her decision to forgo the emotion of love and trade passion for practicality. If only she had some semblance of peace, all of this would be easier, but for reasons unknown to her, peace evaded her.

After paying for her meal, she stretched and remounted her bike. Benito Juárez was where the wonders of the Mexican Sierra began making themselves known. Kendall rode to the local community leader to gain permission to enter the Sierras. This was the custom in the area since they limited visitors to protect the environment. Permission was granted, and she began her trek along the mountain peaks, pedaling at a slow and easy cadence. The view never failed to amaze, and she could see for what seemed like days away. Her legs burned after several kilometers of mostly uphill pedaling, but she pressed on. Part of the trail reminded her of a wild roller-coaster ride through a densely wooded forest. Out here her problems vanished as she concentrated on the ride and the beauty surrounding her. She sucked in deep breaths of the clean, cool, fresh air, and her gaze drank in the pine-tufted mountaintops, the wildflowers, and the occasional squirrel that scampered across her path.

A couple of hours later she reached her destination—almost two miles above sea level. Laying her bike down, she took the seat nature offered on the edge of a boulder and drank in the spectacular views of the Tlacolula Valley. Her heart pounded, her legs throbbed, and her lungs burned, but the end result made the journey worth it.

After catching her breath, Kendall lay back against the rock and let the sunshine warm her face. "God, am I making the biggest mistake of my life? Even if I am, it feels like it's too late." The rest of her life was already in motion, and the momentum grew each day. "I'm so confused, so uncertain." Yet she found herself running just to keep up with the plan. "There doesn't seem to be any way to stop, evaluate, or change the course.

"But the truth is, what I'm doing is selfless, and that's what You are all about—so this must be right, must be Your will." For the millionth time Kendall wrestled with her destiny but didn't come up with any concrete answers—only more muddle.

After another barrage of questions thrown at God, with no answers returned, Kendall assumed she must keep moving forward with their plans—her dad's and Javier's. She shut her eyes against the bright sunshine, and the bike ride and sleepless night took their toll. She dozed under a bright, clear sky.

Sometime later, Kendall—barely awake—swatted at a bug against her cheek. When her hand connected with another hand instead of a fly, her eyes popped open, and she jerked to a sitting position. Her vision took a moment to adjust to the bright sunlight, and she was unsure whether to fight or flee.

"I am so sorry, *amor*. I did not mean to frighten you." Javier ran his fingers across her cheekbone. His familiar broken English calmed her. But his touch never did. She pulled back slightly, and he dropped his hand to his side.

"We walk, yes?" He rose and held out his hand to pull her to her feet.

She accepted, but as soon as she was standing, she tugged her hand away to straighten her hair.

"You need to talk?" His heavy accent laced each word.

Kendall shook her head and followed Javier down the well-worn path. What could she say? *I don't love you. I never have. Your touch leaves me cold. All I want to do is run as fast and far from you as I can.* No, she'd suffer in silence. After all, their match pleased her parents, and Javier adored her. She kept asking God to change her heart, to bless these plans.

Javier stopped and gazed out over the land he loved. "You seem—" He searched for the correct word and glanced in her direction. "Troubled."

She licked her lips, keeping her gaze glued to the valley below for fear he'd see the lie. "I'm okay." Her voice was high and flat. She turned and quickly led the way down the trail, hoping to end this discussion once and for all.

"Your father and I have almost finished translating the book of James in a third dialect."

Kendall paused, and he stumbled into her, taking the opportunity to wrap her in his arms.

"That's wonderful." She slithered out of his embrace. "Only fifty-seven or so dialects to go."

"Thankfully, we are not the only ones working on the translating." He smiled at her, shoving his hands in his pockets.

Her guilt increased. The trail was now wide enough for them to walk side by side. "I'm proud of how hard you and my dad work—the difference you make in people's lives."

He seemed pleased with her praise, and they walked in silence for a while—both deep in thought. He seemed to sense the growing distance between them but didn't appear to know how to fix their problems. Javier, a physically demonstrative man, only intensified Kendall's need for space. He again reached for her hand, and Kendall accepted his offering, fighting the urge to pull away. His calloused fingers intertwined with hers, and she forced herself to oblige him. He seemed content with the quiet as long as he could touch her in some way. So they walked on in silence, his hand caressing hers.

Stopping, he pulled her around to face him. *"Ti gunaa stinnne`."* He whispered the endearment he often used, *my one woman*. His eyes spoke of a deep, abiding love, and guilt nearly strangled her. She looked past him, resting her gaze on the lush green mountains surrounding them. With the tips of his short brown fingers, he brushed a wayward strand of hair out of her face, tucking it behind her ear. He leaned toward her—his lips caressing her cheek in a featherlight touch.

Kendall held her breath, and more guilt weighed her down. *Please don't kiss me. Please. . .*

His lips found hers, and though she begged God almost daily to fill her heart with feelings that matched Javier's, they never came. His respectful kiss left her feeling strangely empty and somewhat disappointed. Never did she savor his touch; she only tolerated it and prayed to love him, truly love him—as a woman should love her man, her *hombre*.

When he pulled back, she smiled, hoping to make up for her lack of response. His earnest brown eyes searched her face. She wondered if he knew, if somewhere within he sensed her distance, her lack of passion, her lack of love.

Surely he must suspect, since she had yet to tell him she loved him.

"We should get back to the village." Kendall pulled free of him and hustled up the trail, hoping against hope that someday she could offer Javier the same deep love he so freely bestowed upon her.

Once they reached the bikes, they headed for home. They wouldn't catch the bus back but would coast down the mountain road from Benito Juárez to Teotitlán. Side by side they rode—their lives woven together with an irrevocable future, yet their hearts miles apart.

Chapter 1

The firehouse tone blared. Brady Cooper threw the kitchen towel on the counter and ran to his locker. The repetitive actions came as naturally as breathing. After a decade, he could get ready for a call in his sleep and honestly had a few times.

Mitch slid behind the wheel and started the ambulance. Brady jumped into the passenger seat, their medic equipment stocked and ready for the call. The sun had set about an hour before, and darkness blanketed the streets.

"Hit-and-run," Mitch yelled over the siren. "Off of College and Sierra."

Only two blocks from the City of Reno Fire Station Number Four, where they spent a large chunk of time each week. They were at the site in a matter of minutes. Brady hopped out of the cab and ran toward the victim, his adrenaline pumping. Her crumpled bike lay a few feet away from where she was sprawled on the pavement. Assessing the situation, he radioed St. Mary's emergency room.

"Female. Midtwenties. Unconscious. Pulse weak. Breathing shallow. Possible broken bones." Brady lifted an eyelid. "Pupils dilated. No ID or medical bracelets."

"Transport immediately," a deep male voice echoed back to him.

"Roger that."

Mitch helped Brady slide the backboard under the young woman. Then they lifted her onto the gurney and rolled her into the back of the ambulance. Brady rode with the patient while Mitch navigated the few blocks to downtown, where St. Mary's Hospital was located. On the ride over, the victim quit breathing. Brady moved quickly, bagging her and squeezing air into her lungs. "Don't die on me," he whispered, staring at the pale but swollen face. Had they not been so close in proximity and had the response time taken longer, she'd have died on the side of that road.

Anger hit Brady squarely in the chest. "How could someone do this to you?" he asked the still form. Why would anyone leave her mangled form in the road to die? Her arms and legs were covered with minor lacerations. A cut gaped near her left eye, and the whole right side of her face was bruised and swollen.

A shiny piece of silver jewelry draped around her wrist caught Brady's eye.

He untwisted it and laid it flat against her sun-darkened skin. KENDALL was engraved in script on the bracelet. "Kendall, you hang in there. We'll find your family, so don't give up."

Once they hit the ER, nurses and doctors rushed the patient out of sight through the swinging doors and down the hall for a thorough exam. Two of the policemen from the scene had arrived right behind Brady and Mitch.

"Did you find any identification, a wallet, anything?" Mitch questioned.

Both men shook their heads.

"Her name is Kendall—at least that's what her bracelet says," Brady informed them and the admitting nurse. "No other info at this time, but two other officers are combing the scene for clues."

"So for now she's Kendall Doe." The nurse typed the information into her computer. "Someone will come looking for her. My guess is she's a college student and her roommate will notice she's missing sooner or later." The nurse sounded so matter-of-fact.

Surely she matters to someone. Brady shrugged, glancing at his partner. "Looks like we're done here."

Brady and Mitch signed off on the case and headed back out into the night. Their shift had just ended, so they drove back to the firehouse to gather their things and go home for a couple of days of R & R.

Brady climbed into his metallic gray SUV and drove up Virginia Street, past McCarran, to his condo sitting on a hillside at the far north end of Reno. Feeling restless but tired, he did some channel surfing in his room after preparing for bed, finally settling on the news. The newscaster shared a few facts about the earlier hit-and-run, asking viewers to contact police Sergeant Frank Cooper Jr. if they knew anything or if a young woman in their lives ended up missing.

"Oh good, Frankie's on the case." Not only did having his older brother involved give him peace of mind that the investigation would be thorough, but Frankie would keep Brady apprised of the progress.

He couldn't get Kendall off his mind and kept remembering when he'd wrecked his dirt bike as a young teen and knocked himself out. When he came to, he was lying in heavy brush, feeling disoriented and quite alone. Finally, Frankie and Cody had found him, but that aloneness had haunted him ever since, and he hated the thought of anyone waking up hurt, alone, and afraid. Did anybody know yet that she'd been hospitalized? Did anybody care? He punched his pillow, hit the POWER button on the remote, and rolled over on his side. However, sleep evaded him much of the night.

The next morning Brady gave Frankie a call. "Hey, bro, what up?" His brother's voice boomed over the line.

"Any new info on Kendall—the hit-and-run?"

"Naw. I saw from the report that you were the medic at the scene. I'll keep you posted. Probably in a couple of days her roommate will figure out she's not just shacking up in the guys' dorm—"

"Frankie, you don't even know her. Why assume the worst?" First the nurse and now his own brother. He felt like the poor girl needed somebody on her side.

"Whoa, bro. A little touchy there, aren't you? You don't know her, either."

"That's right, so I won't make character assumptions."

"Suit yourself, but for a large percentage of college kids, sex is nothing more than a recreational sport. Hey, I'm getting a beep, so I'll let you go and get the other call."

The line went silent after Frankie clicked over. Brady hung up the phone, deciding to grab a shower and head over to the hospital. Maybe Kendall would be awake, and he could help her get in touch with someone.

An hour later, Brady parked his SUV in the lot across from St. Mary's Hospital. He went to the information booth and requested a room number for Kendall Doe. The attendant directed him to the critical care unit on the fifth floor.

Brady followed her instructions. Much of the hospital had been remodeled, leaving everything looking fresh and clean, but he didn't care for the new purple and green color scheme. After his elevator ride, he followed the long hall and breezed through the double doors leading to the CCU.

"Hello, Brady." The greeting came with a warm smile.

"Lucille." He returned the grin. She was one of his favorite nurses. He'd worked this area of Reno for so long that many of the hospital personnel knew him by name.

"Where you been? I haven't seen you in so long I thought you'd found yourself a new woman," the elderly African American joked.

Brady winked. "Not on your life. You're still my one and only. Hey, did Kendall regain consciousness?"

"You mean the hit-and-run?" She shook her head in an exaggerated motion. "No, baby, she's yet to stir."

Brady ran his hand through his hair. "How are her vitals?"

"She's stable—'bout all I can say, bless her little heart. She's got a closed head injury, cerebral contusion, and Doc Anderson is concerned about a possible subdural hematoma."

Brady nodded. "Those often develop slowly."

"She's toting four broken ribs, two broken arms, two breaks in her leg, and her rib punctured her lung. She won't be riding any bikes for a long, long time."

"Any visitors?"

Lucille again shook her head. "Not a one."

Brady hoped by now someone would know. "Do you mind if I go sit with her awhile?"

"You go right ahead." She pointed out Kendall's doorway. "Me, I'll be keeping myself busy with charts and meds."

Brady slipped into the only chair in the glass-encased room. He watched the steady rise and fall of Kendall's chest with each breath. He laid his hand on her arm and prayed that her family would come forward, that her head injury would heal, and that when she woke up, she wouldn't be afraid or alone.

Brady made a point of stopping by the hospital two or three times a day during the next seventy-two hours. Each time he grew more concerned. Kendall's condition hadn't changed and no family had ventured forth.

∞

Kendall heard a guttural sound and realized it came from somewhere deep inside of her. Her head felt as though it weighed four hundred pounds and throbbed. Her eyes were heavy, and though she tried, they refused to open. Every cell of her body hurt. The constant beeping sounds were unfamiliar. She heard some sort of machine purring near her head. Her mouth felt like cotton, and she tried to manufacture some spit to dampen her throat. Breathing in, she realized the scent of rubbing alcohol permeated the sterile air.

"Kendall?" A deep voice spoke softly near her ear. A warm hand touched her arm.

She tried again to open her eyes. Finally, one heavy lid raised and then the other. Everything blurred, and she squinted to gain some focus.

"Kendall?" A man in some sort of uniform leaned over her. His face was earnest and his eyes sincere.

She tried to answer, but her tongue was heavy and uncooperative.

He leaned a little closer. "Can you hear me?"

Her throbbing head wouldn't budge either.

"If you can hear me, blink your eyes twice."

Now maybe that she could handle. With focused determination, she shut her eyes, forced them to reopen, and shut them again. This time they stayed shut. Who was Kendall? She was. . . Her name was. . . She couldn't remember. His voice faded until it was far, far away.

∞

"Lucille, Lucille!" Brady hollered from the doorway.

131

"What's all the commotion, boy? You know I run a peaceful ward."

"She woke up. Even opened her eyes." Brady felt like a kid who'd been given free access to the candy store.

"Well, after almost"—Lucille glanced at her watch—"four and a half days, I say it's about time."

Lucille went into Kendall's room, where she slept soundly once again. She read all the latest vitals from the various machines. "Any response—other than opening her eyes?"

"Yes, she swallowed a few times, opened her eyes and focused on me, then blinked when I asked if she could hear me."

"Blinked, huh?" A skeptical expression settled over the veteran nurse's features.

"At my direction," Brady assured her. "She was aware—I'm sure of it. It wasn't just an involuntary response."

Tiny frown lines embedded themselves between Lucille's eyes. "Why are you so invested in this one, Brady? You're up here more than I am, and they pay me to be here—for twelve-hour shifts." She peered at him over her bifocals, eyebrows raised.

Brady shrugged, shaking his head. "I don't know. For some reason, she matters to me." His explanation sounded foolish, even to him. "And it looks like I may be the only one she matters to. Why isn't anyone looking for her? Where is her family? Her friends? Who did this to her? Was it intentional? All of these unanswered questions plague me constantly." He shoved his hands in the front pockets of his jeans. Then an idea formed.

"Will you keep an eye on her?" he asked.

Lucille lifted one brow. "Again, they pay me to do just that."

"No, I mean a really close eye. Maybe check on her every fifteen minutes or so. I don't want her to be lying in there alone if she wakes up again."

"If I can, I will, but you may notice she's not the only patient in my unit."

"I know, and I appreciate it. I'm heading to the police station. In the meantime, call me if she stirs again."

"You're getting as bossy as some of these doctor types." Lucille reached for the card Brady held out.

"My cell phone number is on there. I'll be back as soon as I can," Brady promised as he rushed through the swinging doors. Hustling through the hospital corridors, he made his way to the entrance, flipped open his cell phone, and pressed the number two. "Hey, Dad, it's Brady." Weaving through the cars on the way to where he'd parked, he continued, "Mind if I stop by your office?"

"Sure, son. I have a meeting in an hour, but I'm all yours until then."

"Great, I'll be there in a few."

The police precinct, where his dad's office resided, was only a couple of blocks from downtown.

Five minutes later, Brady pulled into the station parking lot, climbed the stairs two at a time, and rapped on his dad's partially opened door.

His dad glanced up from a pile of paperwork spread across his desk. "Come on in."

"I came by to ask you some questions about that hit-and-run from the other night. I know Frankie's in charge of the case, but he left me a message saying he'd been up all night on another case, so he'd be sleeping today."

Frank Cooper Sr. nodded. "He mentioned you'd been following the case closely, so he dropped the file off this morning. Said he was pretty sure you'd be by." Concern creased his father's brow. "Why the profound interest in this particular case?"

Brady stood and paced to the window. "People keep asking me that, and I'm not even sure. All I know is that I feel compelled to help her in every way I can."

His dad picked up a file folder off the corner of his desk. "You always were the one who brought home every stray dog and kid you could find. Still are, I guess." His dad flipped open the manila folder and fanned through some paperwork.

"Don't you think it's odd no one is looking for her?"

"At this point, no. My guess is she's an out-of-state student, and her parents haven't realized she's missing. At the beginning of each semester, things are chaotic down at the university, and it takes time to realize who's on first and who's not."

Brady chewed on the information for a moment. "Do you think someone ran her down intentionally—an old boyfriend, a jealous woman, a vindictive roommate?"

"In this line of work, one of those scenarios is never far from our realm of thinking. At this juncture, I can't even guess. Without at least some idea of who she is or who hit her, we can't begin to solve the puzzle because there are no pieces to fit facts together."

Chapter 2

What can I do? With my schedule at the department, I have a fair amount of time off. I know Frankie's working twelve-hour days, and with so many cases open, he doesn't have much time to devote to this one. Why can't we put her face on the national news?"

"We don't have a photo available, and taking a picture of the cut, bruised, and swollen face of an unconscious woman doesn't show the best decorum. From these photos taken at the scene." Frank spread them across his desk, "I don't know that her own mother would recognize her."

Brady stopped pacing and returned to the green vinyl chair facing his dad. "Looks pretty hopeless until she wakes up."

"There were no eyewitnesses, no ID. A smudged tire track is about all we have. The lab is working on that." His dad shut the folder. "They took the pieces of her bike, a smashed cell phone, and everything found around the area. The report says there is nothing notable."

"Can we search around the college area for a car with a crumpled fender and maybe some red paint off her bike?"

"Frankie's already notified the body shops, and I don't have the manpower to do the kind of search you're suggesting. At least not right now. It's been a high crime month, and we have a couple of murders we're trying to solve. As long as Ms. Doe remains alive, she isn't top priority. And honestly, Brady, we have no reason to suspect foul play—at least not at this point in the game." He glanced at his watch.

"Do you mind if I comb the U and check out dented cars?"

"It's your time, but your chances are slim to nil. College campuses are filled with dented cars." His dad rose.

"How about students who haven't done add/drop but haven't shown up for class, either?"

His dad chuckled and slipped into his coat. "Again—next to hopeless. You know that."

"Yeah." Brady sighed. "I'm grasping at anything. How about the national missing person file? Can we access their data and search by first name?"

His dad paused at the door. "Now you're thinking like a cop. Meet me back here at three and we'll see what we can find."

"Deal." Until then, Brady decided to head back to the hospital and sit with Kendall. Maybe she'd wake up again.

Once he was back in her room, he settled into the high-back chair. The room was quiet and dim. He hadn't seen Lucille but assumed Kendall hadn't woken up again.

As was his custom each time he arrived, he laid his hand on her arm and sent up a prayer. *God, You know who Kendall is and every detail of her life. Please provide answers for the police and healing for her broken body.*

His dad was right. Flashing pictures of this bruised and battered woman could serve no purpose. His gaze roamed over her face, wondering what she might actually look like. Her thick dark lashes fanned out from her closed eyes, and thick but well-shaped brows arched above them. Her long raven hair lay in stark contrast against the white pillowcase and only intensified the paleness of her face. Long, slender limbs made him wonder how tall she was.

"No change while you were gone," Lucille stated in a loud whisper from the doorway.

"Thanks, Luce," Brady whispered back. "I'll hang out here for a while. If she wakes up, I'll holler."

"You will do no such thing, Brady Cooper." She placed her hands on her hips. "You will quietly and respectfully come find me, but you will not disturb my unit."

Brady grinned. Lovable Lucille was no-nonsense and guarded her patients with the petulance of a mama bear.

"Agreed?" She demanded a verbal response.

"Agreed."

"Better." She turned and marched away from the door.

Kendall stirred and groaned. "Water. Please, I need water."

Brady touched her arm. "Kendall, I'll go get your nurse—"

"Nurse?" Her right eye opened to a small slit. The confused, contorted face exposed how much pain she was in and how little she knew about her condition. "Hurt. Please—help—me." Her words, barely audible, were filled with pain.

Brady leaned over her bed, brushing her hair off her forehead. "I'll help you. You wait right here, and I'll get help."

You wait right here? How stupid! What else could she possibly do?

∞

Kendall's gaze followed the man out the door. She glanced around the room, trying to make sense of where she was. Nothing seemed familiar. She knew she was lying in a hospital bed in a lot of pain, but why?

"Hello, darlin'." A heavy black woman shined a light into her eyes. "Welcome back."

"Where was I?"

"You were in an accident—with your bike. Do you remember?"

Kendall shook her head. Even that slight movement hurt.

The nice man from before laid his hand on her arm. Her gaze rested on his compassionate face while the nurse poked and prodded.

"I paged your doctor. He should be here any minute. He'll be thrilled to see those green eyes of yours open. You sit tight, and I'll check on you in a while." The nurse turned to leave.

"Am I going to die?" Kendall couldn't help wondering since she was hooked up to who knew what and in incredible pain.

"No," the man with the kind eyes assured her. "It will be a while before you feel like your old self again, though."

Her old self? She couldn't remember what her old self felt like. The whole experience felt surreal—as if this wasn't really her but someone else.

"I'm Brady, by the way." He lifted his hand from her arm and sort of shook her hand.

"Do you work here?"

"No."

He had a nice face.

"I'm a paramedic. My partner, Mitch, and I brought you in."

"Brought me in from where?"

"We picked you up at the scene of the accident and transported you in our ambulance to this hospital."

"I can't remember."

"It's okay. You hit your head pretty hard. It's not unusual for memory loss to occur."

"Kendall, you're awake!" A man in a white coat stood on the opposite side of her bed from Brady.

She nodded.

"You've been through quite an ordeal, young lady. It's good to have you back with us. Did your nurse or this gentleman explain what happened?"

"I don't think so."

"You seem a little disoriented, and it's no wonder. You sustained pretty severe head trauma." The doctor picked up her chart. "Kendall, can you tell me your last name?"

She tried and tried, but nothing came. "I—I can't remember."

"How about your parents' names?"

She shook her head.

"Do you know where you live?"

Panic rose within. "I don't."

"Are you family?" His question was directed at Brady.

"No, sir. I'm the medic from the scene."

"The medic?" His face reflected his confusion.

"Her family hasn't been notified, so I've been keeping an eye on things."

The doctor nodded, but his expression questioned Brady's ulterior motive.

"Since you're not family, I'll have to ask you to leave."

∞

Kendall's head jerked in Brady's direction, and she grabbed his hand that was resting on the bed rail directly above hers. "No, please don't leave me." A panicked look had settled across her features.

Brady glanced at the doctor. "I'm Brady Cooper, Dr. Anderson." Brady offered his right hand—the one Kendall didn't have a death grip on—and the men shook. "My father is Police Chief Frank Cooper. He and I are monitoring this case closely, trying to ID the patient, the family, and the assailant."

"If my patient wants you here, then you are welcome to stay." His tone clearly conveyed his disapproval.

"I do," Kendall assured Dr. Anderson. Then her gaze returned to Brady. "Thank you."

The terror residing in her eyes evoked a silent vow from him that he'd walk through this difficult time with her—no matter how long it took. No one should face this much devastation alone.

"Mr. Cooper can probably fill you in about the accident and what took place at the scene. When you arrived here in the ER, you were in pretty bad shape." Dr. Anderson laid her file on the bedside table.

"You'd been bagged because you'd stopped breathing."

Kendall closed her eyes at the news.

"X-rays revealed multiple arm and leg fractures. The surgeon patched you up with pins and plates. Now that you're awake, we will do further evaluating and get you into therapy services."

"Therapy?" Kendall bit her bottom lip, glancing from Brady to the doctor and back to Brady again.

"Physical, occupational, and possibly even speech. St. Mary's is a level one trauma unit, so you'll have a whole team of specialists determining your individual care based on your specialized needs. But we do know that we need to get you up and moving ASAP."

Kendall looked astounded. "You expect me to get up?"

"Over the years, we've discovered that it's an important component to a fast recovery. Even though you won't feel like it, it's imperative for you to be on your feet. Your team will design a plan based on your injuries. No two people have the exact same injuries, and no two people respond to trauma in the exact same way."

Kendall nodded.

Brady squeezed her hand to reassure her.

"For the next few days, you'll be asked lots of questions, run through the gamut of tests, and at the end, we'll have recommendations for the services needed to get you back on your feet and able to function solo." The doctor grabbed her chart.

"How long? How long before I can walk?"

The doctor's grim expression said it all. "Honestly, it's too early to tell."

"Are we talking weeks, months, never?" Desperation laced her tone.

"A minimum of weeks." He shook his head.

"What about my memory?" Kendall bit her lip.

"Kendall, after an injury like this, there are no guarantees."

She nodded her acceptance of the bad news. Her shoulders drooped from the weight of the truth.

"Any other questions?" Compassion resounded in his tone.

Kendall shook her head, but Brady saw confusion, uncertainty, and a million questions in her eyes.

Dr. Anderson left the room, carrying her chart with him.

Kendall closed her eyes, but not before a couple of tears rolled out. She still had a death grip on Brady's hand.

"You'll be all right." Brady whispered the promise. He gently wiped the dampness from her face with his thumb, a protectiveness rising up within him. "I'll be here with you until we find your family."

"What if I don't have a family?" Her frightened eyes focused on his.

That thought had never occurred to him.

"Why can't I remember?" Panic filled her raspy words. "Who am I? Where do I belong? What's my name? Where do I live? Is anyone looking for me?"

Brady wrapped her in his arms—at least the best he could, avoiding her wires and being extremely gentle with her broken body. He just remembered when he'd been afraid as a boy, his mom or dad's safe arms always made him feel better. He held her and let her cry.

∽

Overwhelmed by the facts, she was a woman with no memory of who she was or where she was—a woman without a past, a woman with severe injuries, a woman with a glum future. This mangled body would take months to recover—if it ever did. Worse, her blank mind might never remember.

Being wrapped in Brady's muscular arms calmed her. His presence made her feel safe. At the moment, it seemed to be the only thing she had to be thankful for. Finally, when her sobs had stilled, she said, "I'm okay now."

Brady loosened his hold. "You sure?"

She nodded and smiled ever so slightly.

Brady pulled a Kleenex from the box on her tray table, dabbing her face dry.

"Will you tell me what happened? Where I was? Just tell me everything you know relating to me and my accident."

Brady tossed the damp tissue into the trash and filled her in on the few facts from her hit-and-run.

Lucille entered the room with some warm broth. "Dr. Anderson said this girl is ready for some nutrition." Setting the bowl on the tray table, she rolled the head of Kendall's bed up some. "You want to do the honors?" She held up the spoon to Brady.

"It's been a while since I've fed anyone," he warned Kendall, accepting the silverware. "My niece and nephew are five and three now, so they don't want my help anymore."

Kendall opened her mouth for her first bite. A small amount dribbled down her chin. Brady grabbed another tissue and wiped the liquid.

"Tell me about you. I've had enough bad news for one day. You said your dad is the police chief?"

Brady spooned another bite into her mouth. "I'm thirty years old and hail from a long line of public servants. My dad—as you already know—is the police chief for Reno, Nevada."

"Is that where we are?"

Brady nodded.

"Why would I be in Reno, Nevada?" She wrinkled her nose. "It doesn't sound right."

Brady shrugged.

"Anyway, go on."

"My older brother, Frankie, is a detective and actually assigned to your case." Brady had become adept at spooning soup into Kendall's mouth and hadn't dribbled any more on her face. "My brother-in-law, Eli, works undercover in narcotics, and my sister, Delanie, is on regular patrol."

"Wow, the whole family."

"Not quite. My mom is a social worker in the adult department, and my younger brother, Cody, is a fireman over in the Tahoe district."

"Where do you fall into the lineup?" Kendall swallowed her last bite of soup.

"Number two of four. Frankie, Brady, Cody, and Delanie."

She smiled at his fast-paced rendition of their names.

Brady glanced at his watch. "I'm supposed to meet my dad this afternoon. We're going to search the missing person files."

Her heart dropped. He was leaving, and she'd be all alone. "For me?"

Brady stood. "Yeah."

"Will you come back?" She hated the pathetic question but had to ask.

He smiled, and for the first time she noticed he was a very good-looking man. His dark hair and blue eyes equaled an appealing combo. "I'll be back." He gave her hand a squeeze. "As a matter of fact, I'll probably be here so much you'll be sick of me."

"I hope so." She couldn't smile well with all the swelling. It kind of hurt, but she forced herself anyway.

He winked and left the room then stuck his head back inside the doorway. "Any idea how old you are?"

She shook her head. Any attempt to recall personal information brought forth a blank screen.

"It'll come back," Brady said with confidence. And he was gone.

∞

Brady got to his dad's office a little before three. "Hey, Dad, she's awake." He couldn't squelch the excitement in his voice.

"That's wonderful. So who is she?"

Brady plopped in his usual chair. "She has no recall, which is fairly common at this point. I did a little reading on head injuries the past few days, and at this point there's no reason to believe she won't make a full recovery."

"So what do we know?"

"Female, somewhere between twenty and thirty is my guess, and her first name."

"Not much." His dad input the information into his computer. "K–e–n–d–a–l–l?"

Brady nodded.

"Just a couple of hits. Thank heaven her name isn't Mary or Susie."

Brady came around the desk to check out the pictures. "It's really hard to guess, but I don't think either of those is her." One woman had spiked blond hair and looked like a motorcycle biker. The other carried a bit more weight in her face. "I mean, it's hard to say. I don't know what she'd look like without the bruises and swelling, but my gut says no to both of these people."

"I'll print them out so you can read the whole profile. And I'll expand the search by a few years in each direction."

Brady ended up reading profiles on five different Kendalls. A couple of them had birthmarks or moles that might help eliminate them with absolute certainty. "Can I take these with me back to the hospital?"

"Sure. And I'll also send out the facts we have over the network."

"Thanks, Dad. I'll see you Sunday, if not before."

Brady grabbed a burger on his way back up to Kendall's room.

"Hey, you." He greeted Kendall and Lucille.

"Brady Cooper, you brought me a hamburger. How thoughtful of you." Lucille grabbed the fast-food bag and winked at Kendall. "This young lady is getting ready to have her own version of a burger and fries—broth and Jell-O."

Brady took the spoon Lucille held out to him. "I don't know if I'll have enough strength without my burger."

Lucille rolled her eyes and shoved the bag back at him. "Men!" She left the room, and Brady settled in his regular spot opposite most of her medical paraphernalia. He laid his burger aside and opened Kendall's Jell-O.

"You don't have to wait. Let's eat together."

Brady fed her a bite and then took one himself. "Tomorrow I start my next shift at the fire station."

"Does that mean you won't be back?" Fear wove its way through the question.

Brady clutched Kendall's hand. "I'll be back every chance I get. The thing is, the next forty-eight hours are not my own, so I can't say for sure when or for how long."

Relief flooded her expression. "Thank you. I know this isn't part of your job description."

"It is now. After all, a promise is a promise." He dipped the spoon in her broth. "And since I hated the thought of leaving you all alone for the next couple of days, I asked my mom if she'd come up and visit with you. Is that all right?"

"Your mom?"

"Remember, she's an adult social worker, so she'll be at the hospital anyway. I can cancel if you're uncomfortable."

Her uncertainty showed. "I guess it will be okay," she said finally.

"I also might be up if we get any calls that bring us here. The good news is that for the two days following this shift, I'll be here all day if you want."

Brady faced a new season in his life—possibly a long cycle of all his free time being donated to a woman he didn't know, but one of whom he felt extremely protective.

Chapter 3

Good morning, little lady." Lucille breezed in and opened the blinds. "You need some sunshine in this room. How you feeling today, sugar?"

"Sore, but I'm alive."

"That you are, and some days that's enough." Lucille wrapped the blood pressure cuff around Kendall's arm—just above her cast. Many of the machines had been unhooked since she woke up yesterday afternoon.

Lucille pumped up the cuff. "Your whole team will be in today. Now that you're awake, there'll be no more lazing around for you. You ready for that?" She removed the cuff and took Kendall's pulse.

Kendall chuckled. "I don't see how anyone is going to get this body to do much moving."

"You'd be surprised what these miracle workers can do. They'll have you out running marathons in no time." Lucille's face grew serious. "Recovery requires hard work, but don't quit until you're well." On that somber warning, she turned and left.

A cloud of hopelessness descended on Kendall. *Am I up for the task?*

"Good morning, Kendall. I'm Marilyn Cooper."

Kendall raised her gaze to the doorway, noting that Brady's blue-green eyes matched his mother's—tranquil, comforting, warm, reminding her of a calm, deep sea.

"Mrs. Cooper, it's nice to meet you. I'm sorry Brady asked you to babysit me. You must have other things to do."

"No—it's my pleasure. I was actually on this floor to check on a case of mine and thought I'd pop in and say hello. May I come in for a moment?"

"Please do."

"Is there anything you need, anything I can do for you?"

A lump lodged itself in Kendall's throat, so she shook her head rather than voicing her answer.

"Do you mind if I pray for you?" Mrs. Cooper placed her hand on Kendall's arm, just the way Brady did.

Did she mind? She wouldn't know if she did, so she shook her head again.

"Father God, we come before You today asking for Kendall's healing. I know her situation must seem daunting, Lord, but it's not too big for You. So we come asking for Your touch of grace, Your peace, Your strength. Be Kendall's all in all. In Jesus' name, amen."

A warmth and peace enveloped Kendall, and she knew God and prayer must be a part of her life. "Thank you. I do feel better, and you are right—everything feels so much bigger than me."

"Kendall?"

She nodded as three new people wearing scrubs entered the room.

"We are part of your medical team and your three new best friends. I'm Tom, your physical therapist. This is Stan with occupational therapy and Brenda from speech therapy."

Mrs. Cooper rose. "Looks like you have a busy day ahead of you. I'll check back with you later today or tomorrow."

Kendall felt as though she was losing a friend. "Thank you—for everything."

Mrs. Cooper smiled. "See you soon." She disappeared past the therapy crew.

"You ready to get started?" Tom asked. He was a big man—tall and muscular with a jovial look about him.

"If I say no?" Kendall half-joked, but she partially wished she could will them away.

"Ah, we don't care," Brenda quipped. "We'll drag you out of that bed anyway." Her middle-aged face sported laugh lines around her mouth and eyes.

"This group has no mercy." Stan rolled a wheelchair up beside her bed. He was the oldest of the three. His head of gray hair and lined face reminded Kendall of a grandfather figure.

Kendall warmed to the trio. "No mercy, huh?"

"None," Tom assured her. "Our first task is to assess where you are and what you need. We start by reviewing your chart, which we've already done. Next on our to-do list is asking you lots of questions, but because of your amnesia, we realize you probably won't have answers."

"Normally," Brenda said from her spot leaning against the wall, "we question a patient and their family extensively."

Only I don't have a family. I don't have anyone. That's not true. Stop feeling sorry for yourself—God provided Brady and Mrs. Cooper.

"Then we take all the information we've obtained and each make our recommendations for services."

"Our goal is for you to have an eventual safe discharge so you can return home and function on your own."

Another wave of panic washed over Kendall. She had no home to return to—at least if she did, she had no idea where.

"Don't you worry." Brenda used a calm, quiet tone. "By then your memory may have returned."

"No use worrying about the what-ifs. A lot will happen before it's time to send you out into the world." Stan's bright blue eyes assured her all would work out in the end.

"How long will all this take? Where will I live?"

"The good news is you'll be moving to the rehab center right here at St. Mary's, so you won't have to go far. Honestly, your recovery period is anyone's guess." Tom shrugged.

"More than a month, less than a year." Brenda grinned.

"So I want to load you up in this wheelchair"—Stan set the brake—"and take you down to the rehab facilities, park you in a conference room, and grill you."

Stan got on one side of Kendall, Tom on the other, and they gently lifted her out of bed. Brenda helped her get settled into the wheelchair. "How's that?"

"Not too bad." Kendall's leg cast went from midthigh all the way down and covered her foot, so they had to prop it straight out. Lucille had been rolling her bed higher and higher, so she'd gotten used to sitting up.

Their destination was farther than Kendall assumed. Nothing they passed looked even vaguely familiar. The fear rose within Kendall and washed over her insides. She echoed Mrs. Cooper's words from earlier. *Lord, I'm so afraid and overwhelmed, so I come asking for Your touch of grace, Your peace, Your strength. Be my all in all. In Jesus' name, amen.*

Again, the simple prayer calmed her and the fear subsided somewhat—not altogether, but almost.

Brenda and Tom each held open a double door to a large gymlike facility. Various machines lined the walls, and the air buzzed with activity as patients and their therapists worked in various areas of the room.

"This will be your home away from home." Tom pointed to the large room they were just leaving. He held open another door, and Stan wheeled her into a conference room. He rolled Kendall up to a table that sat near the center.

After about twenty "I don't knows" from Kendall, the team gave up on the questionnaire. Brenda laid her clipboard aside. "Why don't we just give you a tour of the place?"

"Then we'll take you back to your room and devise a plan." Tom's voice took on a devious tone.

"Oh yes, my pretty." Stan joined the fun. "You're ours, and we shall torture you to our hearts' content."

They rolled Kendall through the facility, explaining each machine's function and laying out her therapy for the first couple of weeks. Then they wheeled her back to her room and helped her get settled into bed.

"Bye." Tom waved from the doorway.

"See you tomorrow." Brenda followed Tom out.

"Bright and early," Stan reminded.

Lucille came in a few minutes later. "Did you see that Mrs. C. left you a little gift?" She handed Kendall a brand-new Bible with a card attached.

Kendall took the offering and ran her hand over the hard cover. This was familiar. "She's a nice lady," Kendall commented absentmindedly.

"Her son's not too bad, either."

Kendall's face grew warm. "No, he's a good man." She met Lucille's probing gaze. "He's become my lifeline to normalcy, and that scares me. I can't expect him to stick around forever."

"You won't need him forever. Just till you figure out who you are, to whom you belong, and where you're going. He'll be here till then. I know that boy. He's as faithful as an old dog."

Lucille's description of Brady brought a smile to Kendall's lips. "He seems to be. How many strangers would pour their life into someone they don't even know?"

"God was watching out for you when Brady Cooper was your medic." Lucille straightened Kendall's bed and tucked the covers around her legs.

"I'm sure what you say is true, but there are times when I'm overwhelmed with panic in the midst of this frightening situation of not knowing."

"I know, baby. I know it's tough, but you keep fighting to get better. And read that there book Mrs. C. brought by. You'll be surprised how much better you'll feel."

Kendall hugged the Bible to her with one casted arm. "I feel like the Bible was a part of my life—and prayer, too. They are the only two things that have any sort of familiarity to me."

"Then you'll be fine, Miss Kendall—come what may, you'll be all right."

"Before you leave, will you open the card that came with the Bible?"

Lucille tore the envelope, pulling the card out and laying it on the tray table. She positioned the table over Kendall's midsection and rolled the head of her bed higher.

Kendall read the note from Mrs. Cooper.

Kendall,

When life feels like more than you can handle, open this book. My favorite place to go when I need comfort or reassurance is the Psalms, which you'll find in the very middle of your Bible.

Even though you don't know who you are, God does. Not only does He know you by name, He knows the number of hairs on your head. Isn't that news amazing and reassuring? He knows each one of us more intimately than we know ourselves. What confidence and courage that knowledge brings me, and I hope it does you, as well.

I'll drop by tomorrow. Until then, may the peace of God abound.

Marilyn

The note and gift flooded Kendall with a certainty that she'd get through this. She and God were on the same team. She was sure of it.

With awkward movements, she flipped the Bible up on the tray table, struggled to turn it around, and finally opened it to the Psalms.

Early in the evening as darkness settled outside Kendall's window, Brady popped his head in the door. "Hey, Kendall!"

Her heart fluttered at the sound of his voice. "Hey." The single word sounded breathless. The sight of him brought a surge of joy and then embarrassment at her strong reaction. She hoped her warm cheeks weren't glowing bright red like hot coals.

∞

"It's good to see you sitting up!" It was just good to see her any old way. He'd missed her today and was thrilled when an accident brought him here to her.

"I didn't expect to see you at all today." She had a sheepish look about her. "I mean, I hoped." Color rose into her face, and she ducked her chin.

"It's okay." He lifted her chin until his eyes met hers. "I hoped, too." Their gazes locked, and emotions shot through him like fireworks on the Fourth of July. Fighting the urge to kiss her, he placed a peck on the top of her head.

Brady cleared his throat and settled into his chair. Unnerved by what had transpired, he took longer than usual to settle in. They'd both declared—with what little they'd said—that this was quickly becoming much more than either expected or was ready for. A week ago they hadn't even known each other.

Brady swallowed and aimed for a lighter tone. "Tell me about your day." He glanced at his watch. "Mitch gave me thirty minutes. Said he'd dawdle down in the ER."

"Your mom came by—twice. The second time I was gone at rehab, but she left me this." Kendall held up the Bible.

"That's my mom." He grinned. "You already started rehab?"

"Tomorrow." Kendall filled him in briefly on what had transpired earlier in the day. "So help me get this straight. A physical therapist works with me on mobility and walking?"

Brady nodded. "All general movement."

"And the occupational therapist is fine-motor skills?" She cocked her head to the right.

"Yep, and the daily acts of living like dressing, eating, that sort of thing."

"What I don't get is the speech therapist. I mean, I'm talking, and I sound fine to me. Do I sound fine to you?"

You sound wonderful to me. "They do more than just speech, and I agree that yours sounds fine. But they also cover swallowing and cognitive skills. Not all types of therapy last the same length of time. You may only need the speech person for a few weeks, but you may need the PT for months." Brady shrugged. "Time will tell."

"I'm moving tomorrow to the rehab center."

"You are?" The news pleased him. "You're making good progress, then."

"And I met with a doctor from neuro regarding the amnesia."

"Neuro? You're sounding like someone in the medical profession."

"Osmosis. You hang around here long enough, you catch the lingo."

He chuckled. Her spirits were high for someone in her predicament, and her wide smile was pretty, even set in her marred face. Somehow he knew that underneath all the bruises, cuts, and scrapes lurked a beautiful woman—inside and out.

"Tell me what he said."

"My amnesia was caused by an injury to my brain during the accident, probably hitting the pavement with such force, even though I had on a helmet. He didn't feel I'm disoriented or confused, but I've suffered profound memory loss. Unfortunately, there aren't any lab tests or a list of conditions to prove or disprove amnesia. You'd think the fact that I don't know who I am would be enough." She shook her head in disbelief.

Brady smiled.

"He did inform me there is neuropsychological testing, and it, along with an MRI to scan the brain, can be helpful in determining the presence of amnesia."

"Is he questioning your amnesia?"

"I asked the same thing. He just likes to verify all the facts before determining a diagnosis. At that point Lucille spoke up."

"Uh-oh, the guy's in *big* trouble. I feel it coming."

Kendall laughed with Brady and did her best Lucille impersonation. "What do you mean—verify? The girl had a head trauma and has no memory. What's to verify?"

Brady laughed harder.

"By her tone and expression, I knew she finished the sentence in her head with the final two words, *you moron*."

"So what did the good doctor say?"

"The young whippersnapper raised his chin and, with as much dignity as he could muster, informed Lucille that he was just about to say those exact words, and given my situation, a diagnosis was inevitable without further testing. So I now officially have what's called retrograde amnesia."

Brady nodded.

Kendall grew somber. "It could take weeks, months, or years for recovery. Once the brain is damaged—it can be slow to heal."

"I know." Brady had done some reading of his own.

"Sometimes the amnesia never goes away." A frightened look settled on Kendall's face.

"But it often does." He reached for her hand. "Don't lose hope this early in the game. Let's aim for weeks. If weeks pass, then we'll shoot for months."

"We?"

"I told you, I'm in this for the long haul."

"I can't ask that from you. You don't even know me. What if I never remember? The doctor said the portion of my brain responsible for retrieving stored information has been compromised. There's no money-back guarantee on this deal, Brady."

He rose and held her head against his chest to calm and comfort her. "I know that, Kendall. I've read the reports in the medical journals. But none of it matters to me. I'm here for as long as it takes. A line from a song says, 'A lifetime's not too long to live as friends.' I'm your friend for life—memory or no memory. It doesn't matter to me. I'm here."

Kendall raised her head. Tears glistened in her eyes. "I really appreciate you. It feels like you're the only thing I have to count on in this whole wide scary world."

She laid her head back against his chest. He closed his eyes and held her close. *Lord, help me to be the man she needs me to be.*

Brady's pager vibrated. He removed one arm from Kendall and pulled it from his pocket. "My partner is ready, so I have to go." Kissing the top of Kendall's head, he shoved the pager back in his pocket.

Her teary eyes made it all the harder to leave. "Hopefully I'll be back tomorrow. If not, the next for sure."

She squeezed his hand. "Thank you," she whispered. "For everything."

Fighting the urge to kiss her lips, Brady turned quickly and left.

"Sorry, Mitch," he said when he reached the ER. "I lost track of time."

"How's the patient?" Mitch asked on their way through the sliding doors and back to their ambulance.

"She's struggling. Can you imagine having no idea who you are?" Brady shook his head.

"No, I sure can't." They climbed into their vehicle. "I've never understood how a person can forget everything about their personal existence, yet can remember how to function in daily life."

"From everything I read, it has to do with the location in the brain. The limbic system is responsible for memory retrieval. Often with amnesia, relational memory is impaired while procedural memory remains intact. So a person with amnesia can't remember their own name but often can do all the procedures they've learned throughout life such as riding a bike, eating, and using a telephone."

"The brain is a complex piece of equipment, isn't it? So what you're saying—in a sense—is that different types of memories are stored in different file drawers. The top drawer may be jammed shut, making retrieval of the stored information impossible, but the other drawers still open and close fine, making their file folders fully accessible."

"You got it, my friend. And Kendall's personal life, her relational life, is stuck in drawer number one."

"What if she's married?"

Brady avoided that line of thinking. "There's no reason to assume she is. Her finger is as bare as mine."

"Not everyone that's married wears a ring."

"True, but don't you think her husband would come looking for her?"

"Unless he was the one who ran her down."

Chapter 4

You've been watching too many cop shows. But by now someone should be looking for her. Frankie ran her fingerprints, and there's no match."

"Well then, she's not a criminal, or at least one who's been caught."

Brady rolled his eyes. They were back at the department. "You are so reassuring, buddy." Brady climbed from the cab, and the conversation ended.

The next afternoon, another emergency call took them back to St. Mary's. He left Mitch to finish in the ER and headed to the rehab center. He found Kendall in her new room reading her Bible. At the sight of her, his heart danced a little jig.

"Hey, you."

Her face lit up. "Brady."

"Love your new crib."

"Crib?" Her brows drew together.

"Digs?" She still looked perplexed, so he tried again. "Pad?"

She smiled. "You mean my room?"

He nodded. "Maybe you hail from some small Iowan farm town or somewhere the ever-changing English language has yet to hit."

"Maybe." She seemed more contemplative than usual.

"How was your day?" He stood in the doorway of her small space, leaning against the jamb.

"Grueling. Between Tom, Stan, and Brenda, I had hours of hard work. Your mom was here at lunch and helped me eat. She brought the flowers." A vase of purple daisies graced her nightstand. "She's very sweet and thoughtful. Makes me wonder what my own mom is like." Kendall shrugged. "Do I even have a mom?"

"I'm sure you do—somewhere."

"In that small farm town in Iowa?" Her sense of humor always kicked in when she needed a light moment.

"Brady, why isn't anybody looking for me? Isn't there a soul out there who cares where I am? Does anyone even know that I'm gone?"

Brady sat on the edge of her bed. He'd been asking himself the same thing, but he needed to be positive for her sake. "It's a little soon for people to wonder. Lives are busy, and people don't keep in touch like they should. Any day now someone will try to call you, get worried, and contact the police. And voilà—you'll be reconnected."

She smiled at him. "You, Brady Cooper, are an eternal optimist. I sure hope you're right. You, my lifetime friend, are the silver lining in the very dark cloud that is my life right now." She reached for his hand and squeezed it. It was the first time she'd initiated affection. She lowered her chin and pulled her hand back, and Brady caught a glimpse of pink highlighting her face.

"I'm in constant contact with my dad and brother regarding your case. They're keeping a close eye on the missing person file, checking it several times a day. My dad has guys checking a list of no-shows at University of Nevada–Reno. Something will turn up." His confident tone didn't reflect his doubt. *It just has to.*

"You're right. Something will turn up sooner or later. Sometimes the fear of the unknown overwhelms me, and I quit thinking rationally. I'll try to get a grip."

Brady glanced at his watch. "I need to get back to the ER in a couple of minutes. Anything else I can help you hash out while I'm here?"

"Yes." Her somber tone caught his attention. "Can I ask you something personal?"

"Anything."

"Are you married?"

"No. You?"

She glanced at her finger. "I don't have a ring or a line from one, so I'd say no." She raised her gaze back to him. "Have you ever been married?"

"Nope."

"I don't feel like I have, either, but I don't really know for sure. How about a girlfriend?"

"Naw."

"Good thing. I don't think she'd appreciate all the time you're spending with me."

"Probably not. You applying for the position?" Her bruised and swollen face grew more beautiful to him each day, but especially when she blushed, which apparently happened often.

Kendall lowered her chin. "No. I just want to know more about you. Knowing something about your life makes me feel better since I know nothing about my own."

Their gazes connected, and the rush of emotion he felt for her shocked him. He broke eye contact, glanced at his watch, and stood. "My time is up," he apologized.

"Thanks for coming. I can't tell you how much your kindness—"

Brady took her face in his hands. "I'm here because I want to be. It's not kindness nor charity." He placed a feather-soft kiss on her forehead.

Brady paused on his way out the door. "And if you ever want to apply for that job—let me know."

He caught a glimpse of her face turning bright red again as he headed down the hall.

∞

Heart pounding, face on fire, Kendall couldn't help but smile. "In a split second, Brady Cooper. In a split second." Something about him felt so right.

One day ran into the next, and no one came looking for Kendall. Soon two weeks had passed, then three. Her hours were full of various types of therapy and daily visits from Mrs. C. Though her memory remained gone, her life felt full.

Dear, faithful Brady kept her busy every free minute he had. Sometimes he read to her, some days they played games, and some evenings they watched television. Brady loved sports, and Kendall didn't mind—as long as they were together. Truth be told, he'd grown to be much more than a friend, but she wasn't sure he felt the same. They flirted some, he often kissed her forehead, and they hugged, but everything else was undeclared.

Today was Sunday, and he promised her a surprise. So she sat dressed and waiting in her wheelchair, wearing an outfit his mother had brought in for her—a jean skirt with one flip-flop sandal on her uncasted foot. Since she had no personal belongings to speak of, she'd been wearing extra scrubs the nurse brought her, but last week Mrs. Cooper had purchased her several outfits. They were even cute. The sage sweater she wore today brought out the green flecks in her eyes, or so his mom said.

Brady walked in decked out in khaki dress pants and a navy blue collared shirt. His presence nearly stole her breath away. He smiled, and her heart did a somersault.

"You look beautiful."

Brady's praise thrilled her. "Thank you." The patient tech had helped her wash her hair and get ready for Brady. "No small feat with these." She held up both of her casted arms.

Brady released her brake and rolled her out into the hall.

"So what's my surprise?"

"I'm springing you from the joint." He'd affectionately dubbed the rehab center "the joint."

Excitement pulsed through her. "Really?"

"Really." He pushed her through the outer doors. A shiny dark gray SUV sat parked at the curb, and Brady rolled up to the back door on the passenger side. "This, madam, is our getaway car."

He clicked a remote and after a beep opened the door.

Placing an arm behind her back and one under her knees, he lifted her from the wheelchair to the backseat so she could stretch out her leg across the seat. He handed her the seat belt, and she awkwardly stretched it around herself as she sat sideways. Then he loaded the wheelchair in the back and climbed into the front.

"Nice ride."

"Thanks. I bought it last year."

"Do they know I'm leaving?" Kendall glanced back at the center as they pulled away.

"Don't worry; this isn't a patient-napping. I signed you out."

"Where are we going? Church?"

He glanced her direction, raising a brow. "How'd you know?"

"Where else would a nice boy like you take a girl on a Sunday morning?" Brady laughed.

Kendall watched the buildings, searching for something familiar, but she felt like a tourist in a strange city. Not one thing jogged her memory. Brady took the on-ramp leading onto the freeway. From the backseat she had the freedom to study every nuance of his profile, and she enjoyed the view.

"I still go to church with my family. I hope you don't mind."

"Not at all. Actually, it will be fun to put faces to names and stories." She wondered what he'd told them about her.

Once in the wheelchair, he rolled her into the nonchurch-looking building. It was large, with rows of seats forming a semicircle around a stage. The back half of the room had risers.

"Hope you're not going to try to roll me up there," Kendall joked.

"Maybe one day, but not today." He rolled her up to the edge of an aisle about halfway to the stage. Mrs. Cooper welcomed her with a hug and introduced her to her husband. Brady took the end seat, between his dad and next to Kendall's wheelchair. As the service began, his other siblings filled the chairs down the row.

Kendall lost herself in the music and preaching. The pastor spoke on God's sovereignty, which couldn't have been more apropos. Church was strangely familiar, and she knew some of the words to the songs. She concluded that she must attend church regularly.

After the service, Brady introduced her to the rest of the crew. "This is Delanie and her husband, Eli. Frankie, his wife, Sunni, and their two munchkins, Mason and Summer. And my brother Cody."

153

Brady's family was warm, welcoming, and talkative. After a few minutes, everyone dispersed, saying they'd see them in a while.

"Are we going somewhere else?" she asked on their way back to the SUV.

"Guess you'll have to stick around and find out."

"Like I have a choice," she reminded him with sass in her tone.

He skillfully lifted her once again into his SUV. She stretched out the casted leg, but she turned her body so she almost faced the seat in front of her.

"If you had a choice, where would you go today?" He pulled out her seat belt and handed it to her, their breath mingling. His eyes grew serious and a deeper shade of blue.

"Anywhere you're going." She hadn't anticipated the huskiness in her voice or the blatant honesty of her answer. Brady stroked her cheek with an index finger and moved his face closer to hers. Her heart pounded. Surely he must notice the loud drumming that nearly drowned out her ability to hear. She anticipated his kiss as he drew near.

Brady stopped short of kissing her mouth and instead planted his lips on her forehead near her temple. Disappointment coursed through her, and she closed her eyes against the onslaught, hoping he wouldn't notice.

He shut her door, and while he walked around to his side of the vehicle, she drew in a couple of deep breaths, trying to clear her head and emotions.

Brady cleared his throat and glanced between the seats in her direction. He appeared unscathed by their encounter.

"You know all the games I've taught you the last few weeks?" He started the car, watching her through the rearview mirror.

Their eyes met. She only nodded, not trusting her voice to sound normal.

"Today you'll put that knowledge to good use." Pulling out of the church parking lot, he headed toward his parents' house.

"Every other Sunday is family day. We start by sitting together at church; then we have lunch either at a restaurant or my parents'. All afternoon we play games, hang out, catch up. I have to warn you, though, we are a pretty competitive group." He rattled on, and Kendall was thankful he wasn't requiring much from her in the way of conversation.

"You ready for the Cooper clan?"

"Sure." But was she? Her stomach knotted.

"My parents moved after all the kids left home. They live in Coughlin Ranch. Does that ring a bell?"

"Nope." She kept her answer short, not wanting him to perceive the confusion flooding through her.

"It's a fairly new development set on the far west side of Reno." Brady turned the corner. "This is where it begins."

Kendall spotted a lake off to the right.

"There's a house for every buyer in here, or so they say." Brady followed a maze of tree-lined streets.

Kendall noted that every yard was manicured to perfection with inviting lawns and lush green plants, but she couldn't help but notice the dry, barren-looking hills not too far off in the distance. They stood as a reminder of her empty, meaningless, barren life.

Brady drove to the end of a cul-de-sac and stopped in front of a gray two-story trimmed in white.

"We're here." Brady made the unnecessary announcement.

Suddenly nervous, Kendall unhooked her seat belt and waited for Brady to help her from the backseat. He lifted her, carefully protecting all of her casted appendages. She studied his strong jaw as he carried her toward the house. "What about my wheelchair?" She glanced at the SUV where the chair remained folded in the back.

"I thought it would be easier without it, especially with a dozen or so of us landing in my parents' great room. Can you press the doorbell?" He turned so she had easy access.

"Brady. Kendall." Delanie threw open the wide front door. "What can I do to help?"

Delanie was beautiful—soft blond hair, Brady's eyes, and a petite build.

"Will you lay a sofa pillow on the coffee table?" Brady carried Kendall effortlessly and set her in an oversized chair, propping her foot on the pillow Delanie had put into place.

"Welcome." Mrs. Cooper handed her a glass of iced tea and settled on the end of the couch closest to Kendall. "Did you enjoy church this morning?"

"Very much." Kendall sipped her tea. "Church feels very familiar to me. That must mean something."

"I hope so." Mrs. Cooper shone one of her encouraging smiles on Kendall. "Lunch is just about ready. Frank is grilling out back. Can I fix you a plate?"

∞

"I'll do it, Mom." Brady sat on the arm of Kendall's chair.

"Okay, sweetie. I'll finish getting everything set up." His mom patted Kendall's knee. "It's so good to see you up and dressed and out of the hospital."

"And thanks for the wonderful outfit. It fits perfectly. In a few months, I'll stand up and model it for you."

"You're welcome." His mom rose.

"You saved me from showing up at church in a pair of scrubs."

"You look adorable in your scrubs," Brady assured her.

Brady moved Kendall to the dining area.

"This is the biggest table I think I've ever seen."

"That's saying a lot coming from a woman who only remembers the last several weeks of her life."

Kendall laughed. "I guess that statement was loaded with irony."

After enjoying pizza, they set up two game boards for Ticket to Ride. Delanie and Eli joined Brady, Kendall, and Cody. Kendall caught on quickly, and they played the game several times.

Mason and Summer were drawn to Kendall. She was very good with them, so the three of them had a game of Candy Land going at the same time.

Brady contemplated the near kiss earlier today. Unfortunately, Mitch's words, "What if she's married?" taunted him. So he aimed for her forehead instead and put some distance between them. However, as this afternoon had worn on, he realized his heart had passed Go and Kendall was much more than "just a friend." He'd fought an inner battle all afternoon and finally convinced himself there was no way she could be married. She'd have a ring. Her husband would be looking for her.

His heart had secretly thrilled when disappointment had etched itself across her face, just as it had etched itself across his heart. She was apparently growing as attached to him as he was to her.

He studied her as she played with his niece and nephew. She'd grown more beautiful each day. The swelling was gone and much of the bruising had disappeared, leaving behind a flawless complexion.

She smiled up at him, and his heart jolted. Yep, either he had some rare disease, or he was crazy about Kendall.

Kendall had to be back at the joint before seven, so they were the first to leave. After many hugs and promises to Summer and Mason that she'd be back, Brady loaded her into his SUV.

"I'm excited, Brady. I know two more things about myself—I enjoy children, and church is a place I know I belong."

"One piece at a time, your life is falling into place."

"I just wish it was faster." She paused. "Hey, thanks for today. I love your family! They're all wonderful!"

"Yeah, me, too. They're the best. I feel blessed in this day and age when so many families are fragmented, even Christian families."

Kendall grew quiet. *She must be wondering about her family.* Brady decided to give her time to think, so they drove the rest of the way in silence.

When he pulled up to the rehab center, he turned off the engine, half-turned in his seat, and placed his hand on her knee. "You okay?"

"After four weeks, I have to face the facts. No one is missing me. No one is searching to find me." She unhooked her seat belt. "Brady, I don't matter to anybody."

"You matter to me." His words carried deep emotion.

"I know—friends for life, right?" She sounded flippant. "But who am I? Where do I belong?" Her voice cracked. "Why isn't anyone looking for me?" A sob escaped.

He went around to her door and pulled Kendall back against his chest, running his fingers through her long, silky strands of hair. "Let's take it a day at a time." He kissed the top of her head.

She twisted her head, raising her gaze. In the dim lights shining into the vehicle from the rehab center, he saw the raw fear painted across her face. "A day at a time sounds easy enough, but I'm fighting a growing hopelessness that sometimes threatens to drown me." She released another sob.

He took her hand in his. "It's okay to cry."

She raised her tear-streaked face. "You don't know what it's like, Brady. You can't possibly understand."

She was right—he couldn't.

"What if I never remember? What if no one ever comes?" Her words were devoid of hope.

Brady had nothing but platitudes to offer, so he remained silent and held her close.

"As a woman without a known past, it's difficult to have hope for a bright future." She sniffed and raised her head. "I am so sorry. Listen to me. I'm swimming in self-pity."

"You don't always have to be brave."

"I do. Your mom's teaching me what the Bible says about taking captive my thoughts. I can't let the fear win. I can't give in to it." Kendall raised her chin in a determined fashion and patted her cheeks dry with the sleeve of her sweater. She glanced toward the rehab center. "I guess you'd better get me inside. They'll think I've tried to escape and send a pack of dogs searching for me."

Brady chuckled and unloaded the wheelchair. After Kendall was settled, they went to the check-in desk. Then he rolled her down the shiny tile floor to her small but private room.

Brady knelt in front of her chair. "You are the bravest person I know, Kendall, but don't beat yourself up because you're afraid sometimes. Of course you're afraid. Who wouldn't be?"

She leaned forward and laid a casted arm on each of his shoulders. "You,

Mr. Brady Cooper, are my knight in shining armor."

Their gazes connected, and Brady felt the warmth of deep emotion spread through him. She leaned farther toward him, and his heart sped into double time.

Chapter 5

Kendall kissed Brady's cheek and whispered near his ear, "Thanks for today. I loved every—"

He turned his head, ever so slightly, ever so slowly, but it was enough, enough for their lips to touch.

This was worth waiting for.

The kiss was long, slow, undemanding. When he raised his face from hers, Kendall felt regret—not at the kiss itself, but that it was over.

"Sleep tight," Brady whispered. Then he left Kendall to ponder the million emotions churning within. It was a long time before she fell asleep. Feeling giddy, she knew a smile must have been planted on her face the entire night.

The following day, Brady and the kiss were very much on Kendall's mind all through therapy. She felt certain she wore a silly grin most of the day, but she couldn't help herself. No one commented or questioned, so she didn't broach the subject.

Shortly after she'd returned to her room from her day's workout, Delanie breezed into the room. "Hi, Kendall. An accident brought me to the hospital, so I thought I'd drop in and see how you are today." She wore her police uniform, and her hair was French braided down the back.

"Hi. Come in."

Delanie took the chair usually occupied by Brady. "I'm so glad you got to come yesterday. Did you have a good time?"

"Yes. You have a great family, and Summer and Mason are adorable." She pictured the two blond cherubs with light blue eyes.

"I'm glad I finally got to meet you. My mom and Brady talk about you all the time."

Kendall's cheeks grew warm. "He does? I mean, they do?"

Delanie giggled. "He does, and they do."

"Can I ask you something?"

Delanie shrugged. "Sure."

"Is Brady always this wonderful? I mean, he seems next to perfect."

"The truth?" Delanie raised her brow.

Kendall nodded, anticipating learning more about the guy she'd fallen for.

He wasn't one to talk much about himself and gave monosyllabic answers to any personal questions.

"He is next to perfect. I love all three of my brothers, but Brady has a special spot all his own in my heart. He is kind and compassionate. More merciful than the rest of our brood."

Kendall grinned. "I thought so."

Delanie studied her, and Kendall wanted to look away but didn't. "Are you falling for him?"

Kendall's face heated up. "I think so, but I'm not sure." Embarrassed, she dropped her gaze to her hands.

"He's easy to care about. Did you know he never even dates? He's just waiting for God to bring the right woman at the right time."

Kendall shook her head. Talk about pressure. "How did you know Eli was the one?"

"Well, I was attracted to him from the first day we met, but as I got to know him and his character, my fluttery feelings of uncertainty grew into a rock-solid love."

Kendall nodded.

"It would be natural for you to fall for Brady. I mean, he saved your life and has stuck by you through this very difficult time."

Kendall sensed Delanie didn't approve of what was happening between her and Brady. "You mean more like hero worship."

"Yes, but not exactly. It's not unusual for women to fall for the rescuers in their lives." Delanie shrugged. "You know, a doctor, a teacher, a pastor. I think as women we are especially vulnerable to men we admire and who rescue us or protect us in some way."

"Maybe you're right." *But I don't think so.* "Maybe I'm confusing gratefulness and admiration with something more."

"Perhaps." Delanie smiled.

It was obvious Delanie didn't want Kendall to fall in love with Brady, and the knowledge hurt. But she'd put on a brave face and not let the pain show. "So how long have you and Eli been married?"

"Six months." Delanie sighed, and a dreamy expression settled over her face. "Six wonderful, blissful months." Delanie laughed. "Listen to me gushing all over the place." Delanie glanced at her watch.

"Guess I'd better run."

"Thanks for stopping by." Her statement didn't feel honest. She'd rather not have had this enlightening visit.

"You're welcome. Do you need anything?"

"Nope, I'm good." *Will you go already? I may need a few minutes to indulge in some self-pity and possibly have a good cry.*

Delanie was studying her again, and Kendall felt like a bug under a microscope. Delanie moved closer to the bed. "I may have been too blunt just now, and I'm sorry. It's not personal."

Kendall nodded. *How much more personal can it be? You don't think I'm good enough for your brother.*

"Kendall, I've hurt you, and I'm sorry." Delanie seemed to struggle with what to say and how to say it, but her expression of regret was genuine.

"I'll be fine." Squeezing the words around the lump in her throat proved difficult, and her voice sounded low and raspy.

"I'm going now before I make things worse." Delanie patted Kendall's hand and left.

A tear rolled down Kendall's cheek. How long would it be before Brady's family convinced him she wasn't that one special girl for whom he'd waited more than thirty years?

∞

Brady, Mitch, and the four firefighters on Shift C were playing Mexican Train on the kitchen table at the fire station. Brady laid down a double two and a two-seven to win the hand.

The buzzer at the front door sounded. "I'll get it while you guys count your points," Brady teased. When he opened the door, there stood Delanie.

"Sis! Is everything okay?"

"More or less." Her expression was troubled. "No big family emergency. I just wanted to talk."

"Sure. Let me tell the guys, and we can sit out here." Brady hollered and excused himself from the rest of the game. Closing the door, he asked, "Everything all right with you and Eli?"

"Yes. More than all right," Delanie assured him. "I wanted to talk to you about Kendall."

"Kendall?"

Delanie sat down on a step, and Brady joined her.

"Do we know who she is? Did someone show up to claim her?" Part of him hoped someone had, and another part of him dreaded what that might mean.

"No, and that's part of what I want to talk about." Delanie sighed and pursed her lips. "She's falling for you, Brady."

He nodded. That much he'd figured out on his own.

"You know?" Delanie's tone carried both frustration and accusation.

Brady stood, feeling too close to Delanie on the shared step. "It's not one-sided, if that's what you're worried about." He turned to face his sister and knew immediately he'd said the wrong thing.

Delanie jumped to her feet. "Not one-sided?" She stood to her full five feet. "That would be good news compared to this."

Annoyed, Brady asked, "What is it with you? You're not usually so reactionary, and you're never this dramatic. Kendall and I share a mutual interest in one another. It's not that big of a deal."

"Brady, it's a huge deal." Delanie had calmed herself and spoke with quiet precision. "We have no idea who Kendall is. Perhaps she's a married woman, possibly the mother of some small children." Delanie scrutinized his reaction.

"If Kendall's married, somebody would be looking for her. She wasn't wearing a wedding ring and had no imprint of one on her finger."

"Brady, think about what you're saying. Maybe she dumped the guy and came to Reno to start a new life. Stuff like that happens all the time."

"She's not that type."

Delanie let out a loud, long sigh. "*She* doesn't even know what type she is. How can you possibly think you do?"

"I know in my gut." Brady ran a hand through his hair. He didn't want to think about all the possibilities. His heart was too involved now.

"What about her belief system?" Delanie challenged in a sure but quiet tone. "Not only might you be falling for some other guy's wife; you might be falling for a person who doesn't share your walk with the Lord."

"I'm pretty sure she's a believer. Church, prayer, and the Bible all feel familiar to her." Doubts were ebbing into Brady's thinking. Perhaps he'd moved too quickly, let his emotions do his thinking for him.

Delanie returned to her previous spot on the step. "Will you at least slow down?" The pleading tone of her voice evoked a promise.

"I'll try." He settled back in his spot next to Delanie. "Here's the thing—I'm in love with her."

Delanie squeezed his hand. "I know what that's like, remember? I fell in love with Eli before he'd committed himself to Christ, but I never acted on it."

"Maybe you're stronger than I am."

"You're Brady Cooper—football star. Biggest muscles in the family, remember? Can out–arm wrestle Cody, Frankie, and Dad—probably all at the same time."

Brady laughed and flexed his arm.

"See. An iron man with an iron will." Delanie grew serious. "You've waited too long for God's best. You were the one who said you'd not follow Frankie's footsteps and marry the first pretty girl to smile at you twice."

Brady nodded. Sunni was beautiful but very selfish and demanding. Frankie's life hadn't been easy. He'd been a big part of Brady's inspiration to wait on God. *Have I quit waiting on You and run way ahead?* He didn't know. Kendall seemed so right. His heart begged God to let her be the one.

"I'll pray for you to be strong and take a step backward." Delanie stood. "Whatever you do, don't kiss her. After that first kiss, resisting is twice as hard."

Brady couldn't make eye contact with Delanie, knowing she'd immediately see through him, so he nodded and kept his head down, staring at the ground.

"You already kissed her! Brady, you've only known her for a month. What were you thinking?" Delanie shook her head. "No wonder the poor girl is so far gone."

Her words jolted his heart. "So far gone?"

Delanie confessed to stopping by to visit Kendall. "It was written all over her yesterday, so I suspected. Today she pretty much spelled it out. If she's not already in love with you, she's right on the edge of the cliff."

In light of Delanie's concerns, the news both pleased and disturbed him.

"If you aren't strong enough to back off because it's the right thing, then do it as a sacrifice for Kendall."

"What do you mean?"

"She's dealing with enough right now, and until we know who she is and what components make up her life, you need to offer friendship and nothing more. It's not fair to her."

Brady sucked in a deep breath. "You're right."

Delanie reached out a hand and pulled him to his feet. "I love you." She hugged him.

"I love you, too, sis. And thanks—I think." He waited until Delanie got in her patrol car and drove away, but instead of returning inside, he settled on the front porch once again and weighed Delanie's advice.

The next morning when his shift ended, Brady ran by his dad's office before going home to catch some sleep. He used his knuckles to rap on the partially open office door. His dad looked up from a case file.

"Brady, come on in." He shook his head. "Still nothing on Kendall."

Brady lowered his tired body into the green vinyl chair. He'd been up most of the night. They'd had one call after another.

"You look like you need to be home in bed."

"That'll be my next stop after I leave here." Brady paused. "I need some advice."

His dad listened as Brady shared about the tenderness between him and

Kendall the night they left his house. "Here's the thing—I'm in love with Kendall and believe she's in love with me."

Concern crossed his dad's features, but he only nodded as Brady continued.

"Delanie paid both Kendall and me visits yesterday, expressing her concerns." Brady shared bits of their conversation. "I have to know what you think."

His dad took his time answering—as he always did. A man of wisdom, he weighed his words before blurting them out. "Worst-case scenario—she's married or engaged. A stranger shows up to claim her—a stranger she should love, but she's now in love with you. You have no right or claim to that love because it belongs to another. What does she do? What do you do? More important, what is the right thing to do?"

He studied his son for a long moment—just the way Delanie often did. "I think until you know the facts of Kendall's life, you must guard your heart and emotions. She's grown to depend on you as a friend already. Maybe you need to slowly step backward and allow her to lean more on her own inner strength and the Lord, less on you."

It wasn't at all what Brady wanted to hear. He'd somehow hoped for his dad's blessing to move forward, but in his heart of hearts, he knew that would never happen. His dad was nothing if not a man of integrity.

"Believe it or not, I still remember those early feelings with your mom. I know this isn't going to be easy, Brady, but until we have answers, it's the best thing for Kendall and for you. So, son, my advice is no more kissing, no more holding her, and no more tender thoughts."

Brady nodded. Knowing his dad and Delanie were right didn't make his task any easier. His feelings for Kendall happened so naturally, he wasn't sure how to make them unhappen. But he made a pact with himself: Knowing how hard it would be, he'd not kiss her again.

"Dad, we haven't talked about her case for a while. What's going on? What are you thinking?"

The expression on his dad's face caught Brady off guard, and fear knotted his stomach. "Has something happened?"

"No, but this is day thirty. The department's stance is shifting from a hit-and-run to attempted murder."

The words sent a chill down Brady's spine.

"Murder?"

"I'm sorry, son, but it looks that way."

Brady struggled to assimilate the news. "Why? Why would you assume someone tried to kill her?"

"She's young. She's beautiful. Not a soul anywhere in the entire nation is looking for her. An angry husband, boyfriend. . ." His dad hesitated. "Possibly a john."

"A john?" Brady jumped to his feet. "You think Kendall's a hooker?" He couldn't believe his ears.

"Brady, we have to be open to every avenue. You know it's a possibility. Girls come here to get a job as a showgirl, and when they get hungry enough, they do what they have to in order to survive. She could be involved in the Mob in some way. There are a million possibilities."

Brady walked to the window and glanced out. To the west sat downtown and numerous casinos. "I know they are all out there—the mobsters, the hookers, the dancing girls, but I never think of them or consider them because they are so far removed from my life. I mean, we occasionally get a call involving one, but I never wonder if someone I meet might be a call girl." He turned and faced his dad.

"Unfortunately, because of my job, they are very much a part of mine. I know you don't want to believe the worst, nor do I. Kendall's grown important to you and your mother."

"Is she in danger?" No matter who she was or what sort of life she might lead, Brady couldn't bear for anything to happen to her.

"We've got it covered."

Brady squinted and stared at his dad. "What do you mean you've got it covered?"

"She's protected."

"Since when?" Brady tried to remember seeing an undercover officer around, but none came to mind.

"A couple of weeks now, and if you haven't noticed, that's a good sign. They're doing their job well."

Brady rubbed the back of his neck. "I can't believe this is happening." He reclaimed his chair. "You believe finding the driver who ran her down will lead to Kendall's identity?"

"Possibly. Sometimes amnesia is a way to escape things people want to forget."

"You don't think she has amnesia?" Brady's mouth fell open.

"I believe she has amnesia, but sometimes amnesia is caused by emotional trauma. Kendall's could be caused by both the wreck and whatever emotional events preceded the accident."

"Dad, this is nuts. I feel like I've left normal life and been dropped into the twilight zone. When did the theory change from Kendall being a college girl who was the victim of a hit-and-run to Kendall being involved in foul play?"

"It's always been a possibility, but as more time passes and all coeds are accounted for at UNR, we have to look outside the box."

"When were you going to tell me?"

"It's all supposition, Brady. Nothing more."

Emotions raced through Brady like cars on the Indy track. What if he'd fallen in love with a hooker or a mobster's woman? Suddenly he understood Delanie's need to warn him to slow down. As a police officer, this was her reality.

"Go home and get some sleep, Brady. You'll be able to process this better then." His dad rose.

They walked together down the hall to the elevator. "I haven't said any of this to your mother." He put an arm around Brady's shoulder.

"It's a lot of information to process." Brady's mind swam through all the facts. He boarded the elevator and bid his dad good-bye.

An attack of guilt hit Brady on his drive home. Wasn't love unconditional? If he really loved Kendall, would her past matter? He was too tired to muddle through the questions.

Chapter 6

K endall hadn't seen Brady in several days. Fraught with insecurity, she realized it was the longest span of time since her accident that they'd gone without seeing each other. Even if he could only pop in for a few minutes, he'd always managed to stop by daily.

I'm sure he regrets the kiss. Kendall found her hope of ever seeing him again dissipating. Feelings of sadness and loss followed.

His mom, however, continued to visit each day. They talked about God, the Bible, and prayer. She brought Kendall books to read, Bible studies to work on, and an iPod filled with Christian music.

Kendall glanced at the clock. Soon dinnertime would be here, and still no Brady. *How will I learn to live without him?* He'd become the high point of her basically nonexistent life.

"I can do all things through Christ who strengthens me." She and Mrs. Cooper had memorized the verse together. Mrs. Cooper encouraged her to recite it when therapy became more than she thought she could bear.

If there is no more Brady, God will get me through. I can do this with Your help. Kendall ran her hand over the leather cover of the new study Bible Mrs. Cooper had brought her a couple of days ago.

"Hey." Brady waltzed in just like always—only a few days later than she'd expected him.

Relief surged through her. "Hey, yourself." She'd never been so glad to see anyone, at least not that she could remember.

Brady had bags under his eyes, but he sure looked good to her.

Remembering the kiss, Kendall felt shy. Her cheeks warmed, and things felt awkward—a first between them. She wasn't sure what to say or how to act.

"I thought I'd spring you from this joint and take you out to dinner. Do you like Mexican food?"

They both laughed at the absurdity of his question, and it seemed to relax them.

"Sorry, wasn't thinking. What do you say? You up for a night on the town?"

"Sure." Kendall was grateful she'd had the nurse help her slip into a pair of sweatpants and a sweater earlier today.

Brady moved her wheelchair against the bed and lifted her into it. She studied his face from her close proximity. He was more than just tired; concern lined his features.

She thought back to her visit with Delanie. Maybe his sister had convinced him to dump her while he had the chance. Kendall feared what verdict tonight's dinner conversation might bring.

On the drive Brady asked, "Do those look familiar at all?"

She shook her head as they passed Circus Circus, a well-known hotel and casino.

"Doesn't ring any bells, huh?"

She gazed at the downtown area. "No. I wish something did."

A few blocks later, Brady turned into a restaurant parking lot. The sign read BERTHA MIRANDA'S.

"We're about to find out if you like Mexican food. This is one of my family's favorites."

He helped her from the SUV. Once inside, the host led them to a small corner table and removed a chair. Brady wheeled Kendall up to the table.

She studied the room. Something about it seemed vaguely familiar—the bright colors, large pots, and tile floors. The waiter approached with two glasses of water. Kendall examined the menu.

"What do you recommend?"

"The tacos."

After they'd ordered, Brady was quiet. He adjusted his silverware for the tenth time.

"Is everything okay?" She partially dreaded his answer but needed to know.

He nodded. "How's therapy going?"

"It's hard, and Tom says we can't go full throttle until the casts are off. But I don't care how much it hurts—I will walk again." Kendall raised her chin, underscoring her resolve.

"I admire your determination. I've heard PT can be grueling."

"When I'm whining at you in a few weeks, remind me of that fortitude."

He smiled and winked. "I will."

A Hispanic family seated at the next table caught Kendall's attention. They had four children probably all under five, and she found herself drawn to the dark-eyed, dark-skinned family. They spoke to one another in Spanish.

Kendall smiled when the mother looked in her direction. "How old are your children?" she asked in their native language. They spoke for a few moments about names and ages and wished each other well.

Turning back to Brady, she saw questions in his eyes. "You speak Spanish?"

168

He cocked his head to one side.

She hadn't even thought about it—it just came as naturally as breathing. "I guess I do." Amazed by the discovery, she grinned. "Wow! I speak Spanish!" She reviewed what she now knew about herself. *I speak Spanish and love kids. Church, God, and the Bible are familiar.*

"Another piece of the Kendall puzzle." Brady smiled.

Every new finding delighted her and gave her hope as she moved another step closer to her true identity. "Has your dad heard anything about my case?"

Brady hesitated then shook his head. His slight delay in responding troubled her.

Brady laid his hand over hers. "I thought we'd drive around after dinner and see if anything jogs your memory."

"The doctor did say sometimes places, people, or things—the familiar—can do that."

"Let's hope."

The waiter brought their hot plates of tacos, beans, and rice. After praying, Brady dug in, not saying anything else. His withdrawn attitude troubled her. Was he feeding her so he could then take her emotions to slaughter?

Kendall toyed with her food more than she actually ate anything. Unfortunately, even after OT, eating was a slow, tedious process. Brady's silence and brooding had robbed her of her appetite. Finally, she pushed her half-eaten plate away.

"Why don't you just say whatever it is you have to say and be done with it?"

Brady looked up from his plate and laid down his taco. It was their first real eye contact of the evening. "I had a rough night, several calls, no rest, and then I didn't sleep much today, either."

Kendall nodded, unsatisfied. Her gaze must have conveyed just that.

"Delanie came to see me after she left you the other day."

Kendall hung her head. Her eyes filled with unshed tears. "I figured as much." Taking her napkin, she dabbed the corners of her eyes as well as she could with her casts in the way.

Kendall hated the rush of emotion that hit her and hated even more the urge to cry.

"Some of the things she said are valid." Brady shrugged.

Kendall stared at her empty ring finger. "Can we have this conversation later in a less public spot?" She pushed her plate away—not the least bit hungry.

He nodded and glanced at her plate. "Are you finished?"

"I am."

Brady raised his hand to call the waiter. "I think we're done. May we get the check, please?"

The waiter glanced from one half-eaten plate to the other. "Sí, señor. Was the meal to your satisfaction?" Concern lined the older gentleman's face.

"Yes," Brady assured him. "As always, it was very good."

The waiter's doubtful expression remained.

Kendall tried to reassure him with a smile. "We are both full."

He nodded, and Brady paid the bill. Then he rolled her back to his SUV. When he helped her from her chair to the backseat, she knew she was stiff in his arms. He kept his movements impersonal.

He drove toward his parents' part of town, and Kendall hoped he wasn't going to drag them into the middle of this. Having him dump her was going to be hard enough, but having the entire family dump her would be unbearable. Kendall decided to wait and see, but if he turned into Coughlin Ranch, then she'd speak up.

The ride was silent, and Kendall's stomach churned in nervous anticipation. After treasuring their first kiss, she now wished it had never happened. That one tender moment, which lasted all of thirty seconds, started a downward spiral that Kendall felt certain would destroy not only their newly budding feelings, but their friendship, as well.

When Brady turned into his parents' neighborhood, her heart dropped.

"I thought we'd take a walk along the lake and talk."

Relief flooded Kendall at Brady's explanation. At least it would only be the two of them. Brady unloaded her chair and then her. Both of them seemed stiff and awkward as the situation forced them into physical contact. She disliked her dependence on him but had no choice in the matter.

"There are some great trails through here. I think a walk will clear both our heads."

Kendall nodded but didn't comment.

Brady pushed her along a paved jogging and bike path that wound through the trees and circled the small man-made lake. They walked for a long time in silence. Kendall kept praying for God to give her the right words. The setting was pastoral—with its trees, flowers, and the sound of the water—so opposite of what was going on inside of her, but the farther they walked and the longer she prayed, the more peaceful Kendall felt. Finally, Brady stopped, parking Kendall facing a bench where he settled across from her, letting out a long, slow sigh. Out of the corner of her eye, Kendall caught sight of a couple of joggers passing by.

Her attention returned to Brady. He looked like a man carrying a heavy burden, and she knew the burden was her. She decided to make this easy for him and for herself.

"I think Delanie is right. I think we should break up." Without waiting for his response, she continued, "I guess that sounds stupid because we weren't ever really a couple. It's just that after the whole kiss. . ." She gazed directly into his sad eyes. "Well, it was special, at least to me." Her voice had a catch in it.

Brady offered a tiny smile and took her hands, but his eyes remained sad.

Kendall sucked in a deep breath, forcing herself to be honest. "Anyway, somewhere in all of this, I started thinking of us as a couple. Maybe even a couple with some sort of future, which is ironic coming from an amnesiac because until I figure out my past, how can I really have a future with anyone? Your sister is right."

There. She'd said it before he could, but her heart was breaking all the same.

∞

Embarrassed hazel eyes looked away from Brady and stared out through the trees. She'd enjoyed the kiss as much as he had. The knowledge made his decision even harder. The conversation he'd most like to avoid was inevitable. He'd hurt her by staying away these last few days, not intentionally, but he'd hurt her nonetheless. He heard it in her tone, saw it in her eyes.

Now in order to clear things up, he'd have to lay his feelings bare before her. Which is what she'd just bravely done. He needed to show her the same respect.

"I'm sorry I hurt you." His gaze roamed out over the lake. "I shouldn't have avoided you. I'm conflicted. . . ."

She sniffed, and he glanced in her direction. Her head hung low, and her long silky hair provided a curtain of privacy. Wiping her eyes with the sleeve of her sweater, she raised her head, her eyes probing the bright blue sky.

"Kendall, before, when I kissed you. . ."

She lowered her gaze to meet his. "Don't say it." She held up her hand like a crossing guard, her bulky sweater hiding the cast. "Don't worry. I get it. I don't have to hear the rejection spoken out loud."

"Rejection? Is that what you think?"

The tears had stopped, and she now glared at him. "Look, Brady, I may have lost my memory, but I'm not stupid. The picture is clear. You don't want me. Nobody. . ." Her voice cracked, and the unshed tears returned, causing her eyes to glisten. "Wants me," she finished with a sob.

Brady lifted Kendall from her chair and carried her to the bench. He sat down and cradled her on his lap as one would a distraught child. She needed holding as much as he needed to hold her. So he held her close to his heart and let her cry. Crying could be cleansing, even healing. There would be time for words later. How frightening it must be not knowing who you are and feeling abandoned.

The front of Brady's shirt grew damp, but he didn't mind. Kendall hadn't broken down since the accident, and the weeks of stored-up emotions came pouring out like water rushing through a dam. Finally, she grew still and quiet except for an occasional postsob hiccup.

At last she lifted her head. "I'm okay now." Her gaze didn't quite meet his. "But you're not." She pointed to the wet spot on the front of his shirt. "I'm sorry."

He smiled at her. "Don't be." He pushed a tendril of hair off her cheek, his fingers lingering there. Their gazes locked, and all sorts of tender feelings spread through him.

Kendall broke their eye contact and slid off his lap, settling on the bench next to him. She carefully put some distance between them and watched the ducks swim on the lake.

In that moment, he realized he'd fallen in love with her—totally, completely, with all his heart in love. And she needed to know, because she felt rejected and abandoned by everyone on the planet. Delanie wouldn't agree, nor would his dad, but he had to tell her, had to reassure her.

"Kendall?"

"Hmm?" She didn't look his way.

"I love you."

∞

Kendall held her breath and replayed his words in her mind. Her heart jumped into overdrive, pounding against her ribs. She faced Brady and saw that his tender expression validated his declaration. But she had to be sure.

"Did you say. . . ?" The words came out breathlessly.

He smiled, and her heart melted.

"I did say. . ." He nodded.

"I don't understand." She thought back over their discussion and the past few days. If he loved her, why did he jump back and put distance between them like a man escaping some near tragedy?

He traced her cheek and jawline with the tips of his fingers. "I'm a man who has fallen in love with a beautiful woman. Who can understand the ways of the heart?" He winked at her.

"But—" She wanted to believe him, but her logic kept arguing.

Brady grew serious. "Here's the thing—I panicked."

"Panicked?"

Brady nodded. "What if you *are* married? I can't risk kissing another man's wife."

Kendall stared at her hands in her lap. "So until someone figures out who I am, or somebody comes forward to claim me, everything is on hold."

He took her hand, gently running his thumb over her knuckles. "It's the right thing."

"What if nobody ever comes? What if we never know?" Kendall felt as though someone had given her a beautiful gift and in the next moment taken it away.

Brady pulled her against him, wrapping his arm around her shoulders. "I have to believe this is all going to work itself out over the next few weeks." Turning on the bench to face her, Brady took Kendall's face between his hands. "I'm here for you, no matter how long it takes—days, weeks, months. I'm not going anywhere."

Relief washed over her like a cool breeze, lifting some of the fear. She studied the earnest face before her, the aquamarine eyes asking for her trust. She laid her forehead against his chest. He ran his fingers through her hair.

"It will be okay. We'll be fine. Together we can get through this."

His presence, his words, his kindness all filled her heart to overflowing. She raised her head and smiled. "Did I tell you that I feel the same about you?"

He laughed. "No. No, you didn't."

"Well, for the record, I think I do." She couldn't bring herself to actually say the word *love*.

He kissed her forehead. "For the record, I'm glad."

"So where do we go from here?"

He took each of her hands in his own. "We take a step back and wait on the Lord."

Kendall nodded. "What does that mean exactly—the whole 'taking a step back' thing?"

"It means we carry this evening in our hearts, to keep us going while we wait."

Dread settled over her. "I won't see you anymore, will I? At least not until—"

"I'll still be around." He kissed her cheek. "I promise."

She closed her eyes, fighting the urge to turn toward his mouth and steal one last kiss. The one from the other night would have to hold her over until things about their future were ironed out. Until things about her life were ironed out.

"After today, we have to go back to being just friends."

"No kissing," Kendall reminded them both.

Brady nodded. "No touching, period."

"Not at all?" Kendall thought about the comfort she received when Brady simply squeezed her hand.

Brady shook his head. "If I hold your hand, then I want to hold you. If I hold you, then I want to kiss you."

His honesty brought joy to her heart, because those were the same feelings and emotions she experienced.

"You look way too happy about this." He tapped her nose with his index finger.

"It's nice to hear you voice my feelings. Misery loves company, you know."

The sun had set, and the evening began to grow dim. Brady rose from the bench and stretched. "I want to drive you by the scene of the accident—see if the place triggers any memories."

"I hope so much that it does."

When Brady lifted Kendall, she rested in his strength. In the same way, she'd rest in his strength to get through the wait. His strength and God's.

Please, Lord, help me figure out who I am.

Chapter 7

Brady drove Kendall back toward the accident site. *Lord, let this place jog her memory. I ask You to touch her, heal her, restore her memory. Let today be the day.*

As they passed the corner where the hit-and-run occurred, Brady glanced in the mirror at Kendall, hoping for a reaction but seeing none. She studied the buildings as they cruised by slowly, but no apparent memory was triggered.

"See anything familiar?" He fought to keep the disappointment from his tone.

She shook her head. "I'm sorry, Brady."

He fought the urge to reach back and grab her hand, giving his typical reassuring squeeze.

"Let's drive through the U. I'll take every street slowly so you can really look around."

"Okay." They rode a few minutes in silence, Kendall studying each building. "Brady, tell me about your family and your life. It will pass the time as we wander the streets hoping to run into my life."

He chuckled.

"If we do run into my life, please don't run over it."

He rolled his eyes at her warped humor.

"So tell me about your parents, your family. Have you always gone to church?"

"Yep. I was on the cradle roll as soon as I was old enough for my mom to leave me in the nursery." Brady drove past some dorms, slowing to a crawl.

"We had a nice middle-class life. My mom stayed at home until Delanie started first grade. Then she enrolled at the U and got her master's in social work. My dad was a street cop and worked his way through the ranks."

Brady squelched a sigh as they passed the last dorm. He sent a meaningful glance in Kendall's direction.

"I'm trying, Brady. I really am, but I feel as though I've never seen any of this before. It's like I'm visiting a strange city for the first time."

"It's okay," he falsely reassured her, needing some reassurance himself. *God, where are You? Why aren't You helping us?* He wanted to hit the steering wheel

175

and yell at the top of his lungs. Why was God silent when Kendall needed His intervention so much?

Brady took a left, deciding to drive past the fraternity and sorority houses.

"So you said your dad worked his way through the ranks?"

"All the way to police chief, which is an elected position. Luckily, he stuck to his plan and got a four-year degree before entering the academy. It served him well and enabled him to go places in the force that he wanted to go. He says he's a man living his dream."

"How about you? Are you a man living your dream?" Kendall shifted her gaze from the passing landscape to the rearview mirror.

Again Brady slowed and crept by the various Greek houses, pondering Kendall's question. Students hung out on the front porches or sat on the grass.

"Yeah, for the most part I am. I've got the job I wanted. I have a great family, some good friends."

"How old were you when you realized you wanted to be a paramedic when you grew up?"

"About twelve." Brady braked for a couple crossing the street. "I was in junior high and doing a ride along with my dad for a paper I had to write. We were called to the scene of an accident, and I watched a medic save a child's life. I knew I wanted the same privilege."

Since the dorm and housing areas hadn't provided any hope, Brady started a methodical approach, taking every block of every street that was accessible by car. Kendall kept her gaze focused out the window, and Brady kept his speed far below the posted allowance.

"I'll drive each street twice, since you can't see both sides of the road at the same time."

"Thanks. How many lives have you saved?"

Brady shrugged. "I don't know. In the early days I used to keep track, but it became a source of pride. So I quit counting because ultimately I'm only a tool that God uses. Nothing more."

Kendall glanced at him and smiled. "Even though I don't know anything about me, I know in my heart that you, Brady Cooper, are one-of-a-kind—a really good man."

Brady pulled over and stopped. "And, Kendall"—he turned in his seat and faced her—"I know in my heart that you aren't a stripper or a hooker or even a married woman. There is something pure about you. I sense it deep in my heart."

Kendall stopped looking at the area and stared openmouthed at him. "A stripper or a hooker?" Lacing her words was the horror of the implication. "Is that what the police—your father and brother—assume?"

"No, of course not." Brady wanted to kick himself for his carelessness. What had he been thinking to let that slip?

The incredulous expression on Kendall's face said even more than she had. "Well, that explains your hesitation earlier today."

"What hesitation?" Brady had no idea what she referred to.

"This morning when I asked whether the police had garnered more information, you hesitated. I don't know what they think or what they've discovered," Kendall said, her voice growing louder, more forceful, "but the idea of my being a stripper or hooker repulses me. I know to the core of my being I'm neither of those things. I may not know what or who I am, but I know what I'm not!"

Under the streetlamp, Brady could see the pulse throbbing on the side of Kendall's neck. "No one is accusing you of either of those professions."

Her expression reflected doubt.

"I promise. Unfortunately, as police, they have to approach each case from every possible angle. There is no evidence tying you to their speculations, but they can't leave a stone unturned."

Kendall looked afraid. "What if I just think I'm a nice person?" Doubts had obviously crept in. "What if I'm a horrible person with an unsavory past?"

Her gaze searched his face.

"I don't believe that for a minute. I don't. There is a sweetness about you, an innocence."

"Maybe you just want to see that. Maybe I just want to believe it, but what if?" Worry lines etched themselves across her forehead. "What if, Brady?"

He raised his shoulders. "Then you start a new and different life with a clean slate. I mean, that's what the Christian life is all about. We're all sinners. We all have things in our past we regret. Every person has deficits that can only be overcome as we surrender our lives to Christ and ask Him to live through us, change us, and make us new creations. That's why we're referred to as born again. We die to our old selves and our old way of life, and we start living a new life with His help and according to His Word."

Kendall laid her head against the window behind her, staring up at the roof. "This nightmare grows worse with each day. First I have no memory of who I am or where I live. Then I discover I've been abandoned by anyone and everyone who might possibly know me. Now I have to face the possibility of discovering that the real me is someone less than desirable." She faced Brady.

"Tell me that your feelings won't change if you discover I'm a topless dancer?"

Brady shook his head, but in all honesty, he couldn't say for sure. He reached for her hand, but she pulled it away.

"Of course they will! I mean, my own feelings about myself will change. How can yours not?" Her tone demanded an answer.

"I don't know, Kendall. I can't predict the future, but my heart says no, nothing will change."

"Everything will change, Brady. Everything." She sighed. "No wonder your poor family wants you to slow down. Imagine their horror that I might be a less-than-honorable catch."

Brady reached for her hand again, just needing to touch her and offer comfort. "Take a deep breath. This whole conversation is nuts. We're talking about the unknown as if it's known."

She did as he instructed, sucking in a deep breath through her nose and blowing it out slowly through her mouth.

"Do that again five more times," he encouraged.

When she let out the last breath, he asked, "Feel better?"

She smiled an embarrassed little smile. "I do. Fear is obviously one of my weaknesses. Once I wrapped my mind around the possibilities, my thoughts ran away and spiraled out of control."

Brady squeezed her hand. "We have to live in the here and now—in the truth that we know. And for us, that means one day and one moment at a time. A few weeks ago, my pastor said fear is an acronym for 'false evidence appearing real.' This whole conversation has been about false evidence."

Kendall nodded. "You're right."

Brady pulled back onto the road. "Study every building, and we'll forget the rest of tonight."

Later that night when Brady rolled Kendall into her room, a cloud of discouragement shrouded them both. They'd covered every accessible inch of the campus, and not one thing looked even vaguely familiar. Brady helped her onto her bed then bid her good night from the doorway, carefully keeping his distance. He knew by the droop of her shoulders that she, too, was discouraged by the lack of progress they'd made today.

When Brady climbed into the SUV, he slammed the door with extra force. "Where were You today, God?"

He headed to his parents' house, knowing they'd still be up. He needed to talk to someone.

Brady let himself in with his garage door opener, finding his dad in the study off the great room.

"Hey there." His dad glanced up from his computer screen. "Everything okay?"

"Do you have a few minutes?"

"Sure." His dad rose, and they left the office.

"Brady, I didn't know you were here." His mom stood at the stove pouring hot water from her teakettle into an oversized cup. "I'm making myself some tea. Can I get you anything?" She studied him a moment in that way moms do. "You look like you could use a cup of hot cocoa." She started the process without waiting for his response.

He smiled, thinking back to his childhood. His mom's answer to all of life's ailments had been hot chocolate, a heart-to-heart discussion, and a time of prayer before heading off to bed. Tonight was no different.

She handed him and his dad each a piping hot cup. "Let's go out on the back porch and enjoy the stars. You appear in need of a mom and dad fix."

Brady laughed. "How can you always tell?"

"I'm a mom."

"And moms always know," Brady finished for her. He and his dad followed her, and they settled into plush, wood-framed lounge chairs.

"What's up, son?" his dad asked, sipping his hot chocolate.

Brady recapped his evening with Kendall. "Here's the thing—I'm in love with her, and I'm trying to heed your and Delanie's warnings, but it's tough. I just know deep inside that she's a single Christian woman. I believe she's the one I've been waiting for."

His mom glanced at his dad, and concern embedded itself in their eyes. "We hope all of that is true, Brady. I've grown to love Kendall, too, and am praying for this story to have a happy ending. I want that for you and for her."

"But," his dad added in his soft, serious tone, "just because you feel it deep in your bones doesn't make it so. I've arrested people and convinced myself of their innocence because I wished it to be, but our hopes can't change facts."

Brady's head knew the truth of his dad's words, but his heart was on a course of its own.

"I'm struggling with my faith." Brady rose and paced to the edge of the porch. He faced his parents. "I'm really mad at God about this whole thing. I mean, He's God. He can do anything. Why doesn't He? He knows who she is. He can restore her memory. He can send someone to claim her. Where is He?" Brady glared up into the black night sky. *Where are You?*

"Those are all questions each believer wrestles with at one time or another, but His Word guarantees He is there, whether you feel Him or not." His dad spoke into the stillness of the night.

Brady let out a long, loud sigh. "I've never had a faith crisis before, and for the first time in my life, I'm not 100 percent certain that God is who I thought He was."

"This is one of those times when you have to return to His Word and stand on what it says."

"What does it say, Mom? Does it say Kendall will ever remember? Does it say she'll be all right?" Brady sat on the end of the lounge chair, resting his head in his hands.

∞

Some mornings Kendall hated rehab, and this was one of those days. "I know it's hard, Kendall, but I promise all your hard work will reap great rewards in the end." Tom wheeled her back toward her room.

"If I live to see the end," Kendall reminded him.

"You will." His voice rang with promise, and she wanted to believe one day she'd be well—her body and her memory; however, doubts plagued her.

As Tom steered her chariot—his affectionate name for her wheelchair—through the door of her room, she caught sight of Brady by the window. Her heart did a happy dance. He and his mom were the two bright spots in her life.

"Brady! I had no idea you would be here!"

"Sorry we're late." Tom set the brake on her chair and faced Brady. "I made Kendall stay after class and work harder than usual. She's my star pupil, and her therapy will be rigorous from here on out." He patted her head like one would appease a small child and headed toward the door, stopping before he exited. "You two have a good night. See you tomorrow, Kendall."

"Bye, Tom," they both called after him.

"Rigorous, huh?" Brady lifted a brow.

"Sometimes, like today, I feel like he wants more from me than I can give."

"You look beat. I planned to take you down by the U again, only this time I thought we'd walk. Maybe we should wait until you aren't so tired."

No matter how worn out she felt, spending time with Brady always held appeal. "A walk—or roll in my case—in the fresh air might revive me. And truthfully, it beats the thought of staying confined to this little room all evening."

"A walk it is." Brady let off the brake and made a U-turn with her chair. "Did you sleep okay?" Concern laced his tone as he rolled her down the tiled hall toward the nurses' station.

"No. I tossed and turned and punched my pillow at least a million times."

"Sounds as fun as my night." Brady stopped at the desk and signed Kendall out; then he pushed her toward the exit doors. "I stared at the clock on my nightstand and wondered if I'd ever fall asleep. I'd force myself to close my eyes, but when I couldn't stand the suspense any longer, I'd peek at the clock, only to discover it was mere minutes later than the last time I'd checked."

Brady stopped beside his SUV. "There's nothing worse than not being able to fall asleep." Each night she hoped for sleep to capture her and carry her off into a land of bliss and peace where she didn't have to wonder about herself. But every morning when she woke up again, her life was still a mystery. Brady lifted her into the backseat and held out her seat belt. She pulled it around her and clicked it shut. Even though he'd instructed her not to think about anything except what she knew for certain, she'd struggled all night with the daunting question of who and what she could be and all the what-ifs that came with that.

Brady climbed into the driver's seat. "The last time I remember checking the clock, it was three in the morning, and my alarm rang at six. Can you beat that?"

Brady had driven the few blocks from St. Mary's rehab unit to the firehouse where he worked. He parallel parked on Ralston.

"Is this your station house?"

"Yep. I thought we'd walk from here. A lot of students that don't live on campus rent places in this area." Brady effortlessly lifted her from the SUV to her chair.

Kendall fought an urge to kiss his cheek and hug him tight. Instead, she diverted her thoughts to the surrounding area. They walked through an older neighborhood, much of it run-down and in need of repair. The houses were small, the yards unkempt. It reminded her of a poor village.

The thought triggered a memory from last night. "I had the strangest dream—almost surreal. I was playing with little children—dark-skinned ones like we saw yesterday at that restaurant. In the dream we all spoke Spanish. I knew them all, and they knew me. We ran through trees in a jungle, playing hide-and-seek. Do you think it's significant or just a dream?"

"I don't know." Brady followed the sidewalk, turning onto a main street. "You do speak Spanish."

"The children were laughing, but I remained still and quiet, hiding up in a tree. Several of them called to me, but they never found me. I kept yelling to them, but they couldn't hear me or see me."

Brady stopped and knelt in front of her. "Maybe it's your anxiety over wanting to be found by someone who knows you."

Kendall nodded, though not completely convinced.

"This is where your accident happened."

Kendall studied every building, the street, but none of it looked familiar. She closed her eyes, willing herself to remember.

She saw headlights coming toward her. Her heart pounded, and a scream tore from her throat. She felt as though all the blood had drained from her body. "No!" she cried. "No! Please don't hit me!" Tears rolled down her cheeks.

Chapter 8

Brady swung by his parents' house the next morning, coming through the garage.

"Hi, sweetheart." His mom kissed his cheek on her way to the kitchen. "The coffee's hot. You want a cup?"

"Sure. Where's Dad?" Brady settled on a bar stool, facing his mom and the kitchen.

"Shaving. He'll be out in a minute." She pulled a bag of frozen blueberries from the freezer. "Have you had breakfast?"

Brady shook his head.

"Dad and I are having smoothies. Would you like one?"

"Sure."

"Morning, Brady." His dad buttoned his uniform shirt as he walked into the room.

"Hey, Dad. I have some Kendall news for you and Mom."

"Did her memory return?" Hope filled his mom's face as she swung around to face him.

"No, but she remembered her accident—at least part of it."

"Does she remember the car—color? make? model?" His dad was always the investigative officer.

"No. Sorry. All she remembers are the headlights coming toward her and the fear that washed over her as she realized someone was about to hit her."

"Still no identity, though—hers or the driver's?"

"Nope." Brady stirred cream and sugar into his coffee. His dad settled on the stool next to him.

"This is huge, though," Marilyn said as she continued adding ingredients to the blender. "She remembers something—a snippet. Surely more will come." She hit START, and the blender hummed to life, mixing and grinding.

"I hope so." Part of Brady feared what they might discover. Sometimes he wondered if she might be better off starting with a clean slate. No memory. No past life. Of course, he knew burying the past never erased it.

"So what brings you by so early this morning?" His dad sipped the hot coffee.

"Not that we aren't happy to see you," his mom added, pouring the frozen drink into three glasses.

"I'm hoping Dad and I can go to the evidence room and sort through Kendall's things. I just need to see for myself exactly what's there. Will you get me in?"

"Sure, if you think it will help, but nothing out of the ordinary was noted."

"I know, and I'm certainly not slighting the reports. It's just that since I know her, maybe something will mean something to me that wouldn't to someone else. Am I grasping at straws?"

"Maybe." His dad set the smoothie down. "But I understand your need to try. And unfortunately, with the recent string of casino robberies, I have no manpower to devote to a hit-and-run investigation, so this might be a good idea." He pulled out his BlackBerry and checked his calendar. "I'm free until a 10:00 a.m. meeting. Drink up, and we'll head over there now."

"Thanks, Dad. I'm hoping against hope that there will be a clue of some kind. Somewhere, somehow, there has to be something. I can't give up, and you and Mom are the best for your understanding and help."

His mom winked at him. "We try."

Brady quickly finished his smoothie.

His dad had gone into the office to gather what he needed to take with him. "You ready?" He had his briefcase in tow.

Brady nodded and hugged his mom. "Thanks for the coffee and breakfast." He followed his dad out the door into the garage. "I'll meet you at the precinct."

On the way over, Brady asked God to give him and his dad wisdom to see what others might have missed. He asked God to prepare both him and Kendall for what might lie ahead. He couldn't shake the dread that settled over him like a dark cloud.

Once parked, he met his dad on the front steps of the building and trailed him through the halls to the locked evidence storage area. All evidence was kept under lock and key with an officer posted outside the room at all times.

"Chief Cooper." Surprised to see the top gun, the officer stood straighter.

"Good morning. How's that wound of yours healing?"

The surprised expression turned to shock. "My wound, sir?" At Chief Cooper's nod, the policeman continued. "I'm doing well, sir. Thank you."

"Glad to hear it. You'll be back out there before you know it." Brady watched his dad fill out the necessary form to enable them to view the evidence. The humility and integrity his dad possessed struck Brady. He accepted no special favors because of who he was or the office he filled.

The officer led them through a locked gate, locking it again behind them. He took them into a room with only a large table and gave them each a pair of white gloves. Then he left, carrying the form his dad had filled out.

"He'll retrieve the evidence and lay it out on the table for us to peruse," his dad explained.

"He seemed surprised that you knew about his injury."

His dad shrugged. "They're my men. I try to keep track of them."

The officer returned, carrying a sealed box. Setting it on the table, he removed the contents and checked each against a master list. Brady moved closer, eyeing each thing removed from the box. This was all that remained of Kendall's life—all that was known.

His dad checked the inventory and signed the sheet. "Ring this buzzer," the officer said, pointing near the door, "when you're finished."

"We will. Thank you."

The officer left, locking them and Kendall's evidence inside the stark room. Brady wasn't even sure where to begin. He walked around the table, eyeing her bike, her helmet, a baggie with her crushed cell phone, another baggie with a chain and some keys. Her clothes had been cut off, their chopped remains lying at the other end.

Brady glanced up. His dad studied him as intently as he studied the contents of Kendall's life. His dad gave him a compassionate, encouraging smile. Brady moved past her riding attire to the pictures from the scene. He picked one up. The sight of his beloved Kendall lying in the rubble and blood nearly did him in—and he was a medic, for goodness' sake. He'd seen far worse, but somehow it was different when a loved one was involved.

His dad moved over beside him, picking up several pictures. He, too, seemed moved by the blood and gore. "We see this sort of thing every day—you and I—but it's different when the victim is someone you care about." His dad laid the pictures down, moved to the other end of the table, and examined her bike. Brady joined him.

The frame was bent. The tires flat and wheels mangled beyond repair. The seat was twisted and torn. Both he and his dad stood bent over the bike, studying each inch of metal.

"This bike looks brand-new."

Brady glanced at his dad. Was he nuts? This bike looked like it had been through a war and lost. "How so?"

His dad pointed to the shaft that held the seat. "Look at how shiny this paint is. No scratches. No fading. And the chrome that isn't damaged is spotless."

Brady nodded his agreement.

Brady's dad picked up the helmet, holding it between his two index fingers. He examined it thoroughly inside and out. The helmet had some bloodstains on it and a dent on the right side.

"See, this doesn't look new. The inside and strap show some wear."

Brady examined it closely, amazed at his dad's astuteness. "Guess that's why you're the cop."

Frank gently returned the helmet to the table and moved on to the clothing. In less than a minute, he made his assessment. "This riding outfit is well worn."

Now *that*, even Brady could see. "What does it all mean?"

His dad shrugged, focusing his attention on Brady. "My educated guess?"

Brady nodded.

"She hasn't been in Reno long. Picked up a new bike when she got here, but she is an experienced biker, probably been doing it for years."

Brady shook his head. "How did you get all that from this?" He pointed to the pile of rubble strewn across the table.

"The bike is new. It's a Gary Fisher, which is a top brand. Serious bikers like good equipment." He picked up her riding shoe. "Not everyone who owns a bike owns a pair of these."

"That's for sure." Brady thought of his mountain bike collecting dust in his garage. He biked in his running shoes.

"Her helmet, shoes, and riding gear all show wear. They are also easier to pack and move than a bike would be."

"Especially if you're a college student and arrived by plane." Brady felt pleased with his deduction.

"Exactly." His dad smiled his "Good job, son" smile.

"But you asked the college for a list of no-shows." Brady rubbed the back of his neck.

"Maybe she hadn't enrolled yet." His dad picked up the cell phone bag and carefully emptied the contents onto the table. "I don't know."

Brady watched as the red phone slid from the bag in three pieces. It had a tire mark across the back of the main body. His dad used his pen to turn the phone over.

"I think this is new, too. Look at the screen. Even though it's cracked, the glass appears new. What isn't scratched or broken is shiny."

Brady didn't quite see it, but he trusted his dad.

His dad pushed the phone back into the baggie and laid it aside. "I'll get this sent to the crime lab and see if they can recover any information from the phone itself. As soon as they can spare a minute, I'll have Frankie and his crew visit every bike shop in the city that sells Gary Fisher. They can take a picture of Kendall with them. Chances are if she bought it here, she paid with either a credit card or check. Between the cell phone and the bike, this might be the lead you've been praying for."

"I hope so." A tiny seed of expectation planted itself in Brady.

"Here's a key and some jewelry." His dad slid a key chain out of the bag. A single key was attached to a small wire circle. "It's a house key."

"To someplace here in Reno," Brady said, tacking on the obvious.

"The girl traveled light," his dad commented as he extracted a silver bracelet inscribed with Kendall's name from the bag. Finally, he pulled out the last item, a plain gold chain with a delicate gold band suspended from it.

Brady's heart fell to the floor, and his chest felt suddenly heavy, as if an elephant had stomped on him. His dad's gaze rose to meet his, compassion filling his eyes.

"Maybe it's not what it looks like. I mean, why would she wear a wedding band on a chain around her neck?" Brady attempted to reason away the facts.

His dad slipped it on the end of his pen and examined it at close range.

"It's inscribed." His dad squinted to make out the words. "In Spanish."

What little hope Brady held on to was dashed to the ground with his father's words. "Spanish?" Brady felt like the wind had been knocked out of him. "Kendall speaks Spanish, and she dreamed about a village with dark-skinned children."

His dad eyed him closely. "Do you think it was a memory and not a dream?"

"I don't know, Dad. Seems more possible all the time." Brady swallowed, hoping to dislodge the fear threatening to smother him.

His dad buzzed the officer at the front. The door opened. "Are you finished, sir?"

"Not quite. Do you read Spanish?"

He nodded and studied the ring. "This is a little different from traditional Spanish. Must be some sort of dialect." He studied the ring closely. "I believe it says 'KB, my future, my life, JG.'"

The inscription sealed Brady's fate. "She's married." If there'd been a chair, he'd have sunk into it. As it was, he leaned heavily on the table. His heart shattered as the reality struck him. He, Brady Cooper, had fallen in love with a married woman, kissed a married woman, held a married woman. Maybe those children in her dream were her children.

Brady felt sick.

Chapter 9

Kendall had Tom park her by the window of her room. Instinctively she knew—she loved the outdoors and spent much of her time there. Her sun-browned skin testified to this fact, as did her heart's yearning to be outside, breathing fresh air, hearing birds sing, and enjoying God's creation.

Kendall saw Brady drive up. Watching him walk toward the building, Kendall knew something was amiss. His shoulders sagged, his step dragged, and his head hung low. Kendall knew for certain he came with bad news.

She didn't know if she could handle anything sad or depressing. "I can do all things through Christ." She whispered the verse over and over, preparing for whatever Brady had today. She heard his footsteps in the hall. As he drew closer, her trepidation grew stronger. When he turned into her room, she held her breath—her back to the doorway.

He waited for several seconds before speaking. "Hey, Kendall." His voice sounded flat.

"Brady." She turned and caught sight of him in her peripheral vision. She swallowed, fighting the fear attempting to choke her. "Will you take me outside?" Maybe out there whatever he had to say would seem less bleak.

He nodded, released her brake, and turned her around. Skirting the bed, he rolled her out through the hall and onto the patio. Large rosebushes grew on trellises. Their scent permeated the air.

Brady sat on a bench, facing Kendall. Sadness lined his face and filled his eyes. Kendall grabbed the arm of her chair, bracing herself against the news Brady had come to share.

Brady pulled his phone from his pocket, and she wondered why he'd chosen now to make a call. After pressing several buttons, he showed her a picture of a ring on the screen of his phone.

She stared at the screen, and a small gold band stared back at her. Though she didn't recognize it, something about it seemed familiar. A wave of emotion hit her: sadness, fear, uncertainty, resignation.

"Does that look at all familiar?" His tone bordered on anger.

She shook her head. "But seeing it brings negative feelings—a lack of peace, an unrest, but I don't know why." She searched his face for some sort of clue.

187

"Where did you see it?"

"It's yours." His voice sounded almost accusatory.

"Mine?"

Brady rose, walking to the edge of the patio, putting distance between them. "Apparently you're married."

"No." Tears rolled down her cheeks. "I can't be, Brady. I just can't be."

"The ring was inscribed in some sort of Spanish dialect. 'KB, my life, my future, JG.'"

Kendall remembered her dream—the Hispanic children. Were they hers? She closed her eyes, wishing to shut out this latest find. "Don't you think if I were married, I would know?"

"Maybe you're trying to forget." Even Brady's voice held distance. "You wore the ring on a chain around your neck."

"That makes no sense. If I'm married, why wouldn't I wear the ring on my finger?" She glanced at her hand. Her finger remained bare and unencumbered. "Did you find anything else?"

Brady leaned back against a porch post, folding his arms across his chest. He filled her in on the contents of her sealed box and the condition of her bike.

Mortified over this newfound information, Kendall asked, "Do you think I ran away? Do you think that maybe I left my husband and children?"

Brady shook his head. "I don't know, Kendall. I just don't know." He sucked in a deep breath. "But what I do know is this is it for us." His words brought an overwhelming sense of isolation to Kendall. "I can't come back anymore."

She wanted to beg, to plead, but didn't. Instead, she nodded her resignation. Tears slid down her cheeks. She attempted to wipe them away, but the bulky cast made the movements choppy and awkward.

Brady's eyes glistened, and somehow the knowledge comforted her. This was hard for him, too.

"Kendall, our feelings for one another are inappropriate. You are married to someone else."

She couldn't argue his logic or the painful truth of his words. Nor could she force words past the lump lodged in her throat, so she nodded her agreement. Silent tears continued to glide down her cheeks and drip off her chin. She gave up trying to stop them or even wipe them away.

"I wish it could have been different." His voice was low and husky.

Again she only nodded.

Brady swiped his cheek. "I'm going to go now, Kendall."

A sob escaped even though she fought hard to hold it in. She covered her mouth with her cast.

"My mom will be here in a few minutes. Do you want to wait here, or should I take you back to your room?"

She shook her head, not wanting to return to the confined space that suddenly felt like a prison cell.

He nodded his understanding. "Good-bye, then." He held his mouth in a tight line.

She sniffed and nodded. Her world crumbled into a hopeless pile of rubble. Seeing Brady walk away tore her heart to shreds, and there was nothing she could do but watch him leave.

Moments later Marilyn Cooper walked toward her. Her compassionate eyes were filled with tears. She said nothing but hugged Kendall close as a mother would her young, and they cried together. When both were cried out, she knelt in front of Kendall and took tissues from her purse. She gently dried Kendall's cheeks and then her own.

Kendall sniffed. "What do I do now?"

Mrs. Cooper settled on the bench facing Kendall and took her hand. "I'm here for you until the end, Kendall. Until the mystery is solved and you're reunited with your family. We'll get through this dark tunnel together, and we'll take it one day at a time."

Gratitude welled up inside Kendall. "Thank you, Mrs. Cooper. I have no one else. I can't even express what your kindness means to me." Kendall tried not to cry again, but a few stray tears insisted on making an appearance. "Will you tell Brady that I'm sorry I hurt him?" She shook her head, still unable to fathom the news. "I didn't know. I just didn't know."

"We all understand that. No one blames you, Kendall. It's just a very unfortunate turn of events."

"If not for you, I'd be completely alone."

Mrs. Cooper patted her hand. "But you're not, and I'll be here every day. I promise."

Kendall attempted a smile. "He was my best friend." Then she laughed, a dry, brittle sound. "Really my only friend."

"I know, and the loss will be hard."

Kendall wondered if Mrs. Cooper understood the enormity of her pain. "I loved him."

"I know you did, and he loved you."

"Yet I'm supposedly married to someone else. Where is he? Where is this husband of mine? Why isn't he searching for me?"

"We don't have answers, but we know the One who does." Mrs. Cooper's tone was strong and sure.

Kendall wanted to ask why God was letting this happen to her. Where was He in her time of need? But she didn't express her struggle aloud, afraid of what Mrs. Cooper might think of her.

Later that evening while alone in her room, Delanie popped her head inside the door. "Do you mind if I come in? I promise not to stay long."

Great, she's come to gloat. Kendall did mind but responded appropriately and motioned Delanie into the room.

Delanie didn't sit down but came and stood next to the bed. "Kendall, I'm so sorry."

Kendall struggled to believe her. After all, this was exactly what she'd wanted all along—Kendall and Brady separate, apart, finished.

"I know you're finding it difficult to believe me, but I'm telling you the truth. I wanted both you and Brady to be happy."

"It's not your fault that I'm apparently married."

"No, but I need you to know this is not what I wanted. I was afraid Brady—both of you—would be hurt."

"And your prediction came true." Kendall didn't mean for her tone to sound so sarcastic.

Delanie's eyes glistened, and Kendall realized she wasn't the enemy. "I'm hoping we can be friends. I know that losing Brady is a huge loss in your life, and I can't replace him, but I'd like to be here for you."

A husky "thank you" was all Kendall could manage.

Delanie squeezed her hand. "How about dinner and a chick flick tomorrow night?"

"Sure."

"On second thought, a chick flick may not be such a good idea. They always have the perfect happy ending. We'll figure out something, though."

"Delanie, thank you. Before you came, I was lying here feeling sorry for myself. I'm a girl with no past, no future, and no hope."

"But not a girl without friends." Delanie smiled, and her words brought the first ray of hope since Brady walked out of her life earlier today.

After Delanie left, Kendall recognized the faithfulness of God. No, her life wasn't going the way she wanted, the way she'd hoped, but God had provided Delanie and Mrs. Cooper. Her plight was hard, but He hadn't left her completely alone. He'd given her two kind women to walk the road beside her. Maybe their motive was pity, but they were here. And Kendall knew they'd stay until the end—whatever that might look like.

Then her mind flipped to her husband. Did she love him? Was theirs a marriage made in heaven? For some reason she doubted either was true.

Chapter 10

The following week, Brady flipped open his ringing cell phone. "Hey, Dad."

"Can you swing by the house this morning? I've finally got some news."

"About Kendall?"

"Yep. We know who she is."

Brady's heart pounded. "I'll be there in about twenty minutes." He snapped his phone shut. He'd missed her this week and was grateful they'd finally figured out her identity.

When Brady arrived at his parents' home, Delanie's car was parked out front. He both anticipated and dreaded whatever news his dad had uncovered.

He nearly ran to the front door. His dad, mom, and Delanie stood around the snack bar that separated the great room from the kitchen.

"Well?" Brady asked.

"The Kendall puzzle has finally been solved," his mom announced.

"And?" Impatience infused the word. He just wanted to know who she was and why nobody had coming looking.

"Kendall Brooks grew up in Mexico as the daughter of missionaries."

Brady nodded. "That explains some things, but what about her husband?"

"She has no husband."

Brady's heart took flight.

"Yet." His dad put extra emphasis on the word. "She is, however, engaged to a Mexican national."

"She's not married?" Brady's mood shot through the roof. He swung Delanie around. "She's not married!"

He laughed and cried and repeated the news over and over.

"Brady, she's committed to another man." His mom tried to reason with him.

"I know, Mom. I know. But she's not married. She still has a choice. I've got to go tell her." Brady grabbed his keys and headed for the door.

"Wait." His dad's voice carried authority. "Would it be better if your mom and Delanie told her? She's still committed to another man."

"Maybe I'm the reason God allowed this to happen. Mom, you say every-thing happens for a reason. I love her. We belong together."

Three pairs of eyes studied him, each reflecting their doubts.

Marilyn spoke up. "I think it's okay to present her with the facts, but until her memory returns, it isn't fair to ask her to choose between you and a man she can't remember."

Brady knew his mom was right. "But how long could that take?"

"Her parents and fiancé are flying in as soon as they can work out the details. Once he's here to defend his position, even if she doesn't remember, she can make a better decision, a more fair decision."

Brady realized he still might lose her, but he had to try. He headed for the door. "I've got to see her."

"Wait, son. At least listen to the whole story so you can fill her in on as many details as possible."

Brady returned to the bar and perched on a stool, feeling like a bird dying to take flight. He tried to focus on the facts of Kendall's life, but the excitement of seeing her again kept drowning out everything else. He couldn't wait to see her expression when he walked in.

As soon as his dad finished outlining the information he'd gleaned regarding Kendall, Brady asked the obvious question. "Why wasn't she on the no-show list at the U?"

"Apparently, unbeknownst to the department, the university only checked the undergrads. Nobody bothered with the graduate students."

" 'When one person does a halfway job, other people pay the price.' " Delanie and Brady quoted their father's often-used phrase and laughed. Brady then hugged his family good-bye and rushed out the door. As he drove the fifteen minutes to the hospital, he anticipated her pleasure at finally having the pieces so she could begin to assemble the puzzle of her life.

Brady parked and jogged to the double glass doors. His heart pounded, and his hope soared. Kendall might one day be his, after all.

He hurried through the corridors to her room, but her bed sat empty. He headed to the nurses' station. "I can't find Kendall. Do you know where she is?"

"She's been going out to the garden early on weekend mornings. Sometimes stays out there till noon. I'd check there."

Brady nodded. *How can you not know for sure where she is? You're supposed to be taking care of her.* He wondered how Kendall even managed to get herself out there.

Turning, he spotted Kendall, now cast free, trudging her way down the hall—at the pace of a ninety-year-old woman—leaning heavily on a walker, yet no one had ever looked so good to him. He stopped to savor the moment. "Thank You, God," he whispered, rejoicing in her progress.

Kendall forced herself to take another step and then another. The pain made her want to quit, but she pushed onward. She had made her way to the patio with her Bible in tow several hours ago. This had become her morning routine, and saturating herself in God's Word made life easier to bear.

A week had passed since the "breakup," but not one day passed without her thinking of Brady, missing him. No news had surfaced regarding her husband, but Mrs. Cooper assured her that Chief Cooper was doing everything in his power to solve this mystery.

Kendall raised her gaze from the floor to see how much farther she had to go. There stood Brady maybe thirty feet away.

She stopped, and their gazes connected. Her mouth went dry, and her heartbeat doubled. *Why is he here?* She knew it would only make it harder in the end.

"Kendall." His familiar voice wrapped around her like a warm blanket on a cold night. In spite of her good sense, tears welled in her eyes and a smile settled on her face. She should yell at him for daring to show up, but the thought of spending a little more time with him brought more pleasure than she cared to admit.

He began to move toward her, a sense of purpose in his step. His eyes remained locked on hers, tenderness filling them. All she wanted was to be swept into those muscular arms and have him hold her forever.

God, forgive me for such thoughts.

She sucked in a deep breath, knowing what she must do. "Why are you here?"

Brady stopped in front of her. "You're not married."

"What?" Her arms gave way, and she swayed.

Brady grabbed her shoulders to steady her. "My dad found your parents, and you aren't married, just engaged."

A plethora of emotions swept over Kendall. She swallowed hard, trying to absorb the facts. She had parents and a fiancé.

"Let me help you to your room, and I'll fill you in on what I know."

Brady swept her into his arms as if she weighed no more than a bag of feathers; then he grabbed the walker and carried them both the short distance to her room. He set Kendall in the only available chair and went next door to borrow another. When he returned, he positioned his chair across from hers.

"So I'm not married?"

"Not yet."

"Why wasn't anybody looking for me? What is my last name? Are they coming to see me? Who am I? What do I do?" She asked every question that popped into her mind.

"Whoa—one question at a time," Brady scolded, but his smile let her know he wasn't the least bit put out by her excitement. His eyes told her what he'd not said aloud—his feelings still ran deep.

"Okay. Who am I?"

"Kendall Marie Brooks—the daughter of missionaries."

She assimilated the information. "Missionaries?" She tried to remember, but no details came.

"You grew up near Oaxaca, Mexico, and had only arrived in Reno the day before your accident."

"At least now I understand why this city is so unfamiliar." Somehow the knowledge brought a certain amount of peace. "Why am I here? In Reno, I mean."

"You came to go to school. You were accepted into the graduate program of Environmental Engineering at the University of Nevada here in Reno."

"Graduate school? That means I've already been to college?" This all sounded like someone else's life, not hers. "How old am I?"

"You're twenty-six, and yes, you must have gone to college somewhere and have a degree. Otherwise you couldn't be accepted into grad school."

Kendall rubbed her forehead. All the straining to recollect gave her a serious headache.

"Anyway, according to what your father told my dad, your plan is to return to Mexico and marry Javier—"

"Javier?" Kendall squeezed her eyes shut, trying to put a face to the name.

"Javier Gonzales—your fiancé." She knew Brady tried to act unaffected, but his tone revealed his true feelings. His jaw was tense; a muscle pulsated in his neck.

"Environmental engineering. That sounds hard. Why would I want to do that?" She shook her head. The idea held zero appeal.

"I guess you and Javier plan to follow in your parents' footsteps and serve the tribal natives. You apparently have big plans to improve the living conditions for the people groups that reside in the outlying areas." Brady's voice carried an angry edge.

"I sound like some sort of saint." She felt mystified, because none of the facts seemed connected to her.

"A real Mother Teresa." She didn't miss the sarcasm lacing each word.

"Why are you angry because my life obviously had purpose? You chose a career as a medic to make a difference. Why isn't it okay for me to make that same choice?" She didn't get his attitude. This wasn't like Brady at all.

He rose and walked to the window and stared out for several seconds, his back toward her.

"The truth?"

"Nothing but," she demanded.

He swung around and faced her, leaning against the windowsill. "I am angry—angry that you have a fiancé, angry that your life will take you far from me, angry that I didn't meet you first."

Her own irritation melted away at his confession. "At least I'm not married," she reminded him in a quiet tone.

"I know, but your plans are already in motion. How would we ever meld our two very separate lives?"

"I don't know, Brady. I don't know." She tucked a strand of hair behind her ear. "I still have no memory of any of this." The frustration of her situation returned.

Brady looked at the ceiling and let out a long, slow sigh. "I know. You and I—as a pair—feel more hopeless all the time."

Kendall couldn't disagree. "When will I meet my parents? Maybe seeing them face-to-face will trigger something. At least that's what the doctor said about the familiar."

Brady nodded. "They're coming, along with Javier. Probably tomorrow. They planned to catch the first available flight."

At Brady's announcement, Kendall experienced fear and excitement. Her stomach knotted in anticipation.

"Here's the thing, Kendall: I'm here against my dad's advice and probably against the voice of reason in my head." He returned to his chair and took her hands in his. "I can't get you out of my mind, and you are rooted deep in my heart." His eyes were intense—his words soft and sincere. "I don't doubt for a second that I'm in love with you, that I want to spend the next seventy or eighty years with you."

Kendall's heart raced. *Are you going to ask me to be Mrs. Brady Cooper?* And in that second, the truth hit her like a brick falling on her head. She'd pledged herself to another. This wasn't right.

"I want you in my future," Brady continued when she failed to respond. "I'm willing to fight for your love or wait for it. I'll do whatever it takes, because I've waited a long time for you, Kendall Brooks, a very long time."

Instead of bringing delight, his words broke her heart. She loved Brady, too, but apparently she loved another man, as well. And Brady was all she knew. Maybe Delanie had been right all along. Maybe she'd mistaken gratitude for love.

Brady slid his hand under her hair and cradled the side of her neck. "You think on all I've said. I know it's been a big day, and you must feel like you're on information overload. I'm not going anywhere. I'll be here again tomorrow and the day after that."

Kendall knew she should tell him not to bother, but she couldn't put a voice to the truth piercing her heart.

Brady leaned in, and though she didn't move toward him, she didn't move away, either. *One last time, just one last time.* She reasoned away her lack of good judgment, but when Brady's lips touched hers, guilt filled her to overflowing.

She pulled back. "Brady, I can't." Not able to face the hurt and rejection she might see in his eyes, she stared at her lap. "Maybe you should leave."

Silence filled the room for a heartbeat. "Maybe I should." Brady rose and carried his chair out of the room. Her heart went out the door with him, leaving Kendall more confused than ever.

∞

The next morning Kendall awoke to the sound of voices near her bed. She opened groggy eyes.

"Kendall! Oh, Kendall!" A gray-haired woman with tanned skin hugged her close. "It is so good to see you."

"Kendall?" Mrs. Cooper's familiar voice came from the other side of her bed. Kendall rolled over and grabbed her hand. She needed something familiar to hold on to. Six expectant eyes focused on her. Six eyes that triggered no recall but instead made her very uncomfortable. Six eyes that studied her like a bug under a microscope. Kendall sat up and pulled her sheet up to her chin. Her eyes struggled to adjust to the bright lights of the room. The two men crowded in close.

"These are your parents, George and Diana Brooks, and this is your fiancé, Javier Gonzales."

Kendall's gaze moved from one to the other. Her mother's eyes were a soft brown, reflecting sadness. Her father's eyes were a shade of gray-blue. He, too, had a gloom about him, but the black eyes that stared at her were most intense. The small Hispanic man wore the look of a lovesick puppy dog. She felt nothing for him, not even a glimmer of attraction. He was nothing like Brady, though she knew she shouldn't compare.

"Ti gunaa stinnne`." My one woman. The endearment spoken with tenderness grated on Kendall. He reached a stubby hand toward her, and she drew back, pulling the sheet a little higher.

Mrs. Cooper wrapped a protective arm around Kendall's shoulder, and Kendall leaned into the safety of her embrace. Hurt and disappointment imprinted itself on the other three faces.

"She doesn't remember you. To her, you are all complete strangers."

Diana Brooks sniffled, and Kendall noticed tears in the woman's eyes, only increasing her discomfort.

"Why don't we give Kendall a few minutes to pull herself together?" Mrs. Cooper herded them out the door. "There's a waiting room down this way." She pointed. They all headed out the door.

"Mrs. Cooper, will you stay?"

Her gentle eyes reassured Kendall. "Yes. I'd be happy to." She turned to Kendall's family waiting just outside the door. "I'll help Kendall get ready, and we'll meet you in a little while."

Mrs. Cooper shut the door before anyone had a chance to respond. She rushed to Kendall's side. "I'm so sorry." She squeezed Kendall's hand. "They caught a red-eye and got in very early this morning. I had offered to pick them up, wanting to be here for you when you met them. I should have come into your room by myself first."

Kendall had grown to love this woman. "It's fine."

"You slept a little later this morning than usual." Mrs. Cooper walked to the closet.

"I didn't sleep much last night." Kendall let out a sigh. "It's not your fault I was still in bed."

"I hated seeing you in such an uncomfortable position." She held up a light-weight wine-colored sweater. "Is this one okay? I know it's your favorite."

Kendall nodded. "I don't remember them. I'm trying. I really am."

Mrs. Cooper removed a pair of sweats from one of Kendall's drawers and laid them across the bed. "You have no control over your memory—no matter how hard you try."

"So they say, but it makes me feel so helpless."

Kendall took her things into the bathroom, returning a few minutes later dressed and teeth brushed. Mrs. Cooper helped Kendall brush her hair. Kendall's movements were still awkward and stiff, and hair care was the most difficult morning task.

"Will you stay with me?" Kendall felt silly asking, but she wasn't ready to be left alone yet.

Mrs. Cooper smiled. "Of course I will. I have an idea. Why don't we go out to breakfast? None of us have eaten, and sitting around a table will give you a chance to get to know them and feel safer."

Kendall nodded. What was wrong with her? They were, after all, her family. Why the apprehension? "When I met you, we were both strangers to each other, and we got to know each other slowly over time. These people know me intimately, but I don't know them at all. They want to pick up where we left off, but I don't know where that was. I don't know how to relate to them."

Mrs. Cooper studied her a moment as she leaned heavily against the walker, waiting to walk out the door. "Do you want me to talk to them before you come down and explain how you are feeling?"

"Would you?" A sigh of relief slipped through Kendall's lips.

Mrs. Cooper hugged her. "You come down in about five minutes. I'll take care of the rest."

"It will take me five minutes longer to get there, even if we leave at the same time." Kendall often joked that her two speeds were slow and slower.

"It will be fine, Kendall; you'll see. God has a way of taking the impossible and working it out." Mrs. Cooper hugged her again, careful not to cause her to lose her balance. Then she started down the hall to the little alcove for visitors.

Kendall followed. *What if I never remember?* She'd placed all her hopes on the fact that seeing them would trigger something, but that hadn't happened. *Now what, Lord? Now what?*

Chapter 11

"What if she never remembers us?" Javier asked in his thick accent. Kendall heard the question as she neared the alcove.

"Then you start from the beginning, getting to know each other again, making new memories." Mrs. Cooper always seemed to have such wisdom.

"You don't understand. She's our daughter—our only living child." Diana's voice carried a pain and a fear Kendall understood.

"I can't completely comprehend what you're going through, but I ask you to remember that this is as hard for Kendall as it is for you. Please give her time and space. She hoped desperately to remember you but didn't. Let things between you happen slowly and naturally."

Kendall rounded the corner, and everyone's gaze followed her into the room.

Mrs. Cooper stood. "Why don't we all go to breakfast? Spend some time getting acquainted."

Everyone agreed, rising, and Mrs. Cooper led them to the parking lot. The Brooks clan squished into the backseat of Mrs. Cooper's small silver sedan, leaving the passenger seat for Kendall. Mrs. Cooper stuffed the walker in her trunk.

She drove to Walden's Coffeehouse near where she and Chief Cooper lived. Delanie had taken Kendall there just last week. Upon arriving, they ordered at the counter and then found a table for five.

Once they'd settled into chairs around the small wooden table, Kendall broke the awkward silence. "I've learned that coffeehouses are very popular here in Reno, and Delanie assures me it's a trend that stretches across the whole nation."

Her parents and Javier nodded and smiled, but a sadness hung over them like dark clouds on a rainy day.

"You know, it's funny how different their English is than mine. So many of the phrases they use, I didn't understand. Delanie and Brady tease me about coming from some unknown Podunk place." Kendall laughed. Now her lack of understanding made perfect sense.

"The villages are much more than a Podunk place. Our family has poured our lifeblood into those people. They matter to us and to Jesus." Her father's expression held disappointment. "They used to matter to you, as well."

"I'm sorry. I didn't mean to offend you." Kendall hung her head.

"You've changed." And she knew from the way he said it, it wasn't for the better.

"Who are Delanie and Brady, dear?" her mother asked, and Kendall knew she must be the family peacekeeper.

"They are my children," Mrs. Cooper responded.

"Oh, I see."

"Brady is the paramedic who saved my life." Just saying his name made Kendall miss him. "The whole family has rallied around me, taken me to church, had me in their home, and kept the monotony of the rehab hospital at bay with their faithful visits."

"Thank you for that." Her mother's kind eyes rested on Mrs. Cooper.

Their name was called, and Mrs. Cooper and Kendall's father picked up the trays, passing out everyone's breakfast and beverage orders.

Kendall felt crushed by her father's harsh response. She decided to get to the heart of the matter, ignoring her breakfast completely. "Where were you?" She directed the question at her father. "Didn't you wonder about me?" Kendall tried to keep the accusatory tone out of her voice, but it sneaked in nonetheless.

"We waited for the call that you'd arrived safely in America, and after speaking with you, we headed into the jungle for a month of intensive work." Her dad filled in the blank.

"As soon as we returned from our trip into Oaxaca to drop you at the airport, *ti gunaa stinnne`*, we received word that many were dying. As soon as your safe arrival was confirmed, we told you of our plan." Javier reached for her hand but stopped himself. Instead, he picked up the butter and occupied himself with his toast.

"You were beginning your studies the following day, and as the four of us agreed, your dad, Javier, and I planned to continue the much-needed work until your return." Her mom spoke in a soft, sure tone, but Kendall read between the lines, believing they must not have wanted her to leave.

"Your father and I worked very hard to dig a new well. The water supply had been contaminated. People were dying." Javier's intense gaze never left her face, and it made her uncomfortable.

"We drove in barrels of fresh water each day and ran the drilling equipment ourselves," her father said, continuing the story. "Your mother cared for much of the village and nursed countless ones back to health."

"The water had caused many to become ill, others to die," her mother explained. "We thought when we arrived home after the crisis passed that we'd have a stack of letters from you."

"But there were none." Javier's words held a note of sadness.

"We became concerned. . . ." Her mother's voice had a catch in it.

"We tried all the next day to get in touch with you, but to no avail." Her father laid down his fork and took a sip of coffee.

"The college had no record of you after you registered, and your landlord said you were a great tenant. He never saw you or heard a peep from you." Her dad cleared his throat. "We finally contacted the authorities and were connected to Chief Cooper."

"He told us of your fate. And as they say, the rest is history. You are here with us now." Her mother patted Kendall's hand.

"Where you belong," Javier reminded her.

How I wish I felt like I really belonged. His words were possessive, and they triggered a memory of him reaching for her while she tried to avoid his touch. Not a good recollection, but one nonetheless. *Why would I duck away from my own fiancé?* The remembrance left her unsettled.

As everyone finished their breakfast, Kendall asked trivial questions about her life. "Was I born in Mexico?"

"No, we moved there when you were two." Her mother's eyes pleaded with her to remember.

"So where was I born?"

"In Texas. I was in seminary," her father answered.

"Any brothers or sisters?"

Silence fell over the group. Kendall glanced from one to the other. All eyes were down.

"Just Patrick," her mother finally answered. "But he died a few years ago."

"Patrick." Kendall said his name aloud, wondering if they were close. "When and how did he die?"

"Patrick died six years ago while you were back in the States for college."

"I'm sorry." It was the only reply Kendall knew to make. Their pain over the loss was evident. She wanted to know more but wasn't sure she should ask.

"Patrick was two years older than you. He stayed in Mexico, having such a heart for the people." Her mother stirred her tea, a faraway expression on her face.

Does that mean I didn't have a heart for the people? Kendall wondered if she imagined the subtle, hidden messages or if they were really there.

"He and I were out in a Jeep, doing some exploring." Javier interrupted her

201

train of thought. "The Jeep rolled, and I was thrown away from the vehicle. Patrick was crushed by it."

"You knew Patrick?" The news surprised Kendall.

"Yes. We grew up together, all three of us."

"When did you and I become—" She couldn't bring herself to say the word *engaged*, for it bound them together in a commitment of the heart. A commitment she didn't feel. A commitment she wasn't sure she could live up to.

"Shortly after Patrick's death."

Something didn't feel right. Did she agree to marry him during a time of mutual grief?

"You came home for the funeral," Javier continued. Kendall tried to remember. She could feel the emotions but could not recall the event.

"I'd loved you forever, even as a small child, but to you I was only your brother's friend. At the funeral you let me hold you and comfort you."

A vision of them holding each other and crying flashed through her mind. When he kissed her, she remained unresponsive, but the fact that she'd let him was enough for Javier. His kiss left her dead inside. Brady's brought her senses to life. The realization fell heavy on her.

"Before you returned to college after the funeral, you agreed to be my wife and partner with me to finish the goals Patrick and I had set."

His words left her cold inside. What had she agreed to? Trying to replace her brother?

"Your father and I were so pleased you'd come to your senses and accepted Javier's proposal of marriage. And doubly pleased that you'd decided to join us as a missionary to the people we've all grown to love so deeply."

The words left Kendall feeling unsettled. Had she tried to lessen her parents' loss by becoming a substitute for her brother? By choosing the life they apparently wanted for her?

Brady and Delanie strolled into the coffee shop. Delanie unwrapped the scarf from around her neck and glanced around the tables. When her gaze fell on them, shock registered in her eyes. She said something to Brady, and he turned to stare. Kendall fought an overwhelming urge to run to him and the shelter of his arms. They both strolled to the table.

"Mom, I thought that was your car. Hi, Kendall." Delanie's smile included everyone at the table.

"Delanie, Brady. What are you two doing here?" Mrs. Cooper jumped up and hugged her children. She hadn't seen them come into the shop because her back was toward the door.

"We stopped in for Delanie's morning tea." Brady's eyes fixed on Kendall's.

"I didn't sleep well and need some caffeine myself."

"First, let me introduce you."

∽

Brady shook hands with Mr. and Mrs. Brooks and then Javier, his nemesis. Then he said hello to Kendall.

"Good morning, Brady, Delanie." Kendall's smile was stiff and forced.

Brady wondered if the awkwardness between him and Kendall was as obvious to everyone else as it was to him.

Both of her parents nodded but said nothing.

"So you are a paramedic?" Javier spoke in broken English, thick with an accent. "And what do you do, Delanie?"

"I'm a police officer." Delanie smiled, but Brady sensed her discomfort, as well. She turned her attention to Kendall. "Did seeing your family trigger any memories?"

"Not really." Kendall's eyes held disappointment.

"I'm sure when we get her back home, things will fall into place."

Kendall seemed surprised by her dad's assumption that she'd be returning to Mexico, but she didn't argue the point. Her gaze sought out Brady's, and he glimpsed all the uncertainty she wrestled with. He gave her a reassuring smile, and her eyes said she was sorry about yesterday.

Mr. Brooks rose. "Brady, do you mind if we take a little walk outside?"

Tension filled the small group. All eyes were on Brady.

"No, sir, I don't mind at all. As a matter of fact, I'd love a word with you, as well."

Brady followed Mr. Brooks out the door and onto the wooden porch. The large man shoved his hands in his pockets and took a few steps away from the windows of the coffeehouse.

"I can't tell you how much Kendall's mama and I appreciate you saving our girl's life."

The conversation went a different direction than Brady had anticipated.

"I was just doing my job, sir. Any medic would have done the same." Brady shrugged off his appreciation.

Mr. Brooks turned and started walking. Brady followed, his gaze resting on the barren, snowcapped hills in the distance.

"I don't want you to get the wrong idea, son. We deeply appreciate all you and your family have done for our girl while we were unaware and unavailable."

Brady sensed a "but" coming. "It was our pleasure. That's what the body of Christ is all about—each of us stepping in to minister to another in need."

"So your family is Christian?"

Brady nodded.

"Thanks for being God's hands. Now that we're here, you all can go back to your own lives and not give Kendall another thought. We can pick up where you left off."

Brady stopped, and Mr. Brooks followed suit. "The thing is, we've grown to care about Kendall. My entire family is invested in her emotionally and spiritually. And we'll still be in Reno long after you leave." Brady decided to ignore Mr. Brooks's earlier pronouncement that Kendall would be leaving the country with them.

"We'll be taking Kendall home with us in the next few days. As soon as we can get medical clearance."

The words brought a sense of loss for Brady. He moved a pebble around with the toe of his tennis shoe and wondered if Mr. Brooks was making all the decisions for Kendall instead of letting her choose for herself. That was sure how it seemed to Brady.

He made eye contact. "Well then, for the next few days, we'd all like to spend as much time with Kendall as we can squeeze in." Brady knew that under the guise of civil conversation, two bucks challenged each other for access to the fair doe.

"I think it might be best for Kendall if you all said your good-byes today. She needs to put her time and energy into getting better and remembering her old life." Mr. Brooks tightened his mouth into an unrelenting line. "She needs time with her fiancé and has no business spending it with another man."

"Sir, I would completely agree with you under different circumstances. But here's the thing: Kendall doesn't remember Javier. My family and I are familiar; you people are not." Brady knew the minute the words were out, he'd said too much.

"You people?" Mr. Brooks's face had darkened to a shade of red. "We are her mother, father, and future husband. We are not *you people*."

"I'm sorry, sir. I meant no disrespect, but she doesn't know you or remember you. You have to put her needs and her comfort before your own desires."

"What are you implying? That I don't care about Kendall's best and only want my own way?"

"That's how it seems to me." Brady ran a frustrated hand through his hair. "I know she's your daughter, but she's twenty-six years old. Why don't you ask her what she wants?"

"She can't know what's best if she can't remember."

"If you want me to stay away from Kendall, I'll have to hear the request from her lips." She'd told him yesterday to go away, but today he'd seen an apology in her eyes. She'd have to tell him again.

"Let's go ask her what she wants."

Brady turned back toward the coffee shop.

Mr. Brooks grabbed Brady's arm. "Why don't we just cut to the chase? I saw the way you looked at her. You have designs on my daughter, but she's engaged to another man."

Brady faced Mr. Brooks, eye-to-eye, toe-to-toe. "I am in love with her. Is that what you wanted to hear?" Brady's voice raised. "And she's in love with me, too. Neither of us knew about Javier until last week. We didn't intentionally disregard her commitment to someone else, but now the feelings are there."

Brady turned to discover that the whole group had heard his loud announcement and all stood gawking at him.

Everyone except Kendall. Her head hung low, eyes focused on the ground, and her hair hid the embarrassment he assumed she was feeling.

Chapter 12

The ride back to the rehab center was quiet, awkward. Shame draped itself like a mantle on Kendall's shoulders. She wasn't prepared for her parents or Javier to hear Brady declare their love loudly enough for the entire world to know.

A few snippets of her memory returned this morning in tiny flashes of segments in time. More than the actual events, she experienced the emotions those situations evoked.

Kendall sensed, more than knowing for certain, that she'd spent her whole life disappointing her parents. A lingering feeling told her she'd never quite lived up to her brother's level of commitment, never quite hit her parents' expectations. Brady's declaration only added to their displeasure. She'd heard it in her mom's gasp, seen it in her dad's gaze before she looked away.

"Well, we're back." Mrs. Cooper tried to sound as if all was well as she parked in front of the rehab center. She got out, retrieved Kendall's walker, and brought it around to her. In the meantime, the backseat had emptied out and everyone was waiting on her.

Mrs. Cooper helped Kendall climb out of the low car and steadied her before letting her stand on her own. Kendall depended on the walker for balance and stability.

Her father stepped forward, right hand extended. "Mrs. Cooper, I cannot tell you how good it was to meet you." They shook hands. "Thanks ever so much for picking us up this morning before the crack of dawn." He chuckled, but no one else joined in. "The wife and I"—he glanced at Kendall's mother—"are so grateful for you and your family's intervention for our little girl."

He glanced at Kendall's mother, and she stepped forward, hugging Mrs. Cooper. "Are we ever! It does a mother's heart good to know another mother cared for her young when she couldn't."

Mrs. Cooper hugged her back and smiled. "It was our pleasure." She wrapped an arm around Kendall's waist. "Kendall is precious to me."

Kendall leaned into Mrs. Cooper's side, afraid if she took a hand off her walker to hug her back she might topple over.

"Guess we'd better get this one back inside." Her father pointed at her. "As

I told your son, we can take it from here. We don't want to impose on your family's time any more than we already have."

Mrs. Cooper squeezed Kendall tight and then released her. A lump formed in Kendall's throat. She wasn't ready to say good-bye or have Mrs. Cooper exit her life.

"I assure you, Kendall's never been an imposition—not for one minute." Mrs. Cooper turned her gaze on Kendall, giving her a reassuring smile. Then she looked back at Kendall's father. "May I help her to her room and tell her good-bye in private?"

The expression on her father's face made his feelings known, but he nodded his approval. "We'll wait in the visitors' lounge."

Mrs. Cooper and Kendall shuffled down the hall at the pace of a snail. Mrs. Cooper kept a reassuring hand on the small of Kendall's back. Kendall fought the urge to cry, but by the time they reached her room, a couple of tears had slithered down her face.

Kendall used her walker to back herself against the edge of her bed so Mrs. Cooper could use the chair, but instead she stood next to Kendall, placing her hand on Kendall's arm.

"Honey, are you okay?"

Through watery eyes, Kendall saw concern on Mrs. Cooper's face. Kendall shook her head, and a few more unwanted tears spilled onto her checks.

Mrs. Cooper slid the walker aside and wrapped Kendall in her arms. That was all it took for what little self-control Kendall had to break and a flood of tears to follow. Mrs. Cooper said nothing. She held her and let her cry.

After a few minutes, Kendall raised her head. "I'm really sorry. I didn't intend to fall apart."

"You have every right to fall apart. Things have happened pretty quickly the past couple of days." Mrs. Cooper released Kendall.

"I'm not ready to say good-bye to you." Kendall tried to swallow away the remaining lump.

"Nor am I, but it sounds like your family will be taking you back to Mexico in a few days." Her astute gaze watched for Kendall's reaction.

"Do I have to go?" Leaving didn't appeal to Kendall, not one bit.

Mrs. Cooper seemed to choose her words with care. "Don't you want to go?"

"The thought of leaving everything familiar to travel to another country with strangers is frightening. Am I wrong to feel that way?"

"Of course not. It's understandable."

"Can they force me to go?" Kendall asked, barely above a whisper. Guilt coursed through her for even wondering.

Mrs. Cooper stepped away, weighing the question for a moment. "No. But maybe in a few days you'll feel differently. They are your family, and they obviously love you."

"But I don't love them. I don't even know them." There. She'd said it out loud.

Mrs. Cooper took Kendall's hand. "Don't make a decision today. Try to keep an open mind." Mrs. Cooper seldom looked worried, but she did at this moment.

Kendall nodded. "Will you please come back? Don't let this be our last visit."

"If that's what you want, but I'm afraid your parents may not be happy if I do."

"I don't care. You are the closest thing to a mom that I have. I need you right now."

Mrs. Cooper gave her a quick hug. "I love you, Kendall, and I will be here as long as you want me to be. Now I'd better run so your parents can visit with you. I'll be back this afternoon."

Her promise made Kendall feel better. "Thank you."

Within a minute or two, Javier entered her room alone. She moved from the edge of the bed to her sole chair. Javier squatted next to her, taking her hand in his. She longed to pull it away but didn't.

"I forgive, shall we say, your indiscretion."

"My indiscretion?" Kendall was incensed and pulled her hand from his, tucking it safely in her lap. "What, may I ask, is that supposed to mean?"

"You gave your heart to another, but I forgive you."

His attitude—as though he was doing her a big favor—only served to rankle her further.

"All is well, *ti gunaa stinnne`*. We shall marry upon our return to Mexico. Within the week, you shall truly be my one woman until death parts us."

Kendall swallowed back the distaste of uniting herself with Javier. Her first impulse was to shout, *"Never!"* but she controlled it. She placed her hands on her head, wanting this whole day to be a bad dream. Meeting her family hadn't solved her problems as she'd hoped, but only created new ones.

"Javier, I can't marry you, not this week, maybe not ever."

He rose, looking down at her. "I have waited a long time for you. First you must finish college; then you must take an internship. Now you must get another degree. I tire of waiting."

He knelt before her, taking her hands in his, much the way Brady did, only her heart's response was very different. "You've given your word, and I have honored mine. The time has come to forget your foolish dreams of more schooling. It is time to get married and start our family."

He moved toward her to claim her lips. She fought the urge to cringe. When their lips met, hers remained closed tight and unresponsive.

Javier pulled back slowly. His eyes reflected disappointment. "You will forget him in time. Your heart will grow to love me once again."

She wasn't sure her heart had ever loved him. Doubt lingered. "It's too soon, Javier. I can't make any promises." She shook her head. Suddenly exhausted, Kendall said, "You must go. I have to rest for one hour. You may tell my parents to come then."

He nodded and left the room, closing the door behind him. She used her walker to get to her bed and lay across it. Closing her eyes, she rubbed the spot on her forehead between her brows. Kendall wished for sleep, but too many thoughts marched through her head for it to come.

Much too soon, a knock at Kendall's door brought with it the realization that her hour of peace and quiet was over.

When she opened her eyes, her parents hovered in the doorway.

"Do you feel better, dear?" Her mother stepped farther into the room.

Kendall wished they hadn't come. She didn't have the energy to deal with them but couldn't very well leave them sitting in the visitors' alcove all day. After all, they'd come a very long way to see her.

"May we come in?" Her dad still stood in the threshold of the doorway.

Kendall nodded. She lay on top of her covers with a light blanket thrown over her.

"We met with your therapist, Tom. He's going to check into what sort of rehab opportunities are available in Oaxaca. He doesn't see a problem with us packing you up in the next couple of days."

Kendall sat up, leaning against her headboard. She pursed her lips, unsure how to navigate what lay ahead. She glanced from her father's unrelenting jaw to her mother's sad eyes.

"I don't think I'm ready to go with you."

"Sure you are." Her mother patted Kendall's hand. "We'll take good care of you, show you lots of pictures, tell all your growing-up stories."

"I'd like to come home for a visit after I finish therapy, but not yet." Kendall tried to reason with them. "I like my therapists and trust them. Tom says trust is an important component to success in rehabilitation. Plus we're in the middle of the plan. A move could cause me a major setback physically."

Her father's jaw tensed.

"Now, dear, I'm sure you can learn to trust a therapist in Oaxaca, too. And

Tom can fill them in on the plan."

Kendall decided to try a different approach. "Javier said something about the trip back from Oaxaca. So you don't actually live in the city?"

"No, but you'd be much closer to home than you are here," her father finally said.

"We'd come see you every chance we get," her mother assured her.

Kendall sucked in a deep breath and decided to speak her mind. "You want me to leave friends I feel close to, therapists I trust, and a place I feel safe for the complete unknown?"

"Oaxaca isn't unknown to you. You grew up near there and know the city like the back of your hand." Irritation wove itself through her dad's words.

"I don't remember Oaxaca. I don't remember either of you or Javier. Don't you understand that my whole life—everything known or familiar—is here in Reno?" Kendall hated the emotion in her voice, afraid her dad would view it as weakness.

"Kendall, you are our daughter, our responsibility. How can you expect us to pack up and leave you here without family or anyone who truly knows you close by?"

"The Coopers know me."

Her mom threw her hands in the air. "They cannot possibly know you. You don't even know yourself."

"You're right." Kendall swallowed hard. "I don't, but until I do, I'm not falling into my old life. I'm twenty-six years old, and it's my life, not yours."

"You are acting just like you did in college—always the rebellious one."

Her father's words struck a familiar chord with Kendall. She wondered what wild things she'd done in college.

"Young lady, it's time for you to grow up and face some responsibility." A vein popped out near her father's temple.

"That's exactly what I'm trying to do—take responsibility for my life, my decisions, and myself." Kendall's voice rose, and she somehow knew she and her father were often combustible.

"You have a responsibility to Javier." Her dad's low tone dared her to deny what he said. "When you said yes to his marriage proposal, you gave your word. The Bible clearly says let your yes be yes."

Kendall let out a long, loud sigh, trying to collect herself. "I don't know him. I don't love him." She glanced from one to the other. "Is that what you want for me—a loveless marriage to a stranger?"

Her mother drew her lips together, and tears gathered in her eyes. "He wouldn't be a stranger forever. You can get to know him all over again."

Tears pooled in Kendall's eyes, and her mother reached for her hand. In less than a day, Kendall knew this precious woman was tenderhearted, gentle, and kind. "Mama, I'm in love with someone else."

"I will not give my blessing to that home wrecker." Her father jerked open the door and left in a huff.

"He didn't know. We didn't know." Kendall whispered the words to her mother.

"Your father only wants God's best for you." She wiped her cheek with the tips of her fingers.

"Do he and I not get along well?"

Her mother made a clicking noise with her tongue. "You're both strong-willed; your wills clash fairly often."

Kendall felt a camaraderie with her mother.

"Did I get into trouble in college?" She couldn't ignore the comment her father had made earlier.

"Your teen years were hard, but once your brother died, everything changed."

"How so?"

Her mom shrugged. "It seemed to ground you somehow. You picked up his dreams where he left off."

Kendall shivered. "What were my dreams—before?"

"Before Patrick died, you couldn't get out of Mexico fast enough. You would have gone to high school in the States if we'd let you."

Kendall only nodded, but she wondered if she'd changed somehow or if she'd just adopted Patrick's life to fill the void for her parents.

"I hope you won't hate me, but I can't be that compliant person anymore. I have to figure out who I am and what God has for me."

Her mother said nothing, only nodded.

"You think I'm wrong, don't you?"

"I don't know, Kendall. I'm not sure you ever loved Javier."

"What are you saying?"

Her mother looked torn between sharing her observations and keeping her mouth shut.

"Because I don't feel like I ever loved him."

"I just wanted you close to home. I hoped in time you'd grow to care about Javier."

Kendall studied her mother. "Have you told Dad any of this?"

Her mother shook her head. "He says I read too much into things." Her mother stood and paced between the chair and the window, biting her lip.

"Mom, if you know something, please tell me."

"All I know is that after Patrick died, you changed your major from elementary education to engineering, which was his major. You suddenly adopted his vision to improve living conditions for the village natives. And just as suddenly, you accepted his best friend as your fiancé."

"I suspected as much. Nothing seemed to make sense or fit." Kendall digested all her mother had revealed.

"Were you just going to let me keep living Patrick's life?"

Guilt oozed from her mother's eyes. "After eight years of power struggles, you and your dad were working together, excited about the future, and close. You'd filled the enormous gap left in his life by Patrick's death."

Her mom lowered her head. "Forgive me, but I wanted you close. If you'd stayed in the States, I'd have lost both my children—one to death and one to distance. I wanted to keep the peace between you and your father, but then I'd see the sadness in your eyes and not know what to do."

"I guess they were my choices, but I can't keep making them."

Her mother smiled a sad, knowing smile.

"Dad will probably hate me."

"He'll get past the disappointment, and he has Javier. In many ways, they've become father and son. Javier's parents died when he was a teen, so he's an orphan in his own right."

"And I guess the truth is, God wants me to be whoever He created me to be and to stop trying to be Patrick."

"You are right, of course."

"Mom, thanks for being honest. I know you risked a lot to tell me the truth. I hope you understand that I have to find my own way now. Figure my life out."

"I do. It's your right and privilege." Her mom hugged her tightly. "I'd best go find your father and calm him down."

"Mom, just so you know, Brady is a really good man."

"I didn't doubt that for a minute. He'd have to be to win your love. Javier tried for years and couldn't do it."

"I feel bad about that."

"Don't. Now he's free to find a woman who will truly love him. He is a good man and deserves more than simply being tolerated."

A twinge of guilt hit Kendall. "Is that what I did?"

"And barely that sometimes."

Mrs. Cooper stuck her head in the door. "Hello. Am I interrupting?"

"I was just leaving." Kendall's mother took Mrs. Cooper's hand. "My husband means well. He's a little headstrong at times."

Mrs. Cooper squeezed her hand. "I know just what you mean. I have one almost just like him at home." She grinned.

"I'll be by later, Kendall. We're staying with a pastor from our denomination while we're here in town." She glanced at her watch. "He's meeting us out front in ten minutes, so if we don't make it back tonight, we'll see you in the morning."

As her mother walked away, Mrs. Cooper asked, "Is everything all right with you?"

Kendall nodded. "Much better. I at least had the chance to connect with my mother on a deeper level."

"She seems like a lovely woman."

"I think she is." Kendall smiled. "You said I don't have to go with them, right?"

"Not as long as you are past eighteen, mentally competent, and don't want to go." Mrs. Cooper's brows drew together. "Do you expect them to try to force you to go?"

"Not my mom, but I'm not so sure about my father. He seems pretty determined."

"That he does." Mrs. Cooper smiled. "Do you want me to step in as a social worker and get things in place to protect you?"

Kendall tipped her head back and stretched her tense neck. "I don't know. I surely don't want to make things worse between my father and me." She paused to think for a moment then focused on Mrs. Cooper with an intense gaze.

"Do you think because I agreed to marry Javier that I should follow through, no matter how I feel?"

Chapter 13

What do you think?" Mrs. Cooper hit the ball back into Kendall's court.

"I don't know. The Bible does say let your yes be yes."

"And your no be no," Mrs. Cooper finished for her. "That's a tough one, Kendall."

"My dad believes I should marry Javier no matter what I do or don't remember because I gave my word."

"You did give your word, but there are extenuating circumstances. I'm not sure what the right answer is. I'd encourage you to go before the Lord in prayer and ask Him."

Kendall ended up telling Mrs. Cooper everything she and her mom had discussed.

"Maybe you should speak with Javier. Perhaps if he knows the truth, he'll release you from your commitment."

"What if he doesn't?"

"Start with what you know to do and see what happens. Don't worry about the what-ifs until they happen."

Kendall giggled. "Brady is always telling me the same thing."

"Smart boy, that Brady Cooper. Speaking of Brady, he asked me to apologize to you for saying too much to your father today."

"Tell him apology accepted. And I will meet with Javier tomorrow. I do want to be honorable before God. After all, He spared my life."

"You're a remarkable person, Kendall."

She felt her cheeks grow warm. "Thank you, but it's you who invested in me and taught me all I know about the Lord and His ways."

"Then we'll give Him the credit."

"My dad plans to leave the day after tomorrow. He has some crucial things going on right now. I'll have to tell him tomorrow that I'm not going. Will you be here when I do?"

"Sure, if you want me here."

"I do. You won't have to tell him; I'll do that. In physical therapy I've learned just how strong I am and how to dig deep. I can do this. I will do this." Kendall wasn't sure if she was trying to convince herself or Mrs. Cooper, but she said the words with conviction.

After saying good-bye to Mrs. Cooper, Kendall spent some time talking aloud to God about all the people she had to set straight tomorrow—in a kind and loving way, of course. The hardest would be Brady. But her mind was made up.

∞

"Dad, I don't know what to do." Brady sat at the bar, watching his dad form raw hamburger into patties. "How do I convince her father that he's wrong?"

"You stay out of it, Brady." His mom had just seconds before walked in from the garage. "This is Kendall's family and Kendall's business. In her father's eyes, you are the other man who disrespected Kendall's commitment."

Brady stood. "That's absurd. I did nothing of the sort."

"At least not on purpose," his mother reminded him, placing her hands on her hips.

"But you did fall for an engaged woman and have encouraged said woman to leave her fiancé for you." Having finished the burgers, his dad washed his hands in the kitchen sink.

Brady swung his gaze from one parent to the other. "All right, I admit it looks incriminating, but I'd never have become emotionally close to Kendall had I known about the engagement. Now we love each other, and I don't know where to go from here."

His mom crossed the great room and walked into the kitchen, standing next to his dad. "It's not your decision, Brady. It's hers, and she has enough people crowding her with expectations." His mom had strong opinions when it came to Kendall. "Don't try to push her, or you may end up shoving her right out of your life." Her expression was stern.

"So you just want me to stand by and watch while they try to force her to marry a man against her will?"

"I think you're both too emotionally charged about a girl who is none of your business." With that announcement, his dad picked up his plate of hamburgers and his long-handled spatula and headed to the patio.

"Kendall's a strong girl." His mom spoke in a softer, less aggressive tone. "No one will force her to do anything she doesn't want to do. And by the way, she said apology accepted."

"Good. At least she's not a grudge holder." Brady settled back on the stool. "I just don't want to lose her, Mom. I've waited a long time for her."

But he couldn't shake the feeling that he'd already lost her. Yesterday she'd asked him to leave, and today his big mouth had brought her embarrassment and pain.

His mom started working on the rest of their meal. He set the table and thought about all that had taken place the past couple of weeks between him and Kendall. What started as an innocent, sweet attraction had become a tangled mess. Of course, if he was honest with himself, his family had warned him from the beginning not to get involved with an amnesiac.

He made a decision. After dinner with his family, he'd drop by the rehab center and apologize in person. Then he'd back out of her life and let her call the shots.

After dinner, Brady loaded the dishwasher, knowing it was one of his mom's least favorite jobs. She enjoyed cooking but not the cleanup.

He bid his parents good night after confiscating a bag full of his mom's brownies. He figured he might need some sort of bribe for the night nurse since visiting hours were ending in ten minutes. It would take him longer than that to drive over to St. Mary's.

Brady buzzed the outside buzzer since the rehab was locked up by the time he arrived. Tiffany, one of the aides who knew him, came to the door.

"You forget something?"

"No." He dangled the bag of brownies in front of her. "Kendall and I had a fight. I just need a few minutes with her. Otherwise I may not sleep tonight."

She grabbed the bag of brownies. "Ten minutes. And you'd better not make a sound walking down the hall."

Brady saluted her as he came through the door. "Yes, ma'am."

She locked the door behind him.

"Why don't you come and get me when you're ready to escort me out? That way I won't have to risk getting caught wandering all over this place looking for you," Brady suggested in a loud whisper.

"I'll be by for you in ten minutes." She headed down the hall to the left, and Brady made his way to Kendall's room. Her door was closed, so he knocked once, softly.

"Come in," she hollered.

She was seated in the vinyl chair with her Bible and a notebook on her lap. When she glanced up, surprise etched itself on her features.

"I thought you were the nurse. What are you doing here?" She glanced at her watch. "It's past visiting hours."

"I know. I bribed the nurse to let me in this late. Can I talk to you? I'll only take ten minutes."

Kendall nodded. "Ten minutes? What did you do, rehearse a speech and time yourself?" She raised one brow.

He laughed. One of the things he loved about her was her dry, sarcastic wit.

"No—no written speeches. Tiffany will be back in ten minutes to give me the boot."

He leaned against a built-in dresser. "My first order of business is to apologize again. I had no right to inform your dad—"

"And half the world," she reminded him.

"Fine. Your dad and half the world that we had feelings for each other."

"I forgive you. Now the second order of business?" Kendall glanced at her watch. "Your time is ticking, mister."

"I love you, Kendall."

Kendall closed her eyes. "Don't, Brady."

His confidence plummeted. "Don't tell the truth?"

She reopened her eyes and focused on his. "Don't make this any harder than it already is."

His heart dropped. "What are you saying? Are you choosing Javier?"

Kendall closed her Bible and sat up straighter. "I'm not picking anyone, Brady. Six weeks ago I suffered major head trauma. I know very little about myself or my life. I have to get to know me before I can know what I want in a man."

"Then I'll wait."

She shook her head. "I don't want you to wait. I don't want anyone in my life with expectations." She pushed her hair behind her ear.

"So this is it?" Brady could hardly believe what he was hearing.

She nodded, and his heart went numb.

"I thought you loved me." He couldn't keep the astonishment from seeping into his voice.

"I don't know." She closed her eyes again for a moment. "I care about you—a lot—but I'm not sure I'm capable of recognizing love at this point in my life. Maybe what I feel for you is gratitude or hero worship. I don't know."

"Well, I know, Kendall. I know that I love you. I know that I've waited a lifetime for you."

"I'm sorry, Brady. I just need time."

He nodded and swallowed hard. "If you ever change your mind. . ." His voice grew raspy.

She nodded. "I know where to find you."

He wanted to hold her one last time, but somehow it seemed pathetic to ask. He struggled to believe this was actually happening. He'd not seen this coming, not at all.

"I guess this is it, then." He straightened, no longer leaning on the dresser.

"Guess so." She pulled her lips together in a tight line.

He had to walk past her to get to the door. He leaned over and kissed her cheek.

She grabbed his hand. "Thanks for everything." Her eyes glistened with unshed tears. He felt sure his probably did, as well. "If it's any consolation, I'll miss you."

He could no longer speak. The lump in his throat prevented that, so he nodded and closed the door on his way out.

He drove straight back to his parents' house. Delanie and Eli were there. He let himself in.

Everyone turned from the game on TV and stared at his tear-streaked face.

His mom jumped off the couch and ran to him. "Brady, are you okay?"

"I am, but my heart's not. Kendall doesn't want me to come and visit anymore."

"Oh, honey." Sometimes there was nothing like his mom's hug, and tonight was one of those nights. He let her hold him as he cried, just like he'd done as a little boy.

∞

As soon as Brady shut the door, the tears fell like rain. She was glad they waited until he'd left. She didn't want to leave him with even a glimmer of hope. She had no idea what or whom the future held for her. No use letting him hang on indefinitely.

And Brady would. He was nothing if not loyal. She had no doubt he loved her. She wished she knew her own heart as well as she knew his. It would have made life much easier—for both of them.

Kendall wrote in her notebook and cried. The cycle continued until well after midnight.

Exhausted, she fell into bed, and sleep claimed her quickly. A couple of hours later, Kendall awoke. She stared at the ceiling. In the quiet stillness of the night, she remembered a fight she'd had with her father. It took her a long time to fall back to sleep.

After what seemed like mere minutes, Kendall was awakened by a knock at the door. She rolled over and rubbed her eyes. She'd told her parents not to come until after PT at noon. She grabbed her watch off the nightstand. It was actually almost eight, not as early as she'd assumed.

Panic shot through Kendall. *What if it's Brady?* She couldn't bear seeing him again—not this soon. She held her breath. Did she dare invite the person in?

Logic won. "Come in." She pulled her covers all the way up to her chin.

The door opened, revealing Mrs. Cooper and Delanie. She hoped they hadn't come to try to change her mind.

"Kendall, we're so sorry to wake you." Delanie stopped just inside her room. "We'll come back later." They both turned to leave.

"No, it's fine. Tom will be here looking for me soon anyway." Kendall sat up, pushing her hair out of her face. "What did you need?"

Both approached the bed. "Brady came by last night after he left here."

Kendall nodded, a knot of dread settling in her stomach.

"My mom and I both were concerned about you." Delanie's words carried empathy, not judgment.

"Even though you and Brady are finished, we are still committed to our friendship with you." Mrs. Cooper smiled.

Kendall should have known these women would not walk out on her just because she'd ended things with Brady. "Thank you. Since I have a limited number of friends at this time in my life, your kindness means the world to me. Is Brady okay with that?"

"Of course he is," Delanie assured her.

"He'd have it no other way, and he understands what happens with us stays between us."

Kendall brought her knees up, resting her chin on them. "I'm so confused."

They both nodded, sympathetic expressions on their faces.

"Late last night, actually more like the wee hours of the morning, I remembered a scene from my life. My dad was angry that I wanted to attend grad school. I tried to reason with him, but he didn't want me to leave."

"But you did leave," Mrs. Cooper said. "So you two must have come to terms."

"I guess." Kendall sighed. "Apparently from ages twelve to twenty, my dad and I didn't see eye-to-eye on much."

"Those are hard years," Delanie said.

"For children and for parents," Mrs. Cooper reminded them both.

"From the few things I remember and the things my mother has told me, my brother was the compliant firstborn. He and my dad shared the same vision and passion. I, on the other hand, had a mind of my own, and my thoughts and my father's were rarely, if ever, aligned."

"Wait." Delanie pulled the chair closer. Mrs. Cooper sat down, and Delanie perched on the arm. Both leaned toward Kendall.

"My mother said I had some rebellious college years. I'm not sure exactly what that means, but honestly it scares me a little. I don't know what I did or why."

"It doesn't matter," Mrs. Cooper said. "It's the past. You and God have started over. Clean slate. Free. Do you know how many Christians wish they could forget their pasts?"

"Of course you're right. My brother died during my junior year of college and I guess at that point in time, I took on his persona, adopted his passions and even accepted his best friend as my fiancé."

Delanie pursed her lips. "Sounds like you were trying to replace him so the loss wouldn't be so hard on everyone else."

"I guess. My mom thinks I somehow blamed myself for his death because I'd strayed from the Lord."

"I think it's easy for prodigals to view God as a harsh judge in the sky with relentless rules just waiting to zap them. In truth, He's a grieving Father just waiting for His wayward one to return."

Mrs. Cooper's analogy warmed Kendall's heart.

"But the truth is," Delanie said, picking up where her mother left off, "bad things often do happen while we're out living life our way. When we leave the protection of God's commands, we open the door for hard consequences to fall on us."

"His rules are to guide us into the safest and best life." Mrs. Cooper hesitated then smiled. "Sorry, we got a bit preachy."

"No. I needed the reminder. I spent the entire night feeling guilty about college years I can't remember." Kendall shook her head. "I guess after I'd made the verbal commitments to pick up where my brother left off, I realized I couldn't do it, so I started running. Apparently Javier and I have been engaged nearly six years, and I've spent the whole time finding one more thing to accomplish before I could actually settle in Mexico and start the life I'd promised everyone."

"Kendall, don't beat yourself up." Mrs. Cooper rose and walked to her bedside. "You were a young woman with good intentions and a good heart."

"And zero wisdom." Kendall chuckled. "Now I have to undo this whole big mess I've made." Her chin quivered. "And hurt and disappoint too many people."

Chapter 14

Kendall lunched alone on the patio, waiting for her parents' arrival. She'd requested to be excused from the dining room, needing some time to pray after PT and before her inevitable meetings with Javier and her mother and father. Being "real" was costly. She was grateful for her past weeks with the Lord and the transforming work He'd begun. She had a feeling the new and improved Kendall might not have liked the old one much. Maybe it was a blessing she'd forgotten her.

Mrs. Cooper arrived first. "You ready?"

"Other than the huge knot in my stomach, I'm fine." Kendall smiled and pushed her barely touched plate of food away. "Thanks again for the visit you and Delanie made this morning. You always manage to keep me grounded."

"If I do, it's only the Lord in me." She settled on the bench next to Kendall's at the round table, the umbrella shading them from the noon sun.

Her parents and Javier came through the doors from the hallway out to the patio. The greetings were kind but a tad stilted.

"We didn't expect to see you this afternoon, Mrs. Cooper." Her dad smiled as he said the words, but they still sounded disapproving.

"Actually, Dad, I asked her to be here. Moral support." Kendall ended on a nervous laugh.

"You need moral support to speak with your family?" Her dad's eyes reflected his hurt.

Her mother laid a hand on his arm. "I know what she means. Yes, we're her family, but we are also total strangers. That's hard to keep in mind, dear," she said to Kendall, "because, of course, we know you so well."

They settled at the table, as well. Javier chose the bench to Kendall's right, and her parents sat across from her.

Kendall cleared her throat. "I asked you all here to explain my position on returning to Mexico and to clear the air, which may be jumbled since I'm not sure I know all the air that needs to be cleared." Kendall smiled, but no one else seemed to get the joke.

"Anyway, after talking to each of you and asking tons of questions, I've made a few discoveries about myself. Some I'm not too fond of."

Kendall looked into each of their faces, faces she should know and love. "Here are the things I do know. I'm not the same person as when you last saw me."

"But you're our daughter—no matter what." Her mom smiled, but her eyes were sad.

"And you're my family, no matter what. The good news is that I love the Lord. I want what He wants for my life. I just don't know yet what that is, but what I do know is that I can't pretend anymore."

Kendall stopped and took a deep breath. "I don't remember my rebellious years, as Mom called them. I have no idea what I did, said, or how I lived."

Kendall felt grieved by the facts she didn't know. She'd hurt her parents, God, and probably herself in the process. "For that, I give each of you a deep, heartfelt apology. I've already been on my face before God, and He's assured me I'm forgiven—even though I have no idea what I'm forgiven for." Kendall wiped the dampness from her cheeks. "How's that for irony?"

They all smiled at her, but they were smiles filled with regret, sorrow, and pain.

"I can't change the past, and I don't want to spend the rest of my days filled with regret." She glanced to her left at Mrs. Cooper. "A wise woman told me that every day is a new day with God, so here's to new days and new beginnings. Fresh starts are underrated. We can't go back because I can't remember what's behind me. I'd like you each to forgive me for the past and start anew with me."

Her mother took a Kleenex from her purse and dabbed below her eyes. "Certainly we forgive you. We already had. Those years were a long time ago."

Her dad and Javier nodded their agreement.

She smiled at each of them. "Thank you, and now I have to ask you to forgive me for compounding my mistakes. You see, I think the guilt I experienced when Patrick died catapulted me into probably the dumbest idea I may have ever had. Most of this is conjecture based on information I gathered from each of you and a couple of snippets of memory."

Mrs. Cooper gave Kendall an encouraging smile.

"I somehow convinced myself that I could make up for all my sin by living Patrick's life instead of my own."

Javier and her parents all appeared confused. "What are you saying?" Her dad's brows drew together.

"You all loved Patrick so much, and though I can't remember him at all, I know from the inflection of your voices and the looks on your faces when you speak of him that he was really special. Each of you were deeply hurt by his death, so I believe my life mission became to replace him the best way I could. I laid my life and my dreams aside and adopted his passions and relationships as my own." Kendall's gaze settled on Javier. "I'm sorry."

She took a deep breath. "I think you all not only wanted his legacy to continue but wanted my life to change, so it was easy to embrace this new me. It was comfortable to overlook what I was trying to do."

Her gaze shifted to her mother. She nodded.

Kendall sniffed, dabbing her nose with the Kleenex Mrs. Cooper provided. "I take all the blame and responsibility for this stupid, stupid idea. As Javier pointed out to me yesterday, I've spent the last six years running from the monster I'd created. I didn't want to be Patrick. I couldn't be Patrick, so I found one excuse after another to postpone stepping into his shoes."

Every eye focused on Kendall—their gazes intense.

"I am so sorry for living a lie and for giving each of you false hope. God has used this accident as a wake-up call. I didn't even realize that in the beginning, but I see it clearly now."

Kendall closed her eyes a moment. *God, please help them to understand.* She raised her gaze to the crisp blue sky and drew in fresh air. "I'm not returning to Mexico."

She looked into each pair of eyes. Javier's were sad yet understanding. Her dad's were hard to read. Her mom's were teary and yet telegraphed her blessing. Mrs. Cooper's gaze was reassuring.

"I'm starting from scratch. A new life in Christ with a new person—me—who I don't really know."

"What will you do?" Concern furrowed her mother's brow.

"I'll stay here in Reno until I'm done with all my therapy. My apartment is paid for until summer—so I heard, anyway. I'm just going to take life one day at a time. God has me in some intense spiritual therapy, too, so hopefully one day in the not-too-distant future I'll be able to walk without a walker and follow whatever path God lays out before me."

Her dad's face had grown softer, and his eyes now shone with excess moisture.

"Early on, I struggled with feeling sorry for myself because I had no past and no people. Now I see myself on the edge of an exciting adventure." Kendall smiled at her God-directed self-discovery. "How many individuals get the chance to start over? My past is gone, literally, and I know after spending hours a day in God's Word, the future He has planned for me is so much more than I can even imagine."

Kendall's mom put her hand over her mouth and sobbed.

Using her walker, Kendall hobbled around to her. "I didn't mean to upset you."

Her mom shook her head. "I'm not upset. I'm rejoicing. I've prayed those very words over your life since you were ten years old."

Mrs. Cooper rose to hug them both. She, too, was crying. "And God has answered the cry of a mother's heart."

Kendall's dad joined the huddle. His face was damp. "Another example of Romans 8:28 bearing fruit."

Kendall agreed. "God has used this in my life for good, even though most people would think it was horrible."

Kendall noticed Javier hadn't moved. He still sat in his spot at the table, head down, arms folded in front of him. Maybe the language barrier had prevented him from fully understanding what had just transpired. Or maybe he understood all too well.

Mrs. Cooper passed out more tissues to everyone, and though there were tears, the feelings in the air were ones of joy and celebration—for everyone except Javier.

"Will you give us a few minutes?" Kendall asked the huddled, hugging group in a quiet voice. The three of them nodded, grabbing their belongings and quietly retreating into the rehab center.

Kendall sat with her back to the table on the bench next to Javier. He hadn't seemed to notice that everyone had left but held the same pose as before, deep in thought.

Kendall laid her hand on Javier's arm. "I'm sorry I hurt you."

He looked up, and in his eyes she saw years of pain and rejection. "We will never marry?" Though a statement, he ended it with a question mark.

She shook her head, hating how the old Kendall had shredded his heart.

"I've loved you since you were six and I was eight."

Kendall's chin quivered, and tears returned afresh. She closed her eyes, wanting to block out the sight of the immense pain she'd caused this man.

"Javier, I do love you, but not in the way of a man and his maiden." She thought back to the romantic love she'd read about in the Song of Solomon, the romantic love she'd tasted with Brady. "I love you as a sister would a brother. You are dear to my heart, and I'll always consider you family."

He nodded, but she could see her words did little to console his bleeding heart.

Unashamedly, she let the tears roll down her cheeks, not trying to hide them or wipe them away. "I was so wrong to mislead you, and I hate that I did that. I wish I could take the pain I've caused you upon myself. You didn't deserve to be hurt. All I can do is ask for your forgiveness. Is that possible? Can you please forgive me?"

He raised his gaze to meet hers. Tears streamed down his face, too. All the love he'd stored in his heart for her, for all those years, was in his eyes for her to see. "Through Christ I will forgive. I will heal."

"Thank you." Her words were merely a choked whisper. He'd offered her the gift of forgiveness, but she knew forgiving herself would be much harder.

Her father's words, *"Let your yes be yes,"* echoed through her mind, and guilt fell on her like a heavy rain. Even though she'd agreed with Javier that they would never marry, maybe she needed to stand by the promise she'd made. Maybe she needed to let her yes be yes.

Her heart pounded. "Javier, I made you a promise. I will honor that promise if you want me to." With God's help she'd be a good wife to him. Maybe she wouldn't love him, but she'd serve the Lord beside him.

Shock and surprise registered on his face. "You'd do that? You'd marry me without love, just to honor your word?"

"I'd do it to honor the Lord."

He wrapped her in a hug, and she hoped she didn't regret her impulsive agreement. *God, if this is what You want for me, I will accept it.*

Javier kissed her cheek. "A part of me will always love you, but your heart does not belong to me. You have given it to another. I will not take what is not mine."

Kendall breathed a sigh of relief. "I'm sorry."

"I knew. Deep inside I knew. Pray that God will bring me a woman who does not hide from my touch. A woman who will give me her whole heart."

"And all those are things you deserve." Ashamed, she wondered how she could have strung him along for so many years. He was such a nice guy—a good guy.

Javier rose. "May the Lord bless you and keep you, Kendall." He kissed the top of her head and went inside the rehab center.

She stayed behind and wept before God.

∞

"How you doing, son?" Brady's dad asked the evening after Kendall had ended their relationship. They'd both just arrived at Peg's Glorified Ham & Eggs to share a meal. Brady needed to talk.

He followed his dad to a table. Once seated, he responded, "I think I'm mad at God." Brady watched his dad's reaction closely, feeling guilty for even saying the thought aloud.

His dad didn't appear appalled or even surprised by Brady's declaration. "Been there a time or two myself."

"And?" Brady felt relieved to know he wasn't the only Christian on the planet to be mad at God.

His dad shrugged. "You work through it. God is God. He's not afraid of your anger or your questions. Don't be afraid of them, either. And certainly don't be afraid to tell Him. So what are you angry about?"

"I don't get the whole Kendall thing." Brady stared off across the restaurant, but in his mind's eye he saw Kendall, remembered her laugh, and missed her all the more.

The waitress approached the table, order pad in tow.

His dad laid down his menu and asked for the same omelet he always ordered when they ate there. Brady wondered why his dad even bothered with the menu. Brady placed his order, and the waitress left to get their drinks.

"Tell me what's on your mind," his dad encouraged.

"A lot, but to start with, why was I the paramedic on duty that night if it was all for nothing? Why did I even meet Kendall? God knew what was going to happen. Is He just trying to torture me? I trusted Him. I committed to wait for His woman in His time. Why did I bother?" He shook his head. "I've waited for God to bring Ms. Right, but He never does. Why?" He beseeched his dad's wisdom, hoping for answers.

"You've got a lot of whys there. Sometimes I do, too. And every single time I find the answers in scripture."

"Do I go to the concordance and look up 'Kendall'?" Brady let out a discouraged sigh.

His dad smiled and shook his head. "No, you just start reading every day, and soon verses will begin to jump off the page and speak to your situation."

"Maybe I'll start in Numbers."

"Numbers might not be my first choice." His dad ignored Brady's sarcasm. "If you can't think of a better place, start in Psalms or Proverbs. You read a chapter or two a day, pray through it, meditate on it. Let it go deep into your heart."

Brady nodded and exhaled a long, slow breath. The waitress returned with two iced teas.

His dad laid his lemon aside. "Can I make an observation?"

"Sure."

"It's the hard things that God really uses. The things we hate going through, the things that push us to our limits. When we look back, we may never want to go through the pain again, but we're grateful for the results."

"Like when Mom had breast cancer?"

"Like then. We're closer to each other, closer to God, and have a heart for others who are suffering. Those results wouldn't have happened in daily life. He threw us a curve ball and used it for His purposes."

Their food arrived.

Brady grabbed the ketchup bottle. "So what you're saying is seek God more for answers, and let Him use this time to grow me into the man He wants me to be."

His dad nodded and closed his eyes. "Lord, bless our food, our conversation, and Brady's future. Amen."

One of many things Brady appreciated about his dad was his concise prayers. No fluff—just straight to the point.

"What do I do with the anger?" Brady dipped a fry in ketchup and popped it in his mouth.

"Keep telling Him it's there and invite Him to remove it. One day you'll wake up and realize it's not there anymore."

"Sounds easy enough."

"But it's not, and I hope I don't sound trite." His dad sipped his iced tea. "Truth is, it's hard work. When your mom was diagnosed with cancer, I was mad, scared, and a million other things. I had to choose every day to keep doing what I knew God wanted me to do—time in the Word, time in praise, and time in prayer. Make a thirty-day commitment to seek Him on a deeper level, and I promise you won't regret it, not for a minute."

Brady nodded and took a bite of his ham. He'd pick up the gauntlet and do what his dad suggested. He had nothing to lose and everything to gain.

Chapter 15

Kendall heard the honk and rushed out of her apartment—at least as fast as one could with a cane and a limp. Tom believed with all his heart that she'd one day walk on her own without any sign of a limp. She hoped so, but this was okay, too. It sure beat turtle speed with a walker.

Delanie and Marilyn Cooper sat curbside in the silver sedan that had taken her more miles than she could count these past three months. Kendall climbed into the backseat behind Delanie. "So this is it—our last lunch at Walden's." Delanie stated the obvious. They'd shared a lot of meals and girl talk, and Kendall would miss them immensely.

"Yeah." Kendall's eyes filled with tears. She had such mixed feelings about leaving.

Marilyn glanced back at her. "Are you all packed?"

"I shipped what little I had last week. What's left will fit into a couple of suitcases, and I'll take those with me on the plane."

"What time is your flight?" Delanie shifted in her seat belt, leaning her back against the passenger door so she could see both Kendall and her mom.

"Six thirty in the morning."

"Am I taking you?" Marilyn had gotten used to chauffeuring Kendall wherever she needed to go.

"No, I'm catching a cab."

"A cab?" Delanie protested. "We can take you. We want to take you, don't we, Mom?"

Kendall shook her head. The tears were gathering again, and she stared at the car roof, attempting to blink them away. "I'd rather say good-bye to you guys today and cry myself to sleep. Otherwise I'll cry the entire flight to Oaxaca."

"Today it is, then," Delanie agreed.

"It will be strange going home, still not remembering anyplace but Reno as home."

"Maybe being back will trigger something," Marilyn said as she parked in front of Walden's. They each ordered their favorite wrap and drink and grabbed the corner table.

"So have you figured out what comes after the summer in Mexico?" Delanie

228

pulled out a chair for Kendall and then one for herself.

"Not a clue, but I plan on spending the summer resting up from all this physical therapy and helping my parents run VBS camps. Tom says I'm ready to tackle my bike again." Kendall settled into her seat, hanging her purse strap and cane over the back. "Remember when the pastor preached a couple of weeks ago on that verse that says God is a light unto our path and a lamp unto our feet?"

Both women nodded.

"Anyway, he said the type of lamp referred to in this passage only provided enough light for the next step, and that's all I can see, my next step."

"Your faith is incredible." Delanie sipped her mocha ole.

"I just keep studying His Word and believing He means what He says." Kendall squeezed lemon into her water. She'd never caught the coffee craze. "I feel like my time in Reno has been not just a time for the physical rebuilding of my broken body, but a time of spiritual rebuilding after a long season of apathy."

They kept their lunch chitchat light, and for that, Kendall was thankful. On the way back to her apartment, Delanie asked, "You'll keep in touch, right?"

"E-mail, instant messaging, cell phones, and maybe I'll even occasionally use a stamp." Kendall climbed out of the backseat when Marilyn pulled in front of her place. Both Delanie and Marilyn got out of the car, as well. The three of them hugged one last time, and a few more tears were shed.

Kendall hurried to her door. Telling them good-bye had been harder than she ever imagined. When she reached the porch, she turned to face them. "I'll be back, maybe not to Reno, but to the States. We'll see each other again." On that promise, she closed the front door, leaned against it, and bawled.

Kendall wanted so badly to call Brady or write him a note, but she'd laid him—and his family—at God's feet. So she couldn't interfere. If God wanted them back together, He'd have to orchestrate it without any help from her.

She prayed that either his mom or Delanie would let him know time was running out. Maybe he'd show up in the morning or even at the airport.

❧

Brady had taken his dad's advice. He'd spent the last six months in an intensive time with God. He'd immersed himself in the Word, and though he still had more questions than answers, they didn't matter so much anymore. His trust in God had grown by leaps and bounds, and he was learning to rest in the Lord.

A few weeks ago their pastor had started a series on the Song of Solomon. The more he read and the more he heard, the more he thought of Kendall. He'd heeded his dad's suggestion and laid her on the altar, but why couldn't he get her out of his mind? Another why. He'd asked God to help him forget, but that wasn't happening.

Pulling out his Bible, he reread part of Sunday's passage—Song of Solomon 3:4. *"I found him whom my soul loveth. I held him, and would not let him go."* Only he read, *"I held her and would not let her go."* He'd done that—held her—but then he'd let her go. His heart just kept saying, *Brady, go get her. You're ready now.* Maybe what God had wanted all along was first place in Brady's life. He now securely had that spot.

Later that morning on his way to the gym, he stopped by Kendall's apartment. He knocked and heard some rustling. The dead bolt clicked. His heart pounded. The door squeaked opened. His mouth went dry.

"Can I help you?" It wasn't Kendall at all, but a young mom with a baby on her hip.

"Uh, is Kendall around?"

"Ain't no Kendall here." She chomped her gum.

He glanced at the address above the door. "This is her place," he insisted.

"I don't know no Kendall. I just moved in last week."

The news nearly stopped his heart cold.

"Don't know none of the neighbors yet, either. Maybe they know Kendall."

Brady nodded. "Well, thank you anyway. I'm sorry to have bothered you."

Last week! He pulled out his cell phone on his way back to the SUV. He punched number three. His mom answered.

"Strangest thing just happened. I stopped by Kendall's, and she no longer lives there."

"Kendall's gone, Brady. She returned to Mexico."

"Mexico?" He almost dropped the phone. "To Javier?"

"Anyway, I thought we'd agreed not to discuss her."

Actually, you agreed, and I abided by your agreement. "Please, Mom, it's important."

"I don't think Javier had anything to do with her return, nor do I think he'll keep her there."

"Thanks, Mom. I need whatever information you have on her." His hope soared.

"Why?"

"Because when I found the one my heart loves, I held her and would not let her go."

"Are you saying what I think you're saying?"

"Yep. I'm going after her."

∞

With the help of his mother, Brady caught a plane for Oaxaca the following week. Thankfully, he already had a passport from a mission trip he'd taken in college, so he didn't have to wait on that.

Brady was more nervous than he'd been in his entire life. He'd never proposed to a woman before, so the daunting task was both exciting and scary. He checked his pocket again for the fiftieth time. Yep, the little velvet box was still there.

Brady had been in touch with the mission organization the Brooks served under. They had given him precise instructions on where to find George Brooks. As God would have it, he was in Oaxaca both yesterday and today to give a presentation and to restock supplies. Brady planned to catch a ride with him back to the village where they lived. Lord willing, he'd be an engaged man before sundown.

Upon arriving at his destination, Brady caught a cab to the mission headquarters. His Spanish was bad—the two years he took way back in high school failed him miserably, but he and the cabdriver somehow made it work.

At his drop-off point, Brady paid the driver and rolled his one suitcase up the sidewalk toward the door. His hand visibly shook when he reached for the handle. He and Mr. Brooks hadn't been the best of friends, so Brady had to trust that this trip was in God's perfect timing. He'd had a complete peace after deciding to come, so he just kept giving the rest of the details to the Lord and put Him in charge of working them out.

The receptionist informed Brady that Señor Brooks was in a meeting. He took a seat in the small lobby and waited, spending the time in praise and thanksgiving. Then he reread a couple of passages from Song of Solomon.

"Brady? Is that you?"

Glancing up, he saw Mr. Brooks standing before him. Brady jumped up and held out his right hand. "Hello, sir."

Mr. Brooks accepted his shake. "This is a surprise. Is Kendall expecting you?"

"No, sir." Brady glanced around. "Is there somewhere we can talk in private?"

"Sure. I have a small office here in the building."

Brady followed Mr. Brooks down a narrow hall. *Small* was right—the room barely held a desk and a chair for visitors. A world map took up most of one wall.

Brady filled Mr. Brooks in on his journey of the last six months or so—the abridged version. "The only thing that hasn't changed about me during that time is the love I have for your daughter. I'd like to ask your permission for Kendall's hand in marriage."

Mr. Brooks smiled, and Brady let out a breath he hadn't realized he was holding. "I would be honored, Brady, to have you as my son-in-law."

Brady had been surprised by the warm welcome he'd received and now sat shocked by Mr. Brooks's enthusiastic response to his proposal.

On the drive to the village, their conversation was comfortable and flowing. Brady was deeply grateful to the Lord for going before him.

When they finally arrived at the small *casa* the Brooks family called home, Brady waited in the car while Kendall's dad helped him set a plan in motion.

A couple of minutes later, Mr. Brooks returned to the car, opening the passenger door. "She's not here, Brady."

"Not here?"

"She's gone to Benito Juárez."

The sunlight was nearly gone. "For how long?"

"She'll return tomorrow afternoon."

So much for being engaged by sunset. Brady followed Mr. Brooks into the house, where he received a warm welcome from Kendall's mother. They dined together and helped him figure out a plan.

"It's her favorite place in the whole world. It will be ideal," Diana Brooks assured him.

So at sunrise the next morning, George, as he'd been instructed to call him, and Brady made the twenty-five-mile trek north from their home village of Teotitlán to Benito Juárez. Brady reveled in the orange ball of fire rising to the east. It wasn't often he woke up early enough to catch the very beginning of a day.

"When we arrive in Benito Juárez, I will take you to the community leader so you can gain permission to enter the Sierras. Then you will have to hike up to El Mirador."

Brady nodded. He was good to go. He had a backpack with food and plenty of water. After the formalities, George left Brady at the foot of the trail. They prayed and Brady started his hike. He spent the time on the trail anticipating and remembering.

As he neared the top, his lungs burned from the exertion—and he was in good shape! This wasn't a trail for wimps. He felt encouraged that Kendall's months of hard work in physical therapy must have paid off. His mom had told him that Kendall said she was stronger than before the accident. She'd spent her remaining time in Reno not only finishing the required PT, but working extra hours on her own.

Finally, he was there.

He saw her bike before he saw her. Then he spotted her. She sat in the cleft of a rock, eyes closed. Brady tiptoed over to her and knelt on one knee.

∞

Kendall let the sun warm her face and rested in the Rock—both literally and figuratively.

"Kendall?"

How strange. She thought she heard Brady's voice.

"Kendall, it's me."

Her eyes flew open. She sat up straighter. "Brady! Is that really you?" She laughed. "What a stupid question. Of course it's you! Unless you're a mirage." She touched him just to be certain her imagination wasn't messing with her.

He had a silly grin on his face. Then she realized he was kneeling. Her heart hammered against her rib cage. In his eyes she saw enough love to last a lifetime.

"Kendall Marie Brooks, I've waited forever to find you."

Excitement bubbled up in Kendall. Anticipating Brady's question, she jumped the gun. "Yes, Brady. Most definitely yes." She jumped up, nearly knocking him over in the process. She pulled him to his feet and hugged him tight. He wrapped her in his big, strong arms, and she knew she'd finally come home.

"Yes, Brady. A thousand times yes."

She gazed into his handsome face. He leaned toward her, and their lips met in a kiss that must have hit seven or eight on the Richter scale.

When they finally separated, Kendall felt slightly breathless and, without a doubt, light-headed.

"You never let me finish my sentence a minute ago." He had an ornery gleam in his eye.

She stepped out of his arms. "By all means, finish what you started." She crossed her arms and played coy.

"I was in the neighborhood and thought I'd drop by and see if you wanted to have lunch with me." He slid his backpack off his shoulders and laid it on the ground.

Kendall laughed and raised her brows. "Lunch, you say?"

Brady nodded. "You know, I never had such an enthusiastic response to a lunch invitation before." He slipped his hand into the front pocket of his jeans, pulling out a small velvet box. "I wonder what you'd say to a lifetime of lunches."

Her heart felt soft and warm inside her chest. Brady returned to his knee. Kendall held her breath in anticipation.

"When I found the one my heart loves, I held her and would not let her go. You're the one, Kendall, and I want to hold you forever and never let you go." He opened the jeweler's box and held it out to her. An emerald-cut diamond twinkled against the black satin that cradled it. He laid the box in her palm. Her hand had a slight tremor as she lifted the ring from its nest and slipped it on her finger.

233

"It's beautiful," Kendall whispered. The moment seemed too reverent to speak out loud. She took a step forward, reaching her hands toward him. He grabbed hold of them, stroking them with his thumbs.

"And, Brady, I want to be held by you forever. I want to grow old with you, have babies with you, dream dreams with you." With her fingertips, she traced his jawline.

He cocked his head. "How many babies?"

She smiled. "Only ten or twelve."

He laughed and rose to his feet. Taking her hand, he led her back to the rock. He sat down and pulled her down next to him. They both stared at her finger, admiring the ring, cherishing the commitment.

"Does my father know you're here?"

Brady laughed and replayed the scene for Kendall.

"Wow. I have to tell you, I'm surprised he was so amicable. But he's been so different since I've been here. My first day he apologized for being so hard on me when I was younger. He said he was too into the rules and didn't work on a love relationship with me. He said it was no wonder I rebelled."

"Guess God's been working on all of us." Brady shook his head. "I know He's sure been working on me. I have so much to tell you."

"Like what?"

"Like how much I missed you, and how God used my grief to lead me toward Him and becoming His man—sold out. You know how He starts convicting you about something and then every message leads to the same point?" His voice was excited as he shared.

"What was the point He was making with you?"

"To really be a man of God would take more time with Him. First my dad told me I needed some spiritual intensive care—sort of like a hospital for the soul. Then I got this crazy e-mail about cell phones. I can't even remember most of it, but the gist was what if you treated your Bible with the same adoration and affection you had for your cell phone? You know, carried it with you everywhere you went, flipped through it several times a day, and responded to the text."

"That's good."

"And a little too true in my case. But again another message about my commitment level. I've loved the Lord ever since I can remember and for the most part made good choices, but I learned I was complacent. My cell phone was more important to me than my Bible. I decided not to live like that anymore. I want God to be number one in my life."

"I want that, too, Brady. For both of us."

"So how soon can we get married?" He sounded more than ready.

"This will probably sound crazy to you, but I'd like to live in the same place and just date for a while."

"Ah—you want the courtship."

Kendall smiled. "I guess I do, and I want us to really know each other well."

"No surprises later, huh? You don't want to wake up and find yourself married to Dr. Jekyll and Mr. Hyde."

"I *am* pretty concerned about that."

"So what are we talking? Six months, a year?"

Kendall thought about it. How long was the right amount of time? They'd been through more in a couple of months than most couples in a couple of years. She already knew Brady better than almost anyone else. "How about next spring?"

"Next spring it is." He dug through his backpack and pulled out a large envelope. "This is from my mom and Delanie." Kendall opened it. "An engagement card." She read the sentiment aloud. "Your mom says, 'If I could have handpicked my daughter-in-law from anyone in the world, it still would have been you. I love you.'"

"What did Delanie write?"

" 'For Uncle Brady and Aunt Kendall—I'm so glad you'll be together forever so you can grow old with my mom and dad. I love you already. Your next niece or nephew.'"

"Delanie's pregnant!" they chimed together and hugged.

Even though most of her yesterdays were forgotten, she had so much more than only today. She had a bright future full of tomorrows with a man who vowed never to let her go.

Epilogue

S pring had arrived, and so had the eve of Kendall and Brady's big day. They'd had their rehearsal and shared dinner with their families and closest friends—a night of fun, celebration, and rejoicing. Of course they'd held the event at Bertha Miranda's.

Now it was just the two of them, walking hand in hand around the lake near his parents' home. "Tomorrow you'll be Kendall Cooper."

"Or you could be Brady Brooks," Kendall joked. "Actually, Kendall Cooper has a nice ring to it."

"Mrs. Brady Cooper." He liked the sound of it. "How long do you think it will take your class to switch from Ms. Brooks?"

"Probably the rest of the school year, but I hope sooner." Kendall had decided to get her teaching certificate. She'd taken the classes she needed in the fall and was student teaching this semester in the second grade.

"Are you still wishing we could have married on the top of El Mirador?"

Kendall smiled, and a faraway look settled on her face. "I would have loved it, but how would we get my seventy-year-old grandmother up there?" No matter how many ways they looked at the possibility, the logistics just wouldn't work. "No, we made the best choice, but I love your suggestion that we go there every fifth anniversary and recite our vows again. I'm holding you to that idea."

"I'm willing to be held." Brady glanced at the time on his cell phone. "I need to get you home. I've heard brides need their beauty sleep."

∞

The next morning Kendall, Delanie, and their mothers had their hair, makeup, and nails done. Delanie brought baby Camden, so they all took turns snuggling with the tiny six-week-old infant. Kendall loved holding him. She was already longing for little ones of her own, but she and Brady had decided to take at least a couple of years to be just the two of them, maybe travel a little, and figure out life as a couple before jumping headlong into parenthood.

"How many of those do you want, Kendall?" Her mother looked with longing at Camden.

Kendall rubbed the back of her index finger softly over the infant's cheek. "That is still on the table for discussion. Somewhere between two and four."

"I just want you to know your dad and I are ready, so whenever you want to get started..."

"Mom!" Kendall blushed. She and her mom didn't have *those* kinds of conversations. But Kendall was very much looking forward to consummating her relationship with Brady. She and Delanie had had those conversations, and Delanie painted a very beautiful picture of the physical love between a husband and wife.

Kendall decided to switch topics, really not wanting to have "the talk" with her mom in front of her future mother-in-law. "Hey, Delanie, did you hear that Cody is bringing a date to the wedding?"

"Yes, and did you hear *who*?"

"Some girl named Lexi." Kendall shrugged.

"Alexandria Eastridge. She's a pretty big name in modeling."

Growing up out of the country made Kendall oblivious to much of pop culture.

Delanie continued. "She's also been on a few tabloids. I hope Cody knows what he's doing."

Marilyn said nothing, but Kendall spotted the concern in her eyes.

After their time at the spa, the girls all went back to Marilyn's house to get dressed. It was a simple affair out by the lake. Nothing fancy, but exactly what Kendall wanted.

∞

At three in the afternoon, Brady stood under a tree facing the lake. He had strict orders not to turn around until the music began to play. Cody stood at his side, both men wearing tuxes. Both Frankie and Eli were ushers. Brady's palms were damp, and he kept wiping them on his pant legs.

The music started. Brady turned. Summer and Mason started down the makeshift aisle toward him, Summer dropping rose petals and Mason carrying the all-important pillow. The rented white chairs seated about sixty guests. It had been hard to keep the guest list so small, but it was what they both wanted.

Once the kids made it to the front, Delanie started her walk as the matron of honor. Brady glanced at his mom in the front row holding Camden. She smiled and wiped a tear away.

The music changed. The guests stood. Kendall came out of hiding, and the sight of her in her dress and veil stole his breath. Their eyes met. She smiled, and he felt like the most blessed man in the world. He got teary, and he wasn't a teary kind of guy.

She moved with grace toward him. Their gazes remained glued to each other. She simply glowed. She'd mastered walking without a cane but still had a barely perceivable limp. He wasn't even sure what was said, but her dad pulled her veil back and kissed her cheek. Then he placed her hand in Brady's and kissed his cheek.

The minister made a few comments. Then it was Brady's turn to say his vows. "When I found the one my heart loves, I held her and would not let her go. Kendall, I will hold you through good times and bad. I will not let you go whether we are rich or poor, sick or well. I will cherish you and honor you all the days of my life."

And he did.

UNTIL TOMORROW

Dedication

To my Lord and Savior, Jesus Christ. Thank You for getting me through this book.

Chapter 1

I'm sorry, Alexandria, but unless you're willing to bend a little here, we've got nowhere else to go." Jamison Price reclined casually in his imposing high-back leather chair as if he'd announced something as unimportant as the weather, not her entire future.

Alexandria Eastridge stared into his cold, calculating steel gray eyes, and she knew she should feel something—sadness, relief, something—but she was dead inside.

"You know, babe. . ." Jamison tapped his pencil against the mahogany desk.

Lexi shuddered at his intimate tone.

"A little give, a little take."

She rose, looking intently beyond Jamison out the window and across the Burbank skyline. Buildings filled with power moguls dotted her vision. "I'm through giving. Probably twelve years too late, but I'm through." She spoke the words in a quiet monotone.

"Your call, sweet thing." Though he still played it cool, Lexi didn't miss the throbbing pulse in his neck or the clenched jaw. "There's a dozen more lined up to replace you—younger, thinner, and prettier. You're a has-been, anyway." He rose and walked to the door, his height nearly dwarfing her almost six-foot frame.

He traced Lexi's jawline. "When you come to your senses, call me."

Lexi said nothing. She passed through the doorway as soon as he opened it and stepped out of her way.

Sure enough, in the lobby sat another young teen and her mother waiting for an appointment with "Mr. Big" in the modeling world—Jamison Price. Lexi saw in the young face all the naïveté she'd once possessed. All the hope. All the dreams.

"Mom, that's Alexandria." The green eyes widened as the teen whispered, gawking at Lexi.

Lexi stopped and faced the wannabe—probably only fourteen or fifteen. "It's not worth it." She shook her head. "The cost of fame is way too high," she warned. "Way too high."

Then she focused on the girl's mother. "Take her and run." Lexi turned and left the office before either had a chance to respond. She strode down the hall toward the elevators, climbing in for the ten-story ride down.

Lexi closed her eyes and leaned against the back wall. *So what now?* There was always clothing, furniture, or fragrance lines, but Lexi had this overwhelming need to walk away from this business and never look back. Maybe she'd feel differently in a few weeks.

Dazed, she exited into the parking garage and made her way to the little silver Miata. She climbed in, lowering the windows and the top. Maybe flying down the 101 to her condo in Malibu with the wind whipping through her hair would bring some sort of feeling, or maybe it would just remind her she was alive.

On the drive home, Lexi weighed her options. One overriding desire kept rising to the top. She wanted to go home. Not home to her parents' place in Beverly Hills, but home to Gram and Gramps.

Thinking of them brought a tsunami of regret and a plethora of longing. She missed them so much. They'd been the still point in her childhood, the place she felt loved, just because. She didn't have to land on any list, have her picture plastered on a magazine cover, or graduate with honors. Those things didn't matter. They just loved her—no qualifiers, no questions—just as she was.

By the time she pulled into her garage, her long locks were a ratty mess, but her plan was clear.

Once inside, the materialism mocked her. She owned the nicest things available to humanity, but what had they given her? She removed her cell phone from her Coach bag and punched the number 2. Her phone speed-dialed her grandparents—just as it did every Sunday evening—in their Nevada cabin at the south rim of Lake Tahoe.

"Hello." The sound of Gram's voice warmed her heart.

"Hi, Gram." She aimed for a chipper response.

"Lexi, it's not Sunday. Are you okay?"

"I'm fine," she lied. "I was thinking of taking a little trip up to see you."

Gram said nothing, but Lexi could tell from the sounds on the other end of the line that Gram was crying.

"Is everything okay with you?" Lexi asked.

Gram sniffed. "More than okay. It's just that you're finally coming. We've waited so long."

Lexi knew Gram meant no condemnation but was merely stating the facts. The guilt, however, pelted her like chunks of ice in a hailstorm.

"Well, I'm going to make up for lost time. How do you feel about having your guest room occupied for the rest of spring and maybe even all summer?"

"The next four or five months?" The glee Lexi heard seeping through the phone line somewhat lightened the load of guilt.

"Is that too long?" She already knew what Gram's answer would be.

"Too long? My heavens, no! It's been five years, honey. That's barely an average of two weeks a year. I'd say you owe us that." Gram laughed—that warm, happy, contagious giggle that warmed Lexi's heart.

Peace settled over her. "I'm excited, too. I'll call you later with my flight info. I can't wait to see you." She was more certain all the time that she'd made the right decision.

"Just so you know right now, I'm going to spoil you. I'll cook your favorite meals, maybe even get some meat on your bones. You're way too thin."

Lexi laughed. Gram said that almost every time they spoke. "I'll be modeling plus sizes by the end of the summer."

Her heart sank as her reality resurfaced. She'd never work as a model again. Her glory days were ending. At twenty-eight years old, she truly was a has-been.

∞

Cody Cooper backed up the wood-filled trailer next to the log home. He put the dual-wheel truck into first gear and turned off the engine, setting the emergency brake. As he exited the driver's side, Alph—his neighbor, pseudograndfather, and the truck's owner—crept out the passenger door.

"Alph, Alph!" Essie, his wife of nearly sixty years, came running around the side of the house—at least as fast as seventy-something legs could go. "Lexi's coming! Lexi's finally coming home!"

Cody's heart lurched at the news. He experienced almost as much excitement as they did.

Alph held his bride close as she cried happy tears. He grinned at Cody. "She's finally coming home. Our sweet girl is finally coming home."

Cody swallowed hard. He'd prayed for this very thing for a long time, knowing how desperately they longed to see their only grandchild again. And a part of him longed to meet her as well. He'd heard every Lexi story known to man—at least a dozen times. He'd perused Essie's scrapbook just as often, admiring the pretty baby, cute little girl, and blossoming young teen into a beautiful woman.

He could see her even now in his mind's eye. Her golden curly locks, reaching well past her shoulders, and her intense blue eyes that had grabbed his heart.

He'd seen every magazine cover she'd graced, watched a video of every runway she'd strolled, and viewed every commercial she'd shot. And somewhere in the midst of the past five years, he'd fallen in love with Lexi—not the model Alexandria Eastridge, but the granddaughter who called every Sunday, the granddaughter who was cherished and loved.

But honestly he had a hard time reconciling the two. He'd seen some of the not-so-complimentary tabloid articles and the string of men she'd been associated with.

"Cody," Essie said with force.

"Huh?" He pulled out of his deep thoughts.

"Where have you been? I said your name several times." She stepped out of Alph's embrace and stood next to him.

Cody leaned against the truck fender, not willing to admit he'd been thinking about Lexi. "I'm sorry. My mind was elsewhere." He winked at Essie. "I'm listening now. What did you need?"

"Would you pick Lexi up at the airport tomorrow?"

He shrugged, acting nonchalant, though inside he was anything but. "If you need me to. I'm off. What time?"

"She called back while you two were out chopping firewood to say her plane lands in Reno tomorrow at noon. Perhaps," Essie said as her eye got that familiar I've-got-a-great-idea glint, "the two of you could enjoy lunch together in the city before you drive her down here."

"Maybe." Cody maintained his cool attitude, not wanting to give Essie any hope. But the excitement inside him could barely be squelched.

"Possibly somewhere quiet and dimly lit so you could get to know each other without anyone recognizing her." Essie was about as subtle as firecrackers on the Fourth of July. She'd been dropping hints—well, maybe not hints so much as suggestions—for years about the wonderful couple Cody and Lexi would make. Somewhere along the way, Cody had bought into her thinking, but he never let on that he'd even be interested, since Essie was the last person he'd ever want to hurt. Sure, he agreed with her that Lexi was beautiful, but that was as far as he'd go. At least verbally.

"This is your chance, Cody. Lexi needs a strong man to love her."

"Essie!" Alph shook an index finger at the woman he loved more than life itself. "You stay out of it."

She stomped her foot. "He's perfect, and you know it."

Alph's expression grew stern. "You let Lexi and Cody alone to live their own lives."

"But neither of them have a prospect on the horizon. Cody's thirty years old, for goodness' sake. He's obviously not doing a very good job of finding someone for himself. He must need my help." Her gaze rested on Cody, daring him to deny anything she just said.

"I date." Though Cody couldn't remember if the last time had been months or more than a year.

"When?" Essie's hands rested on her hips.

He thought for a minute. "Not often, but I do."

His answer brought a smug expression to Essie's face. "The boy needs help." She crossed her arms. "If you'll both excuse me, I have a guest room to air out and spruce up." She lifted her chin and strutted away.

Cody grabbed the gloves out of the truck cab he'd recently exited. "Don't worry. She doesn't bother me." He slipped his hands into the soft leather. "I'm actually flattered that she'd consider me Lexi-worthy." He moved toward the trailer.

"You know she thinks the world of you. Besides, I'm not sure Lexi is Cody-worthy."

Alph's words shocked Cody. He laid down the log he'd picked up to add to last year's dwindling stack of wood resting in the crib. "What do you mean?"

Alph's mouth was drawn into a tight line. "Just not sure what that girl of ours has been up to." Sadness filled his expression. "The world she lives in isn't a moral one."

Cody often wondered if that thought had ever crossed Alph's or Essie's mind.

"Of course, her grandmother will hear nothing of that."

Cody wasn't sure how to respond. "Maybe this is her time to return to her family and her God."

"I sure hope so. Been praying for that one a long time."

"Me, too, Alph. Me, too."

∞

Cody left Stateline, Nevada, early the next morning. Once he hit Reno, he drove his Jeep to the nearest car wash. It didn't get washed nearly as often as it needed. After it was clean and shiny, he met his brother Brady for a cup of coffee, not wanting to arrive at the airport too early.

"How's Kendall?"

"She's great." Brady grinned at the mention of his fiancée.

"You look like the cat that ate the goldfish."

"I think I am. I just can't tell you how great it is to know you're going to marry the woman of your dreams. I want that for you, dude."

Brady and Cody had always been the closest of the four siblings. Only sixteen months apart, they had an ironclad bond—always looking out for the other guy.

Standing in line to order, each purchased a large mocha frappuccino. Then they headed outside and settled at a round table shaded by an umbrella.

"So this is the big day you've been dreaming of?" Brady set his blended coffee on the table in front of him.

Cody heard the thread of disapproval in Brady's tone but chose to ignore it. "Yep." He glanced at his watch. "Just a couple of hours now."

Brady nodded and sipped his drink. Cody watched him wage a battle with himself. "Be careful, I don't want you to end up like poor Frankie."

Cody knew exactly what Brady meant. Their older brother's life was harder than it should be. His wife could be very selfish at times and pretty demanding. "You can't save her or change her—only God can do that."

Cody nodded at his older brother's wisdom, but even his well-intended warnings didn't dampen Cody's anticipation. After five years of praying, he was about to meet the girl of his dreams. Nothing—or no one—could spoil today, so he switched the subject. "And your big day isn't too far off either. What, about five weeks from now?"

A cheesy grin took up residence, and Brady nodded. That's what Cody wanted—a girl who could light up his expression and his world.

They moved on to talk about work and sports. Time crawled, and Cody kept glancing at his watch. Finally he bid his brother good-bye and headed to the airport. After parking he checked the board for Lexi's ETA and gate information. They'd be landing on time, so Cody made his way to the waiting area, watching people come and go.

Finally he spotted her coming toward him. His heart dipped as he glimpsed her in person for the very first time. She was beautiful and almost a head taller than many of the other women in the herd who made their way toward the baggage claim.

She walked with grace and purpose—her curly golden mane bounced with each step, only adding to her aura. Cody swallowed. How does a guy fall for a girl he only knows vicariously?

Her ice blue eyes searched the crowd. Their gazes met. She quickly looked down and stared at the floor as she walked.

When she passed him, he said, "Lexi?" Though she didn't respond, he knew she'd heard him. He'd seen her head jerk up, but she glanced neither right nor left and kept moving at a quick pace.

Cody followed her to the baggage claim belt, not wanting to draw undue attention to her. A few people had already seemed to recognize her and stared or whispered. Maybe it was just her presence. She was hard not to notice.

When she halted a few feet back from the baggage dispenser, Cody stopped next to her.

"Lexi, I'm Cody Coo—"

"I'm sorry, but you must have me confused with someone else." The frost in her tone was reflected in her cold stare that rested on him momentarily. "My name is not Lexi. Now, if you'll excuse me." She walked away from him to the other side of the automated belt that would soon deliver her bags.

Cody figured she was avoiding a possible pesky fan and wasn't put off. He approached her again. "Before you dismiss me again, I'm your grandparents' neighbor and your ride home."

Disappointment settled on her features.

∞

Lexi searched the crowd. *No, they wouldn't send someone else. Not after my being away this long.* But apparently they had. She didn't want to believe this guy, but there was no sign of her grandparents—not anywhere. She swallowed the mass of tears lodged in her throat, but they remained wedged against her windpipe, making normal breathing difficult.

Her shoulders drooped slightly at the realization. "I would have thought they'd pick me up themselves."

"I'm sorry. Your grandfather doesn't like to drive into Reno anymore. He hates the traffic. Besides, I think your grandmother has a little matchmaking scheme going on here." Cody smiled, but Lexi didn't return it. "She asked me to take you to lunch before we head back."

Though he seemed amused, Lexi missed the humor in that idea. "I'd prefer to go straight to their house, if you don't mind." She stood straighter, dismissing the stupid suggestion and the man who made it.

The conveyor belt started, and the first suitcase rolled out, followed by another then another.

"If you show me which bags are yours—"

"I'll get them myself." She hated the curt tone in her voice, but she couldn't leave this man with any romantic notions about her or them—no matter what schemes Gram cooked up.

Cody respected her wishes, though she instinctively knew standing by and watching her lift off six pieces of expensive and perfectly matched luggage went against his grain. She sent him to retrieve a luggage cart, and while he was gone, she scanned the crowd and checked out the airport. She'd forgotten how small and Podunk it was—not even a Starbucks in sight. They had to be at least ten or fifteen years behind in their technology. There was even a guy wearing spurs waiting for his luggage.

Lexi shook her head. This place was hick for a girl who hailed from Los Angeles. She'd gone from chic to bumpkin—all in the course of a morning. Suddenly she questioned her sanity. Was she nuts to come here?

Chapter 2

Cody loaded Lexi's bags onto the cart, not attempting any more stabs at conversation. For that, Lexi was thankful. He led the way through the corridor and out into a warm, sunny day. She followed him through the parked cars until he stopped at a red Jeep Wrangler.

He placed her luggage in the back, handling it with care. What a pain to get all six pieces to fit. He opened the passenger door for her before returning the cart to its place. Lexi couldn't remember the last time a man had opened a door for her. His chivalry touched her, and a tiny fragment of ice chipped away from her attitude.

When he returned, he hopped in and started the Jeep, hooking his seat belt in the process. He never even glanced in her direction. Seemed she'd somehow offended him. No surprise. She'd become an expert at her porcupine personality. She preferred keeping everyone—and especially men—a good distance away.

The area surrounding the airport was old and dated—even the McDonald's looked last century. Cody took the 395 south. Lexi's conscience pricked and wouldn't leave her alone. After all, the guy had come all this way to pick her up. The least she could do was show some kindness. Her grandparents would be horrified.

She held most of her hair in her right hand, trying to keep the wind damage to a minimum. "So you work for my grandfather?" She yelled to be heard over the highway noise.

Cody glanced in her direction. His expression softened a tad. He was actually a nice-looking guy—wavy chocolate brown hair matched his eyes. "No. I live across the street."

"Oh. You're *that* guy." Mr. Wonderful as far as Gram was concerned. The guy did no wrong, and she never stopped talking about him. Lexi hadn't put two and two together—until now.

"So what gives with you?" Suspicion wrapped itself around each of her words.

Cody had the innocent expression down to a science. "What gives?"

"Yeah. Why are you hanging around with my grandparents?" The accusatory tone left no doubt what she thought. She'd wondered many times during the past few years what this guy was after.

Cody pulled off the freeway at the next exit and parked in the dirt alongside the frontage road. Fear shivered down Lexi's back. She wondered if she'd be on the ten o'clock news.

"What are you implying?" A pulse hammered in Cody's jaw.

Lexi refused to back down. She'd learned that if you cower before a man, he'll walk all over you.

"How old are you?" She demanded with boldness.

"Thirty. Why?"

"And you hang around with people almost three times your age?"

"I hang around with my friends—no matter their age. What's your point?"

"I just think it's convenient that you befriend the elderly. What—are you hoping for a mention in the will?"

Cody clenched the steering wheel and sucked in a deep breath, taking his time before answering. She thought for a minute he might be praying. Then he turned and faced her.

"I moved up here for a job. I'm a fireman, and the Reno department wasn't hiring at the time. The home across from your grandparents' house had just gone up for sale." He paused.

The one they'd hoped I would buy so I could be close, at least part of each year.

"I went and saw it and signed a contract on the spot. I met your grandparents the same day. That was five years ago."

"The Reno fire department still has no openings?" Lexi raised her brow. *Oh, come on now.*

"Not that this is any of your business."

She sensed Cody growing impatient with her inference.

"I love it here. Snow ski all winter, water-ski all summer. My only regret is that I miss my family. Your grandparents fill that void for me, and since they miss you, I fill that hole for them. Like it or not, Lexi, I do care about them, and I am a part of their everyday lives."

He pulled back onto the road and onto the on-ramp. She regathered her hair, holding it tight. Cody seemed genuine, and she doubted he'd stick around for five years if he was after their money. Besides, they didn't have that much.

The freeway ended in Carson City. They followed surface roads through the historical town to the Lake Tahoe turnoff. The mountains surrounding them were barren and drab. Just piles of brown earth with no green in sight. To Lexi, they mirrored her life—piles of nothingness. After years of hard work, all she had was emptiness.

Again Lexi fought the emotions rising like a high tide and threatening to sweep over her and knock her down. Discreetly she swiped at a tear, keeping her gaze out the passenger window, staring at the mountains that mocked her. Upon closer inspection, they were covered with a golden, dead-looking grass and small shrubs.

As the road climbed higher, the mountains grew more beautiful. Lexi began to spot life, and trees appeared. The road curved back and forth, and the mountains became dense with pines. Sadly, some of the hillsides carried scars from fires that had left them charred. Another thing they had in common—scars.

The picture planted a seed of hope in Lexi's heart. Maybe here she, too, could find life in the deadness of her soul. Maybe newness might bloom in her scarred and broken heart.

As they rolled over the top of another hill, Lexi caught her first glimpse of Lake Tahoe, and as always, it took her breath away. A tiny gasp escaped.

"It does that to me, too. Every single time. That's why I'm still here."

A million emotions churned inside as she watched the sun dance across the lake, leaving a glistening glow behind. In every direction, majestic mountains stood guard over the body of water. And Lexi's heart cried for home. After running from herself, God, and her shame, she was finally almost there.

Without warning, a dam broke. Tears she'd stored for years burst through, and a deluge ran down her cheeks, dropping off her chin and onto her silk blouse.

∞

Cody knew the moment her emotions gave way. He could hear it in her breathing, and he hurt for her. "Would you like me to stop?"

She kept her focus out the windshield, shaking her head no and sniffing.

He popped open the glove box, leaning across her and catching a whiff of a subtle fragrance. He handed her a napkin. "It's not Kleenex, but it's all I've got."

"Thanks."

She dabbed at her face. He knew from his mom and sister that she hoped to preserve as much of her makeup as possible. By the time he turned into her grandparents' drive, she'd pulled herself together and touched up a few places with a new layer of cosmetics, but there was no hiding the red-rimmed eyes or the Rudolph-looking nose.

Alph and Essie were out their front door before he even rolled to a stop, and Lexi was out of the Jeep and into their arms before his seat belt was undone.

Cody left them in their tearful huddle, making two trips to the guest room with Lexi's luggage. She'd apparently come to stay. Just about every piece of clothing he owned—along with much of the contents of his home—would fit into her bags.

The three of them were just coming into the house as he was leaving. "Cody," Essie grabbed his arm and pulled him back inside with them. "Let me feed you lunch. It's the least we can do. Lexi says she didn't want to stop, and you must be hungry. It's almost two."

He glanced at Lexi, but her expression gave him no indication of her desires. Her arm was intertwined with her grandfather's, and they walked together toward the kitchen.

Cody stopped and gently freed himself from Essie's grip. "I think I should give you guys some time alone."

"Baloney." She grabbed his arm and pulled him toward the kitchen. "Alph, will you please tell Cody that we don't need space from him? He's like family, after all."

Essie's announcement brought Lexi to attention. She was suddenly very interested in what was being said. Her gaze rested on him.

"Be that as it may, I've got some things to do this afternoon." *And your grand-daughter doesn't want me hanging around.* Cody kissed Essie's cheek and winked at her. Then he gave Alph the handshake and half hug they always shared. "Lexi." He couldn't exactly say it was a pleasure. "I'm sure I'll see you around."

"Probably at breakfast tomorrow," Gram threw in.

Lexi's eyes widened, but she held her tongue.

"Cody does most of our chores these days, and in return, we often feed him breakfast or dinner." Alph filled her in on their arrangement. No one actually planned it, but this was what their relationship had morphed into. They fed him, and he helped them. Seemed perfect until today. Somehow, Lexi's raised eyebrows made it feel wrong. She clearly disapproved. He decided he'd best stay away as much as they'd allow. He didn't want to hurt their feelings, but they'd probably get busy with that granddaughter of theirs and not notice much anyway.

After Lexi insisted that her gram let him leave, if that was what he wanted, Cody headed across the street to his A-frame cabin, relieved to have some time to ponder today's events.

His cell phone rang just as he turned off the Jeep. Brady's name scrolled across his screen. Cody flipped it open. "Hey, bro."

"Hey. I was thinking that I might have been a little harsh this morning. Talk about raining on your parade and all."

"It's okay. Your advice was well intended."

"You sound down. You all right?"

"Yeah. . .I guess. . .I don't know." Cody decided to bare his soul to his brother. "Here's the deal: I've spent the last five years listening to all these stories about this wonderful Christian girl."

"And somehow you fell for her." Brady cut to the heart of the matter.

"Was I that obvious?" Cody opened the fridge, wishing he kept it better stocked.

"Yep. You talk about her all the time."

"I do?" Cody thought about that. She was on his mind fairly often. "I guess I do." He pulled out some leftover pot roast Essie had sent home with him and popped it in the microwave. "Anyway, the girl I picked up at the airport this afternoon in no way resembles the Lexi in her grandparents' renditions."

"I suppose I'm not surprised, but I feel bad for you, man."

Cody hit the REHEAT button. "Well, stupidly I was surprised. Her cool distance and borderline rudeness caught me off guard."

"Of course her grandparents would think she's wonderful, but don't they ever glance at those magazines when they're checking out at the grocery store?"

"I guess they assumed—just as I did—that it's all publicity fodder. But the word *shrew*, which I've seen attached to her name more than once, was true of the girl I just dropped off across the street."

"Whoa, that's harsh, bro."

The microwave shut off and beeped, indicating that Cody's lunch was hot. "All I can say is, she's nothing like her grandparents painted her to be. And the sad thing is—the joke's on me, because for all intents and purposes, I'm half in love with a figment of someone else's imagination. If that's not irony, I don't know what is." Cody chuckled at the sheer nuttiness of it all. But truth be told, he had no idea what to do with all the feelings he had regarding a Lexi who didn't exist.

∞

Relief washed over Lexi when Gram finally let Cody leave without too much of a fuss. After Lexi changed into a pair of khaki shorts and a sleeveless top, she set the table while Gram heated up the chicken enchiladas that she had made earlier to serve for dinner that night. "We'll just eat these twice today." Gram set the piping hot pan on a trivet in the center of the table. "They're your favorites anyway."

"Yes, they are." Lexi took her seat and unfolded her napkin, placing it in her lap. "It's my fault we didn't stop for lunch. Cody offered, but lunching with a complete stranger didn't appeal to me." She smiled at her grandparents. "I'd much rather be here with the two of you."

"Honey, Cody is no stranger." Gram served up two enchiladas onto Lexi's plate. "He is quite dear to your gramps and me."

"That may be so, but he's a stranger to me." Lexi took her first bite, savoring the spicy green sauce blanketing the chicken, tortillas, and jack cheese. "These are as good as I remember." She smiled at Gram.

"I promised to spoil you and put some meat on those bones."

Lexi finished the end of the sentence with her, and they laughed. She couldn't recall the last time she'd felt so carefree. Yes, coming was a good decision—except for the Cody part. Eating with him every day might prove difficult. She'd help her grandparents see the light as far as he was concerned.

"That neighbor fellow of yours—what gives with him?"

Both of her grandparents frowned and glanced at each other. "What in the world do you mean, child?" Gramps asked.

"You don't think it's a little strange that a thirty-year-old guy hangs out with the two of you?" Lexi horrified herself with how awful she sounded. "I didn't mean that badly. It's just that most people hang out with other people close to their own age. Is he some sort of freak or something?"

"Lexi!" Gram's tone was shocked. "Do not speak of Cody in such a way. And to think I'd hoped you two would hit it off!"

Well, at least we've settled that one.

Gramps laid down his fork and gave Lexi his full attention. "That's the problem with you young people. Few of you know the value of multigenerational relationships. Friends are far more important to most of you than family."

Lexi knew the conversation had shifted from Cody to her, but she didn't have the courage to tell them it wasn't friends but shame that had kept her away all these years.

"As we've aged, Cody's been a dear to have around. There are so many chores we just can't do anymore." Gram spoke quietly, her eyes begging Lexi to give Cody half a chance. "He's literally a godsend."

"Aging without loved ones nearby creates hardship for older folks." Gramps rested his elbows on the table, and his hands were intertwined near his chin. "When Cody moved up here, he knew no one and missed his family something fierce. We each had a need that could be filled by the other. And your gram loved having someone other than me to cook for."

"He kind of filled a place in our lives that you couldn't, so we'd appreciate your being kind to him." Gram's tone was no-nonsense, but her eyes were filled with hurt.

With Lexi's emotions so near the surface, it was a battle not to cry again. "I'm sorry. I have let you down, and so have my parents. Don't worry—I'll be on my best behavior, for your sake." She smiled and blinked several times, keeping her tears at bay. Her gaze rested on Gram. "However, please no matchmaking. He's not my type; nor am I his." *I'm sure he's way too nice for me.* "How about if after lunch we go for a walk? Remember where you took me last time on that peak where we could see out over the whole lake? Let's go there again."

After the table was cleared and the dishes stowed in the dishwasher, the three of them made their way out the door and started hiking toward Lexi's favorite peak.

Though her grandparents were nearing eighty, they were in pretty good health. Walking two or three miles a day had been their practice since Lexi was a small child, and they were still doing it. The pace may have slowed, but they could still follow a trail up the mountainside.

During the walk, they were all more contemplative than talkative. Lexi was grateful for the silence and the time to think more about Cody. He seemed genuine. And they really loved him. But the relationship still didn't add up in Lexi's mind.

When they finally reached the lookout, the sun hung low in the western sky. Something about the lake always beckoned to Lexi. They each settled onto a boulder and took in the view. No one needed to talk. They just breathed in the fresh mountain air and rested.

No smog. No crowds. No traffic. Just peace.

Then Cody's face rose to the forefront of her mind, and her peace was shattered. How would she spend every day in his presence and be kind at the same time? Why did she have such strong feelings of dislike toward him? She'd get to the bottom of whatever was really going on. She'd expose Cody as the fraud she suspected him to be.

Chapter 3

Lexi opened her eyes and lay staring at the ceiling. She hadn't slept well again and awoke feeling tired. She'd tossed and turned much of the night.

She thought about the past two weeks. She'd done little except hike the mountains and grieve over the mess she'd made of her life. She'd sold herself out for a dozen years of fame that led to nothing but emptiness and regret.

She had no real friends. Oh sure, she'd received many messages on her cell phone these past fourteen days. All from men. Men who wanted to take her to some party or event and flash her around as arm candy. Many were old enough to be her dad, and not one of them cared about her—about the real her, the woman inside. All they cared about was how she looked and that she slept with them at the end of the night.

A tear rolled down her cheek. As a teen, she'd promised God to wait. Somewhere in the back of one of her jewelry boxes was a purity ring that her grandparents had given her on her thirteenth birthday after she'd gone forward at a teen conference and made that commitment.

The guy she'd waited for never showed up, but at times, her bed felt like a revolving door. Each time emptier and less satisfying than the one before.

Several more tears rolled from her eyes and into her hair. At first all the attention had been fun, but even at sixteen, it didn't take her long to figure out they only wanted her body. By the time she was out of her teens, she'd lost count of the men, but she had learned the motto of the business well. *You scratch my back, and I'll scratch yours.* If she hadn't given them what they wanted, she'd never have gone as far in the modeling world or experienced the success she'd known. But in the end, the cost was far too high. If only she'd known at sweet sixteen what she did now.

Lexi rose, wiping her cheeks with her palms. She headed for the shower, hoping to wash away the memories but knowing all the while the act was futile.

Lexi was relieved to find Cody's chair vacant this morning when she glanced out the window to the table on the patio on her way to the kitchen for coffee. He'd been scarce the past fourteen days, and she was glad. He'd actually only dined with them a couple of times, and they didn't interact much with one

255

another. He seemed as bent on avoiding her as she was him.

"I just finished making your omelet." Gram handed her a plate. "Spinach and Swiss. Gramps is still out at the table reading the paper and finishing his coffee. Why don't you join him on the deck?"

Lexi loved that her grandparents ate most meals outdoors. That was something she rarely did in LA.

She carried her breakfast and coffee, taking the seat next to Gramps. Gram followed her out with a small glass of fresh orange juice.

"They're saying that fire yesterday was arson." Gramps looked up from the paper at the two of them.

"I don't get it. Who would do something like that?" Lexi stirred cream into her coffee—an indulgence she'd never allowed herself before.

"And why so close to people's homes? If it hadn't been extinguished so quickly, some of our friends and neighbors might have lost everything." Gram walked over and stood behind Gramps, reading over his shoulder.

" 'Several witnesses report seeing a young woman in the area,'" she read. " 'The police are working with the fire marshal to identify the woman and bring her in for questioning.' Probably one of those high school girls who dresses in all black and wears the weird makeup."

"Just because kids look different these days doesn't make them bad," Lexi said.

"Well, they look bad to me." Gram shook her head. "Anyway, I hope they catch her and she gets all she deserves and more." Gram carried Gramps' empty plate into the kitchen.

∞

Cody read the report from the fire marshal, and his heart sank. The suspect was described as a woman in her twenties with blond curly hair and very tall. He read each witness's account, and though many things varied, each one said the woman was tall and her hair was long and curly. "Dear God, please don't let it be so."

He'd already resigned himself to the fact that Lexi wasn't the Lexi he'd fallen for. He barely tolerated the real Lexi, but surely she couldn't be an arsonist. That would kill her grandparents. He read the report again. The facts were hard to deny. He'd pop in for lunch and see what Lexi had been up to.

He rapped twice on his neighbors' kitchen door and let himself in. "Cody, what a surprise!" Essie kissed his cheek. "You're just in time for lunch. Can you spare a half hour or so? You've been awfully busy lately. Are you avoiding us or our granddaughter?" Essie was never one to hide her true thoughts.

Cody thought about his answer and decided he'd go with the "Honesty is the best policy" theory. "I know you hoped Lexi and I would have chemistry, and we do. We both rub each other the wrong way." Cody chuckled. "I'm sorry, but those are the facts."

Essie nodded and pulled another plate from the cupboard, setting it next to the two others at the bar.

"Where's Lexi?"

"She's out hiking," Alph said as he settled on one of the high chairs at the three-person bar. "Packs her lunch every day and is gone for hours."

More facts stacked up against her. "Every day?" Cody probed.

"Just about." Essie placed a smoked trout salad in front of him. "She didn't hike on her first couple of days here or either Sunday."

Alph nodded. "Both Sundays we all came home from church, ate a big lunch, and took long siestas." He paused to bless the food before they ate.

Cody felt sick. No wonder so many people reported spotting her. She was out walking every single day to God only knew where. "It's not considered safe to hike alone. Do you think it's a good idea?" He took a forkful of lettuce and trout.

"Lexi says the wilderness is much safer than the wilds of LA, and she is probably right. She takes plenty of food, water, her cell phone, and a compass. She also wears one of those big floppy-brimmed hats and sunglasses that cover 75 percent of her face."

Her cell phone was useless in much of the surrounding area. Cody knew that for a fact. "Does she at least tell you where she's going?"

"That she does," Alph chimed in. "Today she is hiking down to Zephyr Cove to swim in the lake."

Great, swimming alone isn't good, either. He wanted to say, "Don't you people get the danger she's putting herself in?" But he didn't bother. Both Essie and Alph seemed nonchalant and unconcerned about Lexi's welfare.

And today she'd gone right down past fire station number three—his firehouse. She'd probably marched right by it on Elk's Cove Road, not having any idea that someone might spot her and notice her description fit the arsonist to a tee. He ate quickly, planning to head down there and read her the riot act.

He hugged Alph and Essie, thanked them for lunch, and hopped in his Jeep. He prayed the entire four miles to the cove. "Please, Lord, reveal who really set the fires and don't let it be Lexi. Her grandparents have served You faithfully for years. For their sake, Lord, let it be anybody but her." But he knew that like everyone, Lexi had a free will, and God allowed all people to choose for themselves.

Cody parked and headed down to the lake. He spotted her lying on the beach in a modest, black, one-piece suit—her golden hair fanned out around her.

A longing hit him. How he wished she'd been the girl of his dreams. He'd never met a more beautiful woman, but it was the inside that mattered most to him. And there, it seemed, Lexi sadly lacked.

∞

Lexi lay on her bright, oversized towel in the beach area. There were a few other swimmers and sunbathers but not many.

As a model, her tan had been the spray-on kind. Her manager forbade sunning due to possible skin damage. For all practical purposes, he'd owned her.

"Lexi." The deep, quiet voice startled her. She jerked to a sitting position. It took a minute for her eyes to adjust to the brightness of the day. She shaded them and squinted. Cody stood a couple of feet from her.

"May I join you?"

Her stomach knotted. She thought they'd reached an understanding and sort of had an unspoken agreement. She assumed their dislike was mutual, so why was he here, ruining her perfectly peaceful afternoon?

"It's important."

She rose to her feet, pulling a wrap over her suit. "Are my grandparents okay?"

He nodded. "It's not them I'm worried about. Where did you hike yesterday?"

"One Hundred Dollar Saddle lookout. Why?"

"Did you hear about yesterday's grass fire?"

She pulled her brows together, trying to remember. "Yeah—sort of. Gram and Gramps were reading an article about it this morning. I wasn't really paying much attention, though. Why?"

He seemed extremely serious and was watching her closely—almost studying her—like one would a bug under a microscope. "Several people reported spotting you in the area."

"Yeah, so?" She shrugged. "I just told you I hiked near there." Now she considered him as intently as he had her.

"You're the *only* person anyone saw anywhere near the area."

Suddenly his implications were clear. Lexi's heart constricted, and fear settled on her like a blanket on a cold evening. The weight of it covered her. "You don't think. . ." Her tone was incredulous. Dizziness overtook her, and she sat back down.

"It doesn't make a difference what I think." His expression was matter-of-fact. He bent down on one knee in front of her, leaning in mere inches from her face. "Did you set that fire?" he asked slowly, enunciating each word. His eyes mirrored the uncertainty of his voice.

"Of course not! Is that what you think? Is that what they think?" She pulled her wrap tighter around her. "Cody, it's not true! You have to believe me!"

But why should he? She'd accused him of something just as bad—using her elderly grandparents. "Please." She closed her eyes momentarily, gulping in a deep breath. She licked her dry lips. "I know you don't think very highly of me, and rightly so. I haven't been very nice, but I'm not a criminal. I'd never do anything like that." She shook her head, horror etched across her face.

She didn't do it. He was sure of it. Her response was pure, unadulterated shock.

"I can't believe this is happening. Do my grandparents think I started the fire?" Her breathing was heavy and slightly erratic.

"They don't even know you're a suspect."

"Cody, I didn't do it." Her eyes pleaded with him to believe her. Her hand quivered as she laid it across her mouth. She squeezed her eyes shut.

"I believe you."

She dropped her hand and opened her eyes. "You do?" Relief flooded her face. "You really do?" Now she studied him.

He nodded.

"Why? Why would you believe me?"

"I don't know. I just feel it in my gut. Either you're a top-notch actress or you're telling the truth. I'm going with the latter." Cody rose to his feet and offered her a hand, pulling her up with him.

"What do we do now?" she asked on the walk back to his Jeep. Funny how they'd suddenly become a "we."

"You need to lay low for a few days. Maybe there's another tall, curly-headed blond around somewhere." Cody opened the passenger door for Lexi. "The police are only collecting information at this point, so there is no warrant or anything."

Cody climbed into the driver's seat and started the engine. "My guess is, it's a case of being in the wrong place at the wrong time. The real arsonist was much more discreet and remained unseen. Please don't hike alone anymore. At least not until this is resolved."

Lexi nodded her agreement. "I won't."

Cody drove her home and walked her to the door.

She paused before going inside, turning to face him. "Thank you for believing me. I couldn't blame you if you didn't."

Their gazes locked. Feelings for the imagined Lexi and newfound compassion for this one collided inside him. He longed to pull her into his arms, assure her everything would be okay, and kiss all the fear away. He, however, did nothing but stand there gawking. She did the same. He wondered if she felt the emotions he did—the unmistakable chemistry, the undeniable pull.

For a moment, Lexi thought Cody might kiss her, and for a moment, the idea didn't repulse her. Instead, he shoved his hands into the front pockets of his jeans and took a couple of steps backward. She swallowed, and the moment dissipated. All that remained was an awkwardness.

"I better get inside."

He nodded his agreement.

She needed to say something more to him, but nothing came.

"Well, see ya." He took another step away from her.

"Bye." She watched him saunter to his Jeep. Once inside, he waved. She did the same and let herself into the house.

Nothing but silence greeted her. Her grandparents must be catching their afternoon nap. She tiptoed to her room, hoping the wood floor wouldn't creak. She needed some time alone and was thankful her room was at the opposite end of the house from theirs.

Lexi changed into a pair of sweats and an oversized T-shirt. She slipped her feet into warm, fuzzy slippers and perched on the side of her bed, picking up the Bible Gram always left on the guest room nightstand.

"It's been a long time." The tears she'd held at bay since Cody's surprise visit refused to lie dormant a moment longer. An army of them marched down her cheeks. At first she tried to swipe them away, but since her efforts were futile, she let them fall where they might.

She grabbed the box of tissues that sat next to where the Bible had been and lay back across her bed, eyes on the ceiling. She pulled a couple of tissues from the box and dried her face then set the box next to her on the bed and laid the Bible on her chest, hugging it against her heart.

"God, it's me, Lexi. Do You still remember who I am?" The words, nothing more than a coarse whisper, sounded silly. "Of course You do. I recall learning that somewhere in the Bible it says I'm the apple of Your eye and my name is engraved on the palm of Your hand. So I know You haven't forgotten me."

Lexi cried harder. How could God still love her? Yet she knew He did. And somehow she knew He was calling her, softly and tenderly, back to Him. Sunday in church, she'd felt that old familiar tug on her heart. He'd gone after that one stray sheep she'd learned years ago in children's church. And this time, the stray was her.

As Lexi thought back over the last dozen years and the many compromises she'd made along the way, she felt physically sick. Curled into a ball on the bed, she recited all the acts she could remember and asked God to forgive each one.

Finally, after she'd laid herself bare before Him, a mantle of peace settled over her like she hadn't known in years. One more thing nagged her conscience, so after she washed her face, she slipped out the sliding door to her private patio and headed across the street. Cody's Jeep sat parked out front, so she was certain he'd be there.

She lifted her chin and forced herself to knock on the door.

∞

Cody went to the door expecting to see Alph, but there stood a fragile-looking Lexi. She'd been crying hard, as her splotchy face, red nose, and swollen eyes testified.

He swung his door open wide. "Would you like to come in?"

She nodded but stopped just inside the doorway, facing him. "I'm sort of making things right with God today, and I felt the need to do the same with you."

"Do you want to sit down?" Cody motioned toward a leather sofa facing a stone fireplace.

She moved toward the couch, and he followed, taking an oversized chair kitty-corner to her. She folded her hands in her lap, staring at them for several seconds. Then she raised her gaze to meet his, sucked in a deep breath, and sent him a tiny, embarrassed smile. "I'm sorry that I've been horrible to you ever since I arrived. I don't have a very good track record with men and struggle to trust or like most of your kind."

Her confession brought an ache to Cody's heart. Probably much of what he'd read about her was true. Men used her and threw her away.

"I forgive you, Lexi." And he did. More lines blurred between the Lexi he'd heard about for years and this one sitting before him. Right now, in her vulnerability, she was precious to him.

Chapter 4

S o you're a Christian?"

She laughed a self-conscious laugh. "I'm sure it was hard to tell, but I once was."

"Then you still are."

"I've wandered pretty far." Lexi picked up one of his sofa pillows and hugged it against her chest.

"When did you become a Christ follower?"

"I was just a little girl—probably six or seven. I asked Jesus into my heart at vacation Bible school."

Cody wasn't sure how much he should ask, but he wanted to know. "So what happened then?"

"My parents are atheists. My mom is my grandparents' only child. I guess they were pretty strict with her when she was growing up, and once she got out of the house, she wanted nothing to do with church or God and little to do with them."

Cody nodded, hoping to encourage her to continue. He knew bits and pieces but didn't know the whole story.

"I've heard Gram say more than once that she wished they'd emphasized God was a loving Father who wanted a relationship and not a set of rules to follow." Lexi seemed a million miles away. "Anyway, I grew up in Beverly Hills. My parents were part of the movie scene—my mom directed and my dad produced. That was their dream for me. I failed them, too." Lexi gazed into the fireplace.

"I started taking acting classes when I was three, but I was never any good. I got a reprieve every summer when they shipped me off to stay with Gram and Gramps. That's when they reinforced the spiritual side of my life.

"Finally, when I was a sophomore in high school, my parents let go of the acting idea and pursued modeling instead. My career took off fairly quickly, and they'd finally found a way to make me *somebody*." Her voice cracked with emotion.

Cody knew by her last statement that she'd never felt loved or accepted until she had a recognizable name and face.

"Why in the world am I boring you with my life story?"

262

"I'm not bored, I promise. It's a world most of us only read about, but few live in it."

"The lucky few." Sarcasm enveloped those three words, and Cody knew Lexi felt anything but lucky.

"What happened with God?"

Lexi met his gaze, her eyes sad. "At the ripe old age of fifteen, I got caught up in the whole idea of fame and fortune and chased the modeling dream. I left Him behind eating my dust." Lexi hesitated, and he wasn't sure she'd continue. She picked at the yarn on the pillow in her lap.

She cleared her throat. "Shortly after my sixteenth birthday, my manager promised me if I did him a few favors he'd make sure I made it to the top. So I compromised my beliefs and myself to climb the elusive ladder of success."

Lexi raised her gaze to meet his. "And as they say, the rest is history."

He reached over and took her hand—his heart aching for her and all she'd been through. "I'm so sorry. No man had the right to use you like that." Cody had an urge to hunt the guy down and pound him into the ground for the shame he'd caused her.

She pulled her hand away. "He didn't force me. I'd failed miserably at acting, so I needed the successes. My parents wanted me to achieve. He offered an opportunity, and I grabbed it with both eyes wide open. For a while, I even convinced myself I was in love with him. That way it didn't seem so cheap and sleazy."

Lexi shook her head and laughed. She rose from the couch. "My goodness—talk about more than you bargained for. I've never shared my story with anyone before."

Cody rose, too. "I'm glad I could be the first, and your secrets are safe with me." He followed her to the front door.

She paused before opening it and faced him. "Would you come to dinner tonight? Gram mopes every time you don't."

He chuckled. "Sure."

"I know you basically changed your whole routine because of me. I promise I'll behave *if* you'll return to the way things were between you and my grandparents."

Cody nodded. "Lexi, I'm not using them or out to take advantage of them. I'm just a man who loves family, and they needed one."

Lexi hung her head. "I know. And thank you." She returned her gaze to his. "You filled a void that needed filling. I'm sorry I said such awful things to you. Will you forgive that as well?"

"I will."

∞

During the next couple of weeks, Lexi reacquainted herself with God through a daily time of devotional reading and prayer. Cody loaned her his copy of *The Purpose-Driven Life*, which for her was a refresher course in God 101. Church still felt exactly the same, only the crowd was much older than before. They still sang the old hymns she'd grown up singing, and her favorite was still "Softly and Tenderly Jesus Is Calling." But the messages always felt more relevant than when she was a kid.

She also heeded Cody's advice and never went anywhere alone. But because of that promise Cody had evoked from her, he ended up spending most of his time off hiking with her. On the days he couldn't, she and Gram took long walks or short hikes. Things with Cody went back to the way they were pre-Lexi, so he was around a lot. Gram was as content as a kitten living in a pool of cream.

Lexi and Gram were almost home from their morning walk when she commented, "You and Cody are sure becoming chummy."

Lexi raised her brows and glanced sideways at Gram. "Chummy?" Lexi shook her head. "We're becoming friends, and I haven't had a real friend in a very long time." Her famous friends came and went, but none were trustworthy. They'd use whomever they needed to gain another rung up the ladder of success.

"But don't you go getting any ideas, Gram. We are friends. Period. There is absolutely no hope for romance." Lexi doubted her heart could ever trust or love again. And Cody deserved someone way better than her.

∞

Cody wasn't on duty today and planned to hike with Lexi later in the afternoon. She and Essie had taken an early morning walk and invited him, but he had some things he needed to get done.

His cell phone rang, and he picked it up off the snack bar dividing his kitchen and living room. It was one of his buddies down at the station. "Hey, Chip."

"You asked me to call if there were more grass fires. One was set this morning not too far from those expensive cabins off Mendon Road."

Cody leaned against his kitchen counter, letting out a long sigh. "What time?"

"Early. Before seven. One of the neighbors spotted the same woman described previously just minutes before she smelled the smoke."

"The tall blond?"

"Yep."

His heart crashed to the floor. "Was she alone?"

"The report doesn't say."

"Any idea about the course of action?"

"The captain said the authorities didn't really pursue the first one, but a second fire with the same MO and suspect? He doubts they'll let this one slide. Sounds to me like some pretty little girl got bored."

Cody's stomach curled, and it was all he could do not to defend Lexi's honor. *Why was she out walking alone? She'd promised.* "Anything else?"

"Naw. Just the usual concerns. Setting the side of a hill on fire is bad enough, but when you're only a couple of football fields from someone's home, that's another matter."

"It sure is. Thanks for filling me in."

"What's your interest in this case anyway?"

Cody paused, scrambling for an answer. "Since it's out in my neck of the woods, I'm concerned. I haven't forgotten the last loon from a couple of years ago over by Meeks Bay. He started at a distance and got closer and closer to homes until several cabins ended up taking a hit."

"That's why the captain thinks they'll put out a warrant sooner than later."

Cody closed his eyes against the onslaught of bad news and said a quick prayer for Lexi and her grandparents. "Thanks for the update. I'll keep my eyes open. If you hear anything else—"

"Call," Chip finished.

Cody shut his cell phone, laying it back on the counter. He mulled over the info for several minutes and had no idea what to think. His mind couldn't wrap around everything and make sense of it, but he sure hoped Lexi hadn't been alone this morning.

Glancing out the window, the large home sitting across the street looked just like it always did. He decided to check things out for himself.

Alph answered his knock on the front door. He opened the door wide. "Cody, come in. I think Essie still has some warm coffee in the pot. You need a cup?"

"Nope. I'm good, but thanks. I thought I'd see what everybody has been up to today."

He followed Alph into the family room.

"Lexi and Essie took their usual sunrise walk. My hip's still giving me fits, so I stayed home and spent some extra time studying for my Sunday school lesson. Our class is in Job, and I want to teach the passage in a way that honors God."

Cody glanced at the stack of commentaries and Bibles next to Alph's chair. The man took the Word seriously.

"Where are Lexi and Essie?"

"Out puttering in the garden. Go on out." He motioned to the sliding glass door.

Cody sauntered outside and paused on the porch, watching grandmother and granddaughter work side by side—their backs toward him. Lexi wore one of Gram's straw hats with a big brim. He wondered if anyone would ever believe that a supermodel enjoyed digging in the earth, nurturing and growing vegetables and flowers.

Just the sight of her warmed his heart. He'd fallen in love with her all over again as they hiked, talked, and laughed. There really wasn't much difference between the real deal and the one her grandparents talked about. He saw more and more of the original as he got to know her better. It seemed the fires had brought with them brokenness and humility. The frost had melted.

"How was your walk this morning?" he asked as he stepped off the porch.

Both turned their heads to see him.

"Wonderful, as always." Essie rose and brushed the dirt off her hands. "I always imagined that models slept until noon, but Lexi assures me that their rigorous schedule included very early days in order to get their hair and makeup done and ready for the next shoot. That explains why she's always up at the crack of dawn."

Lexi rose. "Gram, like everyone, assumes models live a life of luxury and pampering." A smudge of dirt streaked her cheek.

He longed to take the few steps necessary and wipe it off but instead shoved his hand into the front pocket of his jeans. "Hey, you've already convinced me they don't." He focused on Essie. "Those girls really do work hard. Many twelve-hour days. Hot lights. Hours with a personal trainer. Not much time for a life." Cody parroted the facts he'd learned from Lexi during the past weeks.

Lexi got in his face, one hand on her hip and the other shaking an index finger near his nose. "Are you mocking me, buster?"

Cody shook his head in an exaggerated motion. "Nope. No mocking. Just quoting a famous model I once knew." He grabbed her finger and used his to poke at her ribs. She squealed and laughed.

Essie watched their playful banter with delight filling her expression.

Uh-oh. She's taking this in a direction it will never actually head. Lexi has zero interest in me, Cody thought.

∞

Lexi followed the direction of Cody's gaze, realizing they'd given Gram the wrong impression. She'd have to set her straight, because there was more chance of snow in July than her ever settling down and marrying anyone—and definitely never a guy with a spotless past like Cody seemed to have.

They'd both taken a few steps away from the other, and an uncomfortable moment hung between them. Gram gazed from one to the other, watching with anticipation.

Cody recovered first. "I almost forgot why I came by. How would you like to go on a drive around the lake today?"

His suggestion brought a smile. "I'd love to. I haven't done that in years." She glanced at Essie. "I was just a little girl last time, and nothing was more boring than a seventy-two-mile drive around a lake that I'd rather have been in than viewing from a car window. Maybe I'll appreciate it more this time around." She headed for the back door. "I'll wash up and be ready in a few." Stopping at the door, she turned back. Her gaze rested on Gram. "You don't mind, do you?"

"Me?" She waved her hand as if to rid Lexi of such a ridiculous idea. "Of course not."

I bet you don't, you little matchmaker, you.

When Lexi returned a few minutes later, Gram had packed water bottles and lemonade in a small ice chest. Cody grabbed the ice chest, and Lexi led the way out to his Jeep. This time she was prepared; she'd pulled her hair into a ponytail.

Cody drove out to Highway 50 and turned left. In less than two minutes, they'd crossed the state line and were in California. Just past the border, Cody pointed out the Heavenly ski resort gondola.

"It was pretty new the last time I was here. Promise not to laugh?"

Cody nodded his agreement.

"When my grandparents mentioned they were putting in a gondola, I imagined little boats with singing Italian men—not a ski lift up the mountain."

Cody tried not to break his promise but ended up being unable to contain his mirth. "Seriously?"

"Seriously. And might I mention, you're laughing." She really didn't mind. She loved the sound of his rich, timbered chuckle.

Cody pulled into the Starbucks in South Lake Tahoe, just past the base of the gondola. "I figure an LA girl must be dying for chic coffee. What can I get you?"

"You remembered." He sure knew how to impress a girl. On one of their walks, she mentioned her Starbucks fetish. He opened her door and the door to the coffee shop. "Your mama taught you well."

"It was actually my dad. I think some things are caught rather than taught."

They got in line to order.

Lexi realized they'd spent hours talking about modeling—a safe and non-personal topic—but very little time talking about him. And though she tried hard to forget, she'd shared with him, and only him, her deepest, darkest secrets. Things she wished she could erase. But a lightness and freshness had come as a result of confessing her past to someone other than just God.

Cody ordered a large mocha frappuccino.

"A tall skinny mocha latte," Lexi said.

The guy eyed her up and down. "Do I know you?"

Lexi shook her head. "I don't think so. I'm not from this area."

Cody handed him a ten.

Another couple pointed and whispered. She heard them say, "Alexandria." Turning away, she whispered to Cody, "I'll meet you at the car."

He handed her the keys. "I've got a cap and some extra sunglasses in the glove box." He'd bent his head low and spoke softly right next to her ear. His breath danced across her neck, sending shivers down her spine.

"Thanks."

She loved his intuitive nature. He never seemed to miss or forget a thing. Digging through her Coach bag, she pulled out an oversized pair of sunglasses. They covered a good portion of her face, which was the goal. Taking Cody's Anaheim Angels cap from the glove box, she adjusted the back strap and pulled it low on her head. Glancing in the mirror, she decided no one would recognize her now. She barely recognized herself.

Cody joined her in a couple of minutes, handing her the hot drink.

"Cody, tell me about you, your family, and what you've been doing the past thirty years," she said as he pulled back onto the highway.

He shrugged. "Not much to tell." He pointed to a road labeled HIGHWAY 50 that curved to the left. "The Lake Tahoe airport is that way. I was surprised you didn't fly there instead of Reno."

"This girl doesn't like those little planes. No thank you. But I'm confused. I thought we were on Highway 50."

"Believe it or not, there are three different highway numbers on this one road that circles the whole lake. Highway 50 took off toward the little airport, and now we are on 89. At Tahoe City, this takes off toward Truckee, and we'll suddenly be on Highway 28."

"So what do you actually know about Lake Tahoe? Since you're unwilling to talk about yourself, we might as well see who has more useless facts stored up here." Lexi pointed to her head.

"I know we are almost to Camp Richardson. And I know for certain if this was a game of Jeopardy and the category was Lake Tahoe, I'd win." His glance in her direction reeked of smugness.

"I think not. Did you know this lake is twenty-two miles long and twelve miles wide?"

He furrowed his brow for a moment. "I think I did know that. And did you know this is considered the most beautiful drive in America?"

"Not when you're twelve."

He chuckled. "No, I suppose not."

Chapter 5

There's the Forest Service Visitor Center." Cody pointed out the next landmark.

"You read that on the sign. It doesn't count toward our contest to see who knows this lake the best." She used a schoolteacher voice, sounding authoritarian.

Cody pulled into the Emerald Bay lookout. "This is one of the most photographed places in the world, and I'm seeing it with one of the most photographed women in the world." He opened her door again.

She lowered her gaze. "Hardly. I'm small potatoes compared to Tyra Banks and the likes of her."

"You're far more beautiful." Cody's voice took on a husky quality.

Their gazes locked, and Lexi found the simple act of breathing suddenly difficult. Men often told her that, but with Cody, it was different. He was sincere. Today the words meant something to her, and they never had before.

She broke eye contact and didn't respond but admired the beauty in silence, a tenderness settling over her. If she let herself, falling for Cody Cooper would be so easy. Her gaze roamed over the secluded green cove surrounded by mountain peaks. No photo truly did this place justice.

After several quiet minutes, Cody whispered, "You ready? We have to keep moving if we want to see everything."

Lexi nodded, still not wishing to break the serenity. She trailed Cody back to the Jeep.

They followed the road around the lake, leaving the south shore in the rearview mirror. Lexi admired the many views, noting cabins discreetly tucked into the forest and along the edge of the lake. "Seems to me more people live on the California side."

"I think you're right." Cody gazed over the horizon. "Tell me how you became so knowledgeable about Lake Tahoe."

"My grandparents moved up here when I was eleven, so when they were researching the area—geek that I was—I jumped right in to help."

"Geek?"

"I was very studious. Grades were of the utmost importance to my parents."

"I thought acting was."

Lexi shrugged, that old familiar cloud of failure settling over her. "It was—everything was. They wanted a well-rounded child. Smart, talented, beautiful, witty."

"The Stepford child."

"Exactly. Anyway, back to Gram and Gramps. They fell in love with the Tahoe area, and so did I. I know lots of useless facts, like it's the country's largest alpine lake, and the water is crystal clear, cleaner than the drinking water in most U.S. cities."

∞

Cody laughed at Lexi's dramatic rendition of her knowledge of Lake Tahoe, grateful he'd decided to wait to talk about this morning's fire. Otherwise they wouldn't be having such a lighthearted time. He'd determined to wait until after they shared a nice lunch on the bank of the Truckee River. Then they'd have the drive home to process and strategize.

"Lake Tahoe 'must surely be the fairest picture the whole earth affords.'" He glanced in Lexi's direction. "But I'd say you are."

She smiled. "Mark Twain. Very impressive."

"And very true. Every morning I fall in love with this place all over again." He shook his head. "Sounds cheesy, doesn't it?"

"Not at all. Sounds like you're a man with some connection to his own feelings. A rarity in my world." He heard admiration in her tone.

"It's the perfect place to live. I'm an avid outdoorsman. I like it all—sailing, swimming, sailboarding, parasailing, water-skiing, jet skiing, rafting, fishing, snowmobiling, downhill skiing, even an occasional sleigh ride. And let's not forget golf. Sometimes Alph and I drive up to Incline Village for a game. It's a championship course and well worth the drive. You should see it—set on the side of the mountain overlooking the lake. Doesn't get much better."

"Golf with a view."

"Golf with a view—an incredible view. Probably only matched by the area around Heavenly. Those views are gorgeous, too." As they passed Meeks Bay, Cody continued. "This is considered the beginning of the north shore. If you look closely, you'll spot some strategically placed mansions hidden among the trees. Probably less ostentatious than those in Southern California. Up here they have a more rustic look, many built with native wood and stone, but they are mansions nonetheless. Did you know they filmed *The Godfather II* at Ehrman Mansion at Sugar Pine Point State Park?"

"I didn't. I was just thinking what an eclectic place Lake Tahoe is—from the tiniest of cabins to mansions. From the casinos on the south shore to the sleepy villages dotting the west side."

"You're right. And now, mademoiselle, we are approaching Tahoe City—the birthplace of the Truckee River. I thought we'd hit a deli and enjoy lunch on its banks."

"A picnic! How quaint!" Her voice held exuberance, but he wasn't sure what she was thinking.

"You don't like picnics?"

"Oh no, I'm fond of picnics, but I haven't enjoyed one in years. Probably since I was eleven." She laughed.

"Everything happened when you were eleven." Cody slowed for a pedestrian.

"Pretty much. I'd started getting serious about God, and my parents resented my grandparents' influence over that area of my life. They decided I spent way too much time with those 'religious Holy Rollers'—their terminology, not mine—so they limited me to two weeks every summer rather than the whole break. The first year their edict was in force, I cried almost the entire two and a half months. I was home alone every day with the maid." Lexi's voice cracked. "I was a pretty lonely kid, and my best memories were spending three months a year with my grandparents. It worked well for my parents, too. They traveled extensively and didn't have to mess with a snot-nosed kid."

"I'm sorry." Her stories made him even more hesitant to share his life with her. His childhood was the kind every kid should have but many didn't.

"Wow, talk about a downer. I'm the one who is sorry. You should have been a shrink. I have no problem opening up to you—and for me, that's big."

Cody pulled into the Tahoe House. "Glad to be of assistance. I'll send you my bill." He winked. "You ready for lunch?"

"Sure."

"Everything here is fresh—made right on the premises—and really good. They've got soups, salads, sandwiches, and to-die-for pastries. Since your grandmother wants to put meat on those bones, this is just the place to help with that endeavor."

Lexi shook her head. "Gram would turn me into a roly-poly if I'd let her."

They stopped a moment to study the menu. Once Lexi decided, he stepped up to the counter. "I'd like a roast beef on squaw bread, and she'd like the half sandwich—a veggie—and spinach salad combo. Would you throw in a chocolate truffle turtle torte and two large iced teas?"

"A torte?" Lexi raised her brow.

"Hey, just following your grandmother's orders. Besides, it's worth wasting some calories on." He winked. "I promise."

Once they were back in the Jeep with their lunch, Cody followed Highway

89 north. "This highway is now taking us away from the lake, but the river runs right alongside us and is in view much of the way. There's a nice spot up by the Alpine Meadows turnoff where we can eat right next to the river. Then we'll go up to Squaw Valley where the 1960 Winter Olympics were held. Finally, we'll retrace our path back down to Highway 28 and finish our trek around the lake."

"Sounds good. Maybe sometime we can take a rafting trip." She pointed at many bright blue and yellow inflatable rafts floating on the Truckee.

"Looks so peaceful, doesn't it?"

Cody pulled off the road. He and Lexi carried a big blanket, the ice chest Essie had insisted they bring, and the bag filled with their lunch down to the edge of the river.

Lexi spread out the blanket and plopped down on one side. "This, my friend, is the life." She sighed with contentment and lay back. "The sun feels warm and welcoming." She closed her eyes against its brightness.

Cody dreaded ruining this perfect day. She was more relaxed than he'd ever seen her. His news would shatter that for sure.

They ate in silence, enjoying the sights and sounds of nature and watching groups of rafters float by.

∞

Once they finished lunch and stowed their garbage in the bag, Cody asked, "So where'd you guys walk today?"

"Just through the neighborhood." Lexi breathed deep, enjoying the fresh air filled with the scents of pine and water. "I can't believe I found this boring as a kid. It's all so—breathtaking."

"That it is." Cody nodded. "So did you guys stay together the whole time?"

"Huh?" Lexi had only been half-listening. "What guys?" She crinkled her nose. Was he asking about her and Jamison?

"You and your gram. Were you with her the whole walk?"

Lexi's stomach knotted. "Was there another fire?" She searched Cody's face for the answer, but in her heart, she already knew.

He nodded.

"I have never gone anywhere alone, Cody. Just as you requested."

"One of your grandparents' neighbors claimed she saw a woman fitting your description out walking alone this morning."

She wondered if he now doubted her innocence. "Cody, Gram will tell you that I never left her side." Her tone rang defensive.

He grabbed her hand and gave a squeeze. "I believe you, Lex." He must have seen uncertainty on her face. "I do." He said the words with firm conviction. "I should have waited to bring this up—let you enjoy the rest of the day."

"No. You should have told me before we ever left the house. I had a right to know." The bright blue of the sky and the green landscape no longer captivated her. The world, for her, had just turned a bleak shade of gray.

Cody sucked in a deep breath. "I'm sorry. I just wanted to get you away from your grandparents so we could talk in private. I figured the last half of the drive would give you time to process."

Lexi leaned her head back, releasing a long sigh. "How can this be happening again?"

"There's got to be an explanation. We'll find it—whatever it is."

Lexi resituated herself in a cross-legged position, her head hanging low. *I'm afraid.*

"Essie never even stepped away for a second? Maybe to admire a flower, watch a raccoon, or attempt to follow a squirrel?"

"I can tell you've had many a walk with Gram. She does every one of those things, but I don't recall her ever leaving my side. I'm trying to get her to keep walking, so she no longer has time to linger. I try to get my heart rate up at least a little. When she's with me, we don't dawdle. No more nature walks for her."

Cody nodded. "I do understand why during that first grass fire people remembered seeing you. You were out every day hiking somewhere, but if you haven't been alone, why would someone say you were?"

"Maybe it's somebody who looks like me." Lexi stretched her neck—her shoulders suddenly tight with knots.

"Realistically, how many women do you know who are blond with long golden curls and nearly six feet tall?" Cody eyed her.

"Realistically, I know quite a few." She now tilted her head to the side, stretching it down toward her shoulder.

"I guess you would in your line of work. But I've lived in these mountains five years and have never met, or even seen, another woman who fits your description." He paused. "What. . ." He hesitated, seemingly uncomfortable about his line of thinking.

"About an ex?" she finished for him, not wanting to remember any of them. But she ran through the list in her head.

"Did any of them want something you weren't willing to give?"

She thought hard, but nothing came to mind.

Cody cleared his throat. "What about wives or girlfriends who want you to pay?"

Lexi hung her head. She'd never told Cody that she slept with married men, yet he instinctively knew. Shame flowed through her veins, touching every cell of her being. How low she'd fallen.

"Lexi, you've repented. God's forgiven you."

She raised her tear-streaked face and looked him in the eye. "How can He forgive such an atrocity?"

"Because He does, Lexi. Because He does." Cody's face held no judgment or condemnation. It made it easier to believe God didn't, either.

"King David, the man after God's own heart, not only slept with a married woman, but he had her husband killed."

Lexi sniffed. "I haven't done that." How was it he always knew the right thing to say? She looked at him through blurry, tear-filled eyes and decided he was the most attractive man she'd ever met. Someday some girl would be lucky—mighty lucky indeed.

"There are a lot of people who might hate me for one reason or another, and rightly so. Are you thinking this is some sort of revenge?"

Cody shrugged again and shook his head. "I don't know. Nothing else makes sense."

"Maybe I deserve whatever happens to me, even if I had nothing to do with the fires."

"Lexi, we all deserve God's wrath, but He doesn't work that way. He is merciful and gracious to us."

Her much-regretted past, her present reality, the possibility of being punished for a crime she didn't commit, and the loving God who was calling her back to Himself all blended together in this moment in time. Lexi was overcome with more emotions than she knew how to deal with. She tried to hold back, but one sob escaped, and before she could reinforce the dam and hold her tears at bay, the onslaught broke through any restraint, and Lexi wept.

Cody pulled her into his arms, knocking her cap off in the process. He held her against his chest, running his hand over her hair. "It will be okay, Lexi. I promise that somehow it will be okay." He said the words over and over, and she knew that he'd do everything in his power to make it so.

She rested her head against his heart, hearing the steady, calming beat. The last arms she'd cried in had been her gramps's when she was still a little girl. In the circle of Cody's muscular arms, Lexi felt safe. For the first time since childhood, having a man's arms hold her felt good and right. How strange. She'd never before wanted a man to hold her, but she never wanted this man to let her go.

∞

Cody didn't rush her. He knew he'd hold her forever if he could. While she cried, he prayed, asking God to provide answers. When the sobs subsided, he kept her close, waiting patiently until she was ready to pull away. When she finally did, his arms ached with the emptiness. She rose, and they packed up their picnic, neither saying a word.

Once inside the Jeep, Cody drove Lexi to the Olympic site, but he wasn't sure she even noticed. When they arrived back in Tahoe City, he turned left and finished the drive around the north shore. When they hit Incline Village, the upscale community built on the side of some fairly steep mountains, Cody commented, "This is where we golf occasionally."

She nodded but didn't comment.

Leaving Incline Village was his favorite part of the drive, because the route often ran right next to the water's edge. The views of the lake were much better on this side. Nevertheless, he didn't bother pointing out anything else. Lexi was too deep in her own thoughts. He doubted she even saw a thing.

When Cody pulled onto their street, he saw a strange car in front of Alph and Essie's house. He opted to bypass their driveway for his own.

"Lexi?"

She turned and faced him.

"Your grandparents have company. Do you want to freshen up at my place before going home?"

She nodded, checking out the Buick in her grandparents' drive as she headed toward Cody's front door. "I don't recognize that car, do you?"

"Nope."

Cody fetched Lexi a fresh hand towel and washcloth and showed her to his guest bathroom. "Sorry, but I don't have any face soap. Guys don't have special bars for different body parts."

"Thanks. I'll make do."

While Lexi washed away the traces of a broken heart, Cody went out front to unload their picnic items from the car. A woman stood at the bottom of Alph and Essie's porch. He heard her yell, "If you won't do anything about your granddaughter, then I'm sure the police will!"

Cody rushed across the street. "Everything all right over here?" He searched each face for a clue.

"Sybil says she saw Lexi set a fire this morning near her cabin, but I told her Lexi was with me all morning, making her accusation impossible." Gram raised her chin, emphasizing the rightness of her words.

Lexi couldn't have picked a worse possible moment to join them. When Cody saw her coming, he wished for a way to head her off.

When Sybil spotted her, she pointed. "That's her. I knew it was her." She faced Lexi. "If I see you out again, I'll call the police. Don't come near my street!" With that demand, she climbed in her car and sped off.

Chapter 6

That woman is nuttier than a fruitcake," Gram informed them as Sybil drove away. "I mean, I stood here and told her you were with me the whole morning until you left with Cody. She all but called me a liar. And I thought Sybil Green was my friend." Gram turned in a huff and marched into the house.

Gramps followed her. "Can't trust anybody these days. There was a time when folks watched out for one another. Not anymore." He paused in the doorway. "You two coming?"

"Be there in a minute, Alph," Cody hollered and turned to Lexi. "You holding up?"

She nodded. *You precious, precious man. I never thought I'd feel anything positive about your gender—not ever. But you've sneaked into the back door of my heart.*

"What are you thinking?"

That you are a more wonderful friend than I deserve. She shrugged, unwilling to voice her thoughts.

"Are you ready to tell your grandparents what's going on?"

"Not yet. I won't leave the house anymore unless you're with me. We'll drive miles from here to hike."

"Lexi, if this is some kind of revenge, none of those things will stop whoever it is." His gaze was tender and sweet like warm, melted chocolate. "Besides, you'll be miserable under house arrest."

"Not as miserable as I'd be in jail." She laughed, but the sound was hollow and meaningless.

"So you're willing to become a prisoner here, in hopes of stopping the problem?"

She nodded. "If I tell my grandparents, they'll be upset. My grandpa's heart has never fully recovered from his last heart attack. I can't risk what this burden might do to him."

Lexi knew Cody didn't agree with her line of thinking, but he accepted it without trying to push his own agenda.

"All right, Lexi, but I'm counting on you to keep your promise and stay inside. You're just lucky the press lost interest in the grass fire story and let it die.

But all that said, don't you think your grandparents will notice the change in your pattern if you suddenly stick close to home?"

"You're right. As always, I think I'm protecting them by being less than honest. Will you come with me to tell them?"

Cody nodded.

She'd never felt so needy and vulnerable. He must have sensed it, because he pulled her into his arms, wrapping her tight against his chest. "I'm walking through this with you, Lexi," he spoke into her hair. "No matter what happens, no matter how long it takes, I'll be right beside you. And so will God."

"Thank you." She closed her eyes and rested her head against his shoulder. His words gave her the courage she needed to get through this. They stood together in her grandparents' front yard for several minutes. She might have stayed longer, if he'd let her. He kissed her head and released his hold, grabbing her hand and pulling her forward. Just before opening the front door, he paused and turned toward her, placing a hand on each side of her face. Their gazes magnetized, drawing them ever closer.

Lexi's heart beat out its own song against her ribs. She anticipated his lips meeting her own. Never had she wanted a man's kiss more.

He stopped short, resting his forehead against hers. "God loves you, Lexi. Get the idea out of your head that He's trying to punish you through this. The world is full of mean and evil people who affect innocent lives."

"I'm not so innocent, Cody."

" 'Purge me with hyssop, and I shall be clean; wash me, and I shall be whiter than snow.' Lexi, He did that for you. You asked for forgiveness, and He washed you whiter than snow. Like any of us, confessing doesn't erase every consequence, but it frees us from guilt, shame, and condemnation."

He closed his eyes. "Father, enable Lexi to understand forgiveness and all that it brings. May she refuse to give in to the shame and self-condemnation. In Jesus' name, amen."

He hugged her tight for one brief moment and led her through her grandparents' front door. Then he released her hand.

Lexi swallowed hard. "I'll be right back." She moved down the hall and into her bathroom. Bright eyes and flushed cheeks reflected in the mirror. She splashed her face with cool water.

"What a good reminder of how ill-suited you and Cody would be," she whispered. "While he has God on his mind, you have kissing on yours." *What in the world is wrong with me? It's been years since I've wanted to be kissed.*

When Lexi returned from the restroom, Cody and her grandparents were sitting on the deck enjoying iced tea. A frosty glass awaited her. She took the empty seat at the table with Cody on her left, Gram on her right, and Gramps across from her. She took her time squeezing her lemon slice, not sure how to broach the subject that needed discussing. Cody and Gram were conversing about some new wood chipper that was out on the market.

Finally Cody cleared his throat. "I think Lexi wanted to tell the two of you something."

At his prompt, Lexi spilled the whole fire story.

"So Sybil Green is only one of many eyewitnesses who claim to have seen Lexi near the vicinity of a fire," Cody said, summing up her paragraphs of explanation into one sentence packaged with clarity.

Lexi would never forget the horror that settled on Gram's face. Or the fear. Gram sat in stunned silence while Cody explained his theory, at least with the first fire.

As the shock wore off, Gram's spunky personality kicked into gear. She hit her fist on the table with determination. "We'll have none of this. Lexi is innocent, and she won't hide out like some criminal. We will walk tomorrow morning and every morning that follows." She rose. "And that matter is settled," she stated, leaving the deck and going inside.

The following morning, Gram came into Lexi's room and threw the covers back. "Time for our walk. What are you still doing in bed?" She pulled the curtains back. "Rise and shine, sleepyhead."

"I'm not going." Lexi pulled the covers back up and over her head.

"You are going." Determination laced through Gram's words.

Lexi sat up. "I need to spend some extra time with the Lord today. How about if you go without me, at least until I pray this through."

Gram nodded. "I will this time." Lexi knew her unspoken thought was, *But I'll not put up with this for long.*

Gram left the house alone. Lexi went and poured herself some coffee and grabbed her Bible and journal. At Cody's suggestion, she'd decided to record her journey back home to God.

Lexi felt a good cry coming and decided to get dressed and sit on the private porch off her bedroom. She wanted to cry in private and couldn't bear the thought of being cooped up inside on such a beautiful day.

She slipped into a pair of jeans and a T-shirt and sank onto the chaise lounge. "Lord, show me what to do. I have no idea."

Her cell phone rang. It was Cody. "Hi."

"Lexi, where are you?" She knew by the frustration in his voice that there had been another fire.

"I'm on the deck outside my bedroom."

"Alone?"

"Yes."

He let out a sigh. "What happened to not leaving the house?"

"Cody, I'm two feet from it." Her heart was pounding. "Where did it happen this time?"

"Two streets over. Not only do they have an eyewitness, but she named you as the arsonist."

Lexi closed her eyes. *God, where are You?* "She's saying she saw Lexi Eastridge set the fire?"

"Not Lexi Eastridge, but the Newcombs' granddaughter. Get inside the house, and please go sit in the same room with your grandfather. I'll be there as soon as I can."

Lexi did as he asked. Her mouth had gone dry. *God, where are You?* She swallowed against the lump lodged in her throat. *I need You.* She went and sat on the couch in the family room. Gramps was in his chair with commentaries and several versions of the Bible spread on the two end tables placed at the sides of his recliner.

"What's up, Lexi girl?"

She burst into tears. "Another fire—this morning. Someone is saying she saw me light it. Not someone who looks like me, but me."

"That's nuts." Gramps laid his glasses and book aside. "You've been here the whole time."

"I know that. You know that. But how can we prove it?"

"Why should we have to prove it?" His brows drew together. "What happened to innocent until proven guilty?"

"I guess an eyewitness pretty much rules out innocence and establishes guilt."

Gramps drew his mouth together in a hard, firm line.

The doorbell ringing caused both Lexi and Gramps to jump. She glanced at him and saw her own fear reflected in his eyes. He rose from his recliner, and she stood to follow, heart pounding like a tom-tom.

"You wait here, Lexi girl."

She returned to the couch. "God, please help me." She strained to hear, but only a muffle of men's voices came to her. Then she heard footsteps on the wood floor—several sets, drawing closer and closer. She closed her eyes and sucked in a deep breath.

"Lexi." Gramps cleared his throat. His face was ashen. Two policemen stood behind him.

"These gentlemen have a few questions they'd like to ask you." Gramps returned to his recliner, and he motioned for the men to have a seat, but they didn't.

Both stood, watching Lexi with intense eyes—one pair blue and one brown.

"I'm Sergeant Christopher, and this is Officer Elliott. Can you give us your name?"

"Alexandria Eastridge." Lexi's voice quivered.

"We have received several reports that link you with the recent acts of arson." Officer Elliott proceeded to read Lexi her Miranda rights. "Do you want an attorney present?"

Lexi's thoughts whirled. She couldn't think clearly. Three pairs of eyes rested on her, waiting for a response. "I don't think so."

"Fine, then we'll proceed. Where were you this morning, ma'am, between five and seven?"

The front door slammed. Gram stormed in from her walk. "What's going on?" She placed her hands on her hips.

"Everything is all right, Essie. Why don't you have a seat?"

"Ma'am, for the record, will you state your name and relationship to Ms. Eastridge?" The sergeant spoke in a no-nonsense tone.

"I'm Essie Newcomb, her grandmother." Then she settled on the couch next to Lexi and leaned forward slightly as if to shield her from these men.

"Ma'am"—they'd refocused their attention on Lexi—"you may proceed."

"Between five and seven, I was here. I haven't left the house at all today."

"We can testify to that being the truth." Gram leaned forward, eager to help.

"No disrespect, ma'am, but you only just arrived"—the sergeant glanced at his watch—"what, four minutes ago?"

Little did they know Gram didn't give up without a good fight. The woman had the tenacity of a bulldog. "But she was in bed when I left."

"What time did you leave the house?"

"Somewhere between six thirty and six forty-five."

"Did you actually see her with your own eyes or just assume she was in her room?"

"I saw her. I went in and woke her up. We had a conversation." They didn't intimidate Gram.

"And then you left the house?"

She nodded.

"And didn't return until. . ." Again he checked the time. "Six minutes ago?"

"That's correct, but I know she didn't leave."

"How do you know that, ma'am, if you weren't in the home as an eyewitness?"

Gram continued to tell the whole story, and Lexi cringed at how incriminating the facts seemed.

Both policemen kept stoic expressions that Lexi couldn't read, so she had no idea what they must be thinking.

"Sir, were you here in the home all morning?"

Gramps nodded.

"Will you speak your answer, please?"

"Yes, I was here all morning. I awoke around five and haven't left the premises."

"Did you have visual contact with your granddaughter this morning?" The sergeant studied Gramps over the top of his reading glasses.

"Yes, sir, I did. I saw her come in and get a cup of coffee right after Essie—my wife—left on her walk. Then she returned to her room, and I heard her stirring about, probably getting gussied up for the day. You know how women do."

"So though you couldn't see her, you could hear her the entire time?"

"Not the entire time. But often enough to indicate there was life in the house." The sergeant puckered his lips and made more notations on his report.

"Ms. Eastridge, can you tell me what you did this morning and the approximate time you did it? Start at six."

Lexi figured since Gram already told everything, she'd follow suit. "I woke up around five but didn't want to face the day, so I pulled the covers over my head but never quite fell back asleep." She then proceeded to share the rest of the morning, even Cody's phone call.

∞

Cody finally found someone to cover the rest of his shift. He hopped in his Jeep and drove to Alph and Essie's. A million emotions surged through him, but the overriding two were frustration and fear. He wished Lexi had a better alibi for the morning. He'd called his dad earlier, but he was in a meeting. As the police chief in Reno, he would help guide them through this mess.

Turning onto their street, he spotted the police car sitting in front of their house. His stomach knotted. He pulled his phone from the front pocket of his uniform shirt. Staring at the silent cell phone, he said, "Dad, I really need you to call me back."

Cody rang the front doorbell. He figured just walking in might be inappropriate at this point in time.

A few moments later, Alph answered. Concern lined his face. He led Cody into the family room.

His eyes met Lexi's. They were wide and filled with anxiety. She was in the corner of the couch, and he'd never seen her looking more vulnerable. He wanted more than anything to take her in his arms and hold her until all this misunderstanding passed by.

Chapter 7

C ooper, you need something? You're disrupting a police investigation."
Elliott reminded Cody of a cocky rooster, the way he stuck out his chest
and strutted like he was the most important person on the planet.

"I'm a neighbor and live across the street. Just checking on things. Everybody okay?"

Essie resembled an old bear whose cub faced danger. Alph was quiet and contemplative, probably locked into a prayer conversation with God, which was his way. Lexi—ah, sweet Lexi. How he wished he could spare her this, but all he could do was walk through it beside her.

"We'd like to finish up here, if you don't mind." Elliott glared at him.

"Be my guest." Cody folded his arms across his chest and leaned against a bar stool. His stance appeared casual enough, but inside was a lion ready to pounce should they make one wrong move.

"This is a private matter," Sarge informed Cody.

"This is our home, and he's welcome to stay." Alph spoke in a subdued tone but with a firm deliverance.

"Have it your way." Elliott focused all his attention on Lexi. "You're our number-one suspect, and we'll be watching you. We have more interviews to conduct, but don't think about leaving town." The officer reminded Cody of Barney Fife from *The Andy Griffith Show*.

"You can't possibly expect her to stay in Stateline while the investigation proceeds," said Cody.

Elliott glanced at the sergeant. "Well, for sure don't leave the state until this is resolved. Are you clear on that?"

"Yes." Her face was pale and her eyes huge.

"That'll be all then. We'll show ourselves out."

As soon as the front door shut, Cody said, "Lexi, get ready. We're going to Reno to see my dad."

She glanced at her grandparents.

"Alph, you and Essie are welcome, too."

"Not me." Alph rubbed his knee. "These old bones hate making that trip anymore."

"Essie?"

Cody knew she wanted to. She glanced from him to Alph and then to Lexi. Finally she shook her head. "I think I'll pass."

"You sure?"

She nodded. "You two run along."

Cody's cell beeped. "Finally. It's my dad. Will you excuse me?" He walked out the back door and onto the deck.

After filling in his dad on the situation, they set up a time to meet for lunch. While Lexi got ready, he ran to the firehouse and grabbed copies of the reports they had regarding the three grass fires.

He and Lexi arrived at Bertha Miranda's Mexican Restaurant & Cantina a little early. "My family used to come here every Sunday after church during my growing-up years. People stand in line early just so they don't have to wait for a seat later." He opened her car door.

"You have a lot of nice family memories, don't you?" Some of Lexi's color had returned.

He held open the heavy wooden door for her to enter. "I do. I have a nice family. I look forward to you meeting them sometime."

"Me, too," Lexi responded.

Cody's expression was warm and his eyes tender. Just the way he gazed at her made her feel special—even if they were only friends.

"May I help you?" a proper Hispanic gentleman asked.

"Table for three. A booth if you have it." They had arrived a little after the typical lunch crowd, so the place was no longer jam-packed.

The tall, thin man led them to a booth.

Cody pointed at a portrait as they trailed behind the older man. "That's Bertha Miranda," he whispered.

Lexi slid onto the vinyl-covered seat, and Cody slipped in next to her. His closeness wreaked havoc with her senses. Sometimes she longed to lay her head on his shoulder or have him hold her again.

A nice-looking man with graying sideburns slipped into the seat directly across from them. "Son, it's good to see you. And you must be Lexi." He offered his right hand.

"Lexi, this is my dad, Police Chief Frank Cooper. Dad, this is Alexandria Eastridge, aka Lexi."

They greeted one another. Lexi couldn't help but think that the son would be just as distinguished looking one day as his father was today. *He'll make some lucky girl a fine catch—a fine catch indeed.*

"So, Lexi, is there anybody that you can think of who hates you enough to

283

try and malign your reputation, possibly even pave the way to a jail sentence?"

He said "jail sentence" so calmly, so matter-of-factly, but those same words made her want to cry out in terror. "Not that I can think of."

Their waiter came with water and then took their orders. Lexi wasn't hungry but ordered some soup just to be polite.

"Nobody, huh? Possibly another model whom you replaced?"

Lexi thought, but no one came to mind.

Chief Cooper rattled off an entire list of possibilities, but none of them jibed with Lexi.

"I just can't imagine anyone doing this to me or anybody else." She shook her head.

"Sadly, I see this sort of thing all the time. Revenge sounds sweet, though I don't think in reality it ever is." Chief Cooper looked over the notes Cody handed him.

"Here's what I'm thinking: You spend the next few days with a constant companion. Go nowhere without this person, not even the bathroom. Then if your nemesis strikes, everyone will know it's a hate crime."

Lexi didn't say anything, but for an introvert like her, the idea of someone being glued to her hip sounded daunting. *But better than jail.*

"I want you to start making lists of every person you perturbed in any way. Cover every event from junior high on. Based on my experience, I'm certain someone wants revenge. I've seen it too many times, and the pattern is always the same."

"So can they arrest her at this point?" Cody questioned.

Chief Cooper shrugged and leaned out of the way while the waiter set a steaming plate of enchiladas in front of him. "Depends on how confident the DA is that he can make the charges stick. I know the sheriff of Douglas County pretty well. I did him a favor a few years back. Let's head over to Stateline after lunch and meet with him."

Cody bit into one of his ground beef tacos. "That would be great, Dad. Thanks." He smiled at Lexi and squeezed her hand under the table.

Lexi dipped a spoon into the tortilla soup. This whole ordeal felt surreal. "Thank you, sir."

To think several weeks ago she'd perceived Cody as an enemy. Now he'd become her hero and her friend. How grateful she felt to him and his dad.

∞

After lunch Cody held his Jeep door open for Lexi. She'd been quiet through their meal, only speaking when spoken to. The stress of this ordeal was taking its toll.

He longed to draw her into his arms and hold her, reassure her, but he stood back while she climbed in. When she was settled in his passenger seat, he ached to kiss her and promise her this would all be okay. But would it? He wished he knew. God seemed slow in answering prayers where Lexi was concerned.

He shut her door, making his way around to the driver's side of the vehicle. He paused before turning the key, searching for words of wisdom or encouragement, but none came.

Finally he turned the ignition, and the engine growled to life. Shifting into reverse, they started the trek back to Stateline.

"We should have had my dad come to us. Guess I wasn't thinking."

His hand rested on the gearshift knob, and she laid hers on top of his. "Thank you—for everything."

He turned his hand over, and hers slipped into his like it belonged there. "You're welcome."

They drove in silence with his hand holding hers and his heart wanting so much more.

When they pulled into the parking lot of the sheriff's office, his dad rolled in right behind them. Cody and Lexi each took a chair in the waiting area while his dad spoke to a woman at the desk. Moments later the sheriff stepped out from behind a closed door. Cody recognized him from his election poster. He held out his right hand, a grin splitting his chubby face. "Frank Cooper!" They shook hands. "Come on back to my office." He motioned with his head toward the door he'd just come through. A moment later, both men vanished behind the locked door.

"Why does your dad believe me?" Lexi asked. "I mean, he doesn't even know me. For that matter, why are you so sure I'm innocent?"

"The Lord. Discernment. Your character. I'm not sure how I know, but without a doubt, I do."

"Cody, Lexi." His dad stood holding the door open, motioning for them to follow. They both jumped up. Cody paused for Lexi to go first. When her gaze met his, fear radiated from her large blue eyes. He smiled, hoping to reassure her.

"George Howard, this is Alexandria Eastridge."

He held out his right hand and shook Lexi's. Cody noted the recognition in the sheriff's eyes. He must have seen one of her commercials.

"And this is my son, Cody Cooper. He's a firefighter down at three in Zephyr Cove."

"Cody." The man had a firm grip as he shook Cody's hand. "Have a seat, everyone."

Sheriff Howard settled in a chair on his side of the desk.

"Chief Cooper has filled me in on the fact that you're a celebrity. I'd only heard that you were somebody's granddaughter. I agree with the chief; this is probably some type of revenge or hate crime."

∞

Lexi closed her eyes, a tiny ray of hope illuminating her situation. "Thank you." The words were a mere whisper.

"Because of Chief Cooper and his position in our state, we will grant you a privilege not afforded to just anyone."

Lexi nodded. *Another rescue by the Cooper family.*

"Based on our assessment of the situation and the sheriff's wise advice, we are encouraging you to come back to Reno with my wife and me for a few days." Chief Cooper glanced from her to Cody. "We'll see if the fires continue in your absence."

Lexi didn't want to leave her grandparents' place to stay with perfect strangers. She glanced at Cody. He reached for her hand and gave it a reassuring squeeze.

"Maybe Cody can smuggle you out in the middle of the night so no one sees you leaving."

"I'm headed to Reno for the weekend anyway." Cody turned his gaze on her. "My brother is getting married this weekend. You can go as my plus one."

"Great idea." Chief Cooper rose and shook the sheriff's hand. "Thanks for working with us on this. Call me when the next fire happens, or I'll call you when we're smuggling her back up the mountain."

"Sounds good." The sheriff shook each of their hands. "We'll do what we can on this end."

Cody ushered Lexi out the door with a guiding hand on her back. They stopped in the lobby. "Bring her down about three or four, and Lexi, I'd lay across the backseat until you turn toward Carson City on Highway 50. We don't want anyone other than your grandparents aware of this. They need to be discreet. If anyone asks, you're home with the flu."

Lexi nodded.

Chief Cooper gave Cody a hug. "See you tomorrow then. Your mom will have the guest room ready for Lexi. Just show her to it whenever you arrive. We probably won't be up to greet you."

"Sure. We'll see you later in the morning."

Chief Cooper took Lexi's right hand and held it between his hands. "It was good to meet you, Lexi. I'm sorry it has to be under these circumstances, but I'm glad you'll be joining us for Brady and Kendall's wedding. Sleep as late as you like tomorrow, and we'll have a pot of coffee on when you wake up."

"Thank you—for everything."

"My pleasure."

All three exited the building. Cody opened the passenger door of his Jeep and waited while Lexi climbed in and got settled.

Her mind was reeling. What had become a permanent knot resided in her stomach. She just wanted to return to LA, but now she wasn't allowed to leave Nevada. This all felt surreal—Oz-like—as if she'd tripped and fallen into someone else's life.

Cody opening her door surprised her, and she jumped. She'd not realized they'd arrived back at her grandparents'.

As she slid out of the Jeep, Cody pulled her into his arms. He hugged her tight, saying nothing—just holding her.

Lexi wanted to relax in his embrace and give herself over to his affections. But she was much too fragile to handle his tenderness without falling apart, so she remained stiff in his embrace, stepping out of it as soon as he loosened his hold.

She saw the hurt and confusion written across his face. He'd only offered the solace of a friend, and she'd rejected it.

"I just need to get this over with."

He nodded and placed his hand across her back, propelling her forward.

∞

Cody longed to comfort Lexi, but when he'd tried, she'd remained cold and distant. The strain of all this was showing on her face.

He followed her inside, and she settled on the end of the couch, closest to her grandfather's chair. Cody sat on the other end.

"I need to talk to you guys."

Alph picked up the remote and clicked the television off.

Lexi filled them in on all that had transpired.

Essie folded down the footrest on her recliner with force and jumped up out of her chair. "This is not right! You shouldn't have to leave when you haven't done anything." She got teary. "You've only been here a month and promised me the spring and maybe even summer."

Lexi rose and hugged her grandmother. "I'll be back." Her voice cracked with fresh emotion.

"I've heard that before."

Lexi glanced at Cody, as if to say, "What do I do now?"

Cody, too, rose and joined the huddle, taking Essie by the upper arms and turning her to face him. "This isn't Lexi's fault. Do you think she wants to leave you and stay with my family? No, she doesn't, but we are trying to keep her safe. Will you let my dad and me do that?"

Essie sucked in a deep breath. She pulled her lips together in a tight line, and Cody spotted the tears pooling in her eyes. She nodded her head. Cody pulled her into his arms. He'd grown to love her like his own grandmother.

She hugged Cody back—a much better hug than he'd gotten from Lexi. He heard a sniffle, and her body quivered. "It'll be all right."

She pulled back and gazed into his eyes, nodding her tear-streaked face. Then she grabbed Lexi's hand. "You do whatever you have to do. Gramps and I will be here waiting for you to come back." Then her tears fell harder, faster. "Excuse me." She pulled loose from Cody's light hold and left the room.

Lexi wiped at her eyes. "This is about more than me leaving now, isn't it? It's about all the years I never came." She turned toward her grandfather. "It's about the years of neglect."

He nodded.

"I'm sorry, Gramps. So very sorry. It wasn't because I didn't want to be here. I never wanted to hurt you."

She went to his chair and hugged him for several minutes.

"I love you, my Lexi girl." Even Alph's eyes seemed a little shiny to Cody. "And I forgive you. Why don't you go tell your gram what you just told me?"

"I will."

∞

Cody gave Lexi an encouraging smile as she passed him on her way to Gram's bedroom. She longed to cash in on the hug he'd offered earlier, but she didn't let herself. Whenever Cody's chocolate eyes rested on her, her heart melted in response.

Lexi found Gram in her bathroom, reapplying her powder. "May I come in?"

Gram nodded her head.

"Just now, those tears were about more than me leaving, weren't they?" Lexi settled on the edge of the tub.

Gram made eye contact through the mirror. "I'm hurt that you stayed away so long." Gram blinked fast and furious.

Lexi hung her head, fighting her own tears. How much did she dare say?

She raised her gaze back to the mirror. "I'm sorry. I honestly never meant to hurt or abandon either of you."

Gram turned to face her. "I know that, but you did. We got the token Sunday phone call, but you never had time for us. Your friends and your life in LA were obviously more important than your relationship with us."

"Gram, that's not true." Lexi rose, and mere inches separated them.

"A picture is worth a thousand words. And the picture you painted was that we weren't worth the effort."

Lexi felt like a waterfall rolled over her cheeks from the river of her eyes. "I do understand why you would make that assumption, but there was no place I wanted to be more than here. I just couldn't face you."

Gram wrapped Lexi in her embrace. "What in the world are you talking about—you couldn't face us?"

Without being too graphic, Lexi became real with her grandmother. She shared pieces of her life story, bits of her shame, and boatloads of her personal sorrow. They cried together, baptizing the other with their tears. The end result was sweet, bringing healing, forgiveness, and hope for a renewed closeness in the future. Lexi left the bathroom both exhausted and exhilarated.

Cody had long since gone home. Lexi shared a sweet dinner with her grandparents and a tender good-bye scene that evening before they went to bed, promising never to let miles keep them apart for long ever again.

Chapter 8

At three in the morning, Cody crept across the street. Darkness blanketed him. The entire neighborhood was black, and no sign of life appeared. He tapped once on the French door leading to her little private patio. She opened it, motioning him inside. Her bed was made, and atop it sat a large duffel bag and a smaller bag.

"Is that it?" he whispered, pointing to the two pieces of luggage.

"I packed light. Those are my grandparents'." He lifted the large tote over his shoulder and picked up the second bag.

Lexi grabbed her large leather purse, which was almost big enough to count as luggage. He paused at the door, holding it open for her. She led the way into the blackness. He locked and shut the door, following close behind Lexi. She climbed into the backseat of his Jeep while he put her luggage into the very back.

Cody started his car and pulled out of the driveway. He followed Highway 50 to Highway 28. A few minutes later, he announced to Lexi that they'd turned off toward Reno. She sat up.

After a few more minutes, she asked, "Are you sure your parents don't mind me staying there?"

"Not at all. My brother Brady brought home all kinds of strays. I figure it's my turn," he joked, hoping to lighten her mood.

"Strays?"

"Dogs, cats, and kids."

Lexi remained quiet the rest of the ride. Cody had no idea how to ease her anxiety, so he said nothing—just shot up a little prayer for God's peace to permeate.

∞

Cody turned into a neighborhood. The sign said COUGHLIN RANCH. From what Lexi could see, everything was well manicured with grass, flowers, and trees. After a couple of turns, he pulled to a stop at the end of a cul-de-sac. He unloaded her luggage then led her up the sidewalk to the front porch. He laid down her things and fished through the keys on his ring for the right one. Finally he unlocked the door and pushed it open, standing aside for her to enter first. The front door led into a great room. A lamp had been left on, so Lexi could see enough to know Mrs. Cooper had good taste. She liked clean lines without a lot of clutter. The overall effect was warm and welcoming.

Cody led Lexi down the hall, stopping at the second door on the right. He flipped a light switch and laid her things on a chest at the foot of her bed. The bedroom was feminine but not frilly. The brown and pink held great eye appeal.

"The bathroom is across the hall. Knowing my mom, she'll have fresh towels laid out, but I'll double-check." He dashed across the hall. "Yep, you're all taken care of. Do you need anything?"

Lexi shook her head. She'd stopped just inside the door, wishing Cody didn't have to leave, wishing she wasn't in this mess, wishing for a million things that would never happen.

She glanced at Cody. He hovered in the doorway, leaning against the jamb. His eyes reflected her weariness. "Are you driving back home?"

"No. I'll be right down the hall. I'll stay through the weekend and all the wedding activities." His whiskers shadowed his jaw and chin.

"I don't have to attend all the wedding festivities. I mean, I don't even know the couple. It could be awkward."

"I want you to." When she didn't respond, he asked, "Please? I thought about inviting you anyway but just never did."

Their gazes fused, and Lexi felt the connection. Her heart shifted to the next gear. Cody must have felt it as well. He moved toward her—slow, intentional.

She should turn away, step in the opposite direction, but her feet wouldn't respond. They held her in place as if she had cement in her shoes.

Their gazes never separated. Cody slipped his hand around her neck. His head moved toward her in what felt like slow motion. She swallowed. He placed his other hand on the back of her waist, gently pulling her toward him. She complied, and he wrapped her in his arms, folding her against him in a protective hug. His lips met hers, and Lexi knew for certain, at that exact moment, that she'd fallen deeply in love with Cody Cooper.

The kiss was slow, tender, undemanding. The sweetness of it left her wanting more.

When he lifted his mouth from hers, he didn't loosen his hold. Lexi felt dazed by the wonder of his kiss, and she saw the same emotions swimming in Cody's eyes.

He drank in her face with his eyes, making her feel slightly embarrassed. Would he see the flaws and imperfections?

He lowered his head back to her lips, and Lexi anticipated his touch. He took more time with his second kiss, leaving Lexi feeling light-headed.

"I'd better go." He gently pushed Lexi away from himself.

His abrupt change left Lexi questioning his thoughts. She ducked her head so he couldn't see her disappointment and turned away from him, wrapping her arms around her waist.

He turned her back around to face him, his hands on her shoulders, keeping her at arm's length. He gently raised her chin until their eyes met, and he returned his hand to her shoulder.

"I don't want to leave, Lexi, but I have to. I'd never use or take advantage of you, and for that not to happen, I have to set firm boundaries for myself."

His words poured over her broken soul like a healing balm.

"I'm on vacation for the wedding, so I'll see you in the morning. . .and the morning after that and the morning after that. I'm not going anywhere."

This man knew how to connect with her heart on every level and leave her speechless at the same time.

He kissed the top of her head. "Sleep tight." He slipped into the dark hall, closing the door as he left.

Lexi fell across the bed, hugging a pillow against her. Yep, no more doubts or uncertainty. She loved Cody. Many delicious emotions swirled around her as she relived the last five minutes over and over. She fell asleep on top of the comforter, still in her clothes but with a smile on her face.

∞

When Lexi came out into the great room a few hours later, she refused to meet Cody's gaze head-on. He'd barely slept and couldn't wait to see her again. She, however, must be feeling shy or uncertain about the whole incident.

"You hungry?"

"More in need of caffeine." She moved toward the kitchen. "Do you mind if I help myself?"

"Not at all. My parents want you to make yourself at home here." He trailed her to the pot, standing nearby.

"You want a cup?" she asked.

He shook his head. She finished pouring and added some cream. When she turned, she nearly ran into him. He grabbed her cup and steadied it.

"Did you need something?"

He set her cup on the counter and lifted her chin until she finally made eye contact.

"That's better."

A puzzled expression furrowed her brow. Then he kissed her soundly on the mouth. "Just so you know: I'm not a guy who toys with women's emotions, nor am I a guy who kisses every pretty girl I meet. I kissed you last night because you mean something to me."

Lexi stared at the floor. He lifted her chin again. "Caring for someone and sharing affection isn't anything to be embarrassed about."

A tiny smile settled on her mouth. "This is all new to me—not the kissing but the caring."

"So, are you saying you care?" he teased.

"I don't know what I'm saying." She turned to grab her cup.

"Well, here is what I'm saying." He pulled her back around again before she could pick up the mug. "I think you're pretty wonderful."

She smiled. " 'Pretty wonderful.' I like that."

Her smile always caused him to catch his breath. Lexi was in a league of her own. "I wouldn't kiss you unless I thought this thing had places to go."

"What do you mean?" Her brows drew together.

"A future—you and me. I'm way too old for recreational dating and haven't participated in recreational kissing since college."

Lexi looked panicked.

"Don't worry, I'm not asking you to marry me—yet. But one day, I just might." He handed her the cup she'd poured a few minutes ago. "There is some French toast and bacon warming in the oven. If that sounds too heavy, there's yogurt, granola, or stuff to make a smoothie."

∞

Lexi's head spun. No man had ever considered her marriage material before, and the fact that Cody did touched her heart deeper than he'd ever know. But was she? She'd never let her thoughts go that direction. What did she want from the rest of life, now that the modeling had ended?

"Lexi?"

"Huh?"

"You still here with me?" Cody had stuck his face near hers.

"Yeah, sorry." She carried her coffee over to the bar and perched on a stool. "What were you asking?"

"Breakfast? What's your pleasure?"

Out of habit, Lexi almost passed on food, using coffee to take the edge off her hunger until lunch. But her stomach growled. "I think I'll have the French toast. I'm living wild today. Hey, where are your parents?"

"They are both at work."

"So when will we meet?" The later the better, as far as she was concerned.

"Tomorrow at the wedding. You'll meet the whole fam."

His announcement caused Lexi's stomach to drop. "Do any of them read the tabloids?"

Cody wrapped her in his arms. "Doesn't matter if they do, because you are a new creation in Christ—forgiven, washed anew, and loved." Cody kissed her cheek. "Loved, Lexi—more than you can ever understand." His voice had grown husky, and she was pretty sure he meant by more than just the Lord. The mere thought brought a lump to her throat.

I love you, too. Her heart spilled over with tender feelings and gratitude. Maybe she really was a new person and really did have a new life just around the corner. *But not until tomorrow. Not until all this mess is cleared up.*

Lexi felt gorgeous when she waltzed into the great room the following afternoon. Cody's eyes told her all she needed to know. No one else had to think so, but she wanted him to be proud of her.

He rose and met her. "Whoa, baby, you clean up nice." He took her hand and spun her around like they were dancing.

He'd really not seen her in much besides hiking boots and T-shirts. Today she took extra care with her hair and makeup, and she'd donned a gold halter dress—simple yet elegant and modest—hoping to make a good first impression on his family. She'd opted not to attend the rehearsal dinner with Cody last night since Frank had advised her to keep a low profile while here in Reno. They didn't want word to leak that she'd left Stateline. Cody's dad felt the wedding was private enough, but she couldn't deny her nervous feelings about meeting the rest of Cody's clan.

"The bride doesn't stand a chance of being the most gorgeous woman at the wedding." Cody drew her arm through his elbow and led her to the car.

"Guess where the rehearsal dinner was," he said as she settled into his Jeep.

"That restaurant where I met your dad?"

"Yep, Bertha Miranda's. I told you it's the family fave. No wedding would be complete without a little of Bertha's cooking. Both Frankie and Delanie had their rehearsal dinners there, and now Brady. And someday maybe. . ." Cody sent a meaningful glance in her direction. Her heart warmed to the idea.

She opted for a safer subject. "Remind me again who's who."

Cody backed out of the driveway. "There are four of us. Frankie, or Frank Jr., is the oldest. He is married to Sunni, and they have two kids—"

"Summer and Mason."

"Good memory." He stopped at the stop sign and looked both ways. "They are four and six. Brady, the second child, is marrying Kendall today. Her parents are missionaries in Mexico."

Lexi felt intimidated by that. Missionaries gave up everything for others. They were the antithesis of Lexi's family.

"I'm number three, and after tonight will be the only single sibling. The baby and only girl is Delanie. She and her husband, Eli, are both cops and the proud parents of Camden—a baby boy born earlier this year."

"Sounds like a nice family." *Nice and too perfect for the likes of me.*

Lexi had wished a million times for brothers and sisters. Instead, she had nannies and a lonely life except for her wonderful summers with Gram and Gramps.

∞

Once they arrived at the designated wedding spot, Cody made some quick introductions to those who were around—Frankie, Sunni, and Eli. He left Lexi in the shade of a tree talking with Sunni. As the best man, he had obligations to fulfill, but at the reception, other than the toast, he'd be a free man. Free to spend time with the woman he loved.

When he and Brady drove up on the golf cart after pictures had finished, he spotted her immediately. His gut curled at the sight of her. She was beautiful with her hair pulled up, leaving her long ivory neck exposed.

As he approached, their gazes locked. She smiled.

"Hey." He kissed her cheek. "Have you been okay?"

"Fine. You look good in that penguin suit."

He spun around so she could get the full effect. Lexi laughed. "May I seat you, mademoiselle?" He held his arm out, and she linked hers through. Frankie and Eli had already begun seating the early arrivers.

He led her down a grassy knoll. White chairs had been lined up facing a small lake. The weather was perfect, and the setting couldn't have been prettier, green grass in every direction with flowers and trees to accentuate the beauty. An occasional jogger ran past on a nearby path. He guided Lexi all the way to the second row on the groom's side. Sunni, Frankie's wife, was already seated there, and she scooted over one chair.

"I'll see you after." He placed another light kiss on her cheek.

Each time Cody ushered someone to a seat, his gaze was drawn to Lexi. She was, by far, the most beautiful woman at the wedding, and she was there with him!

Finally it was time for the ceremony to begin. Brady took his place next to the minister. The music changed. Frankie walked their grandmother down the aisle. Now it was Cody's turn to walk their mom down the aisle. Then Eli led Kendall's mom to her place in the front row.

Cody took his place at Brady's side. Frankie and Eli sat in the front row next to his parents.

Cody's eyes rested on Lexi. She smiled. In his heart grew tender shoots of love. She was it. He didn't know the whens or hows, but he knew—she was the one. Reflected in her expression was the same wonder he experienced.

∞

Lexi took in every detail of the wedding. There was no glitz but a sweet serenity. As she tried to imagine her parents at such an event, she knew the simplicity would appall them, but honestly, if her day ever came, this couldn't be more perfect. She'd been to a few big celebrity weddings but nothing like this. There were only sixty or so people—all close friends and family. No one on the A-list showed up, no who's who among great American people, but it was precious nonetheless.

After Summer and Mason, Delanie walked down the aisle. She wore a brown dress trimmed in pink. Sunni whispered to Lexi that, sadly, Kendall's lifelong friend was ready to deliver a baby any day now and was unable to make the ceremony. A flutist began to play a classical song. Mrs. Brooks, the bride's mother, stood. The crowd followed suit.

Kendall, on the arm of her father, started down the mound toward her guests gathered at the end of the walk. A lump gathered in Lexi's throat. She wasn't even sure why.

Kendall was beautiful in her white gown. Her dad looked proud. Lexi turned to watch Brady. Love poured out of his expression. A tear rolled down Lexi's cheek. She blinked, not wanting to create a train wreck with her makeup. Cody seemed more than willing to love her like that, but she wasn't worthy of such a nice guy. How disappointed his parents would be if they knew the truth about her.

When Kendall reached the end of the aisle, Brady stepped out to meet her. The minister asked who gave this woman, and her dad said, "Her mother and I do." He then raised the sheer veil, kissing her cheek.

Another tear escaped, and Lexi wiped it away.

Kendall's father placed her hand in Brady's and squeezed Brady's shoulder as he moved toward his seat beside his wife in the front row.

Lexi's lips quivered. Her family was so broken. Her dad would never willingly hand her over to a firefighter from Tahoe. He really didn't care if Lexi married or not, but if she did, he hoped for a power marriage to a man in the entertainment industry.

Lexi shifted her attention back to the pastor and his message. "It's much easier to fall in love than to stay in love. Staying in love requires strategy, commitment, and endurance." He paused, his eyes scanning the audience. Lexi would have sworn they settled on her.

"The strategy is loving each other in daily living, in the small stuff as well as the big. Kendall and Brady, if you don't have a plan and work at it, you will end up in a rut and possibly even with a love that's grown cold. Loving well requires making each other's needs a high priority. It means figuring out how the other feels valued. Strategically keep your marriage above all else in this life—work, kids, friends, hobbies. Keep God on the throne and marriage right under Him. If you live out this strategy, your marriage will be a great source of comfort, joy, and peace.

"Commitment is more than resignation to stick this out until the end because marriage is until death. Commitment is the other side of the same coin, determining this is for life and then making the relationship the best it can be—for the Lord and His glory, for each other, and for the peace that type of commitment brings.

"Last but not least is endurance. This is not a sprint but a long haul. The Bible speaks of love enduring all things, and that is certainly a part of it. Endurance means dealing with sickness, hardship, a job loss, economic crisis—the list goes on. Endurance takes the race one step and one day at a time, always moving toward the long-term goal of survival and finishing the race set before you. But do more than finish—finish well. Finish with victory. Finish with joy. Finish with a flourish."

Lexi pondered the pastor's words while he went on with the wedding vows. *Where do I go from here? I had one goal, to model, and that has ended.* She felt purposeless, but a part of her was also relieved. Definitely a part of her was ready to move on, but to what?

She refocused as Brady recited his vows with a deep, confident voice. "When I found the one my heart loves, I held her and would not let her go. Kendall, I will hold you through good times and bad. I will not let you go whether we are rich or poor, sick or well. I will cherish you and honor you all the days of my life."

The tender words intensified the ache in Lexi's heart. She glanced at Cody, and his eyes were on her. She couldn't deny that she wanted him to be part of the long-range plan, a part of her tomorrow. But with this whole arson thing hanging over her head, did she even have a tomorrow? Fear knotted her stomach. This might turn out worse than anyone anticipated.

Chapter 9

As the wedding party exited, Cody winked at her. He affected her in gentle ways she'd never experienced. The parents followed the bridal party, and then Lexi's row exited.

Cody grabbed her by the elbow as soon as she stepped off the grassy area and onto the pavement of the parking lot. He grabbed Sunni with his other hand. "The wedding party still has a photo shoot. Since Lexi knows no one, would you mind if she hangs with you until we get done? Maybe she can ride with you to the clubhouse where the reception will be held."

"Of course."

Lexi and Sunni spent some time talking during the short drive. She was quite interested in Lexi's life of fame and fortune, wanting to hear all about whom she knew, where she'd been, and why in the world she was at a small-town event in Reno.

"I've been to a few Hollywood weddings, and not one compares to this."

Sunni rolled her eyes. "Please don't tell me they got to you, too."

"What are you talking about?" Lexi couldn't follow her train of thought.

"The holy Coopers." Sunni raised her brow and cocked her head, daring Lexi to deny it.

Lexi felt offended for the family. "They don't seem that way to me. Don't you think they are genuine?"

"I suppose they are genuine enough. I just don't think like they do. Don't get me wrong, I'm a Christian, too. I just don't eat, breathe, and sleep God."

Sunni parked her Impala in front of the clubhouse. They were among the first to arrive. As they walked to the open-air ramada where the reception was set, Lexi continued. "I don't either, but I'm trying to learn. I've done it the other way, and believe me, I've made a bigger mess out of my life than you could ever imagine. I guess you could say one of my biggest regrets is leaving God in my childhood along with pigtails and missing teeth." An ache of remorse filled her heart.

"Why? You've had a great life." Sunni seemed dumbfounded by Lexi's statement. They studied the seating chart and found their assigned seats.

"I have had a great life—by the world's standard. I've had many privileges few are afforded. But you know what I missed? The joy, the peace, the contentment." Her vision blurred slightly. "It's an empty world. You have no idea how lucky you are. A husband who loves you. Two great kids. A family to lean on."

Just then Frankie arrived with Cody.

"Pictures over already?" Lexi asked.

"A few family poses left, so we are going to steal Sunni. Be right back." Cody kissed Lexi's cheek, and the sound of a camera clicked somewhere off in the distance.

The reception was fun. After a nice dinner, Cody introduced Lexi to every guest. They did a couple of line dances and the Funky Chicken. Lexi had a great time and even forgot the trouble hanging over her head.

Dusk was settling, and little tiki lamps were lit. Cody led her to the edge of the dance floor for their first slow dance. He pulled her close, and she draped an arm on his shoulder. Several flashes went off from somewhere beyond the ramada.

"Are you enjoying yourself?" Cody asked as he began a slow two-step.

"Very much. It's the best wedding I've ever attended."

He missed a step, and she almost got his toes. "Really?"

"You sound shocked."

"I am. I thought it might seem rather plain to you. I mean, after all, you've attended some pretty glitzy events."

Lexi laughed. "You sound like your sister-in-law. Most of those events were exciting, even glamorous, but I left feeling empty at the end of the night."

"I'm glad you don't feel that way tonight." With both hands on her back, he drew her against him. His feet stopped as his lips found hers.

Dazed, Lexi opened her eyes at the end of the tender moment. Another flash went off in the dusk beyond the dance floor.

"How many photographers did they hire anyway?"

Cody shrugged. "I think just one and an assistant."

"Seems every time I turn around there are lights flashing." Reality hit Lexi with brute force. "How could I be so stupid?"

"What are you talking about?" Cody's brows drew together.

"The paparazzi. They're here."

Cody glanced around. "I don't see anything."

She hugged him close and whispered near his ear. "Walk with me and act normal."

Taking his hand in hers, she led him off into the darkness just beyond the ramada. *How did they find me?* She didn't know who she was madder at—them for showing up or herself for letting her guard down. She was very camera conscious in LA, but she didn't think she'd need to be in Reno. Once she'd left modeling behind and told no one of her destination, she'd foolishly assumed she was no longer a walking target.

∞

Cody's senses were alert, but he neither heard nor saw anything. She stopped near the edge of the darkness. "Kiss me more, Cody. I've waited all night." She held up a hand, indicating he shouldn't move.

Then she let out a little groan. Flashes lit up the darkness like fireworks on the Fourth. Cody ran toward the closest—only twenty feet or so away behind some bushes. He grabbed the scoundrel by the throat. "What do you think you're doing?"

"Earning a living, buddy."

Cody grabbed his camera.

"Hey, that's mine." The guy tried to grab it back.

Cody yanked and overpowered the guy. "Not anymore." He tossed the camera to Lexi. "Get the memory chip out."

"Won't do you any good. There were three of us out here. You're only getting a third of what we took."

Cody shook the guy. "You scoundrel. You have no right." He longed to punch him square in the face.

"I have as much right as you to earn a living."

Lexi shoved his camera at him. "Not exploiting people's lives, you don't."

Cody grabbed the camera. "Call your friends back over here. You want your equipment back? We need their memory chips, too. We'll erase them and mail them back to you."

"Look, man. They're not coming back."

Cody yanked the guy's cell phone off his belt. "Call them. This is my brother's wedding, and you have no right to take advantage of it."

"We don't care about your brother." He punched in a number. "We're here for her." He pointed at Lexi. "Yeah, dude, they want your memory chips. They're holding my camera hostage."

He paused. Laughed. "Cool. Thanks. I owe you. They'll be right here with the ransom."

Two other young punks showed up in a matter of minutes. Each handed Cody a memory chip. Suspicious, he decided to check them out and make sure they held the pictures of the wedding. He slipped each one into the camera that he still held in his possession. "Yep, sure enough—these are it."

"I'm hurt, man. You don't trust us," the guy with the spiked hair stated in a deadpan voice.

"Give me an address, and I'll ship these back to you."

"Don't bother, man. Keep them as a souvenir of the time you almost made the tabloids. Some would consider that an honor."

"An honor?" Lexi laughed. "Hardly."

"So what's up with you anyway?" The second guy who came back questioned Lexi. "You trading in the LA scene for this dude?"

"My life is none of your business." Lexi glared at him.

"I think it's time you guys hightail it out of here." Cody eyed each of them. "And don't come back. Not tonight, not ever."

They all looked at each other and shrugged. "Guess we're uninvited." Then he looked directly at Cody. "My camera?"

Cody handed it over.

They all walked out into the darkness.

"Cody, I'm so sorry. I had no idea. I feel terrible. No wonder your dad advised me to keep a low profile here in Reno."

He took her hand, and they walked back to the reception. "Hey, it's over. At least we weren't blindsided at the checkout counter with us on the cover. That's why my dad insisted you miss the rehearsal dinner. He hoped the wedding would be a more private affair with less chance of exposure, but thankfully, no one ever has to know. The near darkness and loud music left everyone unaware." He glanced over the unsuspecting crowd. "And I'm glad he agreed you could be my date tonight." He kissed her cheek.

"Me, too, but I'm sure you know that whole paparazzi thing has happened to me before—more than once. And not only do they twist the truth, but the worse they can make a person sound, the happier they are."

Cody guided Lexi back to their table. He held out the chair, and she tucked her dress neatly under her and settled in. "Well, you've gotten to know my family over the last few hours. What do you think?"

"They are all very nice."

"I think I hear a 'but' in there somewhere. Very nice, but. . ."

Lexi squirmed under his scrutiny. She seemed to consider her words with care. "I just can't help but wonder what they think of me. I mean, they are all warm and kind, but they must be questioning what a nice guy like you is doing with a girl like me."

"A girl like you. . ." He ran his gaze over her. "A girl who is beautiful. A girl who is sweet. A girl who makes me glad to be alive." He placed his index finger under her chin, lifting her head, and placed a quick kiss on her mouth. "Yeah. They must think I'm crazy. Not much about you to admire. Not much at all."

Lexi's face grew serious. "You know what I mean. I come with all kinds of baggage, very public baggage. And to top that, I come with men stalking me, and by association your family, with cameras."

"Lexi, they'll grow to love you, just as I have, and none of it will matter."

Love me? You love me? He was still talking, but she had no idea what he was saying. She hadn't gotten past the fact that he said he loved her. He loved her! Wow! No man had ever said he loved her before. Cody said it so casually, so matter-of-fact that maybe he didn't mean it the way she was taking it. She was making too big a deal out of words spoken without fanfare.

"Excuse me." One of the waitresses tapped Lexi on the shoulder. "A guy with spiked hair who said he was your personal photographer asked me to give you this." She held out an envelope.

Lexi's stomach dropped to her shoes. With dread she reached out and accepted the offering. "Thank you."

Cody watched her with curiosity as she tore open the plain white square, pulling out a folded paper from inside. With trepidation she unfolded the note and laid it in front of her. She squinted to read the scribble in such dim light. *Sucker, we'd already downloaded two of the three memory chips. See you around— literally. At every supermarket in the country.* Lexi closed her eyes and sighed.

Cody grabbed the note. "That creep. I'd like to beat the snot right out of him."

Boy, did Lexi understand that sentiment. "Still think your family will *love me*?"

"I won't lie to you—this will upset them, but it's not your fault. They won't hold it against you personally."

"Should we go tell them?" Lexi started to rise.

Cody placed his hand on hers. "Let's wait for tomorrow's luncheon."

"Luncheon?"

"Tomorrow my parents are hosting our immediate family along with Kendall's for a lasagna lunch and gift opening."

"Aren't they going on a honeymoon?"

"They are, but since her parents live in Mexico, she wanted them to be part of the gift opening celebration before they left to go back. Brady and Kendall will leave for Maui the following morning."

Lexi tried to get back into the mood of the festivities, but the articles and implications to come had now overshadowed the joy of the event.

The following morning, Lexi helped Mrs. Cooper get ready for the luncheon. She scrubbed vegetables, chopped a salad, and made some ranch dressing. She was grateful for the time she had spent with Gram in the kitchen. At least she had some skill.

Lexi fought the urge to blurt out the news. Her promise to Cody to let him tell his family was the only thing keeping the news at bay. Lexi wasn't good at waiting. She just wanted things over with.

Cody was staying at Brady's apartment since the place was empty, and he hadn't arrived yet. His mom was easy to be with and talk to, so she didn't mind. Besides, Chief Cooper wanted her to stay through the following weekend. That would be ten days total away from the fire mystery.

She and Cody had called her grandparents several times, but unfortunately and fortunately, no more fires had been set. She knew this only made her appear guiltier. She tried not to think about it to avoid the stress and tension.

"Mom, you're not going to believe this," Frankie said on his way in through the front door.

Lexi spotted a newspaper in one hand and a grocery bag in the other. Her stomach knotted. *Cody, where are you?*

"Pictures of Brady's wedding are in the newspaper this morning."

He sounded excited. Lexi hoped the rest of the family would feel that way. "What?"

"They are really focused more on Lexi than Brady and Kendall." Sunni set another bag on the island next to the one Frankie plopped down. She picked up the paper her husband had just laid down and flipped it open to the local news section. "Here it is."

Mrs. Cooper stopped in the middle of her lasagna prep, wiped her hands, and picked up the paper. Lexi watched as Cody's mom glanced over the article.

"What did it say?" She didn't want to ask but had to.

"Not much." Mrs. Cooper held the paper out to her. "But what it did say wasn't terribly nice."

Lexi accepted the paper. "It never is."

The title was "Saints and a Sinner." Lexi read the caption, guessing where this was headed.

It talked about the fact that yesterday Police Chief Frank Cooper's son married a missionary from Mexico. Then it went on to say that while one son was marrying a saint, the other could be dating a sinner. Lexi laid the paper aside. "I'm sorry."

Mrs. Cooper gave her hand a reassuring squeeze. "Lexi, we are all sinners. There isn't a saint among us, nor is there a reason to be sorry. This isn't your fault."

How did his mom always know just the right thing to say? "Thanks. I appreciate your kind words of encouragement."

His mom smiled. "They aren't just kind words—they are truth."

When Cody arrived, Lexi filled him in. He took his parents aside to let them know this one article in the Reno paper probably wouldn't be the end of it. They both looked concerned, but neither condemned. Each hugged Lexi, reassuring her that they knew she'd put her past behind her and was moving into a solid future with God.

∞

After a weekend packed with wedding activity, Cody prepared to go back down to the mountain Sunday evening. "Can we take a walk before I go?"

"I'd love to." She focused on Mason and Summer who both wanted to start a fourth game of Candy Land. "Guys, I'm going on a walk with your uncle Cody, so you'll have to play without me."

They both protested, but Lexi stood firm in her resolve.

Cody held the door open for her, and she led the way out. "It's pretty out here this evening."

"It is. How are you holding up? You haven't mentioned the whole arson thing since we got here. You doing okay?"

"I'm all right. There's too much activity around your parents' place to think about much."

He nodded his agreement. "How about in the deep of night when there are no distractions?"

"How did you know?"

He pulled her against his side, wrapping his arm around her shoulders. "Your eyes, for one thing. The bags are tattling on you."

She acted incensed. "Don't you know that you never mention a woman's bags?"

"Don't try to change the subject. I know it's hard, but don't worry. I'm confident we'll get to the bottom of this whole thing."

"Lately my mind has been more on the tabloids than the fires." She stopped to sniff a rosebush.

"Mine, too, but it's out of our hands. We just need to move forward and not let it affect us."

"I'll try."

They walked on the trail that led to the lake. He stopped at a bench and pulled her onto his lap. "I'm going to miss you this week." He kissed her cheek near her ear.

"I hate to admit it, but I think I'll miss you, as well."

"Why do you hate to admit it?"

"I try not to get too attached." She ran her index finger over his jaw.

"I'm safe. You can attach to me." He kissed her, and the passion ignited. He stood. "I've got to get going, but know you'll be in my thoughts and prayers this week."

"And you in mine."

When they returned, Cody bid his family good-bye and headed for home. He thought about Lexi the whole drive, a grin plastered to his face. As he pulled into his driveway, he spotted a strange van in front of Alph and Essie's house. There were two men waiting at their front door. The moment Alph swung it open, the camera flashes were blinking.

Cody jumped out of his car and ran across the street. "What do you think you're doing?" He grabbed the guy closest to him by the collar of his shirt.

Chapter 10

Cody jerked the man away from the door. "Get out of here right now! Both of you."

"Hey!" The middle-aged man still standing on the stoop faced Cody. "We're here for the story. Came to see if the grandparents or the boyfriend have a comment on the arson situation. Rumor has it they stopped once Alexandria left the area." The man was cocky, making Cody even angrier. "Comments?" He held out a mic.

"Leave now, or we'll call the police." Cody ground out each word.

"Your choice." The guy shrugged and strutted off. The other man—the one Cody had manhandled—had already climbed into the vehicle, but the cocky guy turned back before he entered the van. "I find a lot of irony that a pyromaniac is dating a fireman."

Essie clutched Cody's arm. "Don't give him the satisfaction. He isn't worth going to jail over."

Cody let out a long, slow breath, releasing some of his pent-up frustration. "You're right. I know you are. Are you two okay?"

"We're fine. Come in and tell us what in the world is going on. We saw some scenes from your brother's wedding on some entertainment show that gossips about the celebrities. They said some awful things about Lexi."

Cody hugged Essie. "I'm sorry, but you know their job is to create sensationalism, not tell the truth."

"Alph and I are worried that the fires stopped when Lexi left. Does that mean we are being watched day and night?"

"I don't know what it means, but you're right—it doesn't look good for Lexi. And now this." Cody let out another long sigh. "How am I going to break the latest news to her? You know it's only a matter of time before she'll hear the implications."

"She sounded worn out when I talked to her earlier today. How is she handling all this?"

Cody shook his head. "It's hard, and now it's going to get that much harder. I need to tell her, and I'd rather do it in person. You guys can pray for wisdom as we walk through this mess."

They both agreed, and the three of them prayed together before Cody headed home. In light of this latest episode, he now planned to head back into Reno tomorrow, which meant finding somebody to cover his shift. He decided to take the whole week off, even though he'd just returned from a three-day hiatus for the wedding. No telling what sort of difficulty they might run into this week as the gossip story broke. Since Lexi was a celebrity, there would be a lot more speculation than if she were a regular joe.

Cody spent the evening doing his laundry, on the phone with his dad, and in prayer. He wanted Lexi to have a really fun day and evening before he dropped this latest bomb.

The following morning, Lexi was home alone at his parents' when he arrived. He found her in the backyard reclining on a chaise lounge and reading a novel she'd borrowed from his mom.

∞

"Hey, beautiful." He held out a bouquet of tulips.

"Cody!" She laid down her book and accepted the flowers. "I thought you were working."

"I decided to take a week off and hang out with you." She studied him a moment, wondering if there was more to it. Then she decided just to take him at face value.

"I thought I'd give you a tour of Reno today. Not nearly as fun as a tour of Lake Tahoe, but it's something to do."

She really didn't care what they did, as long as they did it together. She wavered between feeling crazy about Cody and believing she was not worthy of him. Someday she'd have to settle on one or the other.

She went inside and slipped on a pair of tennis shoes, just in case they did a lot of walking.

"I'm going to give you some choices. Now, don't get too excited. We can go to Fleischmann Planetarium."

She scrunched up her nose. "Anything better than that?"

"Oh, it gets lots better. How about the National Bowling Stadium or the National Automobile Museum?" He raised his brows like he'd just offered her two fabulous choices.

"You're kidding, right?"

"I'm offering you the best of Reno, and you're turning me down?" He acted hurt. "Okay, my last offer is the Sierra Safari Zoo."

"It will do." She gathered up her purse and a sweatshirt and led the way to the door.

After they were in the Jeep and on the road, he said, "I was hoping you'd choose this place. I haven't been there since a school field trip, but it's really cool. It's up Virginia Street—farther north than Brady's apartment, and set at the base of Peavine Mountain."

"These things you people refer to as mountains are not much more than hills."

"Well, they aren't the Swiss Alps, but they're mountains, nonetheless."

"Ya think?" She liked to goad his hometown pride. "You ever been to a real mountain, like Big Bear in Southern California?"

"Heavenly is a real mountain." He gave her his stern look.

"You got me there."

They spent most of the afternoon traipsing through the zoo. Their light-hearted banter felt good after days of heaviness.

"I have to admit, this place far exceeded my expectations."

"May I say I told you so?" He opened the Jeep door for her.

"Seriously, I like the way they have the animals in their own habitats. And not your usual elephants and tigers. So, what now, my gallant chauffeur?"

"Well, I thought we might get a dinner and game night going with Delanie and Eli. Maybe Frankie and Sunni, too. What do you think?"

"Sure, why not?" His family would tolerate her for his sake.

∞

Cody dropped off Lexi at his parents' and ran to Brady's to change, shower, and set the evening's plans into motion. He felt torn, wondering if he should have told Lexi about the upcoming exposé on her activities since leaving LA.

How do you drop a bombshell on someone like that? *Honesty is the best policy.* His dad had said that a million times in their growing-up years. He knew he'd been less than honest with Lexi by not saying anything. He'd withheld information. When they were kids, that was viewed exactly the same as lying—a sin of omission instead of a sin of commission, but still a sin, his parents had assured them.

He and the Lord had a talk during his shower. "I'm sorry. I should have told her. I'll tell her as soon as dinner ends and everyone heads their separate ways. I don't want her to deal with that black cloud during dinner." The guilt pricked. "You're right. I need to tell her ASAP. I'll tell her on the drive over to the restaurant for dinner."

When Cody arrived back at his parents', Eli and Delanie were there. Eli said, "Thought we'd ride over with you."

"Where are we going?" Delanie asked.

"George's."

Delanie rolled her eyes. "You guys did that on purpose so you could watch the game tonight."

Cody shared a conspiratorial glance with Eli.

Lexi came down the hall, and as always, every glance at her made Cody feel like a lucky, lucky man. He smiled, and she returned it. There were no commitments or promises between them, but the fact that she'd softened toward him was enough hope to keep him going. They'd not verbalized much, but if he could read people at all, she was definitely interested.

Lexi greeted everyone, then the two couples exited the house and hopped in Cody's Jeep to go to the grill and oyster bar. Cody realized he wouldn't get the chance to tell her about the paparazzi until the end of the evening. Pulling her aside wouldn't be fair to her. She'd have no time to process or recover.

"Are Frankie and Sunni coming?" Delanie asked from the backseat.

"If they can get a sitter." Cody glanced in his rearview mirror at Delanie.

"Anybody hear from the newlyweds?" Delanie's eyes met his in the mirror.

Eli chuckled. "I'm thinking the family is the last thing on their minds."

When they arrived at George's, the girls headed for the restroom, leaving Eli and Cody to find a table. The place was loaded with televisions showing several different channels, depending on which direction you gazed.

When the girls returned, Lexi took the chair next to Cody, and Delanie settled on her right.

"What are you thinking?" Cody asked Lexi, not glancing up from the menu. He heard her gasp. His head jerked up, and following her gaze, he saw her face lighting up one of the large-screen TVs hanging from the wall. The sound was muted, but as they say, a picture is worth more anyhow.

The word *arsonist* with a question mark after it appeared across the bottom of the screen in bold print. There were photos of her grandparents and of Cody grabbing a guy by his collar and shoving him. Pictures of neighbors, their mouths moving. It didn't take much imagination to know what they were saying. Shots of the burned landscape after the fires that she supposedly set. A picture of his dad and his title printed out across the screen. Cody's name and title followed. Shots of the wedding.

Cody glanced at Lexi. Her hand covered her mouth, and abject horror filled her expression. The story lasted only a couple of minutes, but to Cody, it felt like at least two hours.

∞

Lexi couldn't believe this was happening. Her worst nightmare. Someone had leaked information to the tabloids about the fires. She'd been humiliated by the press before, but this had to be the worst of all time.

When they flashed a picture of Cody in front of her grandparents' home, shoving some guy around, her mortification grew into anger. He knew about this and didn't tell her?

"I need to go." Her tone was sharp and demanding.

Cody nodded. "I'm taking Lexi back to Mom and Dad's. We're going to bow out of dinner."

All four of them were caught up in the slide show of her life the past few weeks.

Delanie was the first to respond. "Of course." She hugged Lexi. "I'm so sorry." Her eyes held sympathy, and her words rang genuine. "If Frankie and Sunni don't make it, we'll just grab a cab."

"I hope this doesn't hurt your family in any way." Lexi's tone held regret.

Everyone said good-bye. Lexi kept her head low as they left the restaurant, praying no one would notice her. Cody held open her door and lingered after she'd climbed in.

"I'm sorry."

"For what?" Lexi snapped. "The exposé or the fact that you knew and didn't tell me?"

"It just happened last night." Cody kept his voice quiet.

"What were you thinking? That you, the big, bad Cody Cooper, scared them off?"

"I just wanted you to have a nice day—I planned to tell you tonight. Look, I know I was wrong, and I'm sorry. I should have told you first thing this morning—"

"This is why you came back down, isn't it?"

He nodded his head.

"Another lie! This is my life, my future. You don't have the right."

"I was wrong, and I admit it, Lexi. I asked you to forgive me."

She looked at him for a long time. "Here's the thing—people have been choosing what they think is best for me for a long time now. I never gave you that right."

Cody nodded and shut the door. She'd spotted the hurt in his eyes that her words had inflicted, but at this moment, her own hurt outweighed his.

The truth was, just like all the men before him—starting with her dad— they all thought they knew best. And with every one of them, trust had, sooner or later, been breached.

She'd known all along he was too good to be true. He was too nice, his family too nice.

When he stopped at the curb in front of his parents' place, Lexi turned toward him. "I want to go home—tonight. To my grandparents'. If you can't take me, I'll rent a car or call a taxi."

"I'll take you, but do you think that's wise?" She could barely make out his silhouette under the streetlamp.

"Don't worry, I'm not sticking around long enough to be accused of any foul play. I'm returning to LA tomorrow."

"But—"

"I'll hire an attorney or do whatever I need to do. I'm not staying here now that the whole world knows where I am."

Cody cleared his throat. "What about us?"

"Cody, there is no us and never was. You're just a nice guy who was there when I needed somebody. We had a few good times, shared a couple of sweet kisses, but that doesn't constitute an 'us.'"

He cringed at her honesty. Boy had he misread her. He climbed out of the Jeep, his heart hurting. He opened her door and followed her up the sidewalk to his parents' front door. "Just so you know, there was an us for me. It was real." He unlocked the front door, pushing it open. He stood back and waited for her to enter.

"Lexi! Cody!" His mom's voice greeted them. She was curled against his dad on the couch. "I thought you guys went out for the evening."

"We did."

Lexi excused herself, and Cody filled them in on the evening's events. His dad flipped on the television and surfed through the channels, but nothing about Lexi appeared.

Lexi carried out her things a few minutes later. The large tote bag was hanging from her right shoulder, her purse on her left shoulder, and the smaller bag in her left hand. She stopped just inside the great room.

"I want to thank you both for your hospitality. You've been more than kind, including me in the wedding and everything. And thank you, Chief Cooper, for trying to help me."

Both of his parents rose and moved toward her.

"Lexi, I don't recommend this course of action."

"I understand, sir, but I can't stay here any longer. I have to regain control of my life and stop this downward spiral."

"I fear you may get hurt by that decision or make your situation worse." His brows drew together in concern.

"With the utmost respect, sir, how can it get worse? Here or at my grandparents', I'm a sitting target."

Cody's mom stepped between them and gave Lexi an extra tight hug. "You be careful. We'll be praying for you."

Lexi's eyes grew glassy. "Thank you." She squeezed his mom's hand. "For everything. I'm sorry your family got tangled in my web."

"Not to worry, dear. We'll be fine. It's you I'm concerned about."

Cody took the bags from Lexi and carried them to the Jeep. She followed, his mom holding her hand. His dad brought up the rear.

After Cody stowed the bags, they all hugged—everyone but he and Lexi. "Be safe, son. Call me." His dad stood by the driver's door, and his mom by Lexi's door. She spoke to Lexi in low tones.

The entire drive home was quiet. Cody contemplated the past six weeks or so since Lexi arrived. Who knew so much would transpire, but it had. He'd found and lost love in less than two months.

∞

On the drive home, Lexi vacillated between knowing she deserved this and wondering why God hadn't intervened. Since the prodigal had returned to her God, life had gone from bad to worse. She had no idea where to turn from here and felt too numb to pray.

Cody's mom was a dear. She'd been kind in spite of everything. The last thing she'd said to her was how sorry she was that things didn't work out between Lexi and Cody. The woman should be sorry Lexi ever entered his life.

When they drove into her grandparents' driveway, the light from the family room window still glowed bright. Lexi wondered if they'd seen anything about her splattered across their television screen.

Cody unlocked their front door with his personal key. "It's just us," he hollered the minute he opened the door. Both Alph and Essie met them on their way to the family room.

"I'll get your bags." Cody went back outside.

Lexi settled on the couch in their family room, telling her grandparents what had transpired and why she'd come home. She heard the front door open and shut again. Cody's footsteps retreated the other direction. He must be putting her things in her room.

"I'm planning on returning to LA tomorrow."

Gram got teary, just as Lexi had expected, but she was fighting the urge to cry, which Lexi appreciated.

"I have to. If I stick around here, I could end up being charged for a crime I didn't commit." Her gaze roamed over each of the two faces that she loved most in the entire world. "I'll be back—soon. I promise."

Both of their expressions were skeptical, and Lexi hated that she'd given them cause to doubt her. Cody entered the room right before her promise, and his face reflected their same misgivings.

Lexi wanted to be mad that they'd question her integrity, but in truth, she knew she'd brought it on herself. This time she'd prove them all wrong. She'd be back before Christmas.

"Cody, will you record that celeb news show? I think it replays several times a day, and I want to know what they're saying about me."

Cody crinkled his brow. "You sure?"

She nodded. She knew by his expression that he thought she should leave well enough alone. He probably subscribed to the theory that what you don't know can't hurt you, but she knew better. In her business, knowledge was power.

Chapter 11

exi, Jamison. I was hoping you'd answer, but guess not. No hard feelings, I hope. Anyway, been seeing your mug a lot lately and have had several calls requesting you for one job or another. I've had to tell them you're no longer under contract, so I was hoping you'd grown weary and bored and would consider some new negotiations. Anyway, love, call me."

Lexi erased the message and closed her cell phone. Restless, she paced around the bed. She'd packed everything except what she needed in the morning. Even though they'd advised her not to leave the state, she had to get out of here. She'd called and secured a spot on a puddle jumper tomorrow afternoon, taking her from here to Reno and then a direct flight to LAX from there. She hated those little planes, but the sooner she could leave, the better. Besides, she didn't want to ask Cody for one more favor.

She glanced out her window, and his lights were still on. On a whim, she trekked across the street to see if he'd caught the story on her. She'd rather her grandparents not have to endure the humiliation if they didn't have to.

She knocked once. Cody's door swung open. He grabbed her arm, yanking her inside and slamming the door behind her.

"What are you doing out roaming around at this hour? In your mind, this situation may be over because you're leaving tomorrow, but you are still a suspect. You still need to keep a low profile, going nowhere alone."

His anger caught her off guard. Of course, she guessed that it stemmed a lot more from her leaving than her midnight wanderings. She'd said some pretty unkind things, and she'd take care of that tonight, too.

"You're right, but I couldn't sleep, and since your light was on. . ."

"So what did you need?"

"A cup of sugar." Her attempt at lightness failed. He didn't even crack a smile. *Right now I need one of your bear hugs.* But she'd burned that bridge. She wrapped her arms around her midsection.

"I wondered if we could check out your recording to see if you caught me."

Compassion filled his stern expression. "It's not worth watching. Take my word for it."

"Nonetheless, I need to." She chewed on her bottom lip. "Please."

He led her to his sitting area. The plasma TV hung above the fireplace, so she snuggled into his oversized sofa that sat facing the television. He picked up the remote, went to his saved list, and hit PLAY. He fast-forwarded to her part.

Lexi watched as pictures of her flitted across the screen. The reporter spouted off a lot of false information, including the fact that she'd been fired as a model. She just didn't want to do the kind of things Jamison had planned for her.

But the part that made her heartsick was the way they shed a negative light on the Coopers—how Reno's elected official had invited a suspected criminal into his home. They also shared the irony of Cody the firefighter taking a suspected arsonist into his arms and probably his bed. Scenes flashed of various kisses they'd shared.

"I'm sorry." She closed her eyes against the onslaught.

"Oh, they aren't through."

Pictures of the wedding flashed before her eyes and a tender scene between them. They went with the sinner-saint angle, asking if Cody would be the person to taint the family by marrying the wild woman and party girl Alexandria Eastridge.

Cody hit the OFF button, leaving a blank screen behind.

"You'd have been better off avoiding me like a bad disease." For the first time that night, Cody made eye contact.

"I won't argue that, just not for the reason you're implying."

He'd opened the door, but did she have the courage to be honest with him? She licked her dry lips.

"I didn't mean to hurt you, Cody." She pursed her lips, fighting the urge to cry. "For a brief moment in time, you and I were pretty wonderful together, but as you now know, I'd drag your whole family through the gutter." A couple of stray tears wound their way down her cheeks. "God may remove our sins as far as the east is from the west, but people remember far longer. And they are far meaner. In truth, my life has gotten far more difficult as I've attempted to return to God. Maybe it's futile. Maybe I'm too far gone."

"No one is too far gone. I promise you that. God redeems broken people and the years the locusts have eaten. He'll do that for you. Please let Him."

Cody went and retrieved a box of tissues for Lexi. She pulled one out and dried her wet cheeks. "I keep begging God to get me out of this mess, but things go from bad to worse."

"Don't beg, Lexi. Claim what you know to be true, and trust Him with what you don't understand. I know that sounds trite, but you are His beloved child. Believe it. Live like it. Nothing is allowed to touch your life unless God permits it. If He allows it, it's for your growth and His glory. Don't let the enemy win, but stand firm, knowing God will use these fires somehow in your life."

Several times during the last few minutes, Cody had started to reach for her hand but had stopped himself.

"I'm so sorry for everything. Please believe me." Fresh tears fell.

Cody drew his lips together in a tight line. She watched his Adam's apple rise and fall when he swallowed.

"I believe you, but this old heart of mine will need some time to heal."

She nodded. *Mine, too. Mine, too.*

She rose from the couch. "I'd better go. I have a 10:00 a.m. flight, so this is technically good-bye."

He stood and followed her to the front door. She stopped before opening it and faced him, wanting to pretend this good-bye meant nothing, but her tears betrayed her.

He opened his arms, and she stepped into them. He pulled her against him as she cried. She wasn't sure, but she thought she felt a tear or two drop into her hair.

∞

Holding Lexi hurt. Cody knew he'd see her again someday but wished he wouldn't. The pain was more than he wanted to bear.

He held her tight, careful not to speak any of the feelings he had for her. When he could bear it no more, he loosened his hold. "I'll walk you home. Promise me you'll stay put, no matter how restless you feel."

She nodded. "I promise." When she looked up at him, her face mere inches from his, he backed out of the embrace and took a deep breath.

"Let's get you home."

He set the pace at a brisk walk, not desiring a slow saunter with chitchat. Before going inside, she kissed his cheek. "Good-bye, Cody." Her tone rang with finality.

"Good-bye, Lexi." *I'll miss you more than you know.*

She seemed to want to say more but didn't. She opened her French door and waved at him before closing it. He stood there a minute. "Good-bye, Lexi," he whispered, turning to cross the street. He glanced back once. "God's best to you."

Cody hit the sack, too tired even to think. Time healed all wounds. He guessed he'd discover if that quotation carried any truth. Right now it felt like the biggest lie on the planet.

Cody's phone rang, startling him awake. He groped for the light and found his phone. It was the fire station.

"Another fire."

Cody jumped out of bed, grabbing a pair of jeans.

"Just a few houses from yours. Same chick."

"Thanks." He shut his cell and slipped on his Nikes. The clock said two thirty. He hadn't been asleep long. He ran out the door and across the street. He could see the fire trucks and headed over there.

"I saw the Newcombs' granddaughter walking down the road at about two."

Cody's heart dropped. A tiny doubt crept in, and he hated himself for it.

A young cop took Mrs. Stark's account and a description of what the suspect was wearing. The exact same outfit Lexi wore to his house. A navy velour jogging suit. He felt sick and leaned against the fire truck, trying to process everything.

Not one fire the whole time Lexi was in Reno, and her first night back, one was set with an eyewitness account. "God, what does this mean?" There were many facets to Lexi; he sure hoped pyromaniac wasn't one. His uncertainty increased as he listened to the report.

"About fifteen minutes after she walked by, I got worried. I mean, I'd heard the stories. I woke up the mister and dragged him outside with me, just in case she was still out there. That's when we saw the flames and called you."

"Good thing you did. Otherwise someone's home could have gone up in a blaze."

"Oh, I know. We've all been a little on edge, and with good reason, so it seems." She shook her head in disgust.

The fire was extinguished quickly, and after questioning the witness, the cop requested a search warrant. By the time Cody had walked toward his cabin, two police cars were parked in front of Alph and Essie's, their lights flashing.

Cody intercepted them. "Let me call and wake them. They are elderly, and Alph's heart isn't in great shape."

"Go ahead, but they need to come straight to the door." There was an officer on each side of the cabin. Cody didn't ask but was certain they'd even stationed one at the back door.

"Alph, it's me. I'm out front with a few of Douglas County's deputies. Can you come to the front door?"

The windows began to light up as Alph traversed the path from his bedroom to the front door. He answered in his robe, thin white legs sticking out below the hem.

"Sir, we have a search warrant." He held out a faxed document.

Alph nodded, opening the door wide. His eyes sought out Cody. He looked pale. Cody led him to his chair. "Wait here."

By the time he'd caught up with them, they were entering Lexi's room, shining the flashlight in her face.

∞

A bright light penetrated Lexi's sleep. She tried to open her eyes, but they quickly closed against the offensive brightness. Her mind wouldn't wake up. She squinted and opened one eye slowly. Blinking, she tried to understand. A flashlight? She screamed and sat up, holding the covers tight against her chin.

A man behind the bright light read her the Miranda rights. *Dear God, no Please let this be a bad dream.* Her heart raced, and fear gripped her.

Another cop flipped on the overhead light. She blinked, trying to get her eyes to adjust. He rifled through her room, stopping short at the overstuffed reading chair in the corner of the room.

"Can you read the description of what the suspect was wearing?" He stood staring at the clothes Lexi had removed just a couple of hours ago.

As the policeman with the flashlight read the outfit described by the eyewitness, Lexi's gaze darted to the perfect match draped over the upholstered chair.

The guy by the chair motioned his partner over. "Think we've got a match."

Both officers studied the jogging suit without touching it. "Yep. Book her."

He whipped out a pair of handcuffs and yanked her from the bed. Before Lexi could protest, her hands were secured behind her back. Lexi was thankful the nights were cool so that she was wearing her long-sleeved flannel pajamas.

Cody stepped into the room. "Is that necessary? She's obviously not a flight risk."

He was dismissed with a glare.

Cody's gaze met hers. She saw sadness, confusion, even doubt. "I didn't do anything. Cody, you have to believe me. I never left here after you walked me home." If he didn't trust her, who would?

He nodded. "I'll call my dad."

The police led her outside and shoved her into the back of the squad car. The sight of her grandparents on the porch broke her heart. Would she never stop hurting them? Tears came again. *God, where are You?*

∞

"Dad, it's me."

"Another fire?" he asked, sounding groggy.

"Yep. Lexi swears she didn't do it. I walked her home about 1:00 a.m., and an eyewitness claims to have seen her around two. She described her down to the outfit she'd had on earlier that night. When the cops entered with a search warrant, the exact outfit lay draped over her chair. An eyewitness is hard to dispute."

"Yes, it is, son. Yes, it is."

Cody could hear his mom in the background, probably wondering who was calling at three in the morning.

"I'll be there in a couple of hours."

"Thanks. I'm staying with her grandparents just to be certain they're all right. Come there, and we'll ride over together to the sheriff's office."

"Will do. And, son, we'll get to the bottom of this."

That's what he was afraid of—that when all was said and done, Lexi would be found guilty. *Love believes all things, hopes. . .* He felt like a fair-weather friend. Once things got complicated, he stopped believing in her. He tried to fight his rising doubt, but it assaulted him at every turn.

He returned to the house, finding Essie in the kitchen making hot chocolate. He knew being busy was her way of coping. Alph was in his chair staring straight ahead. His health concerned Cody.

He settled in the corner of the sofa, near Alph's chair, reaching out and patting the wrinkled arm. "My dad's on his way. He'll do everything he can to help Lexi."

Alph nodded. Essie carried in three mugs and passed them out. The silence screamed of Lexi's guilt. The ticking of the clock nearly drove Cody insane. The worst part of this whole nightmare was the toll it would take on her grandparents.

After what seemed like forever, the doorbell rang. Cody startled then jumped up to answer it. Both of his parents stood on the stoop. The night sky showed the first light of day.

He stepped aside to let them enter, and his mom hugged him tightly. His dad joined in, wrapping his strong arms around both Cody and his mom.

"I'll let her grandparents know we're heading over to the jail."

"I'd like to say hello." His mom followed him back to the family room.

She hugged each of them, placing a kiss on each of their cheeks.

"It doesn't look good for our Lexi girl, does it?" Alph's voice was hoarse. Cody knew he wrestled with a lump in the center of his throat. He'd fought one of those himself several times the past couple of days.

"Don't you worry—Frank will solve this mystery. We all know Lexi is innocent." *How I wish I knew that.*

"Can I make a pot of coffee for you or some breakfast?" Essie offered.

"Maybe later. I want to get over to the sheriff's station and encourage Lexi, but we'll come by again before we head back to Reno."

They said their good-byes. On the way to his dad's truck, Cody said, "Mom, you are something else. I wish I had your faith in people, your exuberance, your compassionate heart."

He climbed into the backseat of the double cab.

"I see all those things in you, much more than I see them in myself. Look at you, willing to love Lexi in spite of her past. If that is not faith in people and a compassionate heart, I don't know what is."

His dad pulled back onto the main highway.

"The truth is, I don't want to believe she's guilty, but all evidence says otherwise. I'm doubting her, and I hate that I am."

"And add to the mix that you are in love with her." His mom read his heart so simply, so matter-of-factly. "That only increases the guilt and confusion."

"Don't be too quick to hang her. She's an intelligent woman. If she left your house to go start a fire, would she wear the same clothes?" His dad parked in front of the sheriff's office. "I don't think she'd make so many careless mistakes."

"Unless she wanted to get caught." Cody climbed out of the truck cab.

"Stop analyzing and start praying," his mom reminded. "Are you coming with me to see Lexi or with your dad to meet with the sheriff?"

"I'll go with you." Cody decided he needed his mom's encouragement as much or more than Lexi did.

She played her social worker card to get them inside the jail. A few minutes later, they brought Lexi in. She wore a bright orange outfit that resembled hospital scrubs. Relief settled on her face when she saw them.

"It's good to see familiar faces. Thanks for coming." She stopped just inside the small room, wishing for the freedom to run to them both and hug them tightly to her.

"Did you think for a minute we wouldn't?" Mrs. Cooper pulled her into a warm embrace. "Frank's here, too, and knowing my man, he has a plan. He'll have you out of here sooner than later." She kissed Lexi's cheek and then sat down at the table, opening her Bible.

Lexi and Cody followed her lead. Lexi took the chair next to her, and Cody sat across from them. Lexi glanced at Cody. Though she didn't deserve it, she needed to know he believed in her innocence. She searched his face.

He smiled at her, but it was a sad and pathetic one. Her heart dropped, as did her gaze. *He thinks I set those fires.* A lump lodged against her windpipe as a little piece of hope died.

Chapter 12

God reminded me tonight on the drive up here about Paul and Silas and their imprisonment. Do you remember that story from the Bible?" asked Mrs. Cooper.

Lexi shook her head. Much had been forgotten during the last dozen years—too much.

"Just like you, they'd been imprisoned, but on top of that, they'd been beaten as well. They didn't complain or even question God. They prayed, they worshipped, and they sang praises to Him. While they sang, an earthquake shook the prison, and the locked doors flew open."

Lexi wasn't sure where Mrs. Cooper's line of thinking was going. Did she think if the three of them sang loud enough the doors would pop open and she'd walk out a free woman?

"The truth is, we all have certain prisons in our lives. Not real jail cells, but there are times we all need deliverance from something. And if the act of praising God set Paul and Silas free, it will do the same for you and me." She began to sing a praise song.

The three of them spent the next thirty minutes or so worshipping the Lord. With each new song, Lexi felt stronger, less afraid. Her faith grew surer. She had no idea what would transpire in her life, but come what may, God would be with her. She knew that for sure at this moment.

"I am going to check on Frank and see if he's made any headway."

"Thank you." Lexi hugged Mrs. Cooper. The guard let her out. Cody made no move to go, so Lexi returned to her seat at the table.

"Lexi, no matter how this thing plays out, I'm in love with you."

Her gaze jumped to him. Though she'd felt pretty sure he loved her, she hadn't expected him to make the big announcement to a girl in orange prison garb. His tender expression made her breath catch in her throat. He rose, moving around the table. His eyes never left hers. Her heart drummed against her rib cage. He reached for her hands, pulling her onto her feet. He placed a hand on each cheek, staring deeply into her eyes. "I love you, Lexi. Not only do I love you, but I want to marry you someday—if you'd say yes."

Lexi closed her eyes. *I love you as well, but we both know I'm not what you need.* A single tear squeezed through her tightly shut lids. He kissed it away. She fought the urge to turn her lips toward his. She stood still, not responding verbally to his proclamations. *Love is putting another's need before my own.* She'd read that somewhere. Today she'd love Cody enough to spare him the humiliation that would surely come if she stayed in his life for too long.

I love you, Cody, but you're way too nice for the likes of me. I've made lots of wrong turns. And you've avoided them. At least until you met me.

Lexi grappled with the irony. She'd had a lot of men she'd never wanted and had to walk away from the one man she truly did.

He held her close a few minutes. She didn't fight it, nor did she join in. Truth be told, she gained strength from him.

"I'll be back," he promised.

Lexi only nodded, but when he retreated, she wished for him already.

∞

Cody ached for her. He'd let the words of the praise songs seep deep into his soul. Like a man hungry for food, his spirit was hungry for the peace of God. The songs covered him like a soothing balm, washing away the trepidation of what was to come. Lexi was in God's hands, and that was where he'd have to leave her.

He searched for his dad and mom.

"I got her out." His dad was filling out paperwork. "According to NRS 193.155, if Lexi was truly guilty, the fires were only gross misdemeanors because the damage was less than five thousand dollars."

"NRS?" his mom asked.

"The Nevada Revised Statutes. They could try to prove intent and charge her with more, but at this point, they won't."

"Only because of you?" Cody stated the obvious.

"Let's just say that in this world, who you know can help." He handed the paperwork to the woman at the desk.

"It'll be a few minutes. Have a seat." She pointed to the hard chairs lining the wall across from her area. The three of them did as they were told.

"So what now, Dad? What keeps all this from happening again?"

"I've been thinking, and I'm trying to come up with a foolproof plan. The thing is, somebody has to be watching her day and night. Probably the same somebody who notified the press where to find her in Reno."

Cody leaned across his mom so he could speak quietly, wanting no one to hear the uncertainties. "How can you be so sure it's not her?"

"I've been doing this job a long time. It's part gut instinct, part discernment from the Lord, and part looking past the obvious because it rarely is."

"So where do we go from here?" His mom turned her blue green eyes toward his dad.

"Somehow I've got to get her under twenty-four-hour surveillance. And that's where you come in." His dad's well-modulated voice was barely above a whisper. The three of them huddled closer. "I can use your house as a base for my operations. Eli just finished a big case he'd been on for months. They made a huge bust. Delanie is still on maternity leave. I'll see if they want to come visit you for a few days."

A jail guard led Lexi through the security door. She now wore the pastel plaid pajamas she'd had on when they brought her in. She had bed head and no makeup but was a beautiful sight as far as Cody was concerned.

He went to her, pulling her into his arms and kissing her temple. Her hug was brief, and she pulled away, moving toward his parents.

"Thank you so much."

They both hugged her. His mom took her arm, and they walked to the truck together. She opened the back door and climbed in after Lexi. That left him to sit in the front with his dad. The morning sun was up, and Cody slipped on his sunglasses.

∞

"I need to figure out who is tailing you and why," Chief Cooper said.

Lexi glanced out the back window but wasn't sure which car he referred to. "You think I'm being followed?"

"Lexi, somebody is a step ahead of you. They have to be watching you at all times. I need you to think. Who would go to all this trouble and expense and why?"

Lexi shook her head.

They pulled up in front of her grandparents' house and unloaded. The front door swung open, and both Gram and Gramps met them on the porch. Their faces flooded with relief. They hugged her tight.

"Thank the good Lord," Gram said, taking her hand and leading her inside.

She glanced back, and Gramps motioned for the others to follow. They congregated in the family room.

Gramps turned to Chief Cooper. "Thanks so much for bringing our Lexi girl home." He shook his hand.

"Can I make everyone a nice breakfast?" Gram offered. "Mr. and Mrs. Cooper?"

"Only if you let me help. And it's Marilyn. Frank and Marilyn." She looked directly at Lexi. "Got it?"

She nodded and smiled. Someday some lucky woman would not only get Cody as a husband but would get Marilyn as a mother-in-law. Lexi had already grown to love her.

The two women headed into the kitchen. Gramps settled into his recliner. Cody and Frank both sat on the couch.

"Guess I'll help with breakfast." Lexi turned to leave, but Frank called her back.

"Lexi, I'd like to strategize with you. Do you mind staying?"

She shook her head and sat in Gram's recliner.

Frank turned to Gramps. "Do you have a garage?"

He nodded.

"And Cody also has a garage. That will help us smuggle people in and out."

"Who are we smuggling?" Lexi asked.

"I'm not sure yet. Depends on who's available. I'm hoping to keep it in the family and not involve the Reno PD. I think between Eli, Delanie, Frankie, and myself, we can get the job done. That is, if they are free and can help."

Gram and Marilyn carried in two trays, one with a pot of coffee and mugs and the other with cream and sugar. They set them both on the coffee table in front of the couch. Frank wasted no time pouring a cup and handing it to her. He continued filling mugs, and the women returned to their breakfast endeavor.

Lexi added a little cream to hers, feeling overwhelmed by this family and their kindness.

"What about the sheriff's office up here?" Gramps sipped the coffee Gram had doctored for him.

"They don't have the manpower, nor frankly, do they have a reason. They aren't, and I quote, 'wasting the taxpayers' money on a misdemeanor with an eyewitness.'"

"Then why are you?" Lexi had to know.

Frank shrugged. "You're a friend of Cody's, so you matter to us. Friends help friends. And it's personal."

"What do you mean?" Lexi set down her cup, giving Frank her full attention.

"I'm tired of people trying to ruin another person's life just because they can. I see it all the time in Reno. Vindictive hate crimes. They are a personal pet peeve, and I don't take them lightly."

Lexi smiled, relieved his answer had nothing to do with her future in Cody's life. "For my sake, I'm glad. I can't thank you enough."

"None of us can," Gramps added.

"It's my pleasure." Frank jotted a few notes down on a small pad he pulled from his front pocket.

"Cody, can we talk for a minute?" Lexi had to clear the air. His proclamation earlier today had been bugging her.

Frank looked up. "Do me a favor. Go stand out front. I want the whole world to see Lexi is out, and it'll give me a chance to watch from the window and see who might be lurking in the shadows."

Lexi led the way through the front door. She walked over to Frank's truck and leaned on the bumper.

Cody asked her to move and lowered the tailgate. They both hopped on it, feet swinging above the ground.

"What's up?" His warm brown eyes probed her face.

"You are the sweetest guy I have ever met in my entire life."

∞

But... He heard it coming—the "let's be friends" speech. His heart hurt, but he'd try to be upbeat about the whole thing.

"You just have to know that I'm not feeling what you are."

He nodded.

"I don't want this whole grand gesture from your family because they assume that one day you and I will marry."

"I've never implied to anyone except you that we might marry." He hadn't intended for the defensive edge to slip into his tone.

"I'm glad. I think it's better that way. But I'd love it if we could be friends."

"We already are," he reminded her.

"Just so you don't expect more from me than I can give. You are the first guy in my life who seemed to like me for me. I got swept up in the idea that a man could care about me in a nonsexual way."

Cody nodded, praying this conversation would end soon.

"I'm sorry."

He forced a smile. "Me, too."

"You two coming in for breakfast?" His mom called from the open front door.

"Be right in," he called back. Relief poured over him. Now he wouldn't have to listen to the same words—*You're a nice guy, but*—said fifty different ways. Cody slid off the tailgate.

"I don't want your family to dislike me, and if your dad no longer wants to help—"

"It's fine, Lexi." He wanted to say, "Maybe I was just caught up in the whole beautiful girlfriend idea." But he knew his motives were wrong, so he bit his tongue. Besides, it was a lie.

They joined the others at the table. Everyone's mood but his was celebratory.

He needed some time alone to lick his wounds and regroup. But as his dad filled them in on his plan, Cody realized he'd have no time alone during the next few days. Not only that, but he'd be Lexi's watchdog by day—never leaving her side. This ought to be a thrill a minute.

"I'm not worried about her safety, so much. Whoever this is, the goal doesn't seem to be to harm, but some sort of revenge." His dad gazed at Lexi. "Has anyone ever threatened you?"

She shook her head.

"Blackmail?"

Shrugging, she laid down her fork.

"Ever been harassed by an ex-boyfriend, a jealous female friend, an old roommate?"

"Nope." Lexi pushed her barely eaten breakfast aside. Cody understood. The thought of food didn't settle well with him, either.

"Anyone angry with you, trying to manipulate you? Anybody want you back in LA?"

∞

Jamison. The thought hit Lexi like an avalanche.

"Who, Lexi? Who?" Frank was like a hound on a scent. "Somebody came to mind. Who was it?"

"Jamison Price, my agent."

"Why? What made you think of him?"

Every eye at the table was on her. They'd all stopped eating, waiting. "He wanted me to resign my contract with—" She paused, glancing at Gramps and then Gram. She searched for words that carried less meaning. "A different kind of modeling in mind." Cody's eyes were compassionate, encouraging.

Her gaze rested on Frank. "I wasn't interested, and he acted like he could care less, but I saw the pulsing jaw and knew he was angry."

"Has he contacted you since?" Frank's gaze was intense. Cody looked a lot like him.

"He left a message on my cell phone last night."

"May I listen to it?"

Lexi shook her head. "I erased it."

"What did he say? What did he want?" Frank's voice took on a demanding quality.

Lexi closed her eyes, trying to remember. "He said something about seeing my face a lot lately and that he'd had several requests for me. He thought I ought to come back to LA for some contract negotiations. I don't know exactly, but that was the gist of it all."

Frank asked for any info Lexi had on Jamison—address, phone numbers, full name.

"The more I think about it, the crazier it would be for him to be involved. He's a very rich man with a lot of clients. He doesn't have time for this sort of thing."

"Did you tell him you were coming here?"

She shook her head. "When I left his office that day, I had no idea where I was going."

Frank rested his elbows on the table. Everyone watched.

"He's processing," Marilyn whispered. She rose and started clearing plates. Gram joined her.

"Take a walk with me." Frank's gaze rested on Lexi.

"I'm still not dressed. Can you give me a minute?" Though her pajamas were beyond modest, Lexi didn't want to parade down the street in them. She'd already sat out front. That was bad enough.

After a quick change and shoving her mass of hair into a ponytail, she found Frank waiting at the front door. She dreaded what this walk might entail.

They walked for a few minutes in silence. Lexi knew Frank had his eye out for somebody tailing her. He reminded her of a cat about to pounce. All his senses seemed alert. She felt tightly coiled herself.

"Lexi, I need to ask some hard questions."

She shoved her hands into the long pocket on the front of her sweatshirt. "I figured you might, but I'll save you the trouble. Yes, in the past we had been—shall we say—more than friends."

"How long has he been your agent?"

"Twelve years."

"And when did things get personal?"

Lexi turned her head away, not wanting to see his reaction. "Almost immediately."

"How old were you?" She thought she heard disapproval in his tone.

She stared at the ground, watching it move with each step forward. "Sixteen."

"How old was he?"

"Almost thirty."

"That snake." Frank wrapped his arm around her shoulders and pulled her against his side. "Lexi, for all men everywhere, I am so sorry. Men like him should be castrated."

He did disapprove, but not of her.

"Who ended it and when?"

"I did. About five years ago."

"Good for you. How'd he take it?"

They'd circled the block and were heading back toward her grandparents' house. "He was angry—very angry—especially because I'd just signed another contract and still had almost five years left."

"After you refused to comply with his wishes, did your job assignments change? Did you get less work?"

"Yeah, but he blamed my age. I'd been doing a lot of teen-related shoots, a couple of music videos, that sort of thing, so I believed him."

The more questions he asked, the more certain he seemed that Jamison was behind the fires. She stopped next to her grandparents' mailbox. "Before we go back inside, I just want you to know how grateful I am that you're helping me. I could pay you."

He smiled. "I'm a public servant and not allowed to accept any sort of compensation, but even if I could, I don't want your money. I just want to help you get out of this mess." He paused to ask one final question. "Was your relationship with Jamison exclusive?"

Chapter 13

Yes. There were no other men—until after." She focused on her shoe.

"How about for him? Were there others?"

She used her toe to move some gravel back and forth. "At the time, I didn't think so, but I found out later that he had slept with almost all his girls on a fairly consistent basis."

"I'd like to slap him with a few charges that have nothing to do with fires."

She raised her chin. "Me, too. He's hurt a lot of people."

"Did you ever think of turning him in?"

"Honestly, no. I grew up in the entertainment industry. This is not that uncommon."

Frank shook his head.

"I also wanted to assure you, you don't have to worry about me and Cody."

He looked surprised. "Who's worried?"

"Well, in case you are, don't be. I let him know this morning that we can only be friends."

"Friends, huh?" He studied Lexi. "Seemed like more than that to me."

She smiled, deciding to play it down. "I think he had a little crush on me."

"And you?" He watched her with that penetrating gaze.

She looked away, watching a bird overhead. "Me?" Searching for something cute to say, she drew a blank. Emotions hit her that she hadn't planned on. Tears she hadn't expected filled her eyes. "Me? I'm going back to LA and away from here just as soon as humanly possible." She glanced at her watch. "I'm booked on the 10:00 a.m. flight today." She attempted laughter. "Guess I won't make that one."

"If you leave, whoever is doing this to you wins."

She wiped at her cheeks. "I don't even know if I care. I just want away from here."

"Boy, do I understand that! If I were in your shoes, I'm sure I'd feel the same. But running rarely solves life's issues. Besides, this place isn't bad, but a man from LA might be."

"You're right." She sighed.

"Will you work with me on this for a few days and see who we can ferret out?"

She nodded. "I guess, but running holds more appeal."

He laughed. "I'm sure it does." He glanced at the house. "Don't run from Cody, either. If what I've observed is real, it's worth fighting for."

Lexi's tears refused to linger any longer. "Why would you want me in your son's life?"

"Grace, Lexi. God's amazing grace. We all have stuff in our pasts—stuff we regret and would like to erase. But God's mercies are new each morning. You've repented, you're forgiven, and you are a new creation in Christ. One I believe my son loves." He hugged her close, and they finished their walk to the front door.

Once they joined the others in the family room, Frank said, "Lexi, I'd like you and Cody to do something very public. Take a hike, whatever. I want as many people as possible to see you're out and about. In the meantime, I'll write a press release and have my office fax it to the Associated Press."

Lexi knew, though the walk fit into Frank's overall plan, he hoped it would accomplish more than just that. But she'd made up her mind. There was no going back.

"Since you'll probably be leaving in the next day or two and we talked about a ride up Heavenly on the gondola, how does that sound?"

A man who remembers his promises. "Sounds great. Give me ten minutes."

∞

Cody dreaded spending part of the day alone with Lexi. Not that he wouldn't love to be with her under different circumstances, but downshifting to just friends took more than a few hours. His dad used to say, *Fake it until you make it.* It was his way of saying—believe it, and your attitude will follow your actions. So, today he'd be the perfect friend. Not the man in love with her, not the man whose heart she just broke, but just a guy along for the ride.

He was foolish to actually think that Alexandria Eastridge—supermodel extraordinaire—would fall for him—Mr. Ordinary. Now, thinking about it, he felt silly hoping she'd return his feelings. Nothing about them could ever work.

When Lexi finally returned, she smiled at him. He tried not to notice how good she looked and smelled. *Two good friends on an outing. Yep, that's all it is.* He opened the front door, waiting for her to exit first. *Doesn't have to be awkward. No sirree. Just two friends burning time.*

Cody drove them across the California line. Knowing she liked Starbucks, he stopped there first. *Good friends can be thoughtful.* "It will probably be cool up there, so I'm getting something hot." He ordered a large mocha latte.

She ordered a tall skinny mocha with no whipped cream.

"Let's leave the car here and walk over. It's less than a block to the ticket booth." They passed by the quaint shops surrounding the resort. They very much

330

belonged in a mountain town with their rugged wood exterior. Lexi stopped a couple of times to peer in windows.

"We've got time if you want to shop."

She smiled. Every time she looked at him, all he saw was sympathy in her eyes. He wanted to say, "Don't feel sorry for me. There are other fish in the pond." Of course he knew there weren't. For him, she was it. Her or nobody. *Looks like it'll be a long, lonely life.*

Cody bought two tickets for the gondola. Since it was a weekday morning, there was no line. The door on the side of the glass bubble opened, and they climbed aboard. He took one side, and she the other.

He wasn't going to say anything, but his chivalry reared its unwanted head. "The view is better from this direction."

"But you're going up backward."

"True, but I'm facing the lake."

"Ah." She moved over onto his bench, careful to leave space between them. "It's beautiful."

"No place prettier as far as I'm concerned."

∞

Lexi had always loved Lake Tahoe, but she couldn't express that to Cody when she said she couldn't wait to leave. The view was pristine. Blue in every direction—the sky, the mountains, the lake. "Thank you for bringing me here. I'd forgotten, and I'm glad I didn't miss this."

"We'll get off at the observation deck then ride on to the top. There is a little restaurant up there, and since you didn't eat much breakfast, I figure you must be hungry."

You're always taking care of me. "I am hungry, and I bet you are, too."

When their gondola stopped, Cody got out and offered his hand.

Habit, I'm sure. She accepted, and he steadied her as she climbed out. The metal beneath her feet wasn't solid, but a grate, providing a place for the melted snow to drain.

She clutched Cody's arm tighter. "Heights aren't my thing."

He wrapped an arm around her back. "My mom's, either, but it's worth the risk." He led her to view one landmark and then another as they slowly made their way around the entire deck.

"Every direction is beautiful in its own way."

"Yeah. This is one of my favorite spots on earth." He gazed out over the lake. "I come up here sometimes when I'm blue. I never leave that way. The beauty just lightens my load somehow."

That old familiar lump was back. He'd probably spend a few sad days up here because of her. How she regretted hurting him. If only she'd listened to her inner voice early on and kept more distance between them. They'd both have been better off for it.

"Remember the praise lesson my mom shared with you this morning?"

"Was that only this morning? It seems like days ago." They were back to where they started on the circular deck that ran around a store and another building.

"I know." He gazed at the beauty surrounding them. "This very place was her first lesson in the power of praise."

"Really, how?" She wondered if his mom stood up here and praised God at the top of her lungs or something equally bold that Lexi would never have the courage to do.

"As I told you, she hates heights. She and my dad came up here for their anniversary the first year it was built. When she stepped off the gondola and onto this grate, her fear kicked into overdrive."

Cody led Lexi to a bench where they faced the lake. Lexi let go of his arm and held on to the gray vertical rails in front of her.

"Anyway, she and a group of women had been studying the power of praise. They called it warfare intercession or something like that. She decided to test it out—you know, kind of a rubber-meets-the-road sort of thing?"

Lexi nodded.

"Just in her head, not out loud, she began to thank God that fear wasn't from Him. She began to claim what she knew the Word said about Him—like she could do all things in Christ. My dad said her legs stopped shaking, and she stepped out unafraid. She did spend most of her time up here mumbling under her breath to the Lord, though."

Lexi laughed. "Your mom is something else."

"That she is. My dad, too. He's a great guy with a heart of gold."

"Don't I know that. The whole family, really." *But most especially you.*

"You want to walk through the little store and then head on up to the top?"

"Sure." The store was tiny but chockful of souvenirs, film, and candy. "Look, they take pictures." She'd really like to have their picture made with the lake in the background but didn't ask. It felt tacky after all she'd said much earlier this morning.

They got back into their bubble, as Cody called it, and floated up to the top. The restaurant Cody spoke of was an outdoor chuck wagon kind of place. The hostess led them to a table covered with an umbrella. The chairs were plastic and mismatched, but something about the place was quaint.

They each ordered a burger. There were Adirondack chairs sitting around everywhere, filled with people.

Cody pointed to the chairs. "People ride up and spend the day. Some hike, some sit. There are usually several forms of entertainment—bands, magicians, whatever. One trail takes you even higher with a clear view of the entire lake."

The waitress brought their water. "Few more minutes on those burgers," she said before leaving.

"Do you want to hike after we eat?" Cody asked.

"I'd rather just claim a chair and watch the world go by. Do you mind?"

"No, we're both running on about two hours of sleep, so I echo your sentiments."

When the food arrived, they both concentrated on it rather than conversation.

After Cody paid the waitress and left a tip, he joined Lexi where she'd claimed two chairs facing the mountain. "So what now for you?"

She'd been asking herself the same question. "I'm not sure. Maybe some deep soul searching. Definitely a career change. I want nothing to do with modeling, acting, or music."

"Then I'm certain you are an atypical American. Isn't that just about everyone's secret dream—fame and fortune?"

"Why, Cody Cooper, I do believe that you are cynical, but it was my dream once, too."

"Was it? Or did your parents convince you it was?"

She thought about that. "I don't even know. It all started when I was so young. What came first, the chicken or the egg?" She shrugged. "The nice thing is that I'm young enough to get a second chance. And I made enough money modeling to tide me over until I decide which direction to go. I read about a school in downtown LA where the kids have to pass through a metal detector to get in. Some students carry guns and knives. I want to find something that matters, make a difference in someone's life. Have an impact on the world for Christ. Just this morning, your dad reminded me of grace. I want to spread some grace around to others, the way God did with me." She paused and took a breath. "I'm sorry, I'm rambling and probably sound corny. Now you probably regret the question."

"No, no, and no to your previous observations."

Lexi grew quiet, enjoying the mountain air and the beauty. Her eyes grew heavy. She closed them—only for a moment. She was so tired.

∞

After Lexi fell asleep, Cody dozed off and on. She slept for about an hour, and he spent part of the time watching her—watching and wishing. When she opened her eyes, he said, "Welcome back, sleepyhead." He held out his hand. "Let's go home."

The ride back down was more comfortable, less awkward. Cody almost believed the friends thing might work. His aching heart, however, wasn't so easily convinced.

When they got back to her grandparents' house, her grandparents told them his dad had done a good job of getting the news out that Lexi had been released due to lack of evidence.

"I've already seen it on several news channels," Frank informed them. "This should turn up the heat. I also made sure to 'leak' the fact that she'd hired a personal bodyguard to stay with her at night. That way nobody will try anything until she's alone tomorrow morning. That bought me some time to get my plan into place and fully operational."

Lexi smiled at Cody. "Your dad has really gotten into this."

He nodded. "It's his job, and he loves it."

At dinner Frank filled them in on his plan. Between bites of spaghetti, he told them that Eli, Delanie, and Frankie were coming down later tonight and bringing some borrowed police equipment with them. He was counting on whoever was watching Lexi to head home for a good night's sleep.

Everyone ate and listened intently.

"The sheriff agreed to thoroughly patrol the area at 4:00 a.m. He's checking every parked car along this block. If he doesn't find anything or anyone, then everyone will quickly man their posts and wait for daybreak."

Cody was impressed. His dad had drawn diagrams and printed maps of the neighborhood off the Internet. "Delanie will man the communications center, since she has Camden and can't be out in the field. I'll set it up tonight once they get here with the needed equipment."

It sounded like a fairly intricate plan to Cody. When they finished dinner, Lexi went in the kitchen to help her grandmother and his mom clean up. He followed his dad across the street to his A-frame cabin. "Dad, I've got two questions for you."

He stopped what he was doing. "Shoot."

"Do you really think Lexi will be safe? I'm worried about her."

"I'd never risk her safety. I promise you that, son. What is your second question?"

"Why are you so invested in this case?"

"Because I hate men who use women like this bum Jamison did. Once I prove he's behind this arson thing, I'm turning him over to LAPD for his sexual exploits with young women. I'm hoping he'll pay his dues behind bars."

∞

Frank and Marilyn spent the night at Cody's place. Frank asked Lexi if she'd mind trading spots with Cody so he could keep an eye on her. She and Marilyn shared Cody's king-sized bed. Frank slept just outside the bedroom door. "That way you have two eyewitnesses—just in case you need them. About five we'll send you home so you can prepare for your walk."

The next morning before the sun had fully risen over the mountains in the east, Lexi left her grandparents' home alone. Only she didn't feel alone because she had an earpiece with Delanie's voice in her head. She'd instructed her not to look to the left nor right, to act normal, and to set the pace as she typically would.

Her grandparents prayed for her before she left the house. She wore the same clothes she'd worn the other day. According to Frank, this should all go down like clockwork. She struggled to imagine Jamison going to all this trouble for her, but Frank seemed fairly certain.

She walked down the road and up and down several neighboring streets, winding her way back around toward home. Her path had been well planned, and Frank had placed people strategically along her way to watch out for her. She arrived back home with an uneventful walk behind her.

"Go on inside. My dad and Eli have a suspect in sight," reported Delanie. Lexi did as she was told, praying that this would finally be the end.

∞

Cody ran down the hill to the guy in the car his dad had spotted. By the time Cody got there, Eli had the guy spread-eagle across the hood of his older model Pontiac. His dad stood nearby.

"Who are you, pal, and who are you working for?" Eli demanded, handcuffing the guy. In truth, Cody knew by what his dad had said that they weren't in their jurisdiction but had received a special dispensation from the sheriff to arrest and book any suspects.

The guy was older and nervous. Cody figured he'd cave easily. "I was hired to tail some girl. Her boyfriend thinks she might be cheating on him, and fact is, she is with some firefighter dude."

"Who hired you?"

"That's confidential information. You should know that."

Chapter 14

His dad checked the man's cell phone. "Jamison Price was the last call you made." He glanced at Cody with a satisfied expression. "Who sets the fires?"

Eli raised the guy up off the car hood and turned him to face Frank.

"I said, who sets the fires? Where's the girl?" his dad demanded in his best "bad cop" voice.

"I don't know nothin' about no fires, and the girl just returned home from her morning walk."

"Let me tell you something—you'd better tell us the entire job you're doing for Mr. Price, and you'd better tell us now. Otherwise, you could be brought up on charges a lot bigger than stalking." Eli tightened his hold on the guy's collar. "You hear what I'm saying?"

"Look, man, I'm a private investigator. I told you before, I was hired to follow the model and report back to her boyfriend. Nuttin' more."

"When and how do you report?" Cody's dad asked.

"I call him every time she leaves the house. I let him know who she is with, what she is wearing, and where she goes."

"That's it?" Eli demanded.

The guy looked puzzled. "It's all he wanted. I'm full service—whatever my client wants, my client gets."

"Delanie, we need all eyes back out there. We have a Lexi look-alike on the loose somewhere toting a book of matches. And notify the sheriff." Then Frank turned to Eli. "Leave him cuffed."

Eli informed the private investigator, "We'll be back for you soon. In the meantime, relax and enjoy a beautiful day."

"You guys got my phone. And I'm still cuffed. Hey, come back here!" he yelled.

"Dad, two streets over, the sheriff got a call reporting a Lexi spotting," said Delanie. "They want the sheriff to check it out."

"We're on it." The three of them sprinted, following Delanie's directions. Eli and Cody rounded the corner neck and neck. They spotted the suspect ahead of them, and Eli gave Delanie a quiet update.

The woman slipped in between two cabins. "You stay on the pavement," Eli said to Cody. "I'll circle around back. One of us will hopefully head her off at the pass." Eli headed off the street, cutting between cabins as well.

Cody sprinted down the street. He saw his dad coming from the other direction. Frank nodded, and Cody pointed to indicate she'd left the road.

Cody stopped a couple of cabins before the spot where he thought she'd turned off. He didn't want to give himself away by making too much noise.

Delanie's voice spoke through his earpiece. "Frankie apprehended the suspect in the act. He's bringing her out and will meet you on the street."

Another couple of seconds, and both Frankie and Eli came from between two cabins. Cody would swear the woman in cuffs was Lexi, but as he drew closer, the resemblance waned.

"Here's your girl," Frankie announced.

She wore a bored expression that roused Cody's anger. The sheriff showed up and read her the Miranda rights. Both the sheriff and Cody's dad stood in the background, letting Frankie and Eli handle the questioning.

"Who are you working for?" Eli demanded.

Everybody knew the answer, but they needed her to say it for the record.

She chomped on her gum and ignored them.

"Your choice," Frankie said. "We'll take you in and book you. We've got no problem charging you with arson. And whoever is calling the shots goes scot-free."

Cody saw a flash of fear in her eyes. Eli handed her off to the sheriff. "Take her in."

"Wait. What will happen if I tell you who I'm working for?"

"I'll ask the DA to go easy on you. Maybe lower your charge to a misdemeanor with a fine." The sheriff acted like he was doing her a big favor, but Cody knew that was all they could charge her with anyway. However, the fear of jail was loosening her lips.

"I'm an actress from LA. My agent hired me to play this part. He promised I wouldn't get into trouble. The fires were just to scare his girlfriend into going back to him."

Why does everyone keep referring to Lexi as Jamison Price's girlfriend?

"Tell us the exact agreement you made with Jamison, how much he's paying you, and how this acting job works," Frankie said, laying out all the information they needed from her.

"Jamison agreed to sign me with his agency if I could convince the neighbors I was Alexandria Eastridge."

She did have Lexi's build but wasn't nearly as graceful or pretty.

337

"He rented me a cabin and stocked it with food. I'm only allowed to leave when he calls me. I go where he sends me and do what he tells me. He promised if I could pull this off without getting caught, he'd get me a starring role. I've been trying to get my career off the ground for a long time." She started to cry. "He promised no one would get hurt." She sniffed.

"How could you believe that?" Cody felt certain no one could be that stupid.

"What are you supposed to do next?" Eli asked.

She sniffed. "Call and let him know someone saw me and that I started another fire."

"Why don't you go ahead with that now?" Cody suggested. "This one is for the Academy Award."

She pulled the cell phone off her belt and speed-dialed Jamison Price. "Hey, it's me." She used a different voice with him than she had with them—sexier, softer, blonder. "Done and done. Yes, sir." She closed the phone.

"Where do we go from here?" Cody asked. They had a lot of pieces, but the puzzle wasn't finished yet, at least not for him.

His dad glanced at the sheriff. "These are small fish, as far as I'm concerned. I'd like to see Jamison Price pay for this and what he does to young girls with the promise of fame attached. He's nothing but a user."

"So what are you thinking?" the young sheriff asked with his brow creased.

"I'd like a little time."

The sheriff nodded.

"Can you spare two men? We'll put these two suspects under twenty-four-hour guard. They can proceed with Mr. Price as if things are normal. I'll get in touch with the LA district attorney and see if he's willing to charge Price with anything."

"Yes, sir. We'll do whatever you need," replied the sheriff. Cody watched with renewed respect as his dad turned over the two they'd arrested to the sheriff and his men. He covered all the details.

Then his dad said, "Let's head back to your place."

The four of them headed back to Cody's and then crossed the street to fill everyone in on the outcome all at once. "I think we need to celebrate!" Essie glowed with her excitement. "Let's have a barbecue, play games, and spend the day together."

Everyone responded with jovial agreements, but Cody was watching Lexi as she sat quietly in the corner of the room, her head bent down. She failed to share the exuberance of the rest of the group. He touched her arm and motioned with his head for her to follow. She did, and they slipped outside.

"I thought you'd be happy. The nightmare is over." He led the way across the street, and they sat on the steps leading to his front porch.

"I am happy, and sad, and a million other things. But mostly I'm angry. This guy manipulated me as an impressionable teen, and a dozen years later, he's still trying to manipulate my life."

"He refers to you as his girlfriend. Any reason he might still think you are?" There was a thread of jealousy in Cody's tone.

"No. I ended that long ago."

∞

Frank headed across the street. He looked like a man with something on his mind. "You have a few minutes?"

Lexi nodded.

"I'd like to speak to you about the case." He glanced at Cody, who rose from his spot next to her.

"You can stay. There is nothing about this you don't know anyway." She smiled at Cody.

He sat back down, and Frank settled on the other side of her. "Would you be willing to testify against Jamison regarding his sexual advances and promises when you were a minor?"

Fear shot through her. If she did, her parents might disown her. But how many more girls would he hurt and take advantage of if she didn't?

She drew in a deep breath. "Yeah. Yeah, I would."

"Are there others who might be willing to follow your lead?"

Lexi thought. Rayanna came to mind. Then Tianna. And there was Claudette. "I think so." Lexi nodded. "I think I could convince a few of the girls he's hurt along the way to stand up and be heard."

"It could get ugly." Frank's expression was filled with compassion. His eyes reminded her of Cody's—dear, sweet, wonderful Cody.

Fear surged like adrenaline through her veins.

"He'll probably make this out to be your fault. Your reputation will be dragged through the mud. Any man you've ever had relations with might be brought in to testify, if the DA will even consider the case to begin with."

Lexi sighed and remembered the young girl sitting in the waiting room the last time she left Jamison's office. "I have to at least try. It's the right thing." With the decision made, peace settled over her. Maybe this would right some of the wrongs in her past.

But she knew in her heart only God could do that. Only He could take what was meant for evil and make it good. Only He could redeem the years the locusts had eaten. Only He could somehow cause these twelve years of sinful choices to work together for good. And in her heart was a ray of hope that He would.

Frank rose. "Then I'm going to make the call, if you're sure."

Lexi smiled, actually tasting freedom. "I've never been surer in my life."

Frank's eyes reflected his approval. He glanced at Cody. "I'll use your cabin and make the necessary calls. It's loud and festive across the street. You two ought to join in the celebration."

"We will." Lexi rose.

Frank disappeared behind Cody's front door. She glanced at Cody. He'd not said much. "You coming?"

He grabbed her hand and pulled her back down on the step next to him. "I just want you to know that I'll walk through this with you, if you'll let me."

His sincere chocolate eyes melted her heart. She had to be strong—more for his sake than hers. She chose her words with care. "I'd appreciate that. I'm sure I'll need some good friends in my corner. Heaven knows all my friends on the LA scene will probably never speak to me again."

When she used the word *friends*, a little of the hope left his face. "I'll be whatever you need me to be." His thumb caressed hers.

I need you to forget me and not gaze at me with such hurt and longing. "True friends are hard to come by in this world, and I know you'll always be there for me. Thank you. Now let's go party." She stood and pulled him up with her.

Frank came out on the porch. "Lexi, before you head across the street, I want you to put in a call to Jamison. I'd like to listen and record it if you don't mind."

Lexi dropped Cody's hand. "You can come if you want—and be my friend to lean on."

∞

Friend? If that's all you'll give me, then I'll take it.

Cody followed Lexi and his dad into his A-frame log home.

"Frankie brought some equipment down so I can record the conversation. We'll be able to hear both of you talking. Are you okay with that?" His dad glanced at him, and Cody knew he only wanted to spare him pain. And protect Lexi's privacy, of course.

Lexi nodded but glanced at Cody, too. Her eyes begged him not to hold whatever he heard against her.

"Lexi, I can meet you at your grandparents' whenever you are through."

She shook her head. "If you truly are going to walk with me through this mess, you'll hear all of it sooner or later—the good, the bad, and the ugly. It may as well start today."

While his dad got everything hooked up and ready, Lexi paced.

"Can I pray for you?" Cody asked.

"Would you? When I walked out of Jamison's office six weeks ago, I never planned to see or speak to him ever again. Having to, especially in light of his latest stunt, makes me feel physically ill."

"I understand. What you're doing is hard and courageous." His heart swelled with admiration for her. He clasped both of her hands in his. They trembled in his hold. "Lord, these next few months will be hard on Lexi. Will You show Yourself real to her? Fill her with Your power, Your peace, and Your wisdom. I ask all this in the mighty name of Your Son, amen."

She smiled. "Thank you." Their gazes connected, and neither pulled their hands apart.

Cody longed to say so much more but couldn't. Lexi had made the boundaries clear, and he'd respect them. Otherwise, he might lose even her friendship, and a little Lexi was better than none at all.

"You ready to get this show on the road?" Frank had just finished hooking up the last wire. He held Lexi's cell phone out toward her. "You've got to sound 100 percent believable—100 percent."

"Remember all those acting lessons you told me about?"

Lexi cracked up, probably alleviating some of her tension. "I told you I was terrible."

Cody winked. "Today you won't be, because it matters." He knew she could do it.

She took her phone with a quivering hand. Taking a deep breath, she closed her eyes and exhaled slowly, deliberately.

She punched one number and put the phone to her ear. Jamison was apparently still on her speed dial. That fact bugged Cody, and he knew jealousy reared its ugly green head.

"Jamison Price Talent Agency. This is Evelyn. How may I direct your call?" She spoke into Lexi's ear but also over a speaker of some sort.

"This is Alexandria for Jamison." She glanced at Cody, and he gave her a thumbs-up. She paced as far as the wires permitted.

"Babe! I've been dying to hear from you. How are you? I've seen the news. Man, I've been worried sick."

I bet you have, you lying snake. Just hearing his voice brought a negative reaction to Cody.

"I've been thinking about you, too." Her words—sounding so sweet and sincere—brought an ache to Cody's heart. "I got your messages."

"Will you come home, baby? Home to your papa bear?" Lexi cringed in disgust, making Cody feel better.

"What exactly are you saying, Jamison?" Again her voice rang pleasant and true—not mirroring her expression at all.

"Baby, I miss you. I wanted to wait and say this in person, but I want you back—all the way back."

"What does that mean?"

"Fly home today, and I'll make sweet love to you all night long. Just the way it used to be. Just me and you, baby. Just me and you."

Cody had balled his hands into fists. How dare that guy?

Lexi sat down. "That's the thing, Jamison. It never was just me and you. You've slept with almost every woman you represent at one time or another."

"I know, but that's in the past. I've sown my wild oats, and I'm ready to be with you for the rest of my life. Fly home to Papa Bear."

"What about modeling?"

"No more, unless you want to. Of course, you can model for me anytime."

The implication made Cody's blood boil.

"I have, however, received a very lucrative offer with your name on the contract. Totally your call, though."

What a piece of work.

"Do you want me to have Evelyn call and book your flight home? I'll even pay."

"You must really want me back." Sarcasm laced itself through Lexi's tone. "You don't ever pay."

"I will from now on if that's what it takes to bring you back."

"I'll tell you what it will take. I need to hear exactly what is on your mind once I get there."

"Baby, you drive a hard bargain."

"I learned from the best," Lexi reminded him.

"Flattery will get you everywhere. I want to live with you and be with you every day from here on out."

"What about a ring?"

"Aw, baby, we've had that discussion. Come on, you know I'm not the marrying kind."

"I want the ring. I want your name. I want a family. And I don't want to model—not ever again. No matter how much money is involved." Lexi seemed to enjoy her newfound power. "Two carats, Jamison. With baguettes."

"Alexandria! You think you can call all the shots?"

"If you want me back, I can. And a prenup that says if you cheat on me, I get 50 percent of your assets."

"Baby, marriage is forever. Who needs a prenup?" His voice was syrupy sweet.

"My assets say I do."

"I'm lovesick. Whatever you want. Meet me in my office tomorrow afternoon, and I'll show you carats and baguettes."

Lexi squealed. "Jamison, you've made me the happiest woman on earth. See you tomorrow." And she closed her cell phone.

Cody wondered if the offer tempted her, and at the same time, he hated himself for doubting her. She'd said she once thought herself in love with Jamison. Now he offered all she'd once longed for. Was she really over him? He searched her face for the answer but found nothing.

"Well played, Lexi. Well played. Will he be surprised when you show up tomorrow with me and the LA DA in tow."

Lexi smiled, but a sadness resided in her eyes, only confirming Cody's fears. She was having second thoughts. She wanted what Jamison was offering. Cody had made the same offer, but she wasn't interested. After all the snake had done to her, she still loved him. How or why, Cody couldn't for the life of him fathom.

Chapter 15

Lexi hung up the phone feeling nauseated. She closed her eyes and tried to regain her equilibrium. Thank heaven her feeling for that man died years ago. All she wanted was to see him pay for all he'd done to her and others like her.

When she reopened her eyes, Cody studied her. He wore a hurt expression. "I'm sorry you had to hear some of that. I'm going across the street to hold baby Camden."

"I'll stay behind and help my dad pack all this up." Frank had already begun dismantling the high-tech communications center he'd set up last night.

"I'll see you in a while then."

Lexi couldn't wait to hold the little guy. There was something so pure and precious about a baby; it was easy to forget her own problems. They just kind of melted away.

∞

When Lexi shut the door, Cody's dad stopped unhooking wires and looked directly into Cody's eyes. "You all right, son?"

Cody blew out a long, slow breath. "Partially. It was hard to hear."

"Because you love her?" His dad raised one brow.

"That and I can't help but wonder how she's feeling about him."

"Ask her."

Part of him feared her answer. "If he does love her and married her, it would right some of his wrongs."

"I don't think so. Your emotions are too close to reason through this. I believe anything she felt for him died many moons ago."

Cody wanted to hope, but doubt flew at him from all directions.

"I was wondering if you'd travel with us to LA. I know you took this week off, and I thought Lexi might need you for moral support. You two seem to have grown close."

"Yeah, I'll go, but I may need you for moral support before all is said and done."

"I'll be there for you."

"Would it bother you or Mom if I did marry a girl like Lexi?"

His dad put the last piece of equipment into the trunk and shut it. "A girl with a past?"

"Yeah."

"Not as long as her future was secure in Christ."

"Grace?"

"Grace. How can we offer less?"

Cody's respect for his dad moved up a notch, and it was already at the top of the chart. He hugged him. "Thanks, Dad. I'll see you over at the Newcombs'."

When Cody walked in, the first thing to catch his eye was Camden snuggled in Lexi's arms. She was alone in the living room in the same rocker her grandmother had rocked her in as a baby. And wafting through the air was a sweet rendition of "Softly and Tenderly Jesus Is Calling" "Come home, come home, ye who are weary, come home; earnestly, tenderly, Jesus is calling, calling, O sinner, come home!" Even from the front door, Cody didn't miss the tear that trickled down Lexi's cheek.

Cody's heart longed to go to her, but he didn't. He joined everyone else in the family room, but he would never forget the sight of her with his nephew. He yearned for things with Lexi that would never be.

∞

Having Cody along for the trip to LA was bittersweet for Lexi. She hated him seeing how low she'd once fallen, but maybe it was a good reminder for him of how unsuitable they were for each other.

They boarded the elevator, all riding together to the tenth floor. Cody, Frank, and Mr. Martinez, the man from the district attorney's office, were all going to wait in the hall until Lexi gained access to Jamison's office.

"Good afternoon, Evelyn." Lexi marched right past the receptionist to Jamison's office door.

"Wait. I should announce you."

"He's expecting me." She breezed right through the door, half-expecting to find him with another girl.

But he was alone, perched behind his desk, his eyes on his computer screen. "Jamison, darling. I'm home." She slipped her purse off her shoulder, and as she did, she punched nine on her cell phone, which would ring Cody in the hall, letting them know she was inside.

Jamison jumped up and came around the desk, sweeping her into his arms. The kiss he laid on her made her want to puke, but she didn't want to arouse his suspicions, so she allowed him to dip her back and lay one on her. Not the position she'd planned to be in when the three men burst through his door, badges out.

"Jamison Price, we are here to question you regarding statutory rape."

At Frank's words, Jamison nearly let her fall on her head. She grabbed hold of his arm and pulled herself upright.

Lexi stepped away from him as Mr. Martinez listed the witnesses. He'd already found two other women—besides her—to testify of his escapades with minors.

He glared at Lexi. "You did this. This is your fault."

Cody stepped between them. "You have no one to blame but yourself. And you deserve whatever happens to you. If you end up in prison, they hate child molesters. You'll get what you deserve."

Cody ushered Lexi out of the office. Two men wearing LAPD uniforms questioned Evelyn. When they climbed into the elevator, Lexi fell apart. Cody pulled her into his arms, kissing the top of her head and whispering words she couldn't hear over her own sobs. The emotion that hit Lexi blindsided her. It was over—all of it. The fires, the ordeal with Jamison, Cody. Today all things good and bad ended.

She longed to wrap her arms around Cody's neck and kiss him long and hard. But love gave more than it took, so today she officially laid down any claim she might have on Cody's heart. This was good-bye, and someday he'd thank her when he found a really nice girl to settle down with.

He led her down the street to the Starbucks. They'd planned to wait there for the other two. This was her chance to say good-bye before Frank and Mr. Martinez met up with them.

Once inside Starbucks, Lexi went in the restroom and wiped her makeup-blotched face with a wet paper towel. When she came out, Cody sat at a table for two with a couple of Java Chip Frappuccinos beckoning her.

He constantly touched her in ways she never expected—thoughtful, sweet ways. No matter where life took her, she knew for certain she'd never forget Cody Cooper.

"You told me this was your favorite afternoon pick-me-up."

She smiled. "And you remembered. I'm impressed."

Cody swallowed, and she watched his Adam's apple rise and fall. "There isn't much about you that I'll ever forget."

Lexi laughed, fighting the urge to turn to mush. "Until the next pretty girl comes along. Then I'll be old news, and you'll replace my info with hers."

"Not likely. Did you know I fell in love with you long before I met you?"

The news surprised her. "And then you encountered the real me at the airport. The shrew. Bet you wished then that you'd run far and fast."

"I wouldn't have missed knowing you for anything." Sincere but sad brown eyes caught her gaze.

You're killing me here. "Are you trying to make me cry?"

He tipped his head to one side in his endearing way. "Nope. Just trying to keep from it myself."

"Cody." Her tone grew serious. "I'm glad I didn't miss you, either. And I'm sure I'll see you again sometime when I visit my grandparents."

He gave her hand a squeeze. "You're not going back with us?"

She shook her head.

"I sort of figured."

His dad and Mr. Martinez entered the shop.

"I'm heading out." Mr. Martinez shook Frank's hand and then Cody's. "I've got your number and will be in touch," he said to her. "I'll need to do an in-depth interview. Not sure how far this will go, but we're willing to give it a shot."

Lexi toyed with her straw. "I'll be around whenever you need me."

The assistant district attorney nodded. "Good-bye, all." He carried his brief-case out the door and was gone.

"How did things go after we left?" Lexi asked Frank.

"Let's just say Jamison Price was not a happy camper."

"Thank you for believing in me and for everything you did."

Frank nodded. "It was my pleasure." He glanced at Cody. "Our pleasure."

"What time is your flight?" Lexi pushed her hair behind one ear.

Frank checked his watch. "We have several hours. Can we see you home?"

"I'll grab a cab. I live a long way from here." Lexi rose.

"Guess this is good-bye then." Frank glanced from Cody to Lexi. Then he stood and hugged her. "Building your future on a lie isn't the best way to start afresh," he whispered in her ear.

He turned to Cody. "I'll meet you at the car. Take your time. We're in no hurry." With that he turned and was gone.

Lexi sat back down.

"Sorry. My family isn't known for being subtle."

Lexi giggled. "Your family's great."

Cody stood. "There is no reason to drag this out."

"No, there isn't." She stood as well.

The moment was awkward. She didn't look into his eyes. Couldn't. "Cody." She swallowed. "Would you kiss me?"

A puzzled expression settled on his face. "Sure." He leaned down and planted a kiss on her cheek.

"That wasn't exactly what I had in mind. I was hoping to erase Jamison's kiss with yours."

Cody's heart thudded a steady rhythm. "You want me to kiss you?"

She nodded. "If you don't mind."

Mind? No, he surely didn't mind. "I guess if I have to," he teased.

"You probably think this is stupid, but it may be years before I get kissed, and I don't want Jamison's lips from this afternoon lingering on mine for who knows how long."

"I thought you still had feelings for the guy." Cody admitted his misgivings.

"Oh, I do—"

His heart dropped after just shooting for the moon.

"Loathing, anger, distrust."

Cody placed his hands on her waist. "The proposal never tempted you?"

"Are you kidding? Not for a second. He is a liar and a loser."

He drew his brows together, certain he'd never figure out God's fairer sex. "Then why the tears?"

"You thought I was pining away for Jamison?" She laughed. "Not on your life." Then she grew serious and stopped looking everywhere but at him.

"I'll miss you and my grandparents. It's been a tumultuous few weeks. But my feelings for Jamison died many years ago."

He moved his hands to the side of her face. "I'll miss you, too, and if things ever change for you, I'll probably still be waiting."

Determined to make the most of this last chance to woo her, he moved slowly toward her, looking deep into her eyes. When their lips met, emotions exploded inside Cody. He took his time, filling the kiss with all the love and tenderness he could muster. When he finally raised his head, she wore a dazed expression. She released a soft, contented sigh.

"Was that your best shot?" He saw the mirth in her eyes.

" 'Fraid so. But I'll try again if you like."

She touched her lips. "No need. Jamison's kiss is gone, and the memory of your kiss will live on." She traced his jaw. "I hate good-byes, so I'm going to the restroom. Will you do me a favor and be gone when I come out?"

He nodded and pulled her into one last hug. "Bye, Lexi." He stumbled over the words. Then he turned her loose and walked away, praying all the while. *God, bring her back somehow.*

∞

With tears in her eyes, Lexi watched Cody walk away, and unbeknownst to him, he carried her heart in his hand. Was she making the biggest mistake of her life? How many days did it take a broken heart to heal? And how long would it hurt to simply breathe?

Lexi sat back down at the table and stared out the window. Feeling lost, she wondered where to go from here. With no desire to stay in LA, where could she go? Even after all she'd been through, her heart still longed to return to the mountains and the most beautiful lake in the world.

Frank said Mr. Martinez would make certain that Jamison Price made a very public apology for all he'd done to slander her name. He hoped it would air on the ten o'clock news tonight. What a good man Frank Cooper was, and Cody was his father's son. The Coopers weren't perfect, but they were the closest to Christlike she'd ever seen, except for Gram and Gramps.

She needed to call Gram to tell her she'd have a courier pick up her things. She should have brought them but took the coward's way out for two reasons. She didn't want to have to mess with luggage while they were dealing with Jamison, and she didn't want to see Gram's face when she discovered Lexi wasn't coming back this evening. But now, in a matter of hours, Gram would know anyway.

She opened her purse to fish out her cell phone. Her little Bible caught her eye, and she pulled it out as well. Gram had given it to her just last week. She unsnapped the cover and flipped through the pages. It smelled new and fresh— the pages pristine and crisp, the gold edges still shiny and new.

A new creature in Christ. That was her. Like the pages of this Bible, she was whiter than snow. The epiphany astounded her. She'd been forgiven and stood before God and the whole world new, clean, and restored to her Father. His grace had been poured into her life. She could see it in the way this whole thing worked out.

A sermon she'd heard recently echoed through her head. She could either live in the forgiveness, live the life of the new creature, or she could remain stuck in the condemnation of her past. Which would she choose? She ran her finger-tips over the cover of her Bible. She raised it to her face and smelled the new leather. Then she hugged it against her heart. Which would it be—free and new or stuck in her past?

∞

"I'm sorry, son. I know you're hurting." Cody's dad slapped his back a couple of times as they went through the tunnel between the airport and the plane to board their flight back to Reno.

"Time heals all wounds, or so they say," Cody said. He found their row in the plane and settled into the window seat. His dad took the aisle seat. The plane wasn't full, so they didn't have a middle passenger.

"Do you think Lexi will ever accept God's forgiveness and forgive herself?" Cody asked once he'd buckled his seat belt.

"She might. The whole Cooper clan is praying for her. Does she stand a chance?"

Cody chuckled. "I hope not, but she may never choose me, even if God gets through."

The aisle was filled with passengers as they stowed their things in the overhead bins.

"No, she may not. She told me once that she couldn't make plans until tomorrow."

"What does that even mean?" Cody's frustration came out with his words.

"I asked the same thing, and she explained that her life was on hold until the whole fire thing was cleared up and she'd been exonerated. In other words, until tomorrow came and she was free, she couldn't move forward."

"Well then today is tomorrow, and she chose not to move forward with me." His dad nodded.

Cody closed his eyes and leaned his head against the side of the plane. *Tomorrow is here. And it will be followed by many more lonely tomorrows.* Days of missing Lexi. Nights of wishing she'd included him in her tomorrows. *Lord, it looks like it will be just You and me for a while longer. Help me get over Lexi and move on to the future You have planned for me.*

"Is this seat taken?"

Her voice penetrated his prayer. Was it his imagination? Did he dare open his eyes, lest he face more disappointment?

"Lexi, you're joining us?" His dad's voice carried enough excitement for both of them.

When he glanced over, his dad climbed out of his seat to allow Lexi to pass through. She shined her biggest smile on him, and Cody sat up straighter.

"Hi." He wasn't sure what to say, and he didn't want to go getting any ideas, so he let her take the lead.

"Hi." She buckled her seat belt, and his dad settled back into his place on the aisle. He wore a face-splitting grin. He obviously believed what Cody dared not hope.

When Cody couldn't stand the suspense another minute, he asked, "Where are you headed?"

"Home." She turned to face him. Something was different. The shadows were gone from her eyes. "I'm going home to stay."

Cody swallowed. His eyes searched her face. She smiled and placed her hand in his.

His pulse increased, and a seed of hope sprouted in his heart.

"I love you, Cody."

It was the first time she'd said those precious words, and he'd not expected them, making the sound twice as sweet.

"You do?" He couldn't hide his surprise. *Lord, this is better than I even imagined.* "You love me?" Sheer joy danced out with the words. "You really love me?"

She nodded and laughed. "Really."

"Dad, she loves me! Lexi loves me." And he loved saying the words. Each time drove the truth home in his mind.

"I know, son. I heard. Now why don't you kiss her already?"

Cody obeyed his dad's suggestion, leaning across her seat and kissing her with awe at this blessing.

"I can't believe you love me," he whispered, her face mere inches from his.

Her expression grew serious. "With all my heart." She laid her hand on his chest. "I'm giving you my very grateful heart, and I'm asking you to treasure it—today, tomorrow, and always."

A promise that would be easy to make and easy to keep.

∞

Cody stood on the observation deck, halfway to the top of Heavenly. His dad, Brady, Frankie, Eli, and Alph stood nearby. For Cody, today truly was heavenly. He and Lexi would vow their tomorrows to each other before his immediate family and her grandparents on this cold, snowy, Christmasy day. Her parents were out of the country and unable to attend.

Lexi's favorite verse was Psalm 51:7, "Purge me with hyssop, and I shall be clean; wash me, and I shall be whiter than snow." So today was an appropriate day for them to wed. The snow would be a constant reminder that she was clean before God, forgiven, free to move into a pure relationship with Cody.

The women made their way out onto the cold deck—all of them but Lexi. Alph went and met her in the small gift shop where she waited. Sunni turned on an iPod, and the wedding march blared out. Lexi came into view, beautiful on her grandfather's arm. Cody had convinced her to wear white, another remembrance of her righteous standing before God because of her relationship with Jesus Christ.

Lexi didn't wear a veil, and her face glowed. Their eyes connected. His heart pounded like an Indian drum during a war dance. When she reached him, he took her hands in his. They faced each other, and tears glistened in her eyes. The snow glistened beyond, covering the earth in a blanket of white.

Cody had never been more grateful for grace than at that moment. Grace that Lexi had accepted. Grace that brought them together. Grace that would fill each tomorrow.

A Letter to Our Readers

Dear Readers:

In order that we might better contribute to your reading enjoyment, we would appreciate you taking a few minutes to respond to the following questions. When completed, please return to the following: Fiction Editor, Barbour Publishing, Inc., P.O. Box 719, Uhrichsville, OH 44683.

1. Did you enjoy reading *Sierra Weddings* by Jeri Odell?
   - ❑ Very much. I would like to see more books like this.
   - ❑ Moderately—I would have enjoyed it more if _____
   _____
   _____

2. What influenced your decision to purchase this book? (Check those that apply.)
   - ❑ Cover
   - ❑ Back cover copy
   - ❑ Title
   - ❑ Price
   - ❑ Friends
   - ❑ Publicity
   - ❑ Other

3. Which story was your favorite?
   - ❑ *Always Yesterday*
   - ❑ *Until Tomorrow*
   - ❑ *Only Today*

4. Please check your age range:
   - ❑ Under 18
   - ❑ 18–24
   - ❑ 25–34
   - ❑ 35–45
   - ❑ 46–55
   - ❑ Over 55

5. How many hours per week do you read? _____

Name _____

Occupation _____

Address _____

City_____ State _____ Zip_____

E-mail _____

BREAK

4

5

7